Cold Blue World

Cold Blue World

A Novel

By Anthony J. Murray

Contents

Chapter 1 7

Chapter 2 12

Chapter 3 21

Chapter 4 34

Chapter 5 48

Chapter 6 61

Chapter 7 76

Chapter 8 87

Chapter 9 99

Chapter 10 109

Chapter 11 117

Chapter 12 131

Chapter 13 143

Chapter 14 152

Chapter 15 160

Chapter 16 171

Chapter 17 183

Chapter 18 196

Chapter 19 210

Chapter 20 222

Chapter 21 232

Chapter 22 243

Chapter 23 254

Chapter 24 265

Chapter 25 280

Chapter 26 294

Chapter 27 306

Chapter 28 320

Chapter 29 331

Chapter 30 343

Chapter 31 353

Chapter 32 363

Chapter 33 373

Chapter 34 385

Chapter 35 395

Chapter 36 405

Chapter 37 415

Chapter 38 429

Chapter 39 439

Epilogue 442

Chapter 1

"Let me get this straight. You planned a dinner with her. She told you at five o'clock that she would 'see you soon' and 'she's on her way.'"

Kameka Ralston never looked away from her screen. She continued her multitask of observing the Andromeda galaxy, recording data, and interrogating her colleague on his dating woes.

"I told you she had a valid reason to not show up." Bartholomew Messner wiped the sweat from his brow with the back of his sleeve. The heavy-set man was prone to sweating, even in the cool observing room at the Keck Observatory. The room was next to the server closet. This meant that the HVAC in that part of the building was cranked making it often too chilly for Kameka's liking.

"Oh yeah you said, her grandmother was sick, and she had to stay home to skype with her." Kameka did not try to hide her skepticism.

"It is a good reason. They are very close. What if it was your grandmother?" There was a lack of confidence in Bart's rebuttal.

"If it were my grandmother, I would have called my date to let them know I was cancelling. I would have answered one of his fifteen text messages. Likely one of the first three or four so that there wasn't a need for fifteen. I would have not ghosted him for the next forty-eight hours."

"Yeah, I guess you are right about that part."

"Just that part?"

For the first time, Kameka spun away from her terminal. Bart heard the clicking of the bearings in her chair as she turned to face him. He slid back from his terminal where he was monitoring at a resolution which would show the lower bound of the estimated edge of the exosphere. The imagining telescope was set to record the live feed.

On the screen just to his right, were images taken by the low-resolution imagining spectrometer, LRIS. As part of his doctoral work, Bartholomew was using the LRIS to monitor the analysis of elements found on Mars for potential habitation benefits.

"What do you mean?" Bart had briefly allowed his work to distract him from Kameka's interrogation.

"You're telling me that you think it was a good idea for you to continue to do the research and collect the data for her thesis paper? Even after she stood you up? After she ghosted you for two days? Despite being behind on your own research? Is that right, Bart?"

"Her grandmother was sick!" Bart felt attacked for his willingness to do a favor for a girl he liked.

"When you went to her room, you heard her inside?"

"Yes." Bart responded.

"You heard a man's voice?"

"Yeah." Both Bart's tone and gaze lowered.

You knocked and she didn't answer."

Bart nodded.

"Then days later, she asks you to help her with her research?"

"I'm her friend. I couldn't say no."

"And where is she now?"

Bart hung his head.

After a few moments he mumbled something incoherently.

"What was that?" Kameka jumped up out of her chair.

Bart was startled but he doubled down and responded louder.

"I said, she has a date!" he roared speedily, spittle ejecting from his mouth.

"No, what was that on the screen?"

"I didn't see anything. What did you see? Was there something in my research screen?"

"No, it was on the screen you had for the exosphere for your little girlfriend." Kameka pointed to his left.

"What did you see?"

"Whatever it was, it was big, and black, and it was on fire." Kameka leaned over the sweaty, heavy-set man with the stained flannel and equally stained anime t-shirt as she anxiously manipulated the keyboard. She was failing miserably at figuring out how to rewind the camera for the recording. All that she accomplished was to develop an idea as to why Keilani was ghosting Bart.

Bart was a nice guy. The aroma of his sweat was mildly pungent and the patches in his unkempt beard were more noticeable from this distance. He was a mouth breather, and she was so close that she could smell the garlic cream and fish that he had in his last meal with each exhale.

"What are you trying to do, Kameka?" Bart was uncomfortable with the woman's proximity as well.

"How do you rewind this thing?"

"You can't. It's the live feed."

"I thought it was recording?" Kameka stepped back.

"It is but it's not a DVR." He quipped.

She placed her hands together over her nose and mouth trying to construct a logical explanation for what she saw. The back of her nose ring nudged into her septum as she inhaled deeply. Both thumbs pressed firmly into her jowl.

"The live feed is all that we have access to here. The recording is done in the other room. We can enter a request in the morning to get permission to access that area. What do you think it was that you saw?"

"Can you shift that to a wider shot?"

"Of course, but..."

"Do it! Focus on the northern part of the sky."

Bart tapped at the keys, clicked the mouse a few times and the viewing field widened. He scanned the sky for something large but didn't see anything out of the ordinary. There was a meteor shower that evening. Dozens of meteoroids entering the atmosphere, crossed the viewing field. None of them were of the magnitude that Kameka had described.

Feeling more than seeing the frustration Kameka wore, he tapped a few more and broadened so that they could see the entirety of the northern hemisphere in a resolution about a dozen times of normal vision viewing magnification. Other than the Orionid, they saw nothing.

"You sure it wasn't like a feed glitch or something?"

It wasn't a glitch. It zoomed past. It took up so much of the field. I've never seen anything that shade of black. Even through the flames. It was like nothingness."

"It was on fire, and it was black?

The girl nodded.

"If it was a meteor, then there should be a report of it touching down tomorrow if it doesn't hit in the middle of the ocean."

"The thing was black, black. Like onyx in a cave black."

"Like Michael Blackson black?" Bart asked.

"How many times have I told you that you can't do that?" Kameka admonished.

"My bad. Well tomorrow we can ask if we can review the recording. I'll put in the request. Once I get the link, I will share it with you."

"We should watch it together. Don't watch it without me, OK?"

"I won't. You really did see something didn't you?"

The girl sat back in her chair and returned to her research.

"Yeah, I think I did, and it wasn't a rock."

Chapter 2

The dark-haired boy with green streaks leaned on the counter, absently fiddling with the Chapstick rolls in the display before him. Leisurely, he glided his hand over them like rollers on a manual conveyor. He tried to make them all show the brand name at once by altering the pressure as his hand moved left and right.

The boy looked up from his idle musing when the bell on the door jingled. His earlobes danced with the weight of the large gauge inserts he had in them. The blonde-haired male walked right to the back. He never acknowledged the canned greeting that the cashier threw at him upon entry.

The cashier noticed that his patron was dressed up. He presumed he was coming from a prom. He ran his fingers through his bangs before whipping them to the side. The boy went straight to the freezers. Rather than grab something from the three doors to the right where the assortment of non-alcoholic drinks was, he veered straight to the left end freezer. There was a suctioning noise as the glass door opened. He reached to the bottom and pulled out a 12 pack of bottles that clanged as he tugged them from the shelf. The boy grabbed a couple bags of chips on his way down the aisle and then set them on the counter, never once making eye contact with the cashier.

"You got I.D.?"

The blonde-haired boy looked up at the cashier. His visage was stern, despite the attempt at a smile. The tone of his voice matched his eyes and not his smile.

"Come on, Roger. I buy here all the time. You know me."

The cashier stared back at him confused. The boy wasn't looking in his eyes. He was glancing toward his shoulder. The cashier turned his head toward his left side, noting nothing amiss with his shoulder but then looked down to his chest. The nametag pinned there clearly displayed the name Roger.

He tipped his head back and smirked.

Things made sense to him immediately. Roger was another cashier that the boss had talked to about getting IDs from people he 'knew were twenty-one' because they went to school together. The manager had tried to catch him selling to under aged individuals, but he didn't really have any evidence. Well now he would.

"Is something funny?"

"I'm not Roger. I am just wearing his name tag because I left mine at home."

"Oh, right. I thought your hair looked different, but I didn't want to say anything. Anyway, I come here all the time and Roger knows me."

"Well, I don't know you. So, I need ID. State law. I don't want to get fired. You understand, don't ya. This economy and all."

"Right. Well, you can just let me slide and I will bring you my I.D. next time."

The cashier pulled the beer closer to him and set it down behind the counter.

"Unfortunately, I won't be able to do that, pal. If you got it in the car or left it at home, you can run and grab it. We are open for another hour."

"Come on. I had a bit of a night. I just want to go home and relax with a few beers."

"Prom date dump ya?" The cashier poked.

"What? No."

The boy looked down at his attire. He realized that it was obvious that he had just come from a prom and was in high school. It annoyed him that he hadn't considered that before coming to get the beer."

"I was at a wedding."

"There wasn't a bar at the reception?"

"There was. But I left."

"Right. Who got hitched?"

"Excuse me?"

"The wedding. Who got married?"

"A friend of mine."

"So you weren't at a prom, on the night of like all the proms around here."

"Why are you being a dick?"

"Listen, I was trying to let you down easily. You insisted on continuing the charade even after I told you I wasn't going to sell to you without I.D. There is no need for name calling."

"What do you mean let me down easy? You are hassling me over an I.D. when I told you I come here all the time. What is that if not you being a dick?"

"Yeah, you can get out."

"What do you mean?"

"I mean you can get your ass out of the store. I know you are still in high school, and you just came from your homecoming dance. I wasn't born yesterday. So, pay for your chips and go. Or just go. Either way I am done with the conversation."

The blonde-haired boy in the suit was clearly flustered. He paced back and forth a moment, hands digging through his previously perfectly coiffed blonde locks.

"Do you know who my dad is? I am the captain of the damn football team!"

"Cool, bro. If this was Varsity Blues, you may have been in luck. $4.86 for the chips. You taking them or not?"

"I don't even know what that means."

"Of course, you don't. Because you aren't old enough."

The cashier grinned at the football player for not getting a football movie reference.

Reluctantly, the boy tapped his card to the chip reader and then shoved the Amex back into his pocket.

"You got a bathroom?"

"Back there, Mox. No whipped cream bikinis when you come out, okay."

Confused and flustered, the boy stormed off to the corner of the store. He locked the door behind him and saddled up to the urinal. His night was not going as planned. His cousin was crowned homecoming queen and he had won king. Someone in the crowd made a joke about incest but he couldn't quite place the voice. His date got creeped out by it and disappeared. He was not going to be getting laid tonight and now he was not able to get any beer. He had a little bit of weed stashed at home in his room, but he didn't want to go there and risk waking his mother.

The boy backed away from the urinal. He made a face at the sound of his crackling steps from the sticky floor. The toilet motion sensor flushed the urine down the drain. He stepped to the sink and swiped a hand under the towel dispenser to activate the reel to roll out a length of paper. He placed his right hand under the soap dispenser to catch the foaming gob that was ejected.

He tossed the gob into the air, his left hand gesturing similarly to his right only from under the running faucet. His startle prompted by a loud crash outside the door. The alarm caused his left hand to redirect water at the crotch of his pants. He cursed aloud, aggressively ripping the towel from the dispenser, swiping it across the front of him. As he crumpled it and tossed it in the bin, he imagined that the Roger imposter had stumbled into a shelf while cleaning up or something. The imagery made him smirk, despite it startling him. As he turned on the water to rinse off the soap residue, he heard a second, louder crash, followed by a scream. There was a third crash, a thump. And then silence.

The boy froze. It sounded as though Godzilla had stomped on the gas station. Since the roof over his head appeared to be intact, he knew that was not it.

Shaking, he crept to the door to listen. His hand instinctively felt for the knob to ensure the lock was in place. Certain that the echo of his rapid breathing would give him away as he was hidden in the restroom, he held his breath. He did his best to assure himself that the commotion all came from a robbery in progress. That the cashier stupidly said something smart or put up a fight. The robber got mad and shoved him into a display shelf and all of that aisle fell down as a result. He thought it over a few more times, convincing himself of the logic.

One thing that he was certain of was that he wasn't about to play the hero. One handheld to his chest, one hand and ear to the door, he listened. Breath held; the boy expected to hear the jingle of the bell as the robbers fled the crime scene. He figured he would just wait five minutes after and then come out.

However, there was no jingle to be heard. Instead, a strange sound could be heard coming from inside the store. At first, it was barely audible. Faint crackling. The boy thought it was all just buzzing in his head from adrenaline. After a few minutes, he could tell that whatever was making the sound was moving around. At times, it even sounded like it was echoing. Eventually, it was directly outside the restroom. It was a clunky, clicking sound. Like the tumblers on one of the traps in the Uncharted movie, but hollower. Like someone turning a big gear underwater. He tried to think of what a robber would bring to a robbery that would make that type of noise. The frightened boy came up with nothing. This served to only heighten his fear.

Sliding to the side of the door, back against the wall, he surveyed the small restroom for weapons. The entire room had white tile, a toilet, urinal, sink and paper towel dispenser. The garbage can was a rectangular, plastic receptacle. There was a support bar on the wall beside the toilet. Other than that, nothing would function as a weapon. The boy doubted that he could get the bar off the wall without alerting whoever was outside the door. He kept waiting for them to try the door handle, but they never did. The room had no windows and the vent in the middle of the ceiling was much too high for him to hope to climb through. He was stuck.

The boy cursed himself for leaving his phone in the truck. It seemed like a half an hour before the muffled clicking sound that moved about the room finally stopped. He waited a bit longer then slowly turned the handle and pulled the door open so that he could peer outside.

The lights in the store flickered. The door to the gas station had been wrenched off the hinges. All the glass from the door was strewn about the floor in front of the counter. The metal frame was crushed against the wall. He thought that perhaps someone had driven a truck through the entrance.

The cashier was nowhere to be seen. There was a small emergency light on the wall that barely lit the room. It was awful to gaze about with the flickering power. The camera on the wall didn't appear to be functional any longer. When he got to the front of the aisle, he noticed that there were long gashes in the countertop. The bags of chips he had paid for were nowhere in sight. He gazed behind the counter and the cashier was not there. His unpurchased twelve pack of blue moon was setting on the floor. The box was crushed and there was a fizzy pool where a few of the bottles had broken.

A light fixture fell to the ground behind him causing his soul to jump out of his body and run to the truck. He thought to run out after it but remembered that he paid for chips. He had no idea why the fright made him think of the chips. Perhaps it was the crackling as the wires crossed sparking from the electric current. He ran over to the shelf and grabbed another bag of each of the brands he had rung up. He dropped them as he snatched them off the shelf because he was gazing at the ceiling for other falling fixtures. He turned to sprint out of the store and had another idea. The boy grinned as he ran back to the cooler. He quickly pulled out a twelve pack and set it on the floor. He grabbed another and set it atop the first. With a bag of chips pinched in each hand and the beer stack hugged tightly to his chest, he jogged out of the store. He was careful not to slide on the chunks of glass that had been strewn everywhere.

    The parking lot was empty aside from his truck and not-Roger's car. He set the beer down in the back of the truck, and then jumped in the driver's seat. His adrenaline was pumping, his hands shaking from the ordeal. He chuckled at the insanity of the scene inside and the fortune of being able to get the beer he originally planned to purchase.

    He reached for the keys that were still in the ignition where he left them. He turned the car over. The exhaust roared as the combustion engine started. He grabbed the shifter to put the truck in reverse when the cashier slammed against the passenger door.

    The boy jumped, shouting expletives brought on by the scare. There were lines of blood protruding from the corners of the cashier's eyes and from his nostrils. His pupils were dilated, and he was foaming at the mouth.

"Jesus Christ!!!" "Dude what the hell happened in your store?"

The cashier opened his mouth as though he were trying to respond. In lieu of words, 4 grey and red tentacles emitted from his throat. The boy's eyes went wide, struck with disbelief. The tentacles struck his window with a force he didn't believe possible for something so close and so small. There were tiny cracks in the glass where they had collided with the window.

The boy depressed the brake and threw down the shifter flooring it in reverse out of the parking spot. Not-Roger slid across the window, smashing off the passenger mirror and falling to the ground as the truck sped from its position. The terrified boy in the driver seat slammed the brakes and shifted the gear stick to drive while it was still skidding. Before he could slam on the gas again, something struck the driver-side door. The boy turned to see more of the tentacles flying at him. They smashed the glass on his window and latched on to his head. The entire world went dark as he was pulled from the truck. As his foot came off the brake the vehicle rolled forward picking up speed before colliding with a light pole, taking it down, rendering the entire station in utter darkness.

Chapter 3

Two Months Earlier

"*Where the hood, where the hood, where the hood at? Have them in the cut, where the wood at? Oh, they actin up? Where the wolves at? You better bust that if you gon' pull that. Where the hood, where the hood, where da...ouch!*"

"Yo, why you flicking me, Bini?" Darius tugged an earbud out and rubbed the spot behind his ear where his cousin's finger clocked him.

The boy didn't respond. His father, gazing in the rearview mirror, answered on his behalf.

"Tunes, if you don't quiet down all that noise, I'm going to make you walk the rest of the way."

"Sorry Uncle Mac. DMX just gets me hyped."

"What do you got to be *hyped* over? We are on a long drive in a car where you are just sitting there. I wish you would listen to something that gets you *laxed* and you would take a nap."

"Nobody says laxed anymore dad. This ain't 1994." Ubini teased at his father's old school lingo.

"I don't know why you listen to that music, Tunes. It is older than you." Ubini reached over and slapped his brother UKeke on the knee. "If you gonna listen to those old head rappers at least listen to something current like J. Cole or Kendrick Lamar."

"Don't involve me in your nonsense. I am trying to finish my book." The boy who was a replica of his brother sitting beside him leaned back in his seat and continued reading the book from the page he marked a moment ago with his finger.

"How much longer, Uncle Mac? We been driving for like 10 hours." Tunes continued to absentmindedly rub the spot where he had been flicked.

"We? You been sitting back there destroying the hip hop of my generation this whole time with your horrible renditions, Darius. It's only been 10 hours, and we would have been there by now if we hadn't stopped almost every hour so one of you could go to the bathroom."

Louise in the passenger seat sat bemused by the nonsense behind her. Her boys and her adopted nephew began to carry on as Bini refused to allow his brother to get back to his reading and Darius aka Tunes, continued to sing aloud despite her husband's admonishment that he would be walking the remaining hundred plus miles of their trip to their new home in Saratoga.

Louise turned her attention to the scenery that whipped by as her husband sped up Interstate eighty-seven in their brand-new Honda Pilot. He took turns with a maroon Jaguar and a white Lexus playing pace car as they weaved in and out of the two leftmost lanes.

This was a common practice in driving along the interstate. A group of cars would decide that the posted speed limit was not for them. They would chase each other along the long journey until a law enforcement vehicle halted their game like a parent stepping into the doorway of a playroom. All the kids would then 'calm' down. This game only worked in numbers because they could simulate an element of the flow of traffic.

A green sign with metallic, white lettering indicated that 'Historic Kingston First Capital of New York' was coming up in a few exits. One bathroom break and a 'you'll just have to hold it' detour brought them to the school where Louise's husband would be teaching when the school year began next month. Her twin boys and adopted nephew would be students at the school as well.

Louise was originally concerned when Mac told her he had begun to apply for positions in New York.

"With the way the political climate is shifting south of the Mason-Dixon, we should try to get out while the getting is good."

Louise had chuckled when he gave that response. She knew he was only half joking about his rationale. Things were getting a bit crazy. Virginia was a blue leaning state. The Governor was a Republican though.

"It's not that bad. It's not like we have a guy like in Florida running the state in Virginia. That man and his people are so afraid of the vagina, it is a wonder why anyone of them would even bother to get married or attempt to procreate." Louise joked.

"Yeah, well the guy we got is proposing to eliminate Martin Luther King Jr. Day from the school curriculum. Plus, he thinks that critical race theory is teaching racism in history. I think we best get out while the getting's good." Mac reiterated the colloquialism.

Again, Louise chuckled.

It was true that the sitting Governor of Viriginia saw critical race theory as racist teaching. It was also true that he proposed to his board of education to remove the holidays of Martin Luther King's Day, Barack Obama Day and Juneteenth from the calendar. Even the white members of the board were puzzled by that. Louise could see why an educator with a mind like her husband's would see that as troubling. However, Mac had other reasons for wanting to move to the Empire State.

William Dubois Wallace, Mac's granddaddy was a Korean War Veteran. He came home from fighting the Korean People's Army of Kim Il Sung expecting a hero's welcome. Instead, he was witness to white folks continued maltreatment of him and his fellow African American soldiers. In the U.S. Army, he had marched and fought side by side with white soldiers in a foreign land. The South Korean citizens he met were appreciative of their presence.

In his home state of Virginia, he and his brothers returning from war were second-class citizens. W.D., as his fellow infantrymen called him, tried to endure it with hopes that the Civil Rights Movement would invoke change. He gave up in 1964 and moved to New York to a town called Pelham.

Willam put his three children through college working on the New York railroad for twenty years. His oldest son took a government job in the District of Columbia and moved back to Newport News, the town where W.D. had been born. There he wed and raised a son named MacArthur. Every summer they spent two weeks in New York at Mac's grandparents' house. They had since moved North to Albany. While they missed the proximity to the big city, Mac's grandparents found the cost of living in Upstate New York more amenable to retiree living. W.D. made a point to show his grandson all the local historical sites. He would take Mac to the Saratoga State Park, the locks along the Erie Canal, and the Lake George Battle Grounds. A few times, they visited the grave of Uncle Sam. They even found a spot in a town called Watervliet where Harriet Tubman had battled police and slave catchers for the freedom of Charles Nalle, a Virginia slave who had escaped north via the underground railroad.

These summers lit the fire of wonder in young MacArthur. It was the obvious choice to his parents when he majored in history in college. Mac became a teacher in the Newport News School District shortly after graduation. Five years later, he caught the eye of the nurse who tended to him after an emergency appendectomy.

Now, they were in upstate New York parked in the lot to the boys' new high school and Mac's new place of employment.

"It doesn't look like there's metal detectors inside. I thought all New York Schools had metal detectors."

Mac glared at Darius in the rear view.

"That's New York City, dummy."

"Hey, Bini. No name calling." Lousie scolded.

"Yeah, how am I supposed to know. I figured all these kids up this way was like Bishop from Juice."

Louise and Mac shared a glance at their nephew's pop culture reference.

"This school looks mad white..." Bini paused at the end, curtailing the insult he had ready to fire at his cousin. His mother was still glowering over her shoulder.

"It does look like a really white school." Keke gazed up from his book to chime in on the conversation. "How many black kids go to this school dad? I hope we aren't gonna be getting escorted like Ruby Bridges."

Louise smiled at her youngest son's joke. He was younger than his brother by thirteen minutes. From conception, Keke took his time.

"Three things, this is not William Frantz Elementary School in 1960. There are three of y'all, so you won't face anything near what that child faced. Third, that child was 6 years old during the Civil Rights Movement. This is the twenty first century."

"However, this is a ninety percent white enrollment school district. I have no idea what the people are like. It will be quite a different demographic from Warwick and the city of Newport News in general."

"So, what you're saying Uncle Mac is that we better not expect Crown's Fried Chicken?"

Everyone chuckled at Darius' joke.

"No Tunes, there is no Crown's in Saratoga. But you will likely be pleasantly surprised by the quality of the pizza."

After a stop by the hospital where Louise would be working to pick up her credentials they headed to their new home. By the time they arrived at Eight Springfield Drive, Darius had switched from singing to dancing. Mac had barely shifted the Honda into park before his nephew had hopped out of the car and headed for the door. Louise jingled her keys out the window at him and he skidded to a halt. He ran back to the car and then took off for the door.

By the time Darius got inside the house, Ubini was standing behind him shaking his head. He watched him fumble the keys trying to find the correct one for the front door lock. Once the door was open, the first boy sprinted down the hallway in search of a toilet. The second boy set his bags down inside the hallway and returned to help his family with the rest of their luggage in the back of the SUV. He turned his shoulders to skirt past his brother who was carrying two bags up the cement walkway. Ubini shuffled two steps then repeated his avoidance technique as his dad trudged along with a knapsack over one shoulder, tugging a large suitcase behind him.

When Ubini got to the rear of the vehicle, his mother was grabbing the last of the items that they had decided to bring with them on the drive up from Virginia. The moving truck wouldn't arrive until tomorrow morning. They brought with them the bare necessities to get them through the night.

Ubini playfully held his arms out before him, emulating the forks on a forklift. His mother smiled at him and loaded the bags across his makeshift forks. When she had finished stacking, he turned sideways for her to plant a kiss on his left cheek. The boy walked mechanically up the sidewalk, turning at a 90-degree angle in kind with the path to the door. His twin brother feigned a trip at him before stepping out of his way. Ubini snapped his head at his brother/ His eyes and mouth went wide in mock surprise.

Ukeke stood at the door, holding it open for his mother. She only had a purse and a coffee mug to carry but he stood rigid like a doorman waiting on her to venture up the walkway to their new home.

"Welcome home, mother."

The boy tried to be stoic. Louise rolled her eyes at his silliness. This brought a wide grin to his face. Louise kissed her son's dimpled cheek which made him giggle.

"Thank you, *Adesusu*." The boy blushed at the compliment.

Louise's great, grandmother Ehiosu was born in Benin. She was of the Edo people. She held the culture and customs dear to her heart. It was especially important because she had been displaced from her home at a young age. Ehiosu had been pawned to a merchant to pay for a debt of an uncle. That merchant brought her to Jamaica. The voyage took twenty days to cross the Atlantic Ocean. During that time Ehiosu served as a maid and a cook for the merchant. She was only sixteen years old and didn't know how to prepare many meals. When she served the same meal for the third night in a row, the merchant beat her on the back with a flogging strap. Her back was split open, and the wounds oozed blood.

The merchant was merciless. He left her wounds untended. With nobody to dress the wounds and unable to reach them herself, Ehiosu had to endure the pain. She had nothing but cold water to run down her back to wash away the blood from her skin.

Her condition did not prevent the merchant from having his way with her on multiple nights. Fearful of being lashed again, she tearfully endured his assault of her body.

Ehiosu's menstrual cycle began after the second night the merchant forced himself on her. This brought him disgust when he learned of it and made her sleep in the cupboard. By the time she arrived at Port Antonio the lashes on her back were infected and her innocence stripped.

Ehiosu exited the vessel, stumbling from weariness; both from the fever and lack of sleep. A local fisherman's wife took note of the blood that crossed the back of her dress and the sweat on her brow. The woman had seen this before in pawned women and slaves. The merchants would whip them to exert dominance and evoke fear. They did not care to dress the wounds. Merchant vessels were not sanitary places for those who could not bathe or dress a wound.

While the merchant went about selling his wares, the fisherman's wife pulled Ehiosu to the side. They snuck off to a hut where the fisherman's wife cleaned the wounds and applied a salve of aloe vera. With a change of clothes and her hair washed and pinned beneath a gele worn to the right, she was able to move about disguised as a married local woman.

The fisherman's wife's name was Kaleisha. Once Ehiosu's wounds were tended and she had a proper bath and change of clothes, Kaleisha took her to a man who helped Ehiosu get transport out of town to a nearby church. The church was used as an escape haven for runaway slaves and servants. There was a trap door beneath the pulpit that led to a hiding space large enough for four people comfortably and up to seven with discomfort.

The next morning the pastor of the church helped her get transportation to Kingston. The merchant was furious by her disappearance but was not familiar enough with local authorities to obtain their help with locating the girl. He didn't pay enough attention to her to give them a good enough description of Ehiosu. They laughed in his face when he said he was looking for a young African girl with no other description. The island was full of them. Not wishing to endure the embarrassment of having her elude him on her first day at port, he abandoned his inquiry. The merchant returned to his ship and left Jamaica minus one pawned girl.

Ehiosu lived in the island nation's capital city for six years. In that time, she learned the native language, she learned the island's culture, and she learned to cook. She also learned English. Ehiosu, at twenty-two years of age saved up money to afford passage aboard a ship to the United States.

Ehiosu knew she would never be able to return to her home. This saddened her. She thought of her mother and her siblings every day. She even occasionally thought of her father who allowed her to be pawned for his brother's debt. Optimistic and thankful for the chance to build a new life, she moved off in a new direction.

While in Jamaica her English became fluent. When Ehiosu arrived in the States, she immediately sought to start a life. She married, had children, and built a home for her family that was brimming with love. Ehiosu taught her children and grandchildren the cultures and traditions of her first homeland of Benin, her second home of Jamaica, and instilled upon them the lessons she learned along her journey. Her story about the Jamaican woman who helped heal her wounds is what inspired Lousie to be a nurse. She wanted to help people in the same way this kind stranger Kaleisha had done for her great grandmother. She wanted to promote the kind of physical and emotional healing that this kind fisherman's wife had for Ehiosu.

Now, Louise was making a trip to a new home of her own. Unlike her great-grandmother, she had her family along for the journey. Her twin boys with their Edo names to represent their culture. Her Jamaican American husband and their adopted nephew. They were embarking on a new chapter in this journey called life. Louise was optimistic that it would be a good decision for her family. She trusted her husband and they had made the decision together. She believed that the experience would bring them much closer together.

Originally the boys were not keen on leaving a home with so much familiarity and so many friends. However, Louise and Mac showed them that with their multiple mechanisms of communication, they could stay connected. This would enable them to keep their old friends as they built new relationships. They could stay in touch and if the distance became more than a physical one, it would be easier to let go over time. Growing apart often happened when people moved away. It was part of life, and she was hopeful that she and Mac could help their boys navigate the emotional elements of the change.

"Mom!! Bini and Tunes are fighting over which room they get!" Keke called from the top of the stairs.

Louise rolled her eyes at the contrast between her hope for closeness and the present scenario inside their new home. Mac was returning from his survey of the backyard. Louise met him in the middle of the empty dining room.

"They're fighting over the bedrooms, dad." Keke reiterated his report to his father.

"Don't worry, we already decided on who would get which room. Let them fight all they want."

Mac wrapped an arm around his wife and the other around his son. For now, their house was empty. Tomorrow the movers would arrive to put their home together, filling it with all their belongings. Over time, they would fill it with memories.

Mac felt it was important to begin by filling it with love. He guided Louise and Keke into the dining room and through the kitchen. He pulled his arm from around his son to open the backdoor. There was a line of trees that marked the edge of their property to the rear. To the left and the right, no demarcation existed. The attached shed just off to the side of the deck was empty. He visually measured the space and presumed he would need to buy some things to fill it up. The first thing that came to mind as he stood in the ankle high grass was a lawnmower. The second, a snowblower. However, the warm air dragged his thoughts to getting a new grill.

Louise gently massaged Keke's shoulders as her husband took stock of the storage capacity of the shed. There was a rumbling of footfalls on stairs that brought all three of them back to the deck. Ubini and Tunes were jostling to get through the doorway. Each eager to be first to plead their case.

"Uncle Mac. I got upstairs first and claimed the big bedroom. Tell Bini I can have it."

"You can't have it, Darius." Mac replied plainly.

"Ha! I told you I get it." Ubini goaded.

"You get it, to share with your brother, Bini." Louise's tone was stern with the second part of her statement.

Keke turned and looked at his mother like she had misspoke.

"Why do we have to share, Mom?"

"Because I need an office space to grade papers and your mother needs a place for her knitting." That second master bedroom is big enough for the two of you to share and you will have your own bathroom. You boys will need to share that bathroom with Darius as well. It is the only shower in the house other than the one in our room and I surely am not sharing with him."

Ubini looked to object. His father's stern look made him hang his head in resignation.

Chapter 4

** Three days after the move**

Darius sat at the edge of the pool. The cool water came up to the top of his calves. His ear buds blasted the melody of Juicy Fruit by Mtume. However, instead of Tawatha Agee singing it was the alternate version by Kima Raynor, Keisha Spivey, and Pam Long, known as the group Total. The dark-skinned boy with box braids bopped his head along to the beat and when the first verse dropped, he sang along word for word. Christopher Wallace's voice prompted him to sway. The meter of deceased rapper's lyrics was the cadence by which the boy danced in place.

Darius Mitchell was in his element when listening to music. As a child, he needed it to sleep. That is how he got his nickname, 'Tunes'. He was two years old and when Louise would put him to bed, he would lay there, arms reaching out. He would say to her, 'Tunes. Tunes'. She had a set of twins of her own, but Louise always showed the boy a special love. She was a nurturer by nature and given his situation, she never wanted him to feel less than in her home. So, each night, she would put on his tunes to which he would fall asleep. Typically, it was local radio. As Darius got a bit older, they would sing together, until she felt the need to retire to her own quarters. Louise would gently kiss the boy on his forehead and turn down the volume to something only he could hear in the quiet of night.

Darius kicked his feet a bit, sitting on the side of the pool. Other than an obsessive audiophile, Darius was an observer. He watched his cousin Ubini chat with a pair of Puerto Rican girls at the other end of the pool. His twin brother Ukeke sat in a chair across the way, reading a comic book. He sat not close enough for Darius to read the cover. However, familiarity with the color schemes of certain heroes, Darius could note that it was a Green Lantern issue. That was Ukeke's favorite. He could have guessed even if he couldn't see John Stewart on the cover. There was a girl laying on the chair to the right of his cousin. She was wearing glasses, so it was hard to tell if she was awake. She laid motionless on the deck chair.

Slowly, Darius lowered into the pool. He studied his surroundings. Most of the kids in the pool were young. There were a few that looked to be teenagers but other than the two girls chatting with Ubini, the high school aged kids were sitting in the deck chairs that surrounded the pool. With each step, Darius could feel the smoothness of the blue pool floor. The cool water splashed up into his armpits that were dry until that moment. He paused, pushing up on his toes to escape the chill of the water. He passed through a group of young boys playing Marco Polo. Darius used his hands to shield his ears from their splashing. He had to pause as one of them lunged before him while eluding a companion with closed eyes and extended arms. When Darius lowered his arms, he noticed a group of boys had arrived and were standing over Ukeke.

He glanced around to see if Ubini noticed but he had not. Darius hopped the dozen steps to the edge of the pool, placed his palms on the ground and pulled himself out. He stood and pulled his shorts away from his legs where they had clung. He jogged off in the direction of his cousin who was entertaining the two girls at the far end.

"What you reading?" The blonde-haired boy in red and white board shorts asked.

Keke glanced up to see him and two others with arms crossed before them. Rather than see them as brutish, he casually responded.

"Green Lantern number twelve. An old issue from last year. They just fought the Anti Guardian. Do you read comics?"

The trio of boys chuckled.

"Nah, that's little kid stuff. But I think you are in my seat, bro."

Keke looked at the boy confused.

"Comics aren't little kid stuff. More than seventy percent of comic book sales in this country are made by men between thirty and fifty."

"Cool story, nerd." the boy in the rear retorted.

The blonde-haired boy who originally spoke to him cast a sly grin at the girl beside Keke. She turned her head away, ignoring the look. Keke picked up on the situation and decided that he was done entertaining these rude strangers.

"I've been here for over an hour. I think you're confused. Go find somebody else to bother." Keke returned to his comic.

"For real. Get up. That's my spot. I want to sit there. Go find another spot to be a geek. Run off to the library or something." The group of boys chuckled once more.

"Brandon, leave him alone and stop being a jerk." The girl in the deck chair beside Keke chastised.

"We're not bothering you, right *bro*?" There was sarcasm in the boy's voice.

Keke caught the sarcasm and closed his comic, setting it down on the chair.

"You're not my bro." Keke stood up. His shoulders were squarer than Brandon's. He was about an inch taller as well, which is not what the boy expected. "And yes, you guys are bothering me."

A second, larger boy squeezed in to show force when his blonde friend wavered. The third boy moved closer in solidarity.

Keke didn't flinch.

Seeing this the girl also stood. Unexpectedly she slapped the large boy in the face with unexpected ferocity. Keke stepped back and chuckled. The other two boys gasped.

"Kellan, what did mom tell you about being a bully?"

"What the hell, Jenna? What did mom tell you about slapping me?"

"She said that if I catch you doing something stupid, I should put you in your place."

"No, she didn't! You only hit me because you know that dad won't let me hit you back."

The boy rubbed his face sheepishly. Rather than provoke his sister further, he turned his attention back to Ukeke. "And what are you laughing at, dude?"

"He's laughing at whatever the hell he wants."

Kellan spun around to find that the boy in front of him somehow appeared behind him with another boy who was slightly shorter. The twin had a stockier build and a less patient demeanor. He walked right up to Kellan until he was chest to chest.

"I would listen to your sister and back off if I were you."

Kellan glanced back and forth from the boy to his sister. Bini could see the intimidation in his eyes, but it was clear that he was too stupid to move on his own accord.

The girl grabbed her brother by the hair and tugged him back out of the confrontation.

"Shit, Jenna! That hurt!" Kellan whined.

"Take your bullshit elsewhere. I don't need it and I don't need your little friends bothering me." Jenna's voice was sinister. Her tone said her orders were not to be questioned.

The girl glowered at the boy she had referred to as Brandon. She hadn't yet let go of her much bigger brother.

"It's getting *dark* over here. We should go."

The meaning in the blonde boy's words was not lost on anyone. Still, the twins and Tunes refused to bite at the provocation.

"See ya around, Jenna."

The large boy wrenched his sister's hand free of his hair and gave her a shove that was only meant to create distance. She stepped toward him a few steps after the push, but he clumsily scurried off.

The three boys and Jenna watched as the would-be bullies marched out of the pool area. The blonde boy cast a last glance over his shoulder before turning out of site.

Bini looked to his twin to ensure he was okay. Keke held out a fist and dapped his brother and his cousin.

"I'm so sorry. My brother and his friends are jerks. Brandon, the one who wanted to sit next to me, thinks he has a chance with me. I have turned that boy down for dates a dozen times and he keeps trying. There are plenty of girls in our school. He should just give up and go for someone else. Not that he hasn't, but he always circles back to me for some ungodly reason."

"It's all good. We've dealt with tougher guys that them." Tunes piped up.

Both twins glared at him, knowing that he had never been in a fight in his life.

"I'm Jenna, Jenna Price. Are you guys new in town?"

"Yes. We just moved here from Newport News." Bini replied.

"Where is that?" Jenna wrapped her towel around her waist covering her tanned figure.

"It's in Virginia. Our dad took a job at the High School here in Saratoga." The twins chimed in unison.

Jenna glanced sideways at them, trying to decide if that was cute or creepy.

"Virginia. That's a big move. Why the change?"

"Our great grandparents lived here in New York. Our dad used to come up here a lot when he was younger." Bini replied.

"That's cool."

"Plus, things in the south are getting a little weird, politically." Keke added.

"I hear that. That Florida governor really has to go. I feel like he will be the next Presidential candidate and he will be like a cross between Trump and Stalin." The girl opined.

"Anyway, I'm Bini. This is my brother Keke and our cousin Darius."

Darius glared at his cousin and stepped forward to offer the girl his hand.

"Allow me to reintroduce myself, my name is...ouch." Bini slapped his cousin on the back of the head.

"What are you doing, bro?" Darius glared once more.

"Don't start with your speaking in lyrics nonsense."

"But you know that's my thing. Ignore my boring cousin. You can call me Tunes."

"It's nice to meet you all." The girl smiled at the interaction of her new acquaintances. "Sorry again about my brother."

"What is his deal?" Keke inquired, tucking his comic into his backpack.

"That was all Brandon. Like I said. He refuses to take no for an answer."

"It seems that pretty girls get their share of harassment wherever you go." Darius replied.

"I would say girls in general. I wasn't always a pretty girl. I was a really chubby as a kid. I would get a whole other type of attention back then. My brother's friends and other kids at school would call me fat and make fun of me because I liked to eat."

"Shoot, I like to eat too." Tunes added.

"He does. All the time. Its gross." Again, the twins spoke in unison.

"Well, I still like to eat. But I had a growth spurt in the summer before high school. My body filled out. I was picked on in eighth grade. A lot, by everyone. I didn't have many friends. When ninth grade began, I was suddenly desirable to the boys, and some of the girls. It was like someone flipped a switch on the hormones in this town. I'm sure a lot of girls would be grateful for the attention." Jenna sighed.

The three boys nodded their understanding and were intrigued by the 'and some girls' comment.

"I never wanted anyone's attention. I simply didn't want their disrespect."

"I get that." Darius replied sincerely.

"The first day of school that year, Brandon came up behind me and hit on me. He didn't know it was me. I had been away all summer. Nobody here knew what I looked like anymore. I had darkened my hair. Brandon used some lame line about coming to him in a dream."

The girl laughed absently as she recalled the memory.

"What happened next?" Darius rested a foot on the edge of the deck chair Keke had been using.

"He said, 'hey babe can I show you a good time?' I replied, well it probably won't be a long time, so I'll pass."

"Oooooooh." The three boys hooted.

"He looked at me sideways like a dog that just heard the word, treat, or walk. Waiting for the next cue or command or the 'just kidding'. Eventually, my voice and face clicked for him. I had already walked away.

He spent the next three months at my house hanging out with my brother every single day.

"That seems stalkerish." Darius chimed.

"You think? Half the time, I wasn't even home. My idiot brother thought that he was just really a good friend. He didn't even see it. Not even after Thanksgiving."

"What happened on Thanksgiving?" Darius squatted down, placed both elbows on his knees, chin resting on his fists.

Jenna chuckled at the boy's choice of posture. His cousins simply shook their heads. The boy couldn't sit still.

She explained the family holiday ritual and how he had weaseled his way in by telling her mother that his parents were both working the holiday. She was subtle with the buildup of how he kept trying to find ways to get her alone and she just ignored all the advances. Finally, she got to the good part.

"In front of my entire family, he asked me to go with him to the winter formal."

The three boys were drawn in. They endured her dramatic pause for what seemed like forever. She took the time during the pause to pack up her stuff in her bag. Once she had packed up, she motioned for them to follow her. Once outside the pool area and away from others Darius caved.

"And?"

"And what?" the girl asked with a coy smile.

"What did you say?" the twins chimed.

"I took a deep breath, took a sip of my drink, stood up in front of my parents, grandparents, aunt, uncle, cousins, and my brother and said, 'I am thankful that you asked me that. I would be happy to."

"What?!" Darius exclaimed.

The twins just stared blankly.

"Everyone at the table smiled. My brother clapped him on the back in congratulations. When all the chatter calmed, I finished."

The three boys followed her to her truck where she tossed her bag in the open passenger seat.

"I would be happy to tell you in front of all my loved ones that I would rather drink construction site porta potty water than be your date to anything. I would rather eat a thousand live crickets. I would rather be dragged face first down fresh, hot blacktop than show my face in public with you. You are shallow, misogynistic, despicable person who is only friends with my brother for a chance to get with me and it is my greatest pleasure in life to know that I can tell you as disrespectfully as possible that you have a better chance at seeing Jesus fly down from heaven on a hippogriff than you do at me ever considering you as a potential date. The white rabbit will be on time before I give any of mine to you."

"What did he say?"

"Nothing. He sat there looking stupid with his jaw open as the whole family stared in disbelief. I left the table and went to my room for the rest of the night."

None of them spoke. The three boys just stood there stunned imagining the scene.

"I'm going to get ice cream. Want to come along?"

Tunes and Bini agreed to go to get ice cream. Despite pleading from his brother and Tunes, Keke chose to take his bike and ride home. He wanted to be alone. He had been content to sit alone and read his comics. Unfortunately, Jenna's brother and his friends decided that they would disrupt Keke's peace.

Keke recognized that his cousin was crushing on Jenna. He felt that being the fourth wheel when they didn't need the third was not helpful to Darius' endeavors. This gave him even more reason to head home.

Keke was lost in his thoughts on route nine when he was startled by the sound of a loud truck. Kellan, Brandon, and their friends raced past him as he passed the Malta Drive In. Without signaling, the truck whipped into a parking lot up ahead.

Keke paused.

He was unsure if they stopped because they saw and recognized him or if that was their intended destination. After a few minutes, he chose to err on the side of caution and ride into the drive-in. Keke did not relish taking measures to avoid a group of bullies. He also didn't care for the idea of them circling back to give him a hard time or following him as he rode past. After ten minutes of waiting, he rode back out to the main road. The truck was gone. Keke kicked his pedals into motion and continued homeward.

He was reading another of his comics on the couch when his father walked in the door. Lousie heard the door and emerged from the kitchen with a sandwich. He informed his wife and son that there is a hiking trail nearby called The Hundred Acre Woods Trails. Mac had spent the morning there.

"I kept hoping I would run into Tigger or Pooh."

Louise rubbed his shoulders while he chewed a bite of the sandwich. Mac smiled at the joke that was ignored by his family.

"After the hike I stopped at the gas station on nine. Some local named Tommy was railing on about how he heard that there was a UFO sighting in the Perseids Meteor Shower. He was trying to convince his buddy that it landed nearby. He was convinced that the ship is currently at the Stratton base being prepared for transport to the Pentagon. Apparently, he knew they had brought it in secretly under the cover of dark and was keeping it in a highly secured hangar."

"Lord, have mercy, Mac. I didn't think you were bringing me to *that* rural of an area."

"Come on Wease. You know there are nuts everywhere. Nobody was paying this man any mind. If anything, they were laughing at his foolishness. Besides, it was the cover story on the National Enquirer on the rack in the store."

"I hope not. There were enough yahoos in Virginia when we went to the rural parts. No need to seek them out here."

"I know, dear. I thought it was comical. I didn't mean to bring this deep seeded trauma to the surface for you." Mac smiled up at his wife.

Keke chuckle on the couch. He loved the way his parents always teased one another. It was such a loving game they played.

He felt lucky in a way.

Not everyone could say that they had a two-parent household where there was love and joy. He and Bini had it good. Darius was not so lucky. He was their cousin the same way his mother was their mother's sister. The bond was built not through blood, but through love.

Lousie had brought Darius home as a toddler when they were young. The three boys grew up together. Keke later deduced that since his mother was an only child, Darius couldn't truly be a blood relative. His belief was confirmed when he woke one night while their parents had friends over. On his way back from a sleepy bathroom stop he overheard the true telling of how Darius came to live with them.

"His mother and I were sorors. Alpha Kappa Alpha at Norfolk State. We were in the same year. I was pre-med she was Urban Affairs. Sabrena was going to change the world. I would joke that I would heal the things she accidentally broke in the process."

Keke sat atop the stairs listening to his mother's voice take on a somber tone.

"Our boys were just 2 years old when I got the call that Sabrena and Maison were killed by a drunk driver. Mac and I were scraping by at the time. They told me that her mother had no wish to bring the baby to Barbados to take care of the boy. Maison had no family that could be found in the country either. I knew I had to adopt him. I couldn't allow my sister's child to end up in the system. It was a small lie that he was my nephew. His mother and I were sorority sisters, and we were closer than any blood sister I could hope to have in my life."

Keke and Bini never treated Darius as other than family. To them, he was always their cousin. Keke knew the truth that his brother wasn't privy to. That was of no consequence. They had been thick as thieves since they were 2 years old. Bini appreciated having Darius to play with when Keke was busy reading. Keke appreciated Darius being there so that Bini wasn't pestering him in those times. Keke and Bini did most of the same things. However, Bini was more social. Keke needed time to himself to decompress from engaging with people all day at school.

"While I was out, I was thinking that maybe we could catch a drive-in movie or go out for ice cream as a family later."

"That's a great idea, honey. Keke, where are your brother and Darius?"

"Oh, they went to get ice cream with a friend after we went swimming."

"Oh, it's so nice that you are making friends already."

The boy nodded and turned back to the comic book.

"So, what is his name?" Louise was pleasantly surprised that her boys were making friends in their new home.

"Who?" Keke asked without looking up from the book.

"The friend that you guys made. What is his name?"

"Oh, I don't know. It's Tunes friend."

"Okay, my dear. I can see that I am bothering you." Lousie gently grabbed the back of Keke's head and kissed him on the forehead.

"Enjoy your comic, Adesusu."

Chapter 5

The next day Keke went for a hike through the trails that his dad mentioned. He rode his bike to the trail. Although the sign stated there was the Luther Forest Mountain Bike Trail, Keke locked his bike up and walked the wooded trail. He wore his earbuds on the ride. Typically, he liked to hear the sounds of nature as he hiked. Today, he elected to keep the music playing as he started out on the trail. After a few songs, Keke stowed them in the charging case that was clipped to his pack and allowed all his senses to be free to experience the upstate New York wilderness.

It was early in the day. Keke made his way through the trails listening to all the sounds of nature that people typically drown out with music or talking or ignore all together.

Halfway through his walk he came to a gazebo. There was a tall, white guy in bike shorts sitting down in the gazebo. As Keke got closer to the man, he could see that there was blood on his shin. The back of his shirt had a few leaves stuck to it.

"Hey man, are you okay?"

"Hi, yes, I think so. Would you happen to have any water to spare?"

Keke pulled a bottle from the small pack on his back and passed it to the man.

"Thank you so much." The man took a sip. He gestured with the bottle and Keke nodded. The man nodded back and then used some to cleanse the wound on his shin.

"What happened?" Keke took a seat across from the man.

"A deer ran out in front of me on the trail. The thing was really spooked. I am not sure what it was that gave it such a stir. I thought it was maybe someone's dog off the leash that scared it. Either way I had to turn quickly to avoid crashing into it. I hit a rock and my bike flipped. When I landed, my water bottle smashed on the ground and all the water leaked out. I limped my way up to here."

"So, was it a guy with a dog?"

"What? Oh, no I have no idea. I never saw anyone until you showed up."

"Is your bike okay to ride?"

"No. I had to push it up here. I need a wrench."

"I have one in my bag."

"That is pleasantly resourceful."

Keke shrugged out of his shoulder straps and set the bag on his lap. He rummaged through pushing items to the side until he found the multitool wrench.

"Why do you have a wrench in your bag while on a hike?"

"Oh, I rode my bike to the trail. I was in the mood for a hike, so I just chained it up to the pole at the trailhead."

Keke pulled the man's bike over to the opening of the gazebo and began to investigate the problem. He flipped the bike onto the handlebars and seat and went to work. The man began to protest but Keke waved him off. The man leaned forward anxiously rubbing his wound to get the bits of dirt out while he watched this unfamiliar boy work on his expensive mountain bike. In a matter of minutes, Keke had the mountain bike back in working order. He grabbed the pedal and cranked the sprocket back a half stroke. He next gave four good forward rotations before releasing the pedal and moving to the rear of the bike to watch the tire spin. He flipped the bike over and spun the pedal while holding the rear of the bike in the air by the seat. Keke clicked the gears to ensure that the derailer properly moved up and down the gears before depressing the disk brake lever to stop the tire from spinning. Once it stopped, he kicked down the stand and dusted his hands clean.

"Wow, where did you learn to do that?"

"My dad taught me." Keke stood staring at the bike with pride, hands on his hips.

Keke sat down once again and began to rummage through his bag. The man watched the boy earnestly. Keke pulled out several objects that he set aside and when he finally found the small case that he was looking for, he popped it open and handed the items inside to the man.

"This is gauze, Neosporin and band-aids. Why do you have these?" The man read off each item as though they were hidden treasures he was surprised to find.

"My mom is a nurse. She makes me and my brother always carry this stuff with us. She tells me that I could help someone in need someday. She will be happy to know that I was able to help you since we always tell her that would never happen. I don't have tape for the gauze, but the band-aids should work."

Keke assisted the man in coating the wound and wrapping the gauze tightly so that it would hold until he got home.

"What is your name, young man?"

"My name is Keke. Keke Wallace."

The man held out his hand to Keke. Keke shook it firmly.

"Keke, I am Wendell Griffin. I am the NYS Assemblyman for the 113th district. My district covers Saratoga and Washington Counties. Please tell your mother, that I said she raised a fine young man. I thank you very much for your assistance."

Keke beamed and affirmed that he would pass on the message.

Over the course of the next week Keke explored the Hundred Acre Wood trail system. He would bring snacks, water, and comics with him. He would sit at the pavilion where he had met Wendell Griffin and repaired the Assemblyman's bike at times. Others he would sit on a stone tablet he found on another branch of the trail. Mr. Griffin was either nursing his wounds or very busy because Keke didn't see him come back during his ventures. In the evening, Keke would return to the woods to run the trails. Bini had come with him a few times. Tunes joined once but he bowed out early.

Mac had told Keke and his brother that they would be going to the school that Friday morning to meet the cross-country track coach to discuss joining the team. He and Bini had run track at their old school. Bini also played basketball. Tunes was the score keeper for the school for basketball and volleyball home games. He wanted to be on the basketball team, but he never made it. Determined that this would be his year, he practiced all off season with hopes of making the team. Keke saw him out at the neighborhood park early mornings as he headed out to hike the trails. He would stop and watch him from the road for a few minutes. His shot had gotten much better, and he now could dribble with both hands. Keke reasoned that he had a shot at making the team depending on the depth of the roster.

When they were in Newport News, the girls in school would flirt with the guys on the basketball team. Bini had started at small forward the last two years and was second in points and assists each year. He led the team in blocked shots last year as well. He never had an issue getting girlfriends but none of them were what Keke would consider serious. A month here, a few weeks there and they would be old news.

Keke and Bini both noticed that Tunes was envious of the ease at which Bini could speak to women and get them to speak to him in return. It was this second part that was difficult for Tunes. Not everyone understood him and his compulsion to speak in song lyrics or his propensity to randomly burst out into song.

For Keke, cross country track was the perfect sport. You were a member of a team, but you could be by yourself. Also, you didn't have the entire school body cheering you on the entire time. He would get an early lead and then he would be free. Just him and Bini and most times their friend Deandre Ware until the final kilometer when it would become a race. Keke and Bini split the top two spots each time. Deandre was always third. Keke was cool with a little competition with his brother and Deandre. It was fun. To the contrary, while he didn't mind playing Tunes in pick-up games, he didn't like all the attention that came with being a top athlete in a school sport like basketball or football.

As a young boy, Keke excelled at baseball. He could hit well, and he was a great pitcher for someone so young. He had great control of the ball and learned different techniques watching online videos. Mac went to all his games. It excited him to see his boys play well. It was the one thing at which Keke was much better than his twin brother. In track, basketball, video games, studies; the difference one way or the other was negligible. For Keke baseball clicked in ways it didn't for Bini. There was some hand eye coordination disconnect, and he couldn't hit as well as Keke. Bini could cover ground. He could play the field well. He just couldn't match up to the offensive aspect of the game like his brother.

In eighth grade, Keke hit a home run in every game of the season. He pitched 5 games and all of them were no hitters. In the third game, he began to feel the pressure for the first time. It was the bottom of the 6th inning. His team was up one to nothing. There were two outs and he hit the third batter in the opposing team's lineup. He threw a slider. The pitch got away from him, and he caught the batter in the shin when it broke earlier than Keke had wanted.

The next batter was the star of the team. This game was the first time that season that he had not gotten a hit every at bat. This didn't bother Keke at all. He was used to striking out good batters. There was no pressure for him. Not until the dugout started to chant for him to strike the batter out. The parents in the stands began to join in. It was all very distracting for Keke. He knew that the tying run was on base and if he gave up a big hit the game was lost. Keke was also wary of throwing the slider again after hitting a boy. The last time he had used his fast ball so the batter would be expecting it this at bat.

His first three pitches were high fastballs. The batter swung at the second one and tipped it back over the home dugout. He didn't swing at the other two and they were called balls. He had expected the fastball, but the higher pitch saved Keke. Keke had been working on a slower curve ball with his dad. He thought that if he could get it to work here the kid would swing at it then he could try his slider on the next pitch.

CRACK.

The curve ball hung over the plate and as it crossed the boy crushed it deep. Keke could only look on as the ball soared toward the outfield fence. Keke knew that it would clear the fence. He didn't even turn to watch it go. He only needed to watch the elated grin on the boy's face as he trotted down the first base line.

Keke felt the stress of the moment had gotten to him and he went with an unknown rather than something that he knew would work. Hitting the previous batter made him second guess himself and all the chanting destroyed his focus.

The world around him was a dull buzz. He could hear the cheers as the game concluded. He turned to walk toward his team's dugout to join his team as they lined up.

A confused sensation became him as all his teammates were storming the field and sprinting toward the outfield.

Keke turned to see his brother evade the other boys as he trotted toward him with the game ball between his thumb and his first two fingers, waving it aloft.

"Did you see that grab, Keke?"

"No. You caught the ball?"

"Heck yeah, I caught it! I saved the home run. That was my first time!"

Keke hugged his twin. In that moment Keke didn't care about his embarrassment at giving up. All that shame that had washed over him had dissipated. He only felt joy for the success his brother had at saving the game. That was a huge deal for Bini who did not excel at the sport the way Keke did. Keke realized that for Bini, the moment was not about saving Keke. He didn't consider that he would fail to strike the boy out. He just knew the game was on the line, so he had to be ready in case his moment came. Seconds later there were eight other bodies in their pile hopping and cheering.

After the game Tunes presented a retelling of the game to the family in a way that only he could. Adding in artist references and lyrics which drew out the story like an extended reprise, he animated how Bini sprinted from centerfield, hurdled the right fielder who had fallen, and then soared up to catch the ball like the ice cream atop a cone before it could clear the fence.

Mac watched his youngest son. He always watched Keke. Keke was the watcher. The pensive one. Mac knew that to understand a watcher, you had to watch them sometimes. They would tell you with their mannerisms, their facial expressions, and other small ways what was on their mind. Bini was the doer. Mac let him do. But with Keke, he was always watching.

At the game. Mac watched Keke after he hit the boy with the pitch. He didn't stand as straight. He fidgeted between pitches. The methodical nature in which he set up his pitches was gone. His pitching cadence was off. Things others likely didn't catch. But a father knows.

Mac looked to the field and could see Bini was poised. The other fielders were relaxed, expecting that a strikeout was a foregone conclusion. Perhaps he could see it in his brother as well. Perhaps Bini had been watching the watcher. Mac knew better. Bini was not the natural at baseball that Keke was. His twins were excellent runners. They both were witty and clever in their own way. Bini excelled in team sports where he could feed off the energy of those around him and strive to be better in the moment. Keke excelled on the mound and at the plate, where he was alone. Mac knew his boys like he knew his own heart and he knew that Bini was poised because he was perpetually ready to be a team player. The other fielders wanted strikeouts because that meant an easy job in the field. Bini was hoping for an opportunity to be great.

When the ball was hit Bini didn't wait. He sprinted to intercept. Almost as if he already knew what would happen. The boy in right field who was supposed to catch the ball, fell. He was not ready to run and stumbled as he began to crossover run to the wall. Bini jumped over him without even looking down. He kept his eye on that ball without looking away for the fence. As the ball descended to drop over the fence, Bini leapt. He told his brother he saved the home run. Unbeknownst to Bini, he also saved his brother from emotional stress.

Rather than celebrate his third no hitter of the season, Keke quietly ate his sundae. Mac said nothing. Not at that moment. Later, he would speak to Keke alone about the importance of a team for when something doesn't go as planned. How they are there to pick you up. Keke explained to his father that he just couldn't concentrate through all the people chanting. He found it distracting.

Mac understood.

The next game that Keke pitched, Mac called him to the fence before the top of the third inning. He handed his son a pair of ear plugs. A 14-year-old Keke stared at the foam oblong objects in his palm. His dad simply tapped both index fingers to his ears and his son understood. He crammed the plugs into his sock. He put them in every time he took the mound and finished the game with twelve straight strikeouts. That was the last season that Keke played baseball.

Friday morning came and the three boys piled into the Pilot with their dad and headed over to what would be their new school for likely the remainder of their high school tenure. There were several other kids there from seventh grade up through twelfth grade. There were six seniors in all on the cross-country running team. Isabella Kisch, Maren Callow, Taryn Callow, Justin Worthington, Marshawn Fields, and Everett Austin. There were four other juniors on the current team: Anika Salei, Katie Lin, Ricky Burns and Kenan Fields. The twins rounded out the seven-person team for the boys' varsity. There was a freshman boy Jaali Mwangi from the JV that would be an alternate should they need him. The prospects for who would complete the girls' team had yet to be decided.

Tunes watched from the bleachers as the coach had the entire team run a couple quarter mile laps as a warmup. The Callow twins pushed out front early. The other girls were no match for them on the moderate distance. Both girls ran the 100 meter in the spring. On the boys' lap, nobody pushed out to the front. They all kept in a pack. They all understood that the warmup was not a race.

After the warm-up, they ran a few miles. When the last runner had finished, the coach called the end of practice.

"Where did you guys move here from?" Mashawn Fields asked the twins.

"Newport News, Virginia." They responded in unison.

"That your brother?" The boy pointed into the bleachers where Tunes was sitting.

"Nah, that is our cousin, Darius." Bini responded.

"He lives with y'all?"

"Yeah."

"Cool. Does he play any sports?"

"He wants to try out for basketball." Keke answered. The boy stood up, wiping the dirt from his hands.

"Cool. Ev and I play hoop. Do y'all play."

"I do." Bini responded.

The other boy had a confused look on his face.

"He likes hoop, but baseball is his thing." Bini explained on behalf of his brother.

Mac had returned and was sitting with Tunes in the bleachers. He noted that his boys were making friends with their teammates. The lot of them chatted while they stretched.

"You wanna be startin' something, Uncle Mac?"

"What you say boy?"

"I said, you gotta be startin something."

Mac shook his head, stood up and walked down the bleachers to the fence around the field.

"It's too high to get over. (yeah, yeah)"

Mac turned to see his nephew who was giggling at his own joke. This made Mac laugh as well.

Between chuckles Tunes managed to spout one last line of the song.

"Their stuck in the middle." The boy pointed at his cousins and their new friends.

"And the pain is thunder." Mac chortled.

He didn't look back at the boy. He simply smiled and headed in the direction of the car.

Tune scooted through the partially open gate, and jogged over to chat with his cousins and the others until they were ready to leave.

On the car ride home, Mac took an opportunity to gauge his boy's enjoyment.

"Well, what did you think?"

"It was cool. The kids seem alright." Keke added the second part knowing that was the intention of their father's question.

"Now Darius we need to find you an activity."

"I'm gonna chill until hoop season, Uncle Mac. Gotta work on my jumper. I'm gonna have them calling me Tunes Curry."

Mac smirked.

"Nobody will be calling you that, I promise you." Bini poked.

"Not a soul." Keke added.

"Man, y'all are just hating. Watch. I'm gonna show y'all. I'll be playing basketball." He leaned forward, singing into Bini's ear.

"We love that basketball!!" The twins chimed.

"Don't y'all dare go ruining a Kurtis Blow classic. I promise you will be walking home."

"Come on Uncle Mac. Basketball is my favorite sport. The honeys like the way I dribble down the court."

"What did I say!?!"

The boys laughed as Tunes continued to ad lib the 1984 track off the Ego Trip Album. Mac felt as though he were being indoctrinated into a cult against his will. Thankfully it didn't last the whole ride home.

Chapter 6

Bini and Tunes spent their final week before the start of the school year hanging out with Jenna. They had quickly become close friends with the girl. Despite her aggression toward her brother on the day they met her, Jenna was a pleasant girl. She was not into drama, and she knew all the cool spots around town. They really appreciated her company.

Especially Tunes.

The two were two peas in a pod. They shared the same love of music. Bini marveled that the girl appreciated the way he spoke in quotes. She even responded in kind. Bini was mostly along for the ride which was a new dynamic for him. He was used to being the center of attention with the ladies. Tunes was usually the sidekick. Bini thought that this role reversal was good for his cousin's self-esteem.

Bini ruminated on how Tunes tried way too hard to get people to notice his value. Not in a pompous or arrogant way. Not even in a needy way. More in a way that told Bini his cousin was hoping for validation for his unique character. Of course, he and Keke appreciated and accepted Tunes. They were family. Tunes wanted something unbiased. Something he could rely on to confirm it was acceptable to be his genuine self. A bond that he could build. Bini was pretty sure he had found that.

The day before school he elected to not join Tunes and Jenna on their planned adventure. They were doing something that Jenna had proposed as a surprise for

'Darius'. She refused to call him Tunes. This did not deter him from correcting her when they were in mixed company. The day before, they had gone to Six Flags Great Escape. Jenna invited her cousin Janet along as a fourth. She was nice and Bini could sense that she was crushing on him, but he was not into her. It was confirmed when she leaned in for a kiss after they stopped at Martha's for ice cream. He dodged and gave her a side hug and pulled away with a kind smile.

However, that wasn't the reason he elected to stay behind the following day. He had not had any alone time with his brother and that was irregular. Keke never minded the alone time. But if Bini was being honest with himself, he began to feel incomplete when he went too long without being around his twin brother. It began to feel like a piece of him was missing.

Bini told Keke that he was going to let Tunes go off on his own so that they could spend the day together.

Keke appreciated this. He had been feeling anxious about starting a new school. Typically, he would have spoken to his twin about something new and different that concerned him. They always used one another as a second voice and sounding board. Someone to calm those irrational thoughts. Quell the moments of doubt that would sometimes creep in. Whenever one of the boys questioned himself, the other was there to pick him up. They were one another's strength. They relied on this dynamic of their bond to get them through tough times.

The two boys played a few games of basketball after breakfast. A couple neighborhood kids joined them and made it a morning of two on two. Bini and Keke won every game. When they were done, they let the kids use their ball with the promise to return it to their porch.

The boys had lunch, then Keke took Bini on his favorite route through the trails. Once they cut through the woods, they rode the perimeter loop. They deviated from the trail to stop and look over the nearby falls. The water was rushing quickly despite the lack of rain. They both stood there in silence for five minutes or more. They just watched the waterfall. Listening to the different calls of water splashing on mossy rocks. After the loop they went home to washup.

"What do you think this school is going to be like?" Bini rubbed his coif of hair with a towel as he made his way across their bedroom to his dresser.

"I don't know. The kids on the track team seem alright." Keke set down his issue of Carnage and sat up on his bed.

"You think they have some good teachers?"

"I'm not sure. Dad was saying that New York is kinda strict with their tenure rules whatever that means. Plus, Coach Halliday was saying that he teaches history. I don't know what grade."

"Yeah, he did say that."

"What if we get teachers like Ms. Benson from fourth grade?"

Bini chuckled remembering the time they wore the same outfits to school, and she tried to have one of them change clothes so that she could tell them apart. When they refused, she tried to get them suspended. When Mr. Simmons, the principal, asked what they had done, he sent the boys back to class. She was pretty sour when she returned after he spoke with her. Four weeks later they had a new teacher.

"I hope we don't see any more teachers like her."

"Hey Y'all! Auntie Louise said it's time for dinner. Was y'all talking about the lady who tried to get you suspended for dressing the same. But Mr. Simmons told her 'Nah, baby not gonna be able to do it, I tried to take you seriously before and you blew it."

"Yeah, that's exactly who we were talking about."

"What did y'all do today?" Bini pulled a t-shirt over his head. "What was the surprise Jenna had for you?"

Tunes held up the bag he was carrying.

"We was pimpin poppin' tags!"

Both twins rolled their eyes and went back to getting dressed for dinner.

"We went to a couple stores that sell vinyl records. It was so cool. There were so many old school albums. It was hard for me to choose which ones I wanted. Afterward, we went back to Jenna's and listened to them. Her brother came home with those guys from the pool that day. That Brandon dude tried to come in and holler at her but when he saw me, he got really salty. Then she hit him with a few dope insults and slammed the door in his face."

"Then what happened?"

"Janet came over for a while. She brought a pizza. She said, when the moon hits your eye like a big pizza pie..."

The boy let the song trail off. Bini gave him a stern look and he quit his jest.

"Yeah, we ate and just chilled. Janet didn't hang out long. She seemed sad that you weren't there."

Bini ignored the smirk on Tunes' face. Keke gave his brother and cousin a probing look.

"He got that dog in him, Keke. You know this."

Keke looked toward his brother whose face told him that Tunes was simply goading him.

"Anything else happen?"

"What do you mean? We just listened to music and talked about stuff. We were both tired after yesterday. You weren't tired from all that walking? What did y'all do?"

"I think what my brother is asking is, are you boyfriend and girlfriend or are you stuck in the friendzone?" Keke stood up and walked out of the room.

"It's not like that! She's really cool. I admit, when we first met her, I was a little Sophie B. Hawkins. But then I realized that we have a lot of common interests. I feel like she really gets me. I'm not used to that."

Bini absently nodded as Tunes confirmed what he had observed.

"Plus, if watching Bini showed me anything, I don't want to throw away friendship on something that might just end a week later."

Bini shoved his cousin out of his room.

"That's cool, bro. But you're not trying to get at that? Really ain't nothing wrong with it if you are. She kinda fine. Probably not a lot of good-looking nerdy chicks around here. You could have it better than I typically do. Like you said, y'all got common interests."

"Why you gotta call her out her name, bro?"

"Nobody called her out her name. What are you talking about? She's cool people." Bini objected to his cousin's characterization of his statement.

She's not nerdy!" Tunes defended.

"What's wrong with being nerdy." Keke turned around in the hallway. One hand leaned against the wall. One leg wrapped behind the other.

"She's not nerdy."

"Yes, she is. Both of y'all are." Bini slid on a pair of slides. "Whether you are a comic book nerd like Keke or a music nerd like you and Jenna, or a history nerd like dad. A nerd is a nerd. No need to get aggro, bro. Just stating facts."

"He's right. Being a nerd just means that you are enthusiastically interested and knowledgeable in a subject. I would say that qualifies you as a music nerd. From what y'all tell me, Jenna is a music nerd too. I believe the term for people like you is audiophile."

"Why y'all gotta be so dang smart all the time?" Tunes marched down the hallway considering what his cousins had just laid out for him. He strongly considered if being a nerd was a good thing or not. Two doors down, he stopped in his room and dropped off his albums.

"One more question, bro." Bini was now standing in his cousin's doorway.

"How the hell are you gonna play those albums without a turn table?"

"Jenna has a spare she is gonna let me borrow."

"Oh, now I see, you got you a sugar momma." Bini jumped back as he finished his verbal jab. Tunes had thrown a physical one in retaliation for the joke.

The boy danced back a few steps, then hurried to join his brother who was already at the bottom of the stairs.

***

The following day Louise drove her husband, sons, and nephew to the high school. She kissed them all goodbye before heading off to her shift at the hospital. They were early and among the first to get there. Only the receptionist and head principal were in the office when they arrived.

Mrs. Zheng, the principal, gave Mac a tour of the school. He already came by the school a week ago to set up his classroom and took the liberty to walk the campus. He found a janitor who let him into a locked rest room in the corridor near his classroom. The janitor was quite chatty and offered to give Mac the grand tour. Despite that, Mac could use a second go around. He also recognized that there was no benefit to not taking the time to get to know his new boss.

While Mac walked the halls with Mrs. Zheng, Carol at the front desk printed out the boys' schedule for them. She also provided them with a map to get around the school to their classes. All three boys had the same lunch period and the same gym class. Keke and Bini were in Geometry, English Language Arts, and AP History together. Bini was taking Accounting 1 and Principles of Engineering. He and Tunes were in the same Chemistry class. Keke was in AP Chemistry, and Spanish. Tunes was taking Digital Communication and Computer Graphics as his electives.

The boys found their lockers and hung out until the first bell. Even with the maps that Carol gave them, they wouldn't have gotten to their class on time if not for Marshawn and his brother Kenan. Luckily, their lockers were nearby. Kenan was in a couple classes with the twins and was also in their lunch period, so they got quickly acquainted. Marshawn was in their lunch as well.

After lunch, Keke had AP Chemistry, his only class alone of the day. He found the lone available seat was next to a slender, dark-haired girl. She had a rounded face, brown eyes, and a French braid in her hair. She didn't see him approaching. Her nose was buried in a book.

Keke noted that she had her chemistry book on her desk and the book she was reading was a hardcover novel. Her fingernails were painted purple with glitter in the paint. As he got over shoulder, he could see that the title was atop the page she was currently tracing her speckled fingertip down. The author's name was atop the previous one. The Hate U Give by Angie Thomas. It wasn't what Keke expected. The boy made a mental note.

"This seat taken?"

The girl did not respond. Keke sat anyway.

"I'm Keke." He turned toward the girl, flashing a genuine smile.

"I'm reading." The girl didn't look up as she spat her dry response.

"It's a good book. One of my mother's favorites."

"I'm reading." The girl repeated.

Keke dropped the matter and took out his textbook. It was the only class that still had a physical textbook. All the others were digital. When the teacher told the class to settle down, the girl beside him casually slid a bookmark into the binding where she left off and pulled a mechanical pencil from behind her left ear.

The teacher, Ms. O'Brien, read through the syllabus with them and discussed the grading structure for the year's curriculum. As she spoke, she strolled about the room handing out copies of the syllabus to each student. There were twenty in total.

When she was finished, Ms. O'Brien took the attendance. Keke recognized the name Anika Salei when it was called out. She was one of the girls from his track tryout. He glanced up to see the hand of the girl at the table nearest to the door go up in the air.

Keke had taken the time to learn the names of all the other students who were at the track practice. When he asked about her last name, she had explained that her parents immigrated from Belarus when they were teenagers. What she didn't tell Keke or anyone else was that her grandparents on her father's side had died from the fallout of Chernobyl. They lived close to the border. Their death left her father orphaned at a young age. He lived with an uncle until he graduated second-day school. He met Anika's mother shortly after moving there. They became close and after high school they fled to the United States to pursue careers in Engineering via visa, and never returned to their native country.

A few roll names later, the girl to his right slowly put her right arm up as the teacher called out, Emma Wakins. Keke was the last student on the roll call.

At the end of class, Ms. O'Brien asked Keke to hang back and speak with her. He didn't notice it at the moment, but the girl Emma also remained in the class.

"I just wanted to talk to you about how you are settling in. Are you finding your way around, okay?"

"Yes, ma'am. My friend Marshawn and his brother Kenan helped us a lot."

"Oh, you know the Fields. I see their mother Jennifer at the gym all the time. Are you related? It is good to have family when you transfer to a new school."

"No, we aren't related, ma'am."

"I noted that you said, 'us.' Do you have a sibling in the high school as well?"

"Yes, ma'am. I have a twin brother, Bini."

"Interesting. It is always good to have someone else with you when you have to go to a new school. My husband was an army brat. He bounced around and he said it was a little easier since he and his sister Tammy were together.

"Yeah, I have a cousin here and my dad works here as well."

"Your dad. Oh wait, are you the new history teacher's son? Oh Lord. I was trying to make sure that you had a support system and here you are with a whole family in the school. Silly of me. I clearly should have done my homework. I'm sorry for holding you up. I will see you tomorrow, Keke. It is nice to have you in my class."

"It's no problem, ma'am. Thank you for being concerned."

As Keke turned to leave, he nearly bumped into Emma who was only just then departing the classroom.

She scurried past him and rushed down the hall. Confused, he jogged to catch up with her.

"Hey, wait!"

The girl stopped and awkwardly did an about face.

"Were you eavesdropping on our conversation?"

"Why would I eavesdrop on a conversation I didn't even know was going on?"

"Then why did you stay after class?"

"I was finishing my chapter, if you must know."

"Your what?"

The girl reached into her bag and pulled out 'The Hate U Give' and waved it in Keke's face.

He leaned back and the girl didn't allow him to interrogate her any further. She turned and stormed off, shoving the book back in her bag as she fled. Keke watched Emma turn the corner. She disappeared and he noted his cousin down the hallway staring at her as well. Tunes turned to Keke, arms upturned and a confused look on his face. Keke wrapped an arm around the boy as he got near to him and shook his head in response to the gesture that was a question. Together, they headed off to find Bini on their way to their gym class.

***

"Wease, I couldn't believe it when the young man asked me about the battle map from the Battle of Bemis Heights that I have hanging behind my desk. Who would have thought that a teenaged boy in this day and age would be a history buff for the American Revolution."

Louise passed the basket of crescent rolls to Bini who was eyeing them from across the table. The boy had been waiting for a pause in his father's story so that he could ask for them.

"He knew about Brigadier General Enoch Poor. The friction between General Gates and Benedict Arnold. I was thoroughly impressed."

"That does sound impressive dear." Louise added to show she was paying attention before ripping a crescent roll in half and dipping it in the broth of the stew chicken in her bowl.

"Wasn't Benedict Arnold a traitor Uncle Mac?" Tunes pushed aside a sprig of thyme before stabbing into a chunk of chicken and shoving the tender meat into his mouth.

Mac stopped speaking. He stared at the boy with a look that they all knew quite well. It was a pensive gaze. Mac used this whenever someone took what he believed to be a complicated subject and attempted to simplify it or repeated someone else's crude simplification.

Mac removed his glasses and set the angled temple tip in the left corner of his mouth. He glanced upward to the ceiling momentarily, as though seeking strength and guidance from a higher power. However, what Mac was seeking was the will to have patience with his adopted nephew.

"Benedict Arnold was a complicated man."

"But he betrayed us, right? He was Washington's right-hand man and he traded sides to the British, didn't he? Scandalous, money greed and lust, in this trife life, there ain't no one you can trust."

"Boy! Damn your public-school education! And stop ruining the music of my generation with your foolishness."

Louise gave her husband a stern look and the grip on her fork stiffened.

Mac took note and softened his approach and his language.

"Darius, people would think that you didn't grow up in the home of a historian."

Mac sighed deeply.

Tunes looked confused momentarily and then dove into his chicken, never taking his eyes off his uncle. Tunes loved it when Mac told stories. Especially new ones. Growing up in Newport News, there were frequent family trips to Williamsburg. Tunes could draw a map of each historical site from memory. The George Wythe House, St. George Tucker House, Bassett Hall, Henry Wetherburn's Tavern, the Benjamin Powell House. They had been to the Jamestown Settlement equally as many times and he could plot the pertinent landmarks just as easily.

Tunes had been to Fort Monroe with the family and on school trips. It is said that the first Africans to arrive in America arrived there on a ship called the White Lion. The White Lion sailed out of the Netherlands and arrive with twenty slaves that were traded for food in 1619. The first African born in America was named William. There is a plaque post that tells of him at the Fort. He always remembered this because the slave baby had his middle name. A young Darius William Mitchell would pretend that he was given that name because of this boy.

Tune didn't remember his parents. They had died when he was just eighteen months old. Killed by a drunk driver. For all he knew his thoughts about the origin of his middle name were true. Then, one day he asked his Aunt Louise about where his middle name came from, and she had told him that was not the case. Still, he loved to hear his uncle weave a tale from history.

"Darius, what you need to know about Benedict Arnold was that he was a complicated man. A man that had a very strong personality. That personality didn't earn the favor of many people. He was average height, but his athleticism and endurance were well above average. His father was a drunkard. This brought shame to what was one of the founding families of the Virginia colony. Benedict Arnold was sensitive to any slight against his character due to the residual shame he felt over his father's addiction. Ironically, Arnold was known to rub it in others' faces when it was he who had disgraced them. He was a tenacious leader who often outperformed his counterparts."

"So, he was a boss on the battlefield? Like, I'm a boss. I call the shots." Tunes chimed.

"Many soldiers who had served with him had the opinion that he was the greatest officer they had ever had the pleasure of service under. In that respect, you could say he was a boss on the battlefield."

"Then he was the GOAT? Dang, then why did he betray his country if he was such a great leader for the colonists?"

"You see Darius, Arnold liked to be flashy. He wanted people to see him as important. A man of means.

He would do things that were advised against to be defiant and to show off. He was investigated for military misconduct by former adjutant general Joseph Reed. In January of 1779, Arnold doubted the cause he had been fighting for due to Reed's investigation and was ready to be finished with the military. Reed was viewed as a patriot, but he was only using his investigation into Arnold to launch his career further."

"Arnold was struggling with money and was suffering with injuries. After all that, the witch hunt by Reed was too much. If that all wasn't enough, then the fact that the British viewed Arnold as some great military mind while the people in the colonies perceived men like him as violent mercenaries had sealed it. Either way, the man went where the money and the respect was at."

"Money, Power, Respect. I dig that."

"The key to life." The twins sung in a deep voice.

Mac went back to his meal, disheartened that what was learned once again simplified a grand concept.

Chapter 7

Saturday came and there was a cross-country track meet with a handful of other schools. The event was hosted by Ballston Spa High School. Tunes was the first person ready. He was showered and fully dressed when Louise got up to put her coffee on. She worked the night shift at the hospital the previous night. Still, she was up making breakfast for her family.

Louise presumed that her nephew was simply hungry and eager to watch his cousins have their first race at their new school. However, when Bini started teasing him about being ready to go, she surmised that perhaps there was an alternative motive, likely of the female persuasion. Neither he nor her boys mentioned anything about this Jenna that he had been spending time with. However, there were a handful of times where they were discussing the girl while Louise was in her knitting room. She could hear every word that was communicated from the bedroom on the adjacent wall. From this she gleaned that Jenna and Tunes were friends and that she went to a different school. She gathered that Jenna liked music as much as her nephew. Louise also gathered that Bini and Keke had been teasing him about their relationship not being more than a friendship. She hoped they would all learn the lesson in this on their own.

The twins had a very small breakfast. Enough to ensure they didn't lose their energy midrace but not so much that they would be hindered during their run. Louise had seen them eat like this for three years. Still, she made a large breakfast as though feeding a family twice their size. Once the family had their fill, she packed up individual 'second breakfast' containers for the twins. Darius had scarfed down enough to sate a grown man for a day, Louise packed a container for her nephew, nonetheless. The containers were labeled by name and placed on the second shelf inside the refrigerator.

Louise dropped the men in her life off at the State Park, wished them well, then headed home to get some rest for work.

Bini and Keke met up with Coach Halliday and the rest of the team at the park. Everyone was stretching near the beginning of the course. The coach explained to the team what the course would be and to make sure they stayed between the boundaries.

Tunes scanned the crowd, looking for Jenna. He immediately found the kids from her school. They all wore purple shirts with the Scotties logo. He didn't see Jenna among the throng of people near them, but he did spot her cousin Janet a short distance away. He went over to meet her but stopped when he saw Brandon and another boy standing with Marty, the boy who was always with him. Marty was there that day at the pool. Marty was wearing the track team uniform. The three boys were pointing in the direction of his cousins and the rest of the Saratoga team. They were leaning in together and snickering. Their plotting was interrupted when the Ballston Spa coach called Marty to come get ready for the race. When he left, the other two boys ran off along the race path.

"What do you think those two are up to?"

Janet smiled upon noticing Tunes next to her and then glanced off where he was pointing.

"Hey Darius. I didn't know you were coming."

"Yeah, Bini and Keke are racing?"

Keke? Oh yeah, Bini has a twin brother, right?" The girl craned her neck, pressing up on her toes, attempting to see the boys through the crowd.

"Yeah. They're over with the rest of the team getting ready for the race. Where do you think Brandon and that other kid are going?"

"Those jerks? He and Robbie always hang out along the route and heckle people as they run. Sometimes they mess with people. They have gotten in trouble for it so many times, but they keep doing it. I don't know why my cousin hangs out with him. Kellan was the nicest boy when we were younger."

"Hmm. Well, that Brandon kid is a real clown. I don't trust him. There is something off about him. He is more than just mean. He seems like the type to force a girl to do things she doesn't like."

"Yeah, I get that vibe from him too. His dad is the sheriff, so he gets away with everything he does. With Jenna, he gets really cringe. He just won't take 'no' as an answer from her. No matter how many times she says it. No matter how rude she is or how embarrassing she makes it for him."

"I've witnessed that. She is brutal."

"Who is brutal?"

They both turned to see Jenna standing there.

"You, girl. Whenever Brandon comes at you with that sweet talk bullshit."

Jenna rolled her eyes at her cousin.

"You would think he would give up. He has a legion of stupid girls at school falling for his charms. I am disgusted by him. I make it known in no uncertain terms. He needs to let it go."

Jenna pulled the bag off her camp chair and jammed the chair legs into the ground.

"Why are we talking about Brandon, anyway?"

"He was just here. He and Robbie were talking with Marty before the coach called him to prepare for the race. They ran off to play their stupid game along the track.

Again, the brunette rolled her eyes.

"Those two are so juvenile. Who gets up early on a Saturday to hang out at a cross country meet to harass people as they run by. They had a game last night. Why not just sleep in. They won. Cherish that. Why come here to act stupid?"

"Janet said they sometimes throw rocks?"

"Yeah, they were kicked out of a few school events for crap like that. They were told last year that they would get suspended if they were caught doing it again.

"Do you think they would try that here?"

"There are a few places where there are no monitors, and it is wooded. They could try something."

"Yeah, but they usually mess with the first few people then try to get to the end. Marty is pretty fast and is usually toward the front of the race."

"Well with Bini and Keke, he won't be." Tunes asserted confidently.

Both girls smiled at the way Tunes championed his cousins.

***

The race started and Bini, Keke and Marshawn quickly made their way to the front of the pack. The three teammates really pushed the pace for this first race of the season. By the first half mile marker they were comfortably alone. The twins were used to having someone keeping pace with them early. It was rare that the person did it with the effortlessness that Marshawn did. They both knew that they wouldn't be pushing away on him late as easily as they have with others in the past. He was faster than Deandre. Unless the third boy gassed himself out, it would be a 3-way race to the end. Everett Austin and Marshawn's brother Kenan were in the pack of boys that were currently vying for fourth place. Marty Frye was among them. At the one-mile mark, Frye pushed ahead of his pack. Not to be left behind, Everett and a few others upped their pace as well. Kenan got a second wind and took off after them with vigor.

The twins and Marshawn didn't speak. The three of them were focused on the race. Keke ran out front, a half step ahead of his brother and their teammate. They came to a turn and Marshawn on the inside, took over the lead spot. The three of them continued this way through the wooded part of the track. As they crossed a clearing, Keke saw movement out of the corner of his eye. He slowed his pace enough for his brother to notice. Keke surveyed the woods attempting to determine what it was that had moved. Bini paced alongside his brother, watching behind for the rest of the runners. The two of them fell a few strides behind Marshawn who didn't seem to find anything wrong with that. He was still pushing onward expecting to win the race. Seeing the pack turn the corner, Bini tapped his brother, insisting they press forward and catch their teammate.

They were a few yards behind Marshawn when the boy was struck by an object in the chest. He spun from the unexpected blow, stumbling to the ground. The twins swiftly moved in to assist their teammate. The boy grabbed at his chest, wincing from the pain of the blow. Bini glanced back to see that Marty Frye and a boy from Colonie gaining ground. His head snapped around as he heard laughter from the woods.

"Can you run?" Keke gazed down at their teammate who was still holding his chest.

"I think so."

"Then let's run." The brothers chimed.

The twins pulled their teammate to his feet. Bini wrapped an arm around Marshawn and helped him jog along. Once he got his bearing, Bini let him go. After about thirty paces he started to fall well behind. Bini stopped to go back for him. Keke stopped as well, but Bini waved for him to continue. There were two boys about forty yards back and gaining.

"You have to go with him." Marshawn urged.

"I am not leaving you. We will do this together. You earned the right to finish. I will help you.

"But the race…"

"My brother will win the race. Come on we have to get running."

Around the corner, there was a race official. When he saw Bini carrying Marshawn, he went to them. There was a bruise that was turning purple on his chest. He radioed that he needed a medic. Marshawn convinced Bini to finish the race. He didn't want to, but the race official told him to go ahead.

Bini was able to catch up and pass most of those who had passed him. After his delay he finished fifth, sprinting the final quarter mile. His brother and cousin were waiting for him at the finish line.

"Did...you...win." Bini gasped, shaking as he attempted to squeeze the water bottle that his cousin passed to him.

"Of course, he won. Twenty seconds short of the course record."

"We need to talk about what happened to Marshawn. Is he okay?"

"Yeah, the race official called for an ambulance for him. Someone hit him with a rock or something from the woods." Bini was still breathing heavily, hands on his hips, pacing about as he answered his brother.

"We have a pretty good idea of who did it too." Tunes stepped aside and Janet was standing there.

Bini bent over taking deep breaths. He didn't notice the girl standing there at all. The girl bravely pushed close to the bent over boy. Gently, she laid a hand on his back. An attempt at comfort. Bini barely noticed her touch. He was glancing up at his cousin waiting for him to continue. It startled him a bit when the girl spoke due to how close she had moved.

"It was definitely Brandon and Robbie. I was telling Darius how they have done this before. They got caught once and were told that if they were caught again, they would be suspended and possibly arrested."

Bini stood up abruptly and walked a few paces away from the girl. She didn't know what to do with her hand that was still hovering over the ghost of the boy and eventually stuffed both hands into her pockets.

"Keke, did you see them?"

"I didn't. I just saw something move in the woods out of the corner of my eye. I couldn't tell what it was that I saw. I was focused on the race."

"Damn. Then it is likely no use reporting it. Not like the police or the school or anyone would take our assumption about them as evidence."

"Especially since Brandon's dad is the Sheriff." Janet added.

"I guess we will just have to handle this ourselves."

"Hey boys! What the heck happened on the course? I just came from the medical tent. Marshawn said the three of you were out front and he got hit with something." Coach Spencer Halliday was visibly angry as well as concerned. Justin, Everett, and Jaali were behind him.

"We didn't see who it was, but someone definitely threw a rock or something at him. I saw a movement in the woods. Which made me slow down a few steps."

"We both did. Slowed down, I mean. Marshawn was a little way ahead of us we caught up to him as he fell. He tried to run after a few moments, but the pain was too much."

"The EMTs said he has a bruise on his clavicle. They took him to the hospital to get x-rays to check for breaks."

"Y'all didn't see who did it?" Spencer asked again. The boys could tell that their coach was looking to get to the bottom of this and took it personally that someone injured one of his runners.

"No sir, I wish we did. We were looking to see but we were concerned with Marshawn and the race." Keke was struggling to hide his anger as he replied through gritted teeth.

Spencer noted his frustration and gave him a reassuring pat on the shoulder.

"Come on, Keke. I'm sorry your first win with our school is tarnished by this situation. But congratulations, nonetheless. Let's go take care of this winner ceremony."

Justin, Everett, and Jaali congratulated Keke on the win as they passed by. Jaali hung back as the others followed their coach.

"Did you guys really not see anything?" The freshman asked Bini who had turned his back, expecting the boy to leave with his coach.

"No, I wish we did."

"But you know who did this?" the boy observed.

"What do you mean?" Bini turned his head to the side as though he were just accused of something.

"I could see it in your face that you and your brother were angry."

"Yeah, we are angry! Someone hit our teammate with a rock."

"How do you know it was a rock?" Jaali casually asked, despite his teammate's raised voice.

"Who is this guy, Bini?"

"Oh, hello. I am Jaali Mwangi. I know, it sounds like 'jolly' like Santa Claus, but it is not spelled the same." The brown skinned boy grinned as he elaborated.

"We do think we know who did it." Janet volunteered.

Bini glowered at the girl.

"Well, we have an idea. Nothing certain. We have leads."

Janet's attempt to make up for her slip-up was not well done.

"What can I do to help?" Jaali asked.

"What do you mean?" Tunes folded his arms, unconvinced they should trust him.

"Your friend here said that you think that you know who did it. You didn't tell Coach Halliday that piece of information. Both you and your brother are visibly angry. More than frustrated or concerned. Your brother was gritting his teeth when he was speaking to the coach. You are now. The way your friend here is posturing, it seems personal. You just got to this school. I was there when you met Marshawn a little over a week ago. I can see that there is something more to this for you all."

"I'm his cousin not his friend! But yes, there is something more for this."

"Tunes, you and Janet go see if you can find out where Brandon and his friend went. Come on Jaali. The girls' race should be ending soon. Let's go cheer on our teammates."

Bini liked the younger boy's astute observation. However, he didn't want to include him in the discussion in case they needed to cover their tracks. The less people involved the better.

Chapter 8

"How are you feeling, bro?" Bini tapped the senior on the shoulder as he approached.

"I'm good. Spent five hours in the Emergency Room for them to tell me the exact same thing the EMTs told me at the park. I don't know why my mom even made me go there."

Marshawn dapped up the twins as they approached his locker.

"Our mom is a nurse. She would have brought us in and checked us out herself."

"They didn't find who threw whatever hit me. I would like to find out who it was. I need to chat with them. I owe them a little something."

The twins grasped the true meaning of their friend's words.

"We might be able to help with that." They both replied.

The twins huddled up with Marshawn and his brother and explained what they knew.

Janet had done some reconnaissance on their behalf. She stopped at Jenna's house first to see if the boys were there hanging out with Kellan. Jenna had told her that her mom asked her to help her with some things in the yard so she couldn't stay for the entirety of the track meet. When Janet told her what happened, the two of them knew where to go.

They went over to Maria Cioffi's house. Maria and Jenna hung out often. Jenna wasn't as invested in the relationship as Maria. The two girls went to school together their whole lives. Maria was very much into the ins and outs of the school social structure. If anyone did anything, Maria would know about it shortly after. The vines of her gossip network grew far and wide.

They weren't there twenty minutes before Maria was telling them about Brandon throwing a rock at some boys from Saratoga during the race to help Marty catch up. Jenna immediately texted Tunes to let him know they had confirmed what was expected.

Marshawn was enraged at learning the motive for his attack. Bini promised to help him get payback. However, Keke advised that they think about it for a bit so that they weren't acting impulsively and getting themselves in more trouble than the boys who attacked them. He pointed out that Brandon's father was the Sheriff. It wouldn't do well for the new kids to get on the radar of local law enforcement.

After lunch, Keke had Chemistry lab. This would be their first experiment. and found that he was again left to sit next to the girl Emma. When he walked into class Anika Salei waved and smiled. Despite never looking up from her book, Emma took note.

"Looks like you are making friends."

"I'm sorry?"

"Anika. She's on the cross-country track team. During the morning announcements they said that you came in first place."

"Oh yeah."

"Well kudos to you."

"Thanks, I guess."

When Ms. O'Brien arrived in the class, she explained the assignment to the attentive students anxious to do their first chemistry 'experiment'. After the instruction, the teacher gave them a few minutes to balance a chemical formula for a ten-centimeter piece of magnesium ribbon, tap water, and ten milliliters of three molar hydrochloric acid. Once they all had their equation balanced, they were instructed to work in pairs and follow the instructions in the lab procedures.

Ms. O'Brien paired them by their tables, pairing Keke to work with Emma. He found the girl was methodical. Meticulous. He watched her trace her finger along the lines of text in the lab procedures. Rather than clutter the desk with a second lab sheet, Keke read the assignment over the girl's left shoulder.

He poured as she read and set the beaker down for her to eye the meniscus of the fluid in the glass. Eight green speckled fingertips pressed to the black tabletop, the girl crouched down, right eye closed assessing the curved rim of the fluid. Keke measured the string then checked with his lab partner. She focused on the lines on the acrylic ruler. She used the tip of her mechanical pencil to tap the incremental marking line to indicate the appropriated measurement, which was exactly where Keke had indicated. She looked up to the boy and then nodded. Emma cut the thread that Keke had pinched at the loose end, holding the other tight to the spool. Together, they quietly completed their assignment. The other groups were chatting along as they worked, incorporating other topics as they went. Since they did not chat casually like the rest of the class, Keke and Emma completed their assignment well before any other group. The two of them were focused on the work so that they didn't have to focus on their previous encounter and neither noticed the chatter that slowed the other groups.

All that was left for them to do was to calculate the percent error and the percentage yield. Emma went to her shoulder pack for her calculator. When she looked back to the table, TI-84 in hand, she found that Keke had pulled the paper to the side and had filled in the first value. The brown-haired girl cocked her head sideways as he moved on to what she assumed was calculating the next value. She quickly typed out the values for the formula for the percentage yield. When she pressed the equals button, she found that the boy had accurately done the calculation in his head, and to the appropriate number of significant figures. She watched as the boy finished tallying for the other two trials. When he was done, she placed her hand firmly on the edge of the paper. It was a silent request to allow her to complete the next questions. Keke put his right index finger on the opposite edge of the assignment and slid it toward the girl. She tugged it at the same time and together they moved the loose page. To the untrained eye, it could have been the planchette of a Ouija board.

Emma completed the last few questions on the lab exercise sheet. Now, it was Keke's turn to nod his approval. He then copied the information they had written on the girl's lab onto his form. The two then walked to the teacher's desk, Emma leading the way. One at a time they set the lab sheet in the basket at the corner. Ms. O'Brien smiled genially at the two of them. Keke and Emma then returned to their table and awaited the end of the class in silence.

***

"I hope that they show up today." Tunes said through gritted teeth. "I wish you would, I, I, I wish you would."

Jenna smacked him gently on the back of his head.

"They have football practice. They aren't going to skip to come harass people at a track meet. So, relax."

"I guess that makes sense. It just makes me mad. I knew they were up to no good last time, and I didn't follow them. I did nothing and someone got hurt."

Jenna wrapped an arm around the boy hugging him close to her.

"You can't save them all, hero."

"They say that a hero can save us...I'm not gonna stand here and wait."

"Well, you will have to wait until the next time they show up Kroger."

He tilted his head away momentarily, feigning disgust. She cupped his chin with her left hand, sticking out her bottom lip in a pouting gesture. Tunes tried to hold the cold gaze. His mouth betrayed him as it slowly turned up into a cheesy grin.

"So, where you want to go to eat after the meet, Clark Kent?'

"Ha ha. Very funny. I don't know. I'm kinda in the mood for pizza."

"There is this place nearby called the Harvest."

"Rachel Ray says it is the best pizza she ever had. At least, that is the claim to fame."

"Fame, lol. Nobody cares about what some white lady on a cooking show thinks about pizza."

"White lady?" Jenna punched the boy on the shoulder.

"Yeah, she's a white lady, right? The one with the cooking show."

"Yes, but why did you say it like *white lady*?"

"I didn't mean it like that. I was just saying. Where I'm from, the real people who know about cooking are the grandmas. The Jamaican grandmas. The Italian grandmas. Those old Greek grandmas. The Chinese grandmas that still look like they're twenty-five. They got all the cooking secrets."

The girl stared at her male friend, trying to discern if he was being rude or if he genuinely meant no harm. The boy did not stare back at her. He was gazing around trying to see if the race was about to start. They were standing by the restraining line in front of the concession stand. If not for the horde of people, they would have been able to see the starting line. They opted to stand where they were because it had a clear view of the finish line. Tunes didn't care where his cousins started the race. The important thing was where they finished.

Jenna could feel the thumping of the boy tapping his foot. She noticed that this was something he did when he was anxious. It first occurred to her the day before school started. She told him she had a surprise for him. The entire time, Tunes thumped on the floorboard of the passenger side of her truck. She didn't say anything to the boy. She just noted it.

Jenna was no stranger to anxiety. Despite her confident exterior, she had experienced anxiety a time or two in the past. The first time her family went to the Six Flags New England, her brother Kellan convinced her to ride the Superman ride with him. When they got up to the platform, she noted that a heavy-set man was disallowed from riding the ride due to the lap restraint not being able to clamp down on his legs. She was a chubby young girl. Her brother jabbed her and joked that she better hope that doesn't happen to her. She remembered sweating profusely. Whenever she got anxious, she would get flush, and her pores would pour. When Kellan noticed, she blamed it on the summer heat. He told her she was gross. In return for the verbal jab, she threatened to rub his face in her armpit if he didn't shut up.

Jenna's pulse thundered in her ears as she approached the two-passenger car. Her brother shoved her from behind and she tripped into the roller coaster car, catching herself on the headrest. She turned around and gazed at him piercing through his dopey smile with her ire. The world seemed to spin out of focus as she sat down into the seat. Her legs were cramped against the narrow space between the seat and the front of the car. She gazed down at the lap bar. With both hands she gripped the black pad and pressed it firmly to her legs. Luckily, the restraint locked into place with only a mild amount of discomfort. Ironically, Kellan's long legs made it difficult for his restraint to lock in. Jenna scooted her feet forward so that he could slide his one leg behind them allowing the bar to lock into place. The attendant had to apply some pressure to shove the bar down far enough to hear it click. She tugged on it a few times to ensure the boy's safety. Jenna mocked him for almost not fitting. He shoved her immediately regretting it as his hand and wrist were slimed by her sweaty arm.

Darius' situation was not the same. Still, Jenna recognized the connection between the action and the emotion. She was empathetic.

Tunes reached into his pocket and pulled out his phone. He connected his splitter that allowed for two auxiliary cables to be plugged in. He pressed play and absently handed his companion a set of ear buds. The girl smiled and slid one of the buds into her ear.

This was also something she could relate to. Like Darius, she used music to relieve stress and eliminate negative thoughts and emotions. Jenna leaned in closer, pulling his hand toward her so she could weigh in on his song choice. He slid the phone into her hand allowing Jenna to select a song. The girl appreciated the gesture. It showed that he trusted her in this moment of worry. She flipped through his playlists and found one that suited her. She pressed play and slid the phone into the boy's pocket.

Tunes tapped the button on the wire to pause the song about twenty seconds in.

"Hey!" She protested.

"What was the other option for pizza?" he asked.

"Oh, we could go to Pizza Works. I think Janet might be working tonight. I could text her and see."

"That'll work. If Bini and Keke come with us, could we stop by the school so they can change?"

"Of course. We can ask them after the race. Looks like it's starting." The girl pointed as the crowd of boys took off running across the damp grass.

The Varsity Boys would run first. Then it would be the varsity girls' turn. The JV would follow. It would be almost seven o'clock before all the races were done. Tunes hoped that coach Halliday allowed them to leave as soon as the final race was over. This would ensure that they got home with enough time to work on his Computer Graphics project that was due in a few days. Tunes needed to recreate The Beach at Saint Andresse by Claude Monet using the techniques they had learned in their current unit. He was almost done but he wanted to make sure he finished with enough time to review and make changes if he wanted. He pressed play on his iPhone and both he and Jenna zoned out. The girl wrapped an arm around his as she commonly did and the two of them faded away into the guitar strumming melody of Slide by the Goo Goo Dolls. It was a song that Tunes recently added to his list thanks to Jenna.

***

That Friday was supposed to be a meet with Christian Brothers Academy and Niskayuna. However, it poured all day on Friday and the meet got moved to Monday. Bini was despondent after his win at the Queensbury meet. He finished first place with a time of 16:04. Keke was right behind him at 16:06. Marshawn didn't run because he was still sore from the rock that hit him in the chest. A boy from Niskayuna finished third with

16:16. Everett and Justin were sixth and seventh. Kenan finished fifteenth. Ricky Burns was nineteenth.

However, it was the girls' varsity team that stole the show. Isabelle, the twins, and Anika finished first through fourth. Isabelle and the twins all broke the seventeen-minute mark. Anika was just shy at 17:02. Katie Lin was in seventh place with a time of 17:37. They scored seventeen and won the meet. For the JV a sophomore named Rosalee Martinez came in second and Virginia Avery finished fourth.

When the boys saw their four teammates out in front, they began to scream for them to push and finish. There was a girl from Niskayuna in the mix, but Anika was able to edge her out for fourth place, thanks to their thunderous support. A second Niskayuna girl finished at 17:35 just ahead of Katie. It was a great showing for the girls who had been the state champs the year prior.

Marshawn was one of the biggest cheerleaders for his teammates as they each crossed the finish line. He didn't get upset despite missing a race in his senior year. He was a positive presence for the team. The boy spent a good portion of the pre-race time coaching his younger brother as to how to focus on breathing and giving him pointers on how to run stronger with less effort. He was elated when his doctor cleared him to run in the next event at his Thursday afternoon appointment. When the rain came, he was forced to wait out the weekend.

Keke woke up on Saturday and felt like a run. His brother was content to sleep in, so he went alone. He was lost in his thoughts and was startled as a deer flew across the trail. The deer had been alerted by the boy's presence.

Keke's earbuds disallowed him from hearing the rustling as the doe noted his approach. The tan and white body flashed across the trail a few yards ahead of him. Keke's eyes went wide, his arms flailed, and he tripped off trail. He managed to save himself a trip to the ground when he clamped onto an oak sapling. He suffered a scrape of his right forearm as he gripped the slippery tree. When his heart stopped pounding, he recognized the irony of not having his pack with him when he was close to getting seriously hurt. He imagined Mr. Griffin happening along to help him to return the favor. Taking the interaction with the frightened doe as an omen, he turned around and headed back to the trailhead where he chained his bike.

Keke stepped to the side of the trail to allow a rider to pass him. A few moments later he found himself doing it for a pair of riders. When a fourth rider approached the trail was a bit wider and he just hugged the left side. Rather than ride past, the rider stopped.

"Keke. How are you doing?"

It was Mr. Griffin, the local Assemblyman. Keke had his eyes to the ground watching his step as he moved off the warn part of the path.

"Hey, Mr. Griffin. How are you?"

"I'm doing well. On the mend thanks to you."

"That's good. It's funny I was just thinking about you." The boy pulled his arm up to the show the elder man.

"Ouch? Don't tell me a deer got you too?"

"Yup. Caught me by surprise. I stumbled into a tree."

"That's bizarre. The two times that I saw you here one of us got hurt because of an encounter with a deer. What are the odds?"

Keke shrugged.

"Hey, was that you I saw won a track meet last week?"

Surprised, Keke affirmed.

"And you came in second the next time. Was that your brother who finished before you?"

"How did you know?"

"A boy with a name like Ubini Wallace had to be related to my friend Ukeke Wallace."

The boy smiled.

"I meant how did you know that I won?"

"My boy, I still read the local sports section every morning. I'm not about to change a forty-year tradition."

Keke laughed.

"Well good luck on the rest of the season. I have to get my ride in. The wife and I are headed to a wedding later."

"Enjoy the wedding, Mr. Griffin."

"Thank you, Keke. Enjoy the rest of your run."

Chapter 9

A few weeks later was the homecoming game for Ballston Spa. The Scotties beat Niskayuna sixteen to thirteen in Overtime. Brandon Gause scored both touchdowns. He was extremely focused on the game. He felt that losing the homecoming game was like the end of the world for a senior quarterback. Jenna laughed hysterically as Brandon's cousin Amelia was crowned homecoming queen during the halftime ceremony. The following night was the homecoming dance. She had heard Brandon brag to her brother Kellan that he planned on being crowned homecoming king many times in the past few weeks. Jenna was willing to bet that he was less inclined to win that title now that his cousin was queen. Then she reconsidered that his arrogance wouldn't allow the shadow of incest to ruin what he had set his sights on.

Maria had convinced Jenna to go to the dance. She was less persuasive and more insistent. It took a few weeks, but eventually Jenna conceded. Jenna was cool with this year's theme, so she wasn't too upset that she had to go. She made the decision early on but still made Maria ask multiple times over the course of two weeks. Maria was shocked at how easy it was to convince her because typically she was very reluctant to attend school dances. That was until Jenna told her she would do it on the condition that Tunes would go along with her. She told Maria that she had to be the one to ask him. She added that it needed to be clear that it was not going to be a date. None of that chivalry or lovey dovey nonsense. They were just going to the same place together.

Maria took it as a solemn task to accomplish. It was a rite of passage to get this boy to go to the dance with her friend. She was at Jenna's house every day for a week waiting for him to show up. Typically, she would just approach him at school, but he did not attend the same school. She felt it was fortuitous when she saw him at the track meet.

Tunes was wary of going along. He felt uneasy when Maria pressed him. He didn't understand why he had to be part of the punishment. He felt uncomfortable at dances. Tunes loved music. He enjoyed mostly old school hip hop and other nineties and early 2000's genres. However, he dabbled in a bit of everything when the mood hit. At dances, he didn't get to choose the music. This was always an uneasy thing for him. If the music didn't match the vibe of the party, he would not be feeling it. If it did, he didn't want it to end. Either he was going to have a great time or a miserable time depending upon the music.

However, Tunes felt he owed Jenna for being such a good friend to him, and showing him around town, so he agreed. Tunes said it was the condition of his participation that Jenna had to accompany him the following week to his homecoming dance. This also would not be a date. Bini was dragging him along and having Jenna there would eliminate the push for him to try to be a wingman for his cousin.

Jenna was not happy that he acquiesced so quickly. She was hoping he would make Maria sweat a bit. Jenna found it sweet that he hadn't, though. It wasn't because

Maria was very pushy, he had a crush on Jenna, or that he truly genuinely wanted to go. It was because he was a genuinely nice boy. He had manners. She was still getting used to that.

Jenna had spent most of her young life dealing with rude or disrespectful boys. While Bini was extremely assertive and had a bit of cockiness, Tunes was playfully self-assured. There was no pomp or arrogance to his behavior. It was refreshing for Jenna. She found that she would catch herself in the middle of the school day wondering what he was doing. It wasn't a crush or desire in an intimate way. She just wanted to be around the boy, as she was happier in his company. That type of platonic adoration was rare. Jenna found it refreshing.

Saturday night came and Tunes paced about the living room. Mac watched his nephew as he circled the couch. Expecting there to be a trail worn in if he did it any longer, he demanded the boy sit down. The twins sat on the stairs where they had a clear view of the doorway. They made sure they stayed up high enough as to where their father couldn't see them. Still Mac knew they were hovering like vultures seeking carrion by the way that Tunes head would not so subtly twist that direction every time he rounded the couch.

When the doorbell rang, Darius snapped up from the couch to a full standing position. His feet were momentarily locked in their place on the floor. Mac loudly commanded his sons to behave themselves. With a head nod, he directed his nephew to open the door.

Jenna came in wearing a hunter green dress. The long, bell sleeves were sheer and flowy on her arms. The bodice clung tightly to her feminine frame. The entire dress had a glitter pattern that sparkled under the recessed lighting of the living room. There was a black pashmina shawl hanging over her shoulders, meant to provide some warmth as the dress was not built for the cool night air. Her hair was done up in a twist with a chignon setting at the nape of her neck. Between the hair, her makeup and the dress, the effect was three speechless, teenaged boys.

"Welcome, you must be Jenna."

"Good evening, Mr. Wallace. It is a pleasure to meet you. You have a lovely home."

"Why thank you. My wife will be pleased that you thought so. It seems that you have achieved something I was hoping to figure out how to do for years."

"What's that Mr. Wallace?"

"Catch this boy with no words to say. I may have to buy myself a green dress."

Tunes blushed. The twins atop the stairs chortled.

"Hey Bini, Keke. How's it going?" Jenna craned her neck to greet the boys who she hadn't noticed when she initially entered the home.

"We're good." The boys said in unison. "You look very nice."

Tunes echoed what his cousins had to say.

"Thanks guys. You don't think the dress is too much, do you?"

She was staring at Tunes from about a foot away. Her Victoria Secret perfume was running its way through his nostrils. Mac could see the boy wavering under the allure of the young girl's presentation. He cleared his throat loudly to snap his nephew out of the trance.

"Uh, no. I think, I think it's, it's, the right amount of much." Jenna, Mac and the twins all chuckled. "One of the most beautiful things in the world..."

"You're too funny! But thank you. I wasn't sure about it when Maria picked it out for me. Look, it matches your tie."

Tunes looked down, forgetting too that he was wearing a white button-up with a black vest and a black and emerald tie.

"Well look at that." Mac said.

"We go out a lot, sometimes we dress the same..."

"Don't finish that verse, Darius or I will slap the tunes out of your head."

The twins chuckled again, adding a few gentle stomps with their stocking feet. Jenna rubbed Darius' back in support of his quirk.

Mac pulled his phone from his pocket and waved them over toward the wall out of view of the window's glare.

"My wife would not forgive me if I didn't get a before pic of the two of you."

They stood awkwardly beside one another awaiting the picture to be taken.

"Come on now. Act like you know one another. This isn't a ransom photo. Move in closer."

Tunes turned to look at the girl. With her heels on she was taller than him. When he stepped toward her, he bumped her shoulder and had to grab her waist to steady her.

"Not that close, Darius." Mac waggled his finger jokingly.

The twins had not left their perch atop the stairs and continued to giggle like schoolgirls.

"Sorry Uncle Mac. Sorry Jenna."

Tunes tried to pull away, but she caught his arm and kept him close. She turned to the camera and smiled big. In that moment, Mac decided that he liked this girl. She was dressed in a short but tasteful dress that he could tell was not her typical attire. Yet, she seemed to be the most comfortable person in the room.

After Tunes and Jenna took off, the twins grabbed their bikes and headed out for their evening plans. Their dad told them that there was a meteor shower and if the cloud cover cleared, you could see it pretty well from the Saratoga Performing Arts Center Lawn. He didn't give them pointers on how to get to the lawn through the locked gate. He only told them that he overheard it from some students in the hallway as he graded papers on his free period.

Mac left it up to them to find a way in. He admonished them that it was private property. However, since there was no show going on that evening, there would likely be nobody there.

When the boys arrived, they found that the gate was guarded. Rather than risk getting a trespassing charge, they decided to find another place to view the shower. It was still early, and the cloud cover hadn't cleared. The boys reluctantly headed towards home. Keke skidded to a halt as they arrived at the drive-in theater.

"What's up, bro?"

"Down there. The artificial lights are minimal there. If we go down all the way in, it may be dark enough to see, if the cloud cover clears."

Bini pulled out his phone to check the weather application on his phone.

"The weather channel says that there is 0% chance the clouds will clear by morning. We should just go home. We can watch football on TV. Have dad order pizza. He probably has a game on and ordered pizza and wings already."

Kiki stared off down the gravel-ridden road. He knew that it would be pitch black back there and he didn't have a flashlight. He didn't expect to need one but that was when they were going to sit outside the amphitheater to watch meteors. Now, he was not so sure. He gazed up to the sky. It was a hazy gray. He presumed that there was not going to be a good view unless the weather changed. His brother had already told him that was not likely.

"Okay, let's go home. We probably won't see anything anyway."

The boys pushed off and headed home.

"Let's stop at the Stewart's and get some snacks in case dad didn't order food."

"You don't have snacks in your bag?" Bini questioned.

"Just some trail mix. I want to grab something else though."

"Cool. We can stop. But let's stop at the Sunoco. They got better snacks in there."

"I'm good with that."

Keke was the first to exit the gas station. The parking lot was completely empty. There was a guy in one of the car wash bays spraying down a muddy, red Dodge 1500. The driver, a man in his early twenties, had the music blaring. Keke was familiar with the tune. It was 1970s rock and roll. Tunes would have known the title instantly. Keke was only vaguely familiar. He wondered how his cousin was making out at the homecoming dance. Jenna looked great in her dress and heels. Tunes and Jenna both professed to only be friends. However, the closeness that he witnessed this evening, looked like something more. Still, it was none of his business. If they both were happy, it was of no consequence to Keke that they had a dynamic and unique friendship.

Keke gazed back to see Bini insert a cup into the f'real shake making machine. He knew his brother would be a few minutes waiting for the milkshake. He scoured the sky looking for a potential break in the cloud cover. He stared off to the south, seeing nothing but gray clouds rolling in. He stared to the North, more of the same. He unzipped his backpack to stow his snacks inside when he saw a bright light rocket across the sky. Keke presumed that one of the meteors had broken away from the others and would be found in a divot tomorrow or the next day.

However, as he watched it traverse the dark sky, Keke noticed that it was falling in a peculiar manner. The path was not elliptical. It looked to Keke as though the object was somehow breaking periodically to regulate its descent.

Each time the object slowed, the light it gave off intensified. This made it seem like the object was glowing.

Keke also noted that the path on which it fell had an odd curve to it. Even with the gray clouds blocking out the stars, Keke could see this.

The door to the gas station slammed as Bini exited. Keke turned to see if his brother noticed the object in the sky. Bini's eyes were down. He was tucking his wallet into his pocket with one hand while he focused on the blue straw jutting from the top of his frozen beverage.

"Did you see that thing!" Keke pointed to the night sky.

Bini glanced up seeing nothing but darkness.

"That gray streak in the sky? Was it one of the meteors?"

"I don't know what it was, but I don't think it was a meteor. This thing fell, different."

Bini laughed at his brother as he pulled on the handlebars to his mountain bike, kicking the stand up, parallel to the frame.

"What do you mean, *it fell different*, Keke?"

"I'm for real Bini. It was like it was trying to control where it went. And, it was giving off this weird bright bluish light every time it slowed down."

"Maybe it was a drone." Bini speculated.

"Nah, this wasn't a drone. It came down from high up in the atmosphere."

"Still could be a drone. They have some that fly really high and really fast."

"Whatever it was, it wasn't really shooting. It looked like it was tumbling through the sky. Like a man would."

"You saying it's Superman up there, Keke?"

"No, I mean like imagine a dude fell out of a plane or off a building. It wasn't smooth."

"Well, someone is going to find it six feet deep in their backyard tomorrow. It will be all over the news and then we will know."

Keke nodded at the likelihood of his brother's statement.

"Come on, Keke, before dad eats all the wings."

The boys weren't out of the parking lot yet when they felt the wave of a sonic boom. The calamity made Bini drop his shake. The sound resonated through them. The power went out all up route nine. The boys stared at one another in disbelief as they watched all the traffic come to a screeching halt in the suddenly darkened streets.

Chapter 10

    Keke was struggling to focus on his AP Chemistry test. Although he had a whole week to study, he hadn't studied as much as he would have liked. Therefore, he was currently being challenged by a routine question on molarity. The sonic boom on Saturday night was all anyone was talking about. Jenna's school dance was ended early after the power in the building was knocked out. There was nowhere to go out afterward since many of the late-night spots in town lost power as well. The one good thing that came of the night was that Brandon was named homecoming king. After his cousin Amelia was nominated queen, it didn't have the same appeal for him. Someone in the crowd called them cousin lovers. While that was not a fair thing to say about Amelia, it was great to see Brandon visibly upset after achieving something he coveted.

    He stormed off immediately after the crowning, presumably to drown his sorrows with his bonehead friends. Jenna didn't care so much that the dance was over. Maria on the other hand, was entirely upset. So much so that she did not go back to Jenna's house with Jenna, Janet, and Tunes when invited. The three friends found that Jenna's parents were still out at the Troy City Music Hall for a Morgan Wade concert. The power had tripped at the house but one flip of the main breaker and everything was back on. There was a similar situation for Mac and the boys at home. Louise ended up working a double shift at the hospital because her replacement was in an accident on her way in.

The following day Jenna, Tunes and the twins went out driving to see if they could locate an area where the police had blocked off or perhaps a house or a neighborhood had been decimated by whatever it was that caused the blast. Keke knew it was a sonic boom. He and his brother had witnessed it when their parents took them and Tunes to see the Blue Angels perform. The four of them were saddened to not find anything of interest during their search.

Monday and Tuesday after practice, the Twins, Marshawn, Anika, and Jaali went out riding around looking for whatever caused the damage. They were certain that it had to be close by. It was all a wasted effort. Coach Halliday told them that it was probably a jet that caused the sonic boom. This sufficed for the others, but Keke had seen the falling object. It was not a jet. He and his brother found it very odd that all the teachers were going to great lengths to redirect all conversation related to the incident. If they really believed it to be a jet, then why the avoidance? They both knew that adults did that to redirect from things they could not explain. They understood that being an adult didn't mean you had all the answers, nor were you required to. Their father had taught them that.

Due to these distractions, Keke went down to the wire with the test. It was even worse that Emma sat anxiously beside him tapping her pen as he was the final student to finish. When he laid it on Ms. O'Brien's desk, she had a blank look on her face. Keke only had to sit in that awkward silence for a few minutes before the bell rang. He was careful not to make eye contact with any of his classmates as he exited the room. Tunes could see the stress in his face as he approached him.

"Brother, brother, brother..."

"Not today, Darius."

"Damn, you using the government name? You want to talk about it, cuz?"

"It's nothing. I just had a test."

"So, you always do good on tests." Tunes rubbed Keke's shoulders.

Keke shrugged his hand off.

"Come on let's just get to gym class."

The day got worse from there for Keke. He took an elbow to the face playing basketball and had to go to the nurse. He developed a headache from the hit. The nurse wasn't authorized to give him anything for the pain, so his mother came to pick him up from school. She brought him home and gave him a concussion test and examined his nose. When she was finished Keke changed into a clean shirt while his mother made him a sandwich and some soup.

When his mother was satisfied that he did not have a concussion, she stopped fussing over him and headed out to the school. She told Keke that dinner was in the oven and that all they needed to do was turn it on after his brother got home from practice and the timer would let them know when to take it out. She kissed her youngest son on the forehead and left to pick up her husband so that he could drive her back to work for the remainder of her shift. That would be the last time for this trade off because they had agreed to go used car shopping as they would need a second vehicle for the family.

After Keke finished his sandwich, he decided that he needed a run to clear his head. He left his dad a note regarding the instructions for dinner that his mom would no doubt have given to him when he dropped her off. Still, he wanted to make sure he was responsible in case she didn't tell his dad and he didn't make it back before the end of practice. He stuck a refrigerator magnet over the note. It clung to the door. He pulled his bicycle from the shed in the backyard and headed off to the trails.

***

Kameka ran to the observing room, expecting to find Bart. He wasn't there. Instead, there was a dark-haired girl sitting at the terminal.

"Oh, hey Keilani. Have you seen Bart?"

The girl turned to roll her eyes at Kameka. Without responding she turned back to her terminal.

"Hello? Did you hear me? I asked you a question?"

"And?"

"What is your problem? Have you seen Bart? I have something really important to speak with him about."

"Why is that my problem."

"You're a bitch, you know that. I don't know what Bart sees in you. You need Jesus....and a bath 'cuz you smell like onions."

Kameka barely heard the girl suck her teeth as she gasped in disbelief. She was already out the door. Kameka searched the observatory for Bart but did not find him. She decided to check for him at home.

When she arrived at his room, the door was ajar. She pushed it open slowly. She found that he was packing up his belongings into a suitcase. He wasn't folding any of his clothes. He was shoving and slamming in other possessions haphazardly. He swiveled back and forth scanning the room, shuffling left and right like a crazy person.

"Bart! What the hell!!" Kameka slammed the door as she crossed the threshold.

"Holy shit! Jesus! Wha, wha, why…? Are you trying to give me a heart attack. You scared me! What are you doing here?"

Kameka ignored the question and stormed across the room. She slipped her hand under the edge of the suitcase and flipped it closed. She then waved her arm around the room. Her hand was turned up toward the ceiling. Her neck craned to and fro, mimicking the sway of her arm.

"What are you doing?" Kameka slammed her hand on the suitcase. "And, where are you going?"

"I'm going back to Pasadena. Tonight."

Bart opened the suitcase once more, shoving past his fellow graduate student as he gathered his belongings from the bathroom.

"Bart. Bart! Slow down. What is going on?"

"I can't slow down. I have to catch a flight at Hilo."

"Why?"

Kameka was confused. She was annoyed, and she had enough. When Bart attempted to push past her a second time, she shoved the big man backwards alarming him as he stumbled into the dresser.

"Knock it off!" The burly man rubbed the spot on his lower back where he collided with the corner of the dresser.

"No. You tell me what is going on. I went to the observation room to talk to you about the recording of the feed from last night. You said that you were going to requisition it before our observation time tonight. When I got there, your little girlfriend was there, and you weren't. She was bitchy and wouldn't tell me where you were. I come here to find you packing up like the fat scientist from the first Jurassic Park movie."

"Keilani is not my girlfriend."
There was a tone of defiance in Bart's voice. It didn't go unnoticed that he was eying his suitcase and not looking at her.

"She was probably being bitchy because I told her that you made me stop doing her work for her because she stood me up for our date."

"I didn't make you do anything. I told you that you should, but I didn't make you. You're a big boy. You can make your own choices. You should have told her you can't do her work for her because you have your own work to do, and she is using you and she is a horrible person. That's what you should have told her. Besides, you were still doing it last night."

"Well, she was begging me to do her work tonight, so I had to tell her something." Bart looked away sheepishly.

"I don't even care about it. She can be mad, stay mad, run and cry, run tell dat, whatever. I really don't care. What happened with the recording of the live stream from last night?"

"Nothing. I gotta, I gotta go." Bart again attempted to step toward his suitcase. Again, the young woman impeded his path.

"Why?"

"Why what?"

"Are you kidding me? Why what? What do you think? Why do you have to go? Why are you going home to Pasadena when we have another week and a half here? Why are you so keen to fly out of here in the middle of the night? Why have you not told me what you saw on the playback?"

"Why all that?" Bart inquired feigning ignorance.

"Yes, Bart. Why all that?"

There was a dramatic pause while Bart weighed his options. Kameka watched him wiping sweat from his brow, hand on his hip, he fidgeted back and forth. He glanced at his watch a few times before he made his decision.

"It was some type of UFO."

"I beg your pardon?"

"A UFO. U – Fricken- FO. An unidentified flying object. An object from space flying or crashing into our planet."

"No shit?" Kameka was not sold.

"No shit."

Kameka spun around; hand cupped over her mouth. She absently walked toward the window. Thoughts swirled through her mind. It was hard to focus. What could it mean that she had seen a UFO enter the atmosphere?

Not like one of those nuts on the internet that have pictures and videos of blurry lights in the sky. A legitimate UFO entering the atmosphere and falling to the Earth.

She wondered where it landed. Whether anyone else had seen it as it fell. Whether there was anyone around as it touched down. Realization struck her as she remembered that the feed was recorded. Bart had retrieved it for her that morning. He watched it. He saw what she saw. He was a witness to her findings. So that begged a singular question.

"Bart why are you lea…" Kameka turned to find herself alone in Bart place.

Chapter 11

"I can't believe you were just going to leave and not tell me!"

Kameka and Bart sat crammed in the back of the taxi with Bart's suitcase bouncing between them as the sedan rumbled along the rugged road on the way to Hilo International Airport. Bart was already inside the car when she found him outside his place. The driver had already put the car in drive when she caught up to them. Kameka tugged the door open and jumped in, much to the surprise of Bart and the driver.

"Auwe!" the driver exclaimed.

"Listen Kameka, I'm not stupid. I have read enough conspiracy theory reddit threads. It's time for me to go. Get out and just let me go."

"You're crazy, Bart! I'm not getting out. We need to go back. Driver, please take us to the Keck Observatory."

"No! Take us to Hilo. I have a flight to catch."

"No, Bart. You aren't leaving until you tell me what happened after you watched the video of the *UFO.*" Kameka hissed the end of her statement.

"Just go back and request permission to watch it yourself."

"No, just tell me!" Kameka leaned toward Bart, grabbing a handful of his sweat dampened shirt.

Bart swatted her hand away, the moisture aiding in extracting his polo shirt from her grip.

"Listen, I called a friend at SETI to see if Hat Creek picked up a transmission for your sighting, Okay?"

"And?"

And, I figured that with an object of that size entering the atmosphere, there was likely some type of transmission that they picked up well before it arrived.

"What did your friend say?"

"He said, they recorded a recent group of transmissions that emanated from Beta Centauri. There were three transmissions in total. They were all abnormal. The first one was two months ago. The next two were a week later. All three had bizarre travel speeds. Among other things."

"You're not just gonna gloss over *'they were all abnormal.'* What was abnormal about them? What was bizarre about the travel speeds?"

"Well, in space, radio waves travel at the speed of light or 299,792,458 meters/second, usually."

"I know what the speed of light is, Bart. We both are in the same field of study."

The boy put his hands up in defense expecting her to lunge at him once more.

You said, usually. What do you mean usually?" She redirected.

"Well Beta Centauri is about 390 light years from Earth. Radio Transmissions from that far away would be from a sound emitted 390 years ago. He said that the radio waves continually bounced back to the Earth at unimaginable speeds over the past eight weeks."

"Is he sure that they are from the same source?"

"Yes, they had the same radio frequency signature."

"OK. They identified signatures from an object from 390 years ago. They had speeds that they never saw before. What does that have to do with this insistence to leave town? What does that have to do with the sighting from last night?"

"The radio fingerprint was recorded at 520 Terahertz! He said they believe that they were recent transmission according to the radio fingerprint."

"And that means what?"

"The radio frequency tops out at THF, tremendously high frequency. The perceived limit was believed to be thirty terahertz. A radio frequency of this level is unheard of. It is unimaginable. The stuff of fantasy. The top minds at Hat Creek couldn't surmise how something could emit such a fingerprint. The consensus was that their system had a virus. They continued to track the radio signal, while their IT department went through all the appropriate analysis and debugging measures. The system was clean, but the readings simply did not make sense. Well, that was until..."

"Until what?"

"Until the object fell from the sky, and I reported it to them. They were running and re-running tests and the data was still giving them the same conclusions. They thought that perhaps another entity was sabotaging their work. They disbelieved their IT when they said the system was clean.

Their leadership contacted the government. You know the alphabet boys; CIA, DHS, FBI. They were there when I called."

"There were agents in your friend's office?"

"Someone from DHS got on the call and interrogated me. They then told me to send them the video. I told them that I didn't have the ability to do that. Then they asked me where I was."

"And you told them?"

Until that moment, Bart and Kameka had forgotten that there was someone else in the car with them. Both of their heads snapped forward toward the driver who had been listening intently to their conversation as he winded his way down the road toward their destination.

"Mind ya business." Kameka admonished the driver.

"Listen lady, y'all got me involved with this. I'm just a cabbie." The driver shot back.

Accepting that the man had a point she returned to her conversation.

"Well, did you tell them?" the brown skinned woman questioned.

"No, but Peter did. He was in the room with them. I could hear him say it."

"Then what happened?"

"Then they told me to stay put and not to leave town."

"Then what?"

"Then they hung up and Keilani was there confronting me about her data from the night before. I told her I didn't have it and she flipped. Eventually I told her that you told me not to do it for her and that I had to go."

"Forget Keilani. If the DHS agent told you to stay put, then why are you flying home? That seems wildly suspicious, don't ya think?"

"Lady, do you want to end up at Guantanamo? You should also fly home."

Again, Bart and Kameka glared at the driver.

"The two of you are so screwed. If you saw a real-life *UFO*, then they are coming to get you." The slender man in the front seat with the fisherman's hat had whispered the acronym, mocking Kameka.

Thirty minutes later, they arrived at Hilo. Bart paid for the ride and didn't give a tip. Kameka noticed and shook her head. While her fellow grad student dragged his suitcase from the car and scrambled through the doors of Hilo, Kameka passed the driver a twenty-dollar bill. He nodded.

"Mahalo nui loa."

"You're welcome. Are you hanging around? I am likely going to need a ride back to Keck later."

"If I don't get another pick up to go back, I'll be here."

"Okay, I may be needing your services."

Kameka ran through the doors. Inside she quickly identified Bart. He was one of the maybe fifty people in the main lobby of the airport. He was hustling toward the TSA checkpoint. She caught up to him as he queued up behind a pair of elderly ladies in Hawaiian shirts and oversized glasses. Kameka chuckled because their ensemble reminded her of cartoon elderly people.

"Dude! You can't go home. We discovered something big."

Bart turned to Kameka. His face glistened with sweat from hurrying up to the checkpoint. He had been looking back and figured that she simply stayed in the car and gone home. He was exasperated that she had not given up.

"You don't know how big of a discovery it was. Kameka, just go away. Go get your stuff and book yourself on the next flight out of here. Nothing good is going to come of this discovery."

Kameka scowled at him.

"Or don't. Whatever. I don't care. I'm getting on this plane."

"Actually, you're coming with us."

Bart turned to see two men and a woman in suits standing behind the TSA agent at the desk. The one who spoke stepped forward and flashed a DHS badge. Bart turned and scowled at Kameka as if to say, 'I told you so.'

***

"So how did y'all find us?"

Kameka was aggressively curious. Bart beside her in the back of the SUV, was sweating and shaking. He was convinced that they were going to end up in a ditch.

"We have our ways." The agent in charge who identified himself as Special Agent Swain replied.

"Come off it. Your tracked Bart's phone."

The woman in the suit with the FBI credentials smiled. She liked Kameka. She was gritty. Kameka didn't give any appearance to know the gravity of the situation. Or if she did, she wasn't fazed.

"We tracked Bart's phone." She confirmed.

DHS Agent Swain scowled at her for volunteering the information. He was set on playing the cagey omniscient secret agent man. Agent Swain liked to hold all the cards, or at least give the impression that he did. FBI Agent Dawn Bush had just ruined that for him.

The agent in the front driver seat tapped Swain on the shoulder with the knuckles of his index and middle finger.

"By the way partner, you owe me fifty bucks. I knew they would go for Hilo and not Kona."

"We never made any bet."

"I said I bet you. I was right."

"That isn't how bets work Smarten."

"Whatever."

"So, you were just about to tell us why you picked us up." Kameka redirected.

"No, we weren't." Agent Swain was stern in his response. He glared over his shoulder at Bush.

"Are you guys going to kill us?" Bart whimpered.

Kameka screwed up her face and cocked her head to the side in disgust.

"We promise, we won't tell anyone what we know."

"We? I don't even know anything. You ran out before telling me."

"No, I told you about the UFO and the 520 Terahertz and the Beta Centauri."

"Looks like you have a problem with not telling people what you know, Bartholomew." Agent Swain did not turn around as he pressed Bart.

Kameka baited Bart and the look he gave told her that he caught on.

"Look, we need to see what it is that you saw at Keck. That is why the Agents in Mountain View told your stoic friend here to stay where he was. We needed to see the video evidence of the object entering the atmosphere. We asked that he send it and he said that it wasn't possible to send. Therefore, our only option was to come here." Agent Swain volunteered.

"So, you just want to see it. Imagine that, Bart?" Kameka quipped.

Bart clung tightly to his suitcase.

"There was a miraculous finding and you had evidence of what happened and rather than let them see it, you ran off. I can't imagine how they would be upset. I would think that it would be understandable that doing such a thing would make them come find you."

"Okay, Kameka. Yes, I ran out on you. It was your finding and when I saw the evidence, I called my friend and then ran out before I got you the playback. What did you expect? I thought they were going to come here to kill me."

"We're not the CIA chief." Agent Smarten joked.

"What? I knew they did that! See Kameka? They were there when I called SETI. They are going to take me out after I tell them everything I know. This is why I was going home."

"Listen buddy, if the federal government was going to kill you, it wouldn't be because you had video evidence of what might be a UFO. We would have to kill a third of the population."

Agent Swain gave his partner a look that told him that he wanted him to quit with the glib commentary.

They arrived back at the Observatory shortly before dusk. The staff that were on the night shift were puzzled by the men in black suits that paraded Bart and Kameka through the corridor to the Replay Recording Room. When they arrived, they found the door locked. Bart, who had his suitcase clung tight to his chest stood aside nervously.

"Well?" Agent Swain stared at the disheveled man who was coated in sweat.

"It's locked."

"Okay."

"Well, are one of you gonna kick it down? I'm certainly not strong enough." Bart's inquiry was nonsense, but he was serious.

Agent Smarten chuckled, but Agent Swain was not amused.

"Or," Kameka stepped forward from the rear of the pack. "You could go get the key."

"But I don't have permission. I didn't put in a request." Bart shuffled back and forth unsure of where to stand.

Kameka hooked her thumb towards Agent Swain who was looking rather gruff, his patients running thin.

"You can take Agent Smith with you. The Oracle won't say no to him."

Again, Smarten chuckled. Agent Bush cracked a smile.

Agent Swain scowled at Kameka who wasn't at all fazed by his tough persona. The Matrix reference was a solid joke, and she knew it. His stern look couldn't rob her of that. Not with the smile on Agent Bush's face beside her.

Agent Swain motioned with a wave of his hand for Bart to lead the way. As he turned, Agent Swain tugged on the handle of the suitcase and tore it from Bart's grasp. He set it down in front of the door of the Replay Room. It annoyed the senior agent how the man clung to the luggage like a safety blanket.

When they returned twenty minutes later, Agent Swain looked somehow even more ornery. Bart looked somehow more uneasy. Kameka noticed that there was a third member of the party. Director Matsuda stepped forward and unlocked the door for the agent to enter. Bart attempted to follow him but Agent Smarten put a hand on his shoulder holding him back. Director Matsuda gave the agent a disapproving glance and he released Bart, allowing him to enter the room.

Once the entire party was inside of the small room, Bart pulled up the desired footage. The six of them watched in awe as a black spaceship, larger than a cruise ship, engulfed in fire, jetted toward the planet's surface. Director Matsuda held both hands to his mouth when a smaller object broke off the larger. Agent Swain had Bart rewind and zoom in to see what it was that had broken off. Kameka stole a look at the director and they both nodded that they understood the nature of the second object.

"Holy shit!" said Agent Smarten crudely articulating his surprise.

"Agent Smarten! Let's act like we represent the United States Government and not some UCLA Fraternity."

"Sorry Swain. But was that a..."

"Alien. Little Man from another planet. An extraterrestrial. Yes, it was." Kameka finished what the agent was reluctant to say.

"That man from another planet didn't look so little, Kameka." Bart croaked.

"Whatever it was and wherever it was from, I saw it first."

"Don't worry young lady, we will let you name it after yourself or your dog or your grandmother or whatever. But first, we need to discover where it touched down." Agent Swain assured.

"And were there more inside that ship." Agent Bush added.

"That looked like a flying strip mall." Exhilaration began to replace Bart's uneasiness.

"It was a rather large vessel." The director too was excited over the discovery. "You are quite lucky Miss Ralston."

"We will be needing a copy of this footage Mr. Matsuda." Agent Swain turned to his partner. "Apparently, a copy of the recording could have been requisitioned and then sent to us via encoded cloud server. *Somebody* would have just needed to explain who was requesting it and submit the form."

Bart shuffled backward, trying to slink into a corner.

"As I said, it is a relatively standard procedure to request replay footage. I generally have a handful of requests on my desk each week. Mr. Messner has submitted half a dozen to support his own research. I am surprised that he did not think to do so. It would have saved you folks a long flight here and back."

"Well, we only flew in from Honolulu. However, we will have to take the long trip to the mainland to establish where the ship landed and where the..."

"Extraterrestrial being." Kameka volunteered.

"Yes, where the extraterrestrial being landed. My guess is that there won't be much of it to scrape up. But we will need to quarantine the area. It could be host to alien bacteria or virus that could cause a problem if it came in contact with people or livestock." Agent Smarten never looked away from the screen with the still frame of the alien figure ejecting from the burning craft as it plummeted toward who knows where.

"I can tell you where it landed."

All the occupants of the room turned toward Kameka.

"How do you know where it landed?" Bart turned to her in disbelief. "You hadn't even seen it until a few minutes ago."

"Yes, Ms. Ralston. That seems a bit curious to me as well that you would be able to provide this information." The senior agent added.

"Well, I don't know where it landed, yet. However, I can tell you where it landed, possibly using a least square minimization formula."

"Go on."

Agent Swain leaned back against the doorframe. Both Agent Bush and Director Matsuda smiled.

"It shouldn't be too difficult."

Kameka glared at Bart, daring him to interrupt again. He remained silent.

"When I *discovered* the alien ship, it was on the screen in the observation room. Bart was monitoring the exosphere for his little girlfriend's thesis work. He wasn't looking at the screen nor the screen with his own research because I was interrogating him.

"Interrogating?" Agent Bush asked.

Kameka waved off the question as inconsequential.

"Anyway, I saw the object enter the atmosphere. It was moving so fast. It cleared the screen in the blink of an eye."

"And how does this help us?" Agent Smarten chimed from behind Agent Swain.

"Patience." Was the simple retort from Director Matsuda. He nodded to Kameka to continue.

"Director Matsuda, if you could get me the data on where the telescope was pointing in this video, I could use the multi-parameter phase curve modeling program that I developed."

"But those are used to calculate pre-atmospheric orbits of meteorites." Bart interrupted.

"Patience, Mr. Messner."

"Thank you, Director. That is true Bart. However, the program I developed is not designed to extrapolate the prior heliocentric orbit of the object. I modified the formula to forecast the end point given the rotational speed of the Earth. I typically need about twenty seconds of video to have had the known height at two separate points in time. That would give us a ninety-percent confidence of the data. Given we only had about ten seconds in the wide frame, I am only able to give it with about seventy percent confidence."

"And what does that mean in English?" Agent Smarten inquired.

"It means I can give you an estimate somewhere within a 500 km radius." Kameka responded to Agent Smarten's ignorance of the presentation of her capability.

"That seems like a huge guess, lady."

"Well with the size of the craft in the video, if I tell you to check Chicago and there is a news report about it touching down near Cincinnati, St. Louis or Detroit, then that is your confidence interval."

Agent Smarten thought to interject with another quip but Kameka didn't let him get the words out.

"However, given that there were no reports of sightings on the news, the internet or social media anywhere, I am going to hypothesize that it landed in the Atlantic Ocean somewhere. But come along chief, let's get to my laptop so that I can figure out where our space invader fell."

Kameka walked out of the room, slowly curling, and uncurling her index finger in the agent's face winking as he swiped to knock her hand away.

Agent Bush decided that she definitely liked the girl. Even Agent Swain smirked at the gesture.

Chapter 12

Bini sat beside the hospital bed weary from lack of sleep. He insisted on staying up all night. He checked the time. It was 9:30 am. He should be in school right now. Given the circumstances, his mother let him skip. Across the room his cousin Darius was slouched in a chair. The brunette girl at his side slouched in a not so comfortable repose with her head on his shoulder. Bini smiled to himself at the thought of how awkward they would be when they woke up.

But they were not who he was hoping would awaken.

The faux leather upholstery on the chair he was sitting in did not allow for overnight comfort. Bini shifted many times in the past twelve hours. This was his second evening of night watch and he cursed himself for not thinking to bring a pillow for his seat. The teen stood slowly, stretching high. He reached his arms down toward his lower back, rubbing the circulation back into his buttocks. Standing there over his brother in the hospital bed, his heart was burdened by worry.

Keke laid in the bed with wounds that none of them could explain. Bini leaned over his brother's body. Gently he placed his forehead to the forehead of the sleeping boy. Eyes closed, wishing him a swift recovery in the native language of his great, great grandmother. The words were a prayer they had heard their mother recite many times. The gesture was one that the twins would exhibit toward one another as young children whenever they were apart for any extended period. It became habitual as they grew older. The gesture evolved into a rite, a wish for health and favor. They would do it before a test. It was their pregame and pre-run ritual. Whenever an occasion arose, the twins would press their foreheads to one another. Some would laugh the first time they saw them display the gesture. Neither of them ever wavered. Their mother had explained to them that if there is a way that they choose to show love, they should never let another person or persons sway them from it for any reason. The world was not overflowing with acts of love. She taught them to never shy from showing or accepting genuine kindness or support.

"Kòyo." The boy's voice was raspy, barely audible.

Bini glanced down uncertain he had heard it at all. Keke groggily looked up at his brother. A dry lipped smile on his sickly face.

Bini pushed the rolling table beside the bed out of his way and dashed off into the hallway. As he went, Bini called out for a nurse. The sudden clamor awakened the pair of teens sitting in the far corner of the room.

"Keke! Jenna, he's awake. Keke, you're awake."

The boy in the bed was groggy. His mouth was too dry to speak beyond the single word greeting he presented to his brother. He pointed toward the table Bini had pushed away. His arm was restricted by the tube which fed into the intravenous needle taped firm to the back of the extended hand. Still, the girl in the corner took Keke's meaning. A brown pitcher sat next to a stack of tiny plastic cups.

"I think he wants water Darius."

"Oh, you're thirsty, oh, you're thirsty." Jenna glowered at the boy for the sing song in such a serious situation. Tunes frowned back sheepishly.

He nodded that he understood the look was an admonishment to be serious. Darius poured a cup of water and held it up to Keke's mouth to allow him to sip slowly. A few moments later, Bini came running in with a nurse in tow.

The next forty minutes, the room was chaos. A second nurse came in to assist the first nurse in taking vitals, removing his catheter, and changing out the fluid bags. Shortly after the second nurse arrived, Louise hurried into the room to check on her son. She did not interfere with the care the other nurses provided. In that moment, she was only a mom.

Keke's doctor showed up shortly after Louise and began to ask all the questions. What do you remember? How did you come to be in your condition in the woods? Were you with anyone?

Keke told the doctor that the last thing he remembered was on Saturday, he went for a run in the Hundred Acre Wood Trail. He was up on the ridge over the waterfall when he heard something scurrying off the trail. He explained how on a prior run he had been startled by a deer that he couldn't hear so now he ran with one ear bud in for awareness for creatures. Louise gave a look to her other son to see how much he knew about Keke's past runs. The boy didn't look back at her as he was focused on his brother.

Keke explained that the sound was a frightened fox sprinting away from a chorus of raucous voices. The voices turned out to be a group of high school kids chasing the poor animal. Keke stood in the middle of the trail to cut off whoever it was that was coming from around the bend. He figured that he could buy the fox time to make it back to his den. The group of delinquents turned out to be Marty, Robbie, and some other boys that he did not know.

Not expecting to see anyone blocking their path, the boys quieted down when they saw Keke standing there, arms folded. Marty brazenly stepped forward and told him to get out of their way.

Keke didn't move.

His tone was purposefully belittling as he called them out for chasing a defenseless animal. He turned his attention away from the doctor and toward his mother as he confessed the name that he called the group of boys which was a euphemism for a part of the female anatomy.

Louise shook her head disapprovingly.

Again, she glanced to Keke's brother and then to her nephew. This time they both were keenly aware. The second of the two boys stepped back behind the shoulder of his female companion to interrupt the eye contact. Bini simply lowered his head, silently scolded for the Keke's chosen language as though it were his fault as the older brother.

Realizing that their numbers didn't scare Keke the way they did the fox, Marty drifted back into the cluster where he felt braver at a distance.

Noticing the absence of their pack leader, Keke asks why they were not off hanging on Brandon's coattails. He again confessed to using another euphemism. This time, for male genitalia. Marty became momentarily somber and then angry as he confided that his friend has been missing since the night of the prom. Keke thought about this for a second, recalling the sonic boom from that night. He starts to wonder if Brandon's disappearance had any correlation with the object he saw falling. The wonder was short, and he came back to the moment, shrugging as he abandoned the thought.

One of the other boys in the back stepped forward, annoyed at Keke's cavalier nature. He poked a finger in Keke's face and suggested to the rest that he thought they should use Keke as a replacement for the fox that Keke allowed to escape. Keke smirked as the boy extends his finger toward him. Keke stared the boy directly in the eye, ignoring the outstretched finger.

The boy said they can call the new game 'runaway slave'. This won him a round of laughter from his buddies. While the boy was turned toward his friends, soaking in the accolades for his joke, Keke shifted his stance to get out of direct line of the still extended finger and to get a more defensive posture. He quickly sizes up the rest of the chuckling boys. Before they could turn their attention back to Keke, there was rustling in the woods. The sound caused the nearby boy to shift his stance. Keke noted his tightened base and wasted no time. He shoved the broad-shouldered boy as hard as he could. His foot placement and the force of Keke's shove caused him to stumble awkwardly into Marty and another boy. None of them were anticipating the collision. Marty tried to step aside. This did not prevent his feet from getting tangle with the feet of the shoved boy. The collision caused Marty, the boy Keke pushed and the third boy to crash to the ground.

Robbie held out his hands attempting feebly to catch his companions.

Angrily, they looked up to where Keke had been standing only to find the boy had taken off running.

Even though it was late in the day, the windy path that led back toward the waterfall overlook did not slow him. Keke was quite familiar with the trails. He had run them a few times a week over the past two months. He could navigate them without getting lost. He knew where roots jumped up in the path and where branches encroached on the head space. He didn't need to look back to know that he was putting a great deal of distance between him and the group of boys. The sound of their voices was waning. The fastest of them was likely Marty. From experience, Keke didn't presume he would want to be out in front and to be the first of them to catch up to Keke alone. He knew that even if he were out in front, he was not as fast as Keke. A fact also learned from experience in cross country races. Lastly, their yelling would mean that they were not properly breathing and would likely slow to a halt quickly.

The trail widened a bit at the approach to the overlook and sloped into an upgrade. Keke looked back to find that he was alone. He rested a minute expecting the goon squad had given up. He truly wanted to finish his run that way. Going around the loop to the side trail would add twenty minutes to his run and he was getting hungry. Still, there was a chance that the boys would hangout around the entry closer to his house expecting him to come back that direction.

Once again, their voices began to carry into earshot. Keke decided to just loop down along the falls and cross the bridge and head back up toward the bike trail. He turned and started off down along the steep edge where a simple nylon rope warned of the dangers of the slippery slope beyond. The trail narrowed beyond the falls overlook. The sound of the boys screaming nearly inaudible slurs made something scurry, rustling the leaves. Whatever it was, it was large enough to snap a branch on a small tree along the trail. Keke's awareness heightened, but he didn't see anything other than a falling branch. The sound of an unseen animal stumbling through the brush alerted him. He stole a glance at the forest floor so as not to trip and stumble. As he did, he crashed into something solid and warm.

The force of Keke's body colliding with the unseen animal was enough to send them both tumbling down the steep embankment. In his second unsteady somersault the boy smashed his head on a rock. The animal's weight added force to the blow. The location of the wound felt wet and began to sting. The two were lost in a deadly tumble which was about to terminate in a forty-foot drop to a shallow pool. It would likely be a terminal fall for one or both of them. The world around Keke spun from his tumbling while his head swirled from striking it on the rock. The boy struggled to stay conscious as his body was battered on the rugged surface. His misfortune was exacerbated as he was struck with intense pain of something stabbing into his chest just below his left clavicle. He cried out as the thick blunt object impaled him.

He presumed it was a deer antler given the thickness and the weight of the beast.

He threw his arms out in desperation. Keke envisioned catching hold of a tree. As though commanded by his will, his hands connected with a young red maple. Unfortunately, his left hand was facing the opposite direction. His right wrist collides abruptly with the stubby trunk, fingers unable to latch as the bones in his left wrist shifted, the collision with the trunk resulting in a boxer's fracture upon impact. Desperately he clawed for grip with the fingers on his right hand, ignoring the pain of the shattering small carpal bones as they forced his hand into an awkward bend. Thankfully, the momentary purchase he gained from grabbing at the tree slowed him enough to pull himself free of the deer. His relief of the weight was brief, ending with the sight of the cliff edge a handful of feet away.

Keke knew what was below and knew he had to fall wide of the cliff edge to have any chance of hitting the pool of water below. Keke spun with his momentum, kipping as his shoulders smacked down in his roll. He landed on one foot and was able to press the other to the cliff wall, pushing off into a dive, hoping to land in the water or perhaps in the mud along the opposite shore and not on the nearby rocks.

Keke thought he had passed out as he fell, as there was a sudden bright light and then darkness. He recalled the pain of landing flat backed into the water. He was too dazed to swim and could feel the oxygen fleeing his lungs as he sank.

Keke didn't recall anything after that.

The doctor confirms that the boy's injuries match his recollection of his fall. There was a deep gash on his head. There was a fluid in his wound that they thought might be mercury and they grew concerned. Tests for mercury were negative but the sample dissipated before they could examine it, further. The lab found this to be curious, but the doctor was satisfied that the mercury test was negative and focused on the other injuries. Keke's left wrist was braced, his scaphoid and capitate both had hairline fractures from hitting the tree. The right wrist had a large bruise, but the x-rays showed no broken bones. His ribs were wrapped and the wound in his chest where the antler punctured his flesh was stitched. The same mercury-like fluid was in that wound as well. The doctor was able to flush it out with iodine and there did not seem to be any type of infection developing.

Keke was exhausted after the telling of what he remembered from two nights ago. His mother suggested that perhaps they should give him some alone time to get more rest. The doctor agreed but informed Keke that the man that found him was back and was hoping to check in on him. He inquired if they would like to meet him.

Louise nodded to the doctor and the doctor left to get the man who was waiting down the hall. To Keke's surprise, it was Assemblyman Wendell Griffin who followed the doctor into the room.

"Mr. Griffin. What are you doing here? Are you the one who found me?"

"I certainly am. It was quite fortunate that I did. You were in terrible shape." The middle-aged gentleman nodded a greeting to Louise. The grateful mother stepped toward Mr. Griffin and hugged him much tighter than he expected she could. Tunes shot a surprised look at Keke when Bini joined his mom in her show of appreciation.

When Louise and Bini released the Assemblyman, he took a moment to straighten out the wrinkles in his suit coat. He moved in close to Keke's bedside and began telling his portion of the story.

"I was riding along the trails as you know I am oft to do. It was a particularly late ride for me. I had heard yelling and got curious, diverting my ride down in the direction of the voices. It was in a wide part of the trail, just beyond the bridge to cross over the stream that I came across Keke laying in the middle of the path. He was dripping wet, the ground all around him was muddy. His head, his neck, his chest, were all covered in blood and dirt. His clothes were torn. It was difficult to tell if he was breathing."

"I was extremely worried." Mr. Griffin had turned to Louise. She took his hand in hers and gently squeezed.

"I immediately dialed 911. I gave them the best guess of where we were in relation to the closest trailhead. Since that first time we met I began to carry a small first aid kit whenever I remembered. Luckily, I had it that day. I used what I had to clean out the wound on Keke's chest and applied gauze wrap to his head. It was not quite enough so I rummaged through Keke's shoulder bag and found a bit more. The tape was drenched but the plastic that held the gauze kept it dry. I tore a piece off and applied some iodine to press over the stab wound in Keke's chest and wrapped the rest around his torso, tying it in a knot under his arm to hold it in place. I took off my riding jacket and pulled it on over the dressing to add a bit more pressure. It was a snug fit, but it did the trick. That was enough until the EMS arrived."

Wendell segued to telling Louise about the day that Keke helped him after his own fall. Louise rubbed Keke's arm, proud of her son for helping a stranger in need.

Bini grilled the assemblyman about seeing the boys who chased his brother. Louise gave her eldest twin a stern look. Wendell merely smiled, taking no offense to Bini's frustrated inquiry. He cordially informed the young man that nobody else was around, although there was a moment when he felt he was being watched.

"How did Keke get out of the water?" Tunes asked curiously.

"I am not sure young man. When I found your brother, he was on a part of the trail that was a good distance away from the water."

"He's our cousin." The Twins said in unison, which made Wendell chuckle.

Keke quickly recapped his fall story for Mr. Griffin who was not pleased to hear that there were delinquents running the woods, shouting racially charged insults toward this fine young man who was clearly of far more favorable character than these other boys. Bini watched as Mr. Griffin made a mental note when names were mentioned.

Once Mr. Griffin was brought up to speed, he acknowledged the merit in Tunes' question. The group of them became engaged in a discussion about how Keke got to where he was on the trail. The best explanation was that he had gotten himself out of the water and walked as far as he could.

Keke was weary from having overslept and not eaten any solid food in days. In the middle of their discussion, he fell asleep. When he woke up, the doctor and his parents were there asking if he felt up to going home.

Chapter 13

The next day Keke woke up to Darius bringing him breakfast in bed. On the nightstand to his left sat a small stack of new issue comics for him to read. Darius explained to Keke that the team heard about his accident. They asked Bini what they could do to help. Darius suggested they get him some comics. They thought it was a good idea and the group of them chipped in and got him some reading material to keep him busy until he was back on his feet. Tunes pointed out that Anika had gone to pick them up and got a few special issues that were on top of the pile.

Keke spent the day reading the comics and completed them all before Darius and Bini got home from school. After dinner, Bini helped him into the bathroom to wash up. His mother worked late but still got home before he fell asleep. With help from Bini, she changed his bandages. It was a surprise that his stitches looked good and showed no sign of inflammation. She commented that the surgeon did a good job of sewing him up. She ran her hand across them gently and noted that the wound looked close to healed already and that he shouldn't have much of a scar.

The following day, he had more energy and asked Bini to help him downstairs. It was a warm day for October. Rather than be cooped up for another day, he convinced Bini to help him outside to the yard where he could sit in the sun. Bini asked how he would get back in the house and he told him that he would manage. Bini was concerned but Keke insisted. Bini pressed, informing his brother that he could barely walk. He also noted that he ate a pretty big breakfast. Keke rolled his eyes at his brother's insinuation that he would need to move his bowels soon. He slowly stood up and showed that he could move if needed. The healthy twin smiled, walked back to his brother touching forehead to forehead.

An hour into being home alone, his brother's forecast of a need to use the bathroom came true. Keke's bladder felt as though it were a balloon dangling from the end of an outdoor faucet. He could feel it growing and growing. At any moment it would burst and blow out the side of his abdomen.

He slowly made his way to the downstairs bathroom. His hips and thighs were bruised in the fall and the bones in his legs were still very sore. After five or six steps he considered whether it was worth it to urinate on himself to save the pain of walking.

He managed to make it to the bathroom after an excruciating five minutes. He rested on the toilet for a while before making his trek back to the deck. Keke stopped to sit on a stool at the kitchen counter on his way back. He got himself a drink from the refrigerator, took the pain killers that the doctor prescribed and rested a few moments longer before shuffling back to the lawn chair on the deck. Out on the deck, he flopped down in the chair so hard that he nearly toppled it. He was exhausted and his legs burned. To think just a few days earlier he was running through the woods with little effort.

Mac stopped home to check on him around lunch. He found Keke sleeping in a lawn chair at the edge of the deck. The boy was soaked in sweat and had a fever. He tapped Keke at first, and then shook him when he didn't stir. Flush with worry, Mac scooped up the boy. He carried Keke into the house and laid him in on the couch in front of the air conditioner. When Keke still didn't wake up, Mac called his wife and informed her of Keke's condition.

She listened as he panted between words on the other end of the line. She calmly told Mac to get him into a bath of cold water. Mac slid his phone in his pocket and lumbered up the staircase, one arm under Keke's back the other cradling his knees. Louise listened to the muffled sounds of her husband stomping as he schlepped their boy up to the tub. Mac didn't even remove his clothes. He just sat the boy down into the fiberglass basin and turned on the water. Louise in his pocket listened as her husband's foot falls rumbled, Mac leveraging the railing as he hastened down the stairs. She heard his stomping as Mac took the stairs once more, returning from the kitchen with a bucket of ice from the icemaker.

After he dumped the bucket he sat down on the toilet, remembering that his wife was on the call. Winded, from his labors, Mac couldn't get any words out. Louise on the other end was concerned but remained calm. She was a boy mom and a nurse. She was accustomed to these situations. She explained to her husband what the next steps were and what symptoms to watch for. She told him to call 911 if Keke didn't wake up after the temperature drop. Mac informed her that he understood, and she hung up the phone, fully trusting that her husband would handle the situation at home while she finished her shift.

After twenty minutes in the cold water, Keke became alert. His temperature dropped way down. Mac helped him out of the tub and into his room where he changed out of his sopping clothing. Mac texted his wife to let her know that the bath had worked.

Keke was extremely alert, showing no sign of fatigue or residual effect. Louise, surprised that the bath had worked so well but relieved to find that her son had recovered, convinced Mac to go back to work and finish his day. She explained that she will be home to tend to their son soon. Keke told his father that he was feeling a lot better. He stood and showed that he could walk far better than he had earlier in the morning. He was certain that the morning walk made him weary and sitting in the sun overheated him. Mac reluctantly returned to the school to finish his day.

Two days later, Keke returned to school. He wanted to go back a day sooner, but Louise insisted on another day of rest. Keke was never one to argue with his mother. In AP Chemistry, Ms. O'Brien assigned his lab partner Emma to assist him in getting up to speed. It was more of a request but in a way that Emma really couldn't say no. There was a quiz in a few days, which will be prep for their unit test that will be the ending grades of the marking period. Despite the strong insinuation in the request, Emma agreed to help Keke. They spoke briefly after class and planned to meet in the library at the end of the school day.

The next day, they were granted permission to use their study hall to catch up on the lab that Keke missed on pH titration. Ms. O'Brien was in the lab when the two arrived. She had set up everything and laid out all the necessary materials for them. She quickly explained the directions which were written on the board and in their lab manual. They told her that they understood, and she departed for her class that period.

Emma had previously done the lab just a few days prior, so they were able to move relatively quickly through the setup and steps. Most kids would likely copy the work that Emma had done and get it over with. However, Keke wanted to do the assignment. Emma, wishing to hold to the integrity of the assignment, was pleased that he wanted to earn his grade. A small part of her feared that he may ask to copy to get it over with.

The two had been lab partners for a few weeks. While they worked well together, they weren't particularly friends. Their interactions in class were oddly transactional. Neither wanted to admit that their initial encounter on the first day of school was such that it created a barrier to them being more than polite classmates. However, it was true that there was something that lingered. Regardless of the unmentioned first impressions, they had respect for one another's intellect and work ethic.

The lack of small talk that would have happened in a more friendly engagement enabled the two youths to make quick work of the assignment. When they finished, Emma reviewed her notes from the prior class to ensure that there were not any added tasks that may not have been in the lab manual. Once she was satisfied that all requirements were met, the two of them cleaned up their work area.

Keke balanced a 50 ml burette and a 25 ml pipette inside a 50 ml beaker. One hand haloed around the long glass; he carefully transported them to the sink and placed them inside. The burette didn't fit longways so Keke elected to leave it in the beaker and balance it against the corner of the sink while he rinsed the pipette with acetone.

Meanwhile, Emma returned the stand and clamps to the metal cabinet next to the eye wash and shower station. Keke was on his way back to their station, so she turned to walk up the next row. As she turned, she caught the tip of her elbow on the edge of the tabletop. The blow to the nerve endings at the edge of her humerus, brought out a quick wail. The girl stumbled backward into the shelves beside the cabinet. A plastic bottle of four molar sodium hydroxide solution toppled off the shelf, tumbling toward the table in front of her. The force of hitting the shelf and the pain of her arm going numb dropped the young girl to her knees, her opposite hand cradling the spot where the table had connected.

The entire series of events was slow motion for Keke. The elbow hitting the table, the exclamation of pain, the crash into the cabinet and fall. He had only taken one step toward the girl when he noticed the falling bottle. His initial thought was that it would land on the girl. It looked to be nearly full and likely weighed enough to cause more pain. He lunged, hoping to catch it or at least deflect it. He watched as it cleared the girl but crashed on the table cap first. The hard plastic cap shattered, flinging the fluid in a spiral pattern. The bottled bounced spilling on the table. Keke hit the ground with a knee and threw himself over the girl who was in the direct path, shielding her from the spray.

Keke held his head tucked into the crease of his elbows which were embracing the girl. The back of her head was pressed to his chest as he used the breadth of his back and shoulders to cover her small frame from the splash of the basic fluid.

The sound of the plastic bottle careening to the floor snapped everything back into real time. Emma swiftly realized what Keke had done when she felt his body on hers. The girl pushed him up off her and shoved him into the nearby shower. She turned on the water dousing him head to toe. After ten seconds of splashing, he reached for the handle and shut off the water.

Emma checked herself for potential moisture but felt no burning. Her eyes were on the bottle that rolled across the floor. She stepped carefully past the puddle to see exactly what the contents had been. With the tip of her shoe, the shaken girl rolled the bottle over until she could see the label on the container. Once she saw that it was 4M NAOH, she jumped past the puddle and grabbed the sopping wet boy and spun him 180 degrees.

"You're burned!"

"No, I'm good."

"No, there's holes, in your shirt. It burned through."

Emma yanked on the tight wet cloth of his shirt tail pulling it up to his shoulders. She examined his back but found no burns.

"How?"

"You shoved me in the shower just in time."

"But it burned your shirt. It should have burned your skin."

"Are you disappointed?" He asked calmly. Water dripped down the boy's face.

"What? No. I'm relieved. You saved me. Why did you do that?"

The stress of the situation caused tears to well up in the girl's big brown eyes. Keke looked into her freckled face. He felt concern for the girl whose bottom lip had begun to quiver.

"I'm okay. We're okay."

The girl just blinked, as the shock of what almost happened set in.

Keke grabbed her gently, cradling the elbow that she had smashed on the table in his palm. He pulled her a few rows back and sat her down.

Ms. O'Brien returned a few minutes later, shocked by the scene. She found Keke, gloved and goggled pouring Vinegar into a pool on the table to neutralize the sodium hydroxide that had spilled. There was a pile of white towels from the spill kit covering the puddle that was on the floor.

When asked, Keke explained that they were putting stuff away and the bottle of sodium hydroxide fell off the rack and cracked open when the top hit the desk. He added that he got splashed and Emma pushed him in the shower and turned it on preventing him from being burned.

Ms. O'Brien began to express how Miss Wakins had employed quick thinking. Emma simply sat there saying nothing. Before the teacher could dive further into questions about Emma's condition, Bini entered the lab with a pair of gym shorts, a t-shirt and slides.

"This was all I had." Bini stared at his twin, trying to gather how he had gotten so wet.

"Shower." Keke pointed, reading his brother's face.

"Okay. I gotta get to class." Bini touched his head to his brother's still damp forehead.

"Me too. Emma, you coming?"

"Huh?"

"We have to get to our next class. Are you coming?"

"Oh, yes."

Emma got up and started towards the front of the room, staring at their teacher the entire time. As she passed her, she paused, ran over to the table where they had been working and grabbed Keke's lab. She scurried back toward Ms. O'Brien.

"Here. This is his. We finished." She pointed to Keke who was standing at the door turned and trotted quickly out of the room.

"You good to get to class alone." The boy asked.

"What?"

Keke stepped toward the boy's restroom and pushed the door open.

"I have to change before I go. If you wait, I can walk you."

The girl turned red in the face at the idea of having a boy walk her to class.

"Oh, no. Thank you. And thank you, for, you know. Bye."

Keke watched as the girl scurried off. He noticed his brother down the hall, watching him, watching her before he disappeared into the bathroom.

Chapter 14

An hour later, Keke sat in the cafeteria wearing his improvised outfit. He was eating the lunch his mother packed for him. Keke picked the orange out of the bag and dug his thumb nail in to peel it. From nowhere, Tunes jumped into the seat beside him. He grabbed Keke's left arm. The orange dropped down smushing his sandwich as Tunes tugged on his arm. Keke said nothing. The look on his face said it all.

Tunes began to apologize but he took note of Keke's attire and stopped. The boy pulled his head backward on his shoulders as he craned his neck to the side, squinting his near eye in confusion. Again, Keke responded with a facial expression of his own. After a moment, Tunes simply shrugged.

"You'll never guess what the news is saying about the blackout!"

"Since the blackout four people have been reported missing."

"How did you know?" Tunes was disappointed that his cousin had already heard.

"Do you think you are the only gossip in this school?"

"Y'all talking about the missing people?" Bini took the seat across from his brother. Marshawn, Anika, and Jaali sat in order to his left. Kenan claimed the one to Keke's right.

"Yeah, and did you hear who one of them was?"

"The weird mini mart worker at the gas station on Route Fifty?" Anika questioned. "I think his name is Ethan or Evan."

"What? No. Well, maybe. But I was talking about Brandon Gause."

"No way!" the twins said in unison.

"Who is that?" Jaali leaned forward, nearly knocking Anika's lunch tray off the table. She scowled at the boy who quickly waved his hands in apology.

"He's the quarterback for the Ballston Spa football team." Bini replied.

"He's a racist jerk." Tunes added.

"He's the one who hit me with a rock at the race at the state park." Marshawn rubbed the spot on his chest where the bruise had only just gone away.

"No shit?" Anika scrunched up her face in disgust at the news. "Good riddance to him. I hope he never comes back."

The girl gently rubbed her teammate's arm in solidarity. Marshawn returned the affection with a warm smile.

The group began a spirited discussion of conjecture about the blackout. Through the talk of aliens, Russians, and cyber hackers there was plenty of laughter. Every time Tunes burst out into song, they all groaned, shoved, or shushed the boy. This did little to dissuade him. Lost in the conversation was Keke's funky attire, which suited him just fine.

As they were getting up to head to their next class, the twins were halted by the head of security. The tall militant man looked grumpy. He sized up Keke's apparel, gave his brother a strong look over and then put his hand firmly on Keke's shoulder.

"You're coming with me."

Keke was surprised by how difficult it was to shrug away from the man's grip. He was assisted as the man stumbled a few steps landing on the table.

"Keep your hands off of my brother!" Bini growled.

He put his whole body into the shoving maneuver. The large man had not expected it and tumbled easily. Bini and Keke postured to defend against retaliation. The security guard stepped toward them aggressively then paused. The entire cafeteria around them had gone silent. The sound of him crashing to the table had brought all eyes to him. Anika had her phone out recording. Keke turned to see his cousin and Marshawn ready to pounce behind him. The entire room was watching them. Even a few of the lunch ladies had their hands on their hips in disapproval of the security officer's aggressive tactic.

"Where do you want me to go?" He asked the guard.

"The principal sent me to get you."

The man scowled attempting to seem fierce. He watched as a dozen other students pulled out their phones to record the encounter.

"Lead the way." Keke replied.

The man stood there momentarily considering whether to push the issue. He knew that if he forced the boy there would be plenty of video evidence to cost him his job. As much as he hated the defiance this boy displayed toward him, his alimony payments kept his anger in check.

"That's not how it works. You walk ahead of me."

"You heard my brother, high and tight. Lead the way. We'll follow."

"The assistant principal only wants him." He jabbed a finger at the air between him and Keke.

"You can't always get what you wa...aant..." Tunes crooned.

"We're all coming." Keke nodded to Marshawn who voiced his in solidarity.

"Yeah, all of us." Anika added.

The Callow twins scowled from across the room as half of their track team strode off to the office after a scuffle with the head of school security.

***

When Keke and his entourage arrived at the principal's office, they found that one of their track teammates was sitting on the bench outside.

"Ricky, what are you doing here?" Jaali asked.

The boy lowered his head avoiding his teammates' gazes. He looked entirely uncomfortable. Carol saw that the security chief was accompanied by a group of kids, and he looked even more sour than usual. She buzzed the assistant principal immediately. When he came out, he ordered the kids to go back to class. They stood defiantly. His fury was not as scary as Principal Zheng. She had a way of looking straight through you when she was angry.

He stepped toward the group of teens attempting physical intimidation like the security chief had. He was met with the same rebelliousness.

"You send this goon to put hands on my brother and then you have the nerve to try to scare us off with a stern look?" Bini was seething at the conduct of the assistant principal.

"Ukeke, in my office, now!" He demanded.

Ubini stepped forward.

"We're not going any further until you call my dad."

Assistant Principal Paul slammed both hands on his hips deciding on what to do.

"Martin, grab that boy and drag him in my office!"

Martin Ridgefield looked to Carol who shook her head in admonishment.

She hoped that the understanding that the boys' father was a teacher at the school would encourage cooler heads.

"Listen, Mr. Paul. If you or your bulldog put their hands on my brother, you will have hands put on you when our dad gets here."

"Your dad some type of tough guy?" Ridgefield puffed up his chest stepping toward the defiant twin.

"Ask him yourself. Here he is."

Ridgefield and Paul craned their necks to gaze out to the hallway. Tunes was galloping toward them. He was anxiously glancing behind him. Ridgefield, thinking it a ruse, stepped chest to chest with Bini. The chief of security grabbed hold of the boy's shirt just as his cousin burst through the doorway.

"You think you're funny, punk?"

The security chief was staring straight into the bold eyes of the boy, hands gripping tight to his shirt. He did not see McArthur Wallace march through the opened door.

Without a word, Mac slid an arm between his son and the man. He snatched the left wrist of the ogre gripping his son, applying pressure between the joints of Ridgefield's thumb and index finger. The guard's grip immediately loosened. Mac shouldered the man back a few yards, grabbing the left elbow with his free hand. He swiftly flipped his hand over top and applied pressure to the wrist, wrenching Ridgefield to the side. Mac kicked his near leg out from underneath him. The kick was all that was needed to take him to the ground. Never releasing the wrist or elbow, Mac leaned down and growled in the man's ear.

"Who told you it was a good idea to put your hands on my son?"

The scream that escaped Carol's diaphragm caused by the aggressive move, alerted another security officer in the hallway. He rushed in, surprised by the sight of his boss pinned to the floor by the new history teacher. He looked to the Assistant Principal who was equally stunned by the scene.

"He did Dad!" Bini pointed to the assistant principal. "He told him to drag Keke into his office. Drag."

Mac glanced at his eldest son following his extended arm to Bertrand Paul.

"Is that so?" Mac asked the guard, tugging more strongly on his arm.

Ridgefield nodded.

Bertrand Paul looked to Kenny the security officer, nodding toward the two men on the ground. Bini stepped in front of him, pointing to the window where Anika was recording.

Mac stood up, pulling the guard up by the arm.

"I don't ever want to see you put your hands on another child in this school again, you hear me?" Adrenaline rushed through Mac's veins as he growled at the confined guard.

"Now apologize to my son."

Mac spun not even waiting for the man to speak and stepped to Bertrand Paul.

"Where is Principal Zheng?" Mac's chest was heaving with fury.

"She is out today." Bertrand's voice cracked. Despite his bravado and ire with Bini and Keke, he truly worried for his safety.

"Carol, call the police. I want to report an assault on my son at the direction of a school official."

"I, I, I,..."

"Spit it out Bertrand." Mac poked.

"I sent for that boy..."

"Keke. My son's name is Keke. Not that boy. Keke."

"I sent for Keke. A student reported that he had lit a fire in a classroom."

Mac examined his youngest son and saw that Keke wore a confused grimace.

"What student?" Bini exclaimed.

Without a word Assistant Principal Paul betrayed the trust of the boy sitting on the bench outside the office.

Anika, Marshawn, and Jaali outside the door glowered at their teammate who was doing his best to make himself look invisible. Bini could see the three of them mouth some version of 'what the hell?'

"That is still no reason to have this man put his hands on my child or any child. I will have words with the Superintendent about you. Now let's go into this office and get to the bottom of this. Kenny, please invite Mr. Burns to join us. Bini, get a copy of that video from Miss Salei. Our lawyer may want to pursue legal action depending on the result of this meeting."

None present was confused about who was in charge of the situation at that moment. Bini looked toward Anika who nodded and began typing his name into her phone to forward the recording.

"I thought I told you to apologize to my son?" Mac called to Ridgefield over his shoulder. The man mumbled his apology with little effort.

Mac shooed the assistant principal toward Principal Zheng's office, put an arm around Keke, who he had just realized was wearing an odd outfit, and lead him into the office. As Keke took a seat, Mac shared a look with Carol before nodding to his son and nephew to head out. Kenny escorted Ricky Burns in behind them. He chuckled as his supervisor marched out of the office, after being embarrassed by the history teacher.

Chapter 15

The large Principal's Office felt very small with the heavy tension that hung in the air. Kenny was standing in the corner. He shifted his weight to his other foot, bumping into a filing cabinet, breaking the uncomfortable silence.

They all looked over to see him holding one hand out before him the other to his chest, mouthing an apology.

"Mr. Burns. Tell us what you saw."

From behind the desk, protected from Mac's immediate reach, Bertrand Paul had regained his authoritative poise.

"I was walking down the hallway and I heard voices in the chemistry lab. I looked in and I saw a spark from a fire. Then I saw two people hugging on the floor."

Mac, who had since calmed himself and returned to a cordial demeanor, peered toward his son who was watched Ricky as he told his story.

"Who did you see set the fire?" Assistant Principal Paul asked, his tone accusatory as he stared at the boy in the gym shorts and T-shirt.

"It was Keke. He was the only person who could have lit the fire. Emma was already on the floor."

Keke sparked up at the way the boy said Emma's name. He felt something weird as though experiencing déjà vu. It disoriented him. He was nauseous to the point he almost vomited. Unable to hide the pain, he doubled over in the chair beside his father.

"Looks like someone's guilt is getting the best of him. I think we have heard enough. Where is the lighter Mr. Wallace?" Bertrand asked smugly.

Mac stared a hole in the man. Betrand swallowed a lump that arose in his throat out of nowhere.

Keke didn't respond. The sensation that burned through him was burning his insides. It was like when he woke up in the bathtub. Perhaps it was a residual infection because of his injury. His father leaned in and whispered something in his ear. Keke could not comprehend what was said. There was a discussion that began in the room around him, but it was all a blur in the nausea. The moment of déjà vu returned but instead of himself, it was an image of his father in the hallway on the other side of the school. He was speaking to another teacher, and he was seeing Ricky Burns come out of the bathroom and go into a classroom nearby. Mac slid his sleeve aside to see his watch face. It was just before the first lunch.

Suddenly, the sick feeling washed away and there was an amazing sense of clarity.

"Ricky, what were you doing in that hallway?" Keke's question cut through the chatter around him.

"I am asking the questions here!" Bertrand cut in before the boy could respond.

"Then ask Ricky why he was in that hallway when he had class on the other side of the school."

Ricky looked at Keke shocked.

"My dad saw you last week at that time you were walking down the hall going into Mr. Karkowski's math class. Right dad? It seems a bit out of the way to be just casually walking down the hall across the school."

The boy began to stammer. Mac was surprised that his son knew this because he didn't know how, but he immediately recalled the day. It was as though the memory was forced into his mind.

"Indeed, I did. Sheila Brown was there in the hallway with me. Why were you all the way over on the north end of the school?"

Bertrand Paul started to interject but Mac held up his hand.

A chuckle escaped from the corner. Again, Kenny apologized.

"Well, I, umm, I was looking for..."

"For Emma?" Keke finished what the boy was reluctant to say.

"What he was doing there is of no consequence. It doesn't change the fact that you started a fire in school. You are getting expelled."

"I beg to differ. And I didn't start a fire. There was no fire. You can ask Emma. You can ask Ms. O'Brien. She was in the room right after. Don't you think she would have noticed evidence of a fire. Wouldn't there have been an aroma of smoke."

"Hand over the lighter." Bertrand pressed.

"I don't have one." Keke stood up and slammed his hands on the desk in frustration. Principal Paul jumped in surprise as did Kenny in the corner. Mac grabbed his son's shoulders firmly and set him down in a chair.

A moment later, there was a knock on the door. Kenny crossed the room to open it. He stepped aside and in walked Bini. He had Emma in tow. Emma had her hands in her pockets. She was noticeably nervous. It occurred to

Keke that this may be the first time his chemistry partner had ever stepped inside the principal's office. She looked extremely sheepish and unassuming. That was until she set eyes on Ricky Burns.

"What are you doing here?" Her voice screeched as though she were consumed by discomfort.

"It's not what you think!" The boy leapt up from his seat, arms extended out before him.

"What are you doing here Miss Wakins? Why aren't you in class?" Bertrand Paul also stood, raising his voice as he addressed the girl.

Emma turned to Bini who had brought her to the office and then to Keke, who shrugged.

"He told me that you accused his brother of starting a fire in the lab." The girl jabbed a finger at Ricky. "I came to tell you that did not happen."

"I saw him!" Ricky retorted.

"How? Were you following me again?"

"Again?" Both twins echoed.

"Kenny stepped forward to be a body between Emma and Ricky, as the girl looked ready to pounce at him.

"I wasn't following you. I just happened to be in the hallway, and I heard a voice that sounded like yours and I looked in the classroom and saw the spark."

"A hallway that you weren't supposed to be in." Keke challenged.

"Why were you following me?" Emma demanded.

"I wasn't. But it was a good thing I did. He tried to burn you."

"I did not! You're crazy!"

"I saw it."

"Prove it! You can't. Because it never happened."

"It did, you tried to light a fire in the chemicals."

"He saved me from the chemicals you idiot!"

"No. I save you! I get to be your hero!"

The realization of the words that escaped his mouth hit Ricky in a wave. One moment he was enraged and the next he was embarrassed, gazing at the ground.

Kenny took the opportunity during the silence to provide an opportunity for resolution.

"Sir. I think I know how to solve this."

"And how's that?" Mr. Paul was extremely irritated that his first day of acting for the Head Principal had suddenly turned upside down.

"That room where the lab is, that is one of the rooms monitored by security. We installed the cameras in that room three weeks ago. We could watch the playback. Just log into the administrator account for the security software and I can show you.

Keke and Emma shared a look. They knew that the story they told didn't match the exact way things transpired. Hopefully, nobody would compare the playback with the incident report Mrs. O'Brien would be submitting.

It took ten minutes to login and figure out how to use the playback function. Kenny offered to show Bertrand how to do it, but the man insisted that he could manage. Ten minutes later they all exited the office. Assistant Principal Paul was doing his best apology tour to Mac, Keke, Bini and even Emma. Ricky Burns hung back with Kenny while he escorted them out.

During the initial viewing of the incident, Ricky stood in the corner by the window while Mac, Kenny, and Keke watched the events over shoulder.

Emma returned the stand and clamps to the metal cabinet next to the eye wash and shower station. Keke approaching her. Emma turning to walk up the next row. Emma banging into the edge of the tabletop. Emma falling backward holding her arm and stumbling into the shelves beside the cabinet. The plastic bottle of four molar sodium hydroxide solution toppling off the shelf, tumbling toward the table in front of her. Emma dropping to her knees, rubbing her elbow.

Keke lunging to catch the bottle. The bottle crashing on the table, cap first. The hard plastic cap shattering, flinging the fluid in a spiral pattern. The bottled bouncing and spilling on the table. Keke on one knee throwing himself over the girl who was in the direct path, shielding her from the spray.

Keke pressing the girl's head to his chest, protecting her face from the splash of the basic fluid. As the fluid spun there was an intense glow that looked as though it came from the spinning fluid that lasted for a flicker. Despite how intense it was, it was only a second. There were no flames as Ricky described.

The video continued with Emma pushing Keke off her and into the shower. She turned on the water dousing him head to toe. After ten seconds of splashing, he reached for the handle and shut off the water.

That was where Bertrand Paul stopped the tape. Mac leaned on the desk next to him glowering upon the man who without a desk between him and without evidence to confirm his actions, once again felt small.

Bini, Emma, and Ricky were shown the playback the second time through. Emma was startled by the brightness of the light. In her mind she was puzzled because she knew that there was nothing else present to cause a reaction. A shared look with Keke told her he was puzzled by the same thing.

"Well maybe you couldn't see the lighter?" Ricky was overwhelmed with desperation.

"You would have seen it in his hand when he stepped out of the shower. With his arms wrapped the way they were in defense of the girl, it is impossible that he could have lit a lighter above them and there is no logical reason for him to have thought to do it." Kenny interjected to save further confrontation.

Out in the corridor, Emma said nothing as she hurried back to her class. Mac gave Tunes a disapproving look for not going to class. It was just as well. He told the boys to gather their things from their lockers as they would be leaving for the day.

Mac returned to speak with Carol and asked her for Principal Zheng's personal cell phone number. Carol denied his request but offered to dial it for him and let him speak to her. He accepted the compromise and left a message for her to call him when she did not answer.

**

The dinner table was a raucous scene that evening. Tunes and Bini took turns giving play-by-play of how Mac took down Martin Ridgefield in the principal's office and then punked the assistant principal for telling him to put hands on Keke. Louise gave Mac condemning looks at the telling of how he employed violence to solve a problem in his workplace.

He felt as though he was being falsely accused and that his actions were justified. When he could take it no longer, he jumped in, cutting his nephew off.

"Look, honey. That man had our boy by the shirt. I watched as he stepped up chest to chest threateningly and then grabbed ahold. He had menace in his eyes. I was not about to allow that."

"But what type of example are you setting?"

"That you protect family when someone attacks them." Mac glanced at each of the three boys to drive the point home.

"Yes Sir." The three replied.

"Keke?"

"Yes, Mom?"

"You are being quiet. What is on your mind?"

"The flash."

"After today's events you are thinking about comic books?" Tunes asked confused.

"No dummy. Not *The Flash*. The flash. The one in the video. It was weird."

Bini cocked his head to the side and screwed up his face in mock disgust. He shook his head at how simple his cousin could be. His mother's stern gaze brought him to fix his face as he realized he had insulted Darius in front of his parents.

"Yeah. How did it happen. There was just a splash of NAOH solution. It's basic. It's a non-combustible solid and even in water the solution should not ignite. There was nothing in the air that it would react with."

"I am just happy that your friend was quick enough to shove you in the shower, so you didn't get burned by it. You just came back from one hospital stay. You do not need another."

Louise's statement carried a tone of finality. Mac changed the subject by asking about her day. After dinner Bini and Tunes went into Tunes' room to play video games while Keke did his homework. When Bini came to bed Keke was already sleeping, his chemistry book laying across his chest. Bini gently lifted the book and slid a bookmark into the page where his brother had left off in case it was important. He quietly switched into his bed clothes and turned out the light.

That night Keke dreamed of running through the woods. Not on the trails but through the wooded area. He was hiding from someone. There were voices. Hikers. It was a cool night, but he didn't feel cold. He felt worried. He was not afraid, but wary for some reason. A deer startled him as it foraged behind him. He was stunned that a deer would come so close.

Distracted by the deer, he had allowed the hikers to come within sight of him. One woman and two men. He stared at them from between the trees. The hikers immediately noticed the deer to his right and began to whisper. He thought it odd that none of them noticed him standing there or engaged him. The hikers crept closer to see if they could get a better view of the deer. Slowly the woman pulled out her phone and took a picture of the deer. She did not notice that the flash was still on. When the deer scampered off, he too ran swiftly through the woods.

Keke awoke to Bini shaking him profusely. He was drenched in sweat to the degree that Bini couldn't get a grip of his flailing arms.

"Keke!" Bini hissed.

"Huh? What is happening?"

"You were dreaming. I think you were running in your dreams. I heard you panting and then when I looked over I saw your arms and feet pumping on your bed."

"I was dreaming that I was running in the woods."

"Well, your bed is soaked. How long were you running?" Bini joked.

"I'm not sure."

A door creaked.

"Shoot. Here comes mom. Quick, pretend you were sleeping. I'll go into the bathroom and tell her I made the noise."

"Why not just pretend you are asleep too?"

"Because she'll come in and lean on the bed to kiss us good night and she will see that you are soaked."

"If I'm sleeping then she might do that anyway."

"True. Then you go into the bathroom. Bring a change of clothes with you so you don't look like you were in the pool."

Keke touched foreheads with his brother and hurried into the bathroom.

No sooner did the door close than his mother open the bedroom door and peek in. Louise noticed that the light was on in the bathroom and Keke's bed was empty. She considered going to check on him, but a moment later there was a flush followed by the faucet. She didn't want her boys to think she was being a helicopter mom, so she quietly shut the door and headed back to bed.

Chapter 16

That Saturday was an important meet. The meet was hosted by Saratoga Springs. If the girls placed first, then they would secure first place in the conference. They were currently ranked third in the state despite being the defending champions. They had won every meet so far and the girls were growing stronger as runners. Especially Anika who had been working out with Marshawn, Justin, and Kenan. She placed second in the last meet, edging out Maryn and Isabella who had been fighting to stay ahead of her most of the race. Sectionals were in two weeks.

It was a great day for a run. There was a slight breeze. The day was extremely overcast but warm for a fall day. It was bearable for shorts. The girls were all locked in during their warmup period.

It was tense in school for the remainder of the week. Principal Zheng had been out all week. There were early whispers that she may have disappeared the night of the sonic boom blackout. As soon as Carol caught wind of the rumors, she quickly quelled them by informing the kids that she was simply on an anniversary vacation with her husband. Bertrand Paul was acting principal in her absence. Ridgefield kept a watchful eye over the twins. He was always outside their classroom or lurking near their locker. Tunes had given the head of security a look each time their paths crossed. When Tunes felt he was hovering too close he would ask the guard if he wanted him to call his uncle. This gave Ridgefield pause. The twins pretended like he didn't exist.

Marshawn, Everett, and Justin pushed out to the front to get an early lead to begin the race. This would be their last home meet as seniors. They intended to make it a good showing. All three had been pacing under the sixteen minutes mark on track runs. They were hoping to match that today. Bini pushed the pace with his teammates. A boy from Christian Brothers Academy did as well. Bini glanced about for his brother who was atypically not at his side. Slowing to look back, he caught sight of Keke. Bini saw that he was several meters behind the lead. He began to slow to check on him. Keke waved him onward. Bini reluctantly upped his pace to catch the lead.

Keke was feeling nauseous, and his equilibrium was wavering. At first, he thought maybe he was getting a stomach bug or the flu. His insides were in knots, he was struggling to keep his pace. In the first half mile, Keke had fallen to the middle of the pack. He had his normal breakfast, but for some reason he felt extremely sluggish and drawn. There was a buzzing in his ear and his heart felt as though it were pumping sludge. His feet felt like anchors as he lifted them and slammed them down. He imagined that everyone watching the race saw him as Benjamin Grimm. A man of bricks and stone, lumbering forward by will alone.

Kenan became concerned as he easily passed him by. Keke through up a lazy arm to wave off the look. When he rounded the next turn, he glanced back to see about a dozen runners behind him. This told Keke that he was running faster than he felt. Still, the dysphoria that spun through his head was threatening to make him pass out.

Keke was convinced it was fever. He was barely aware of the course as he continued to run. The breeze that ran across his face had a glowing aura to it. He could hear squirrels chittering in the trees along the course. He could smell a sweet perfume somewhere nearby. Most intensely he could feel that his brother was worried about him and was not concentrating on the race as he should. He tried to connect through the sensation to communicate that he would be alright. He knew that it would not be a message received but he was hopeful that his brother would come to the realization on his own and win the race.

The cloud-cover broke, bathing Keke and the surrounding area in a warm glow. The sun felt good. Keke soaked it in. He could feel the UV waves penetrating his skin. His senses intensified. He could feel the ground beneath him with every thumping footfall. He could taste the cool air as he inhaled and exhaled. The field ahead narrowed as his vision tunneled, focusing on the path forward. The cluster of stimuli was distracting. He considered that perhaps it was delirium setting in.

Up ahead, his cousin and Jenna wore worried looks. Keke came out of the fugue as he approached where they stood along the track. Keke pumped his arms a bit stronger. Drove his knees harder. Elongate his stride. No longer just trudging along. He was galloping.

Tunes called out to him when he got within earshot of them.

"What's wrong?" Tunes yelled.

"Nothing, I'm fine." Keke managed to mutter.

Tunes held out both hands in front of him, palms upturned. He waved toward the pack way ahead and then back to Keke.

Keke didn't address the unspoken question. Realization set in that he was indeed fine. The sun's warmth had invigorated him. It was as though the glow penetrated inside him. And began to shine out. It fueled him. Powered him as it was absorbed into every cell. Keke basked in it. He was rejuvenated. A few moments earlier he was ready to walk. He now felt like he could fly.

Keke upped his pace, running more than jogging. He passed Kenan so fast that the boy was startled. He rounded the next turn and saw a group of boys heading up an inclined section of the course. At the top of the incline eclipsing the hill was his brother and teammates out in front. He sped up, graduating toward sprinting up the hill. The clouds pushed farther apart and the warmth he felt stimulated him further.

Keke was running at a full sprint as though it were the last few hundred yards of the race. Yet, there was over a mile to go to finish. He eclipsed the crest of the upslope quick enough to see Justin round the bend. He was following behind a small pack of boys. Keke lengthened his stride, increasing his speed in pursuit of the leaders.

Keke passed Justin right as he had overtaken the three other boys, all from Columbia. With roughly half a mile remaining. Marshawn, Bini, Everett and the boy from Christian Brothers Academy were the only runners ahead of him. His goal was to catch up and place in the top three. He felt he had the stamina to do so. He just needed to push onward. He was one hundred yards behind and closing.

Anika and the twins were standing along the course halfway between them. When they saw Keke and how fast he was running they began to shout his name. Despite their worry that he was going to burn out at the pace he had set, they encouraged him onward. Unlike the baseball game where Bini saved the homerun, the cheering didn't distract Keke in the slightest.

Bini had heard his teammates shout his brother's name and was encouraged. Marshawn and the CBA boy were really pushing the pace. Bini didn't dare look back and lose a step. Everett had fallen behind a few yards but was still pushing with all he could.

Meanwhile, Keke continued to close the distance. One hundred yards was cut in half and then again twice more in ten seconds. A few more seconds and he was ahead of Everett and on the heels of his brother and the other two runners.

Bini was shocked when his brother motored past him. It seemed too incredible to be real. The trio had heard the stomping steps as he approached. The CBA boy was in disbelief of Keke's speed as he surpassed them. He didn't just catch up and move ahead. He zoomed past the three of them with extreme ease. Anxious for the win, the CBA boy opened into his best sprint as well. Marshawn and Bini followed suit.

The three boys pushed as hard as they could. Their final hundred yards were at full sprint. Each of them, their lungs burning, collapsed after the finish.

It was a fight for second place. Each one of them pushing to break out in front of the others. There was no chance to catch up to Keke who had left them all behind. Bini and Marshawn shared a quick glance when they watched as Keke crossed the finish line a solid forty seconds ahead of them after falling way behind to start the race. The final result was Keke way out in front, Bini second, the boy from CBA and Marshawn a half step behind Bini. It appeared to be a tie for third, but Marshawn was able to edge him out by virtue of a longer stride. Everett finished next and Justin was seventh. The boys had won the event.

Bini was still on the ground panting beside Marshawn who was on all fours beside him.

"We all finished sub-sixteen minutes." The two boys found that Keke was squatting beside them, offering them each a water.

"Bro, where did that come from?"

"Yeah, and what was your time?"

"They said officially 15:09.13." The three boys looked up to see Anika beside them. "Keke, I never seen anyone do what you just did."

Keke was silent. The girl took the silence for modesty.

"You two should have seen it. Keke sprinted the final half mile to catch up with you guys. He must've gotten a burst of energy or something."

Keke knew that he had sprinted much more than that but didn't correct the girl. Before Keke could offer up an excuse for his bizarre performance, Coach Halliday was there beside them.

"Anika, you have to go get ready for your race! Keke, Bini, Marshawn! Awesome job! Keke, you were behind when I saw you turn the first corner. Did you just turn it on after that?"

"Yeah, something like that, Coach."

"Well, whatever you did, your time was amazing. That time was close to a section record. Listen there are some scouts here to watch the girls. I convinced them to speak to Marshawn, Justin, and Everett. I suggest you and your brother meet with them as well. 15:09. Just, wow!"

***

The atmosphere in Cusato's was rowdy. The aroma was heavenly. The smell of garlic and butter, sauce and cheese and chicken wings. The entire team had met at the shop to celebrate the victory. The girls had crushed their run and Keke had run an amazing time. Both the boys and the girls came in first and were looking to celebrate.

All the seniors except Marshawn had left already. He and his brother stayed to hang out with the twins. Jaali stayed too. Jenna and Tunes joined them as the seniors were heading out. They occupied the two corner booths. The vibe was lively. There were several other patrons inside. Typically, the owner would be kicking them out. However, Tunes and Jenna ordered food when they arrived, and he knew that the kids had something to celebrate.

Keke slid out of the booth and made his way toward the bathroom. He had one too many drinks and his bladder was begging to be emptied. While he was away, a few members of the team took the opportunity to voice their concerns.

"So, is Keke taking PEDs or something?" Jaali asked.

"PEDs?" Bini was confused by the question.

"Performance enhancing drugs. You know like steroids or something."

"No, he would never. What the hell is the matter with you!" Bini was insulted by the suggestion.

"I'm just asking. How do you explain what he did today? He was way behind."

"He didn't look great when I passed him on the race." Kenan added.

"You passed him on the race?" Marshawn was surprised.

"Yeah. Almost all the runners had. Then a minute after I passed him, he came sprinting by.

Bini looked toward Tunes who was nodding eyes wide. Jenna too nodded across the table from him. He was not comfortable with his teammates discussing his brother in his absence. However, the information they were providing was concerning.

"What other explanation do you have for his ability to hold that speed for that long. He would have had to sprint for two plus miles." Jaali who was propped up on one knee in the next booth did his best to not be accusatory in his tone but was failing.

Bini didn't have an opportunity to respond because Tunes redirected his attention.

"Holy shit! Look who just walked in."

The group of them looked toward the door to see a dark-haired boy with green streaks in his hair standing by the doorway. The boy glanced around the room staring at every group of patrons. It was as though he was looking for someone.

"I think that's the guy who works at the gas station by my house that went missing." Anika added.

"What? No, not him. Him!"

Tunes directed his attention to the counter. A blonde-haired boy was probing the crowd as well. He stared at the boy by the door who took the non-verbal cue and moved on up the street. The blonde-haired boy turned to leave.

"Is that Brandon? Wasn't he one of the people who they said disappeared." Bini asked Jenna who was still twisted around, unable to believe her eyes.

"Yeah, his mother reported him missing. My brother has been so upset. He would be the type to fake disappearing to get attention."

Bini nearly fell to the ground as the boy to his right jumped up from the booth and marched off in pursuit of Brandon. Tunes and Jenna reached for him, but neither could get a handhold. The entire group knew it was Brandon who had hit Marshawn with a rock at their first race of the season. Kenan in the other booth wasted no time scrambling off after his older brother. Seconds later, they all were rushing out after their teammates.

"Hey! You! You like to throw rocks at people?" Brandon stopped and rounded to face Marshawn. He scrupled the boy's face. There was no anger. No sign of a smirk. His expression was blank. Marshawn noticed none of this.

"What's wrong? Not so brave when you aren't hiding in the woods.

Kenan arrived to stand beside his brother.

"I have no familiarity to you." He responded.

Brandon stood there a moment and then turned to walk away. This enraged Marshawn who sprinted forward and with both hands shoved Brandon who slid forward on his chest smacking his chin on the pavement.

Chest heaving, Marshawn stood over him.

Bini and Tunes arrived and were tugging him back as there were witnesses watching.

They dragged their friend back toward the pizza shop. Meanwhile, Kenan stood defiantly watching as the boy stood up and began to walk toward them.

"You should not have done that."

Marshawn wormed out of Bini's grip and ran full speed at Brandon. The blonde boy's chin was bloodied but he didn't seem to notice. Marshawn swung a long winding haymaker that missed its mark. Brandon ducked underneath the other boy's momentum. With his right shoulder pressed to Marshawn's hip, he grabbed hold of his knees and flipped him over. Marshawn tumbled through the air and crashed down on the pavement. The air exited his lungs so hard that none came back in.

Before Brandon could turn on Marshawn, Kenan rushed him. Brandon side-stepped him slamming him into the hood of a Toyota Corolla parked beside them. He stared the younger boy down before turning back toward Marshawn.

Jenna ran forward and stepped in front of him. The boy stopped, not expecting to see her there.

"What are you doing? He's down! You made your point." She screamed in his face, her voice full of reprimand.

Anika took the opportunity to slide in behind her to tend to Marshawn who was still struggling to get a breath.

"Seriously, I said back off." She placed a hand in the boy's chest and shoved him back a step.

His countenance stayed blank as he grabbed the girl by the throat and tossed her backward. Surprised by the aggressive act, she lost her balance as the back of her thighs collided with Anika and she too hit the pavement.

Brandon had no sooner dropped his arm to his side than did Bini strike him with a left hook that sent him stumbling past the fallen Marshawn. Before he could turn Tunes tackled him to the ground. The two boys tumbled across the sidewalk. Brandon came out on top. He put a forearm in Tunes' chest Tunes threw a right cross that landed sending the boy rolling off him. Before he could get up a kick to the chest from Bini sent him tumbling. The boy sat up but didn't try to stand. Bini walked over to Brandon and Tunes joined him.

"Just stay down." Bini admonished.

None of them noticed that the boy with the green streaks in his hair had returned. He shoved Kenan aside, grabbed Bini by the throat pinning him to the wall. Tunes punched at the arm holding his cousin to the wall. With surprising dexterity, the boy grabbed Tunes with his free arm and pinned him next to his cousin. Both boys swung frantically trying to break free of the grip. Neither was successful. Bini began to lose consciousness and his eyes rolled in his head. There was a sudden jolt and both he and

Tunes slumped to the ground. His elbow slammed the cold sidewalk sending his right arm numb.

Tunes sprung up, driven by adrenaline and helped Bini to his feet. Standing a few feet from them was his twin brother. Keke, who had been in the restroom when the fight started, had arrived in time. The boy with the green streak in his hair was out cold on the pavement. Brandon was standing over his unconscious body. He still stared at them blankly. Behind them Marshawn had gotten to his feet with Anika's assistance. Jaali, who had not been involved in the fray stood by the doorway to the pizza shop with a few other patrons. He watched all his friends engage in a melee against these two individuals who he did not know. He was shocked when Keke slipped by him with great speed and force. He knocked out the boy who had pinned his brother and cousin to the wall effortlessly.

Now the one boy was lying face down on the pavement and the blonde-haired boy whose presence was the catalyst for the event was standing there with a bloody chin staring at Keke.

"We should get out of here before the police show up."

The words weren't out of Keke's mouth before the sirens sounded in the distance. The group of them took off around the corner. Jaali watched the blonde-haired boy. He stood expressionless as they departed. The freshman shared a look with Kenan as he passed by him.

"PEDs."

Chapter 17

Agents Swain and Smarten left the campus of SUNY Oswego. They had spent the better part of the weekend interviewing students getting the wildest, most over embellished stories about what crashed in Lake Ontario. The object lit up the sky before it splashed down. The object had landed a few weeks back and gossip had spread. It was easy to weed out who had seen it and who hadn't. Unfortunately, they had to interview them all. College kids were all at that age where they wanted to be part of something special. An unidentified object of massive size and unknown origin plummeting to Earth was a magnet for attention. Most were swayed by knowing there was a meteor shower that night. In the end, the two people who the agents wanted to interview were the most difficult to find.

Almost every student interviewed had said the object was black as night. There were a few who had said nonsense about little green men coming out of the water. Agent Swain summarily dismissed them. However, many of those who were outdoors during the event had used terms like, 'so black it was invisible'. 'Like darkness, but on fire.' 'A black hole burning through the sky.' This all spoke to what they had gathered from the local police reports from other onlookers and those they gathered from Rochester to Oswego. There was currently divers heading out to look for whatever it was that plummeted to the bottom of Lake Ontario. The object was the size of a cruise ship. The timeline for confirmation was a matter of days.

The two witnesses that mattered to Agent Swain were two delinquents who got drunk at Gibby's pub and decided they would steal a boat from Wright's Marina and go for a cruise on the lake. According to the local police, they recorded the splashdown. The force was enough that it nearly capsized their boat even though they were roughly five nautical miles away. They had only taken the boat out far enough to where they couldn't be seen from the shore. The wake from the crash flooded the marina parking lot near Cahill Pier.

The officer who took the police report assumed that it was a giant piece of space junk that had fallen, and they had just exaggerated the size. The Homeland Security Agents learned otherwise when the National Guard and Navy divers confirmed the size with the echo location devices. Still, they allowed the local authorities and everyone else in the town of Oswego to assume the space junk theory to be the case.

To justify their reason for seeking out the two students to be interviewed by homeland security, they had given a story that there may have been hazardous materials on the space junk that could have radiated the sky and contaminated the water as it crashed down. They explained that there was a special division of the Red Cross that would need to examine to rule out the chance of a threat to the health of the two individuals. They cautioned that nobody should go out on the lake or into the lake until the Red Cross, Navy, and Coast Guard had completed their examination.

The FBI and DEC had already set up shop and established a perimeter at all known marinas and piers.

Those that were privately-owned were told the same story about contaminating the water. They brought in crews to take samples of the water and the local news had communicated their advisory to the public.

What the FBI, DEC, or locals didn't know was that the DHS agents had information that they did not share. Agent Swain had informed his partner that it would be best not to tell anyone that there was a secondary site. The piece that had broken off the ship and had fallen as though in control of itself. The piece that everyone in the room back at Keck was convinced was an alien. None of that information was conveyed to anyone outside of the group. Agent Swain was hopeful that finding the ship would conclude that it was not a ship and that no creatures were inside of it. The size and location of where it fell made getting that proof impossible.

In the absence of evidence to the contrary, Agent Swain had to move forward with the most likely of truths. An alien ship had crash-landed in Upstate New York and somewhere out there were the splattered remains of the creature that piloted said spaceship. It was also likely that the creature was one of many beings on board and others leapt from the ship as this one had. If Ms. Ralston's calculations were right, those remains would be located within a fifty-to-one-hundred-mile radius of Hunter Mountain. She had done the calculation based on zero wind resistance and without any understanding of the object's ability to control its path. Given that there were reports of an unseen object that created a sonic boom in Saratoga Springs area on the same night that the ship landed, he reasoned that her calculations were accurate.

No other instances matched that description so either this creature was the lone passenger, or the others perished in the crash.

Agent Swain noted that his partner was uncomfortable with the discovery. From the moment that he had seen the humanoid figure tumbling through the sky, he had been off. When they landed at Albany International Airport, FBI agents were waiting for them to offer a ride to the local bureau office. Agent Swain had already learned of the crash landing in Lake Ontario while they were at the Cal Tech Research Facility where Ms. Ralston did her calculations using the program she had spoken of at Keck.

When she was done, Agent Swain offered her and Mr. Messner a choice. They could come along as liaison in their investigation, or they could stay at their school with a DHS officer watching over their every move. They would not have access to their mobile devices and would not be able to communicate anything related to the investigation or else be detained. Ms. Ralston agreed to come along and assist with the investigation with the caveat that she could sign into the zoom versions of her graduate course lectures.

Mr. Messner declined to come along and was left in the care of another pair of agents. Ms. Ralston was now in Albany with Agent Dawn Bush awaiting their return before they continued their investigation.

There was little discussion between the Agents Swain and Smarten for most of the two plus hour drive back to the capital. Both men spent time processing how to bring the news to their leadership that the idea of beings from another planet arriving on Earth was no longer a hypothetical situation. As senior officer, that duty would fall to Agent Swain. He was positive that the military brass would want to find a way to blame the Russians or the Chinese or possibly the South Koreans for this.

No scientists had identified the possibility of this occurrence. Ms. Ralston was certain that this was not one of the Near-Earth Objects being tracked. She confirmed this with a review of the database at Caltech. Rick Swain was hopeful that he could report back that the object was some large rock that surprised the locals but was of no consequence. Now he would be communicating to the Secretary of DHS that they should hand this one off to the Joint Chiefs. However, that could wait. There didn't appear to be any immediate threats to national security. Rick Swain decided that he was going to see through the remainder of this investigation. This was something straight out of an X-Files episode and it intrigued him. He found it impossible that he and Agent Smarten would come across little green men. However, he relished the thought of being on the forefront of a discovery that delivered solid proof of life in the universe out there in the stars.

While Agent Swain contemplated the magnitude of the scientific relevance, Agent Smarten was riddled with worry. His thoughts were of an Independence Day, War of the Worlds type of invasion being imminent. The quiet of the ride back to Albany had allowed the man to slide down a rabbit hole of rabid imaginative thoughts. The Cheshire Cat at the end of it was this body of a fallen extraterrestrial of which they were at that moment racing down interstate ninety to go locate the remains. He recalled seeing those movies about alien invasion as a kid and not once did he find them anything but horrifying.

***

Keke was awakened by a strange sensation. He felt an unknown presence close by. At first, he thought he was dreaming. However, the off-key noise that was his cousin singing in the bathroom adjacent to the bedroom he and his brother shared told Keke that he was awake. With a sudden sense of alarm, he snapped upright in his bed.

Bini glanced over from where he was putting on his socks at the edge of the opposite bed. The boy was bewildered by the way that his brother had flung his upper torso upright like the Undertaker. Bini did not know what was going on, but he knew his brother was not alright.

He watched as Keke scanned their bedroom twisting his head right and left. It reminded him of the BBC special he watched with his mother a few weeks back. Keke looked like one of the Springbok that sensed a cheetah in the distance. Bini all but expected him to start bouncing in the air as a sign of warning.

Keke was alerted to the presence of someone or something. It made the hairs on his arms stand up. It was like a movie where someone was watching you from the shadows. The camera would be concentrated on the individual, moving with them in personification of the watcher. Only there were no shadows here and no camera. Whatever it was, it loomed so close that it could be inside of him. He swung his legs off the bed and hopped into an upright position. Bini monitored out of the corner of his eye, saying nothing. Keke crossed the room to the closet. He paused in front of the door glancing at the door to the bathroom. Keke slowly set his hand on the knob, placing an ear to the closet door. The boy listened for a moment. When he finally was convinced that there was nobody there, he turned to find Bini standing there with him.

Bini grabbed the base of Keke's skull and leaned his forehead toward his own.

"Bro, what is going on with you?"

"I sensed someone was here."

"Sensed? Like a presence in the Force?"

"I could sense them. They were here, near me. Like I could reach out and put my hand on them. And then they weren't."

Bini pressed the soft part of his wrist against his brother's forehead. There was no fever. He pulled him away to arm's length checking his pupils. Properly dilated. Lastly, he placed a hand to his brother's chest, feeling his heartbeat.

"There is something different. You are different."

"What do you mean?"

"You have been acting strange lately."

"Yeah, you have. I am glad you said it Bini!"

The twins turned to see their cousin standing in the doorway; bare chested and enshrouded in a cloud of steam. He gently rubbed the hair atop his head with the towel in his left hand.

"What are you guys talking about? I am fine."

"Okay. First, let's talk about the race yesterday. One moment you can barely keep up with the slow kids and then a minute later you're Wally West. Then last night, you came out of nowhere and KO'd that rainbow haired freak!"

"Shhhh." Bini admonished his cousin to keep his tone down. They had not told their parents about what happened at the pizza shop and did not give the particulars of how Keke had won the race. All they had said was that they had won.

"Why didn't you say Jay Garrick?"

"Who?" Tunes was lost on the question.

Keke waved him off as to say never mind. Keke should have known better to expect his cousin to know the original flash from the 1940's.

"Seriously. Bini, that dude was freakishly strong. He had us both. Nobody can grab you like that. He was Mark Henry in Pete Wentz's body. But Keke knocked his lights out like he was Saitama."

Keke said nothing.

"Cuz, are you on steroids?"

"Steroids? What? No. What is the matter with you? Where the hell would I get steroids and why would I use them. It's not like I'm in the gym working out."

"Well maybe there are running steroids that help you run fast."

"Running steroids?"

The twins responded together to their cousin's statement with a matching degree of disbelief. He began to continue his argument when both boys shoved him back a step and turned and headed down to breakfast.

After breakfast, Jenna arrived at the house. Louise was ecstatic as it was her day off and she had not been there to meet Jenna the night of her prom. She spent more time than Darius was comfortable gushing over how great the two of them looked. Most of the comments were directed at Jenna's dress and her hair. The family assumed that she sprinkled in compliments about Tunes to be polite. Mac whispered something to that effect to his nephew as he passed by to place his dish in the dishwasher. Tunes responded to his uncle's jab with a dirty look.

Mac looking to get some quiet time at home, told his wife to stop fussing over Darius' girlfriend and let the kids go out and enjoy their day. Again, Darius gave his uncle the look. This time, Jenna gave it to him as well. Keke, who had been busy eating more than the rest of the family combined and Bini who had been watching him shovel all the food down, cracked up at their father's comment.

Louise shushed them all, patted Jenna's hand between hers and told her not to let these boys make her into something other than the gorgeous young lady that she was. Jenna responded with a simple 'yes ma'am'.

Bini, Tunes and Jenna headed out the door. Jenna invited Keke to join them for an afternoon at the outlet malls in Lake George. He politely declined. Bini scrupled his brother momentarily before blowing a kiss to his mother. She caught the flying kiss in her left hand and used her right hand to pull the closed fist to her chest, pressing the gesture of love into her heart.

"Why didn't you want to go with them, dear?"

Louise rounded the table and rubbed the top of her son's head before tugging it backward to plant a kiss on his forehead.

"I think I'm going to go for a hike."

"That sounds like a good idea. Maybe I will join you."

"Well, I wanted to go into town. I was thinking of riding my bike. I wanted to grab some new comics."

"Oh, then I will just find something else to do. I am not about to spend an hour sitting outside that store while you get lost inside."

Louise gave her husband a look. She had missed the cue that her son wanted to go alone and the mention of riding his bike after the offer of company was enough for Mac to take the hint. In some ways, Louise knew the boys better than he did. However, in this he was certain that his boy wanted to be alone. He just had to present it in a way that his wife didn't pry too much. Like he always had, he watched his watcher.

Keke nodded to his father and then spun around to head back upstairs.

Keke got wet on his bike ride into town to buy new comics. A mile into his trip it started to sprinkle. By the time he arrived at the comic bookstore, it was raining pretty hard. The cold November rain chilled Keke's fingers as they gripped the handles of his mountain bike. He alternated putting his fingers inside his sleeve. Cuffing the sleeved fingers up to his chin, Keke warmed them with hot breath.

Keke arrived at the store and took a moment to get inside. He felt extremely depleted as though he hadn't eaten in days. He thought that maybe the rain was giving him a cold. Then he chuckled to himself. His mother was a nurse. Keke knew that twenty minutes in the cold rain wouldn't immediately deplete your immune system. He slipped inside hoping the warmth within the store would take care of the effects the cold wet weather was having on him.

After a short time browsing, Keke had only grabbed a few of the comics he had gone to buy. He was feeling worse than before and thought back to when his brother asked if he was feeling alright that morning. Did Bini sense that he was getting sick?

No, that isn't what he meant. There were a lot of unexplained things happening to him lately. This was just another one of them. The sensation he had as he rode home was similar to the feeling in the beginning of his last race.

Like the last time, Keke had eaten a decent breakfast. Also like with the race, Keke had engaged in cardiovascular exercise. While he wasn't riding the bike extra hard, he was pedaling along at a good pace when the rain picked up. He reasoned that he may have to monitor how long he allowed between eating and activities in the future if the pattern persisted.

The rain began to pick up and he didn't want the comics in his backpack to get ruined, so Keke pulled into the gas station before the turn off for the trails to wait it out under the awning. It became evident that the rain was not letting up. Keke stepped into the store and stood by the door for a moment. The clerk looked at him with judgmental eyes.

"Hey, do you mind if I wait in here and call my dad for a ride. The rain is pretty bad out there."

The clerk said nothing. He didn't even look up from his magazine. He simply pointed at a sign up above the counter. It read 'Buy something or Go.' Keke thought it was odd how the 'B' and the 'G' were capitalized.

Keke didn't argue.

He went to the counter across the way and grabbed a hard paper cup. He poured himself a cappuccino and brought it up to the counter. The clerk glanced up at the cup and the plastic card in Keke's hand. He tapped a disgustingly long fingernail on the counter beside where Keke had placed the cup. Under the laminated surface was a piece of cardboard. On the cardboard was a crudely scribbled message. The message told Keke that he had to spend another three dollars and forty-nine cents. There was a five-dollar minimum to use a card.

Keke huffed.

He reached over and grabbed a KitKat bar and tossed it next to the steaming cup. Still $1.51 to go. Keke had begun to shiver from the cold. As a chill ran through him the clerk looked at his face. The boy looked sickly. The clerk's demeanor changed. He typed in another number and the total came to $5.11. Keke shot him a confused look.

"Grab cup of soup. You look unwell."

Keke turned to see where the man had pointed. Next to the cappuccino dispenser was a microwave. In an aluminum rack beside the brown oven with preset buttons was a stack of noodle cups. Keke's father had told him that it was unhealthy to microwave styrofoam and then eat out of it. However, Keke's sickly feeling got the best of him, so he nodded.

Keke followed the instructions on the back of the cup. He filled the cup with hot water from the dispenser on the cappuccino machine. He pressed the preset button for three minutes. He was feeling even more weary than when he had been out in the cold. The sound of the rain on the metal awning of the store reminded Keke of a steel drum.

The clerk had gone back to his magazine, content that his suggestion had been a help to the boy. Keke set his hand on the microwave oven to steady himself. He was starting to second guess his previous conclusion. Perhaps it was possible for him to get ill from being out in the rain for that short of a period. A crack of lighting outside lit up the sky. The thunderous boom that followed it startled Keke. The shock of the noise radiated through his body. There was another loud crack, a blinding light and a concussion of air struck him. He flew onto the shelf behind him smacking his head on the tile floor.

Chapter 18

Keke slowed to a walk as he approached the top of the wooden staircase that led down to a walking platform that traversed the narrow stream and surrounding brush area. Immediately after the incident at the gas station, he rode his bike to the trail. He had awakened to the very nervous clerk standing over him shaking his shoulder. He couldn't recall where he was initially. The face above him seemed familiar but there was a buzzing noise that was extremely distracting. It didn't take long for Keke to realize that the buzzing noise was inside him. Or more accurately, it was him. Every single one of his thirty-seven trillion cells was reverberating.

Keke sat up and noticed that the microwave was blackened and there was a white foam dripping from it. The extinguisher in the clerk's right hand told him that the microwave had caught fire. The image of him touching the apparatus with the soup he purchased warming inside appeared in his mind. He recalled the sound of the thunder as the lightning crackled through the afternoon sky. There was a jolt within him as his synapsis reacted to the shock of the sound. The energy navigated its way to his extremities. There was a concussion of air as the charge that flooded from his palm into the tiny oven overloaded the circuits. The energy release blasted him into the Moon pies and Nutty Buddies. He was unconscious before he crashed down on the pile of Hostess Donettes.

The clerk postured fearfully as he hovered over the boy. He was certain that his microwave had killed a patron, and he would be imprisoned for it. There was little relief when Keke woke up. The boy attempted to stand, and the clerk abruptly shoved him to the ground. He implored Keke to lay down while he called an ambulance. Keke assured the distressed clerk that he was alright.

That was not accurate. He was not alright. He was superb. As awful as he felt earlier at the comic bookstore and up to when he walked into the gas station, he felt equally magnificent in that moment. It was like he had received an elixir. He was a Kryptonian in the radiance of the Earth's sun. He was a Korbinite who found Mjolnir and was able to wield it. He was Max Dillon turned into a living capacitor. He was Prince Adam with the Sword of Power in his grasps.

Keke pushed the clerk aside and stood up. He walked outside, leaving the confused clerk to ruminate on the events that had unfolded. He snatched his bike and before mounting up he felt the proximity of that presence from this morning. Only this time, it was not some feeling tickling the back of his mind.

It was a clear picture.

Keke knew what direction it was and how far away. He was drawn to it like a magnet. The force of its pull was unlike anything he had ever encountered. It was ethereal. It was extraterrestrial. He imagined himself Pepe Le Pew being carried on the wind of a female cat's scent. He chuckled at the thought.

Whatever the thing is, it drew him to these woods.

Keke believed that his connection to it came from within himself. He didn't know when it got there but the sensation which he felt that morning had turned into a beckoning.

Keke slowly descended the staircase. He tapped the bud in his right ear, pausing his music. He softened his footfalls as he pulled out the round black plugs and stowed them in their case. Earnestly he listened to the sounds of the surrounding woods.

Birds; the song of a Gnat Catcher calling out in the distance. Its song a lullaby to her recently hatched young. Its soft, melodious call carried hints of the Meadowlarks that are also native to this woodland.

Keke focused to block them out. He had no idea how he knew the things he did about the bird and their song, or how he knew that there was a couple dozen field crickets adding to the cacophony of woodland sounds that clouded Keke's ability to discern if there was anyone nearby. However, he felt their presence and could tell he was getting close to his target. All of his senses enhanced with every step. He approached the diamond-shaped center of the walk. A shimmering atop the opposite flight of stairs caught his eye. At first, he thought it was a branch flowing in the wind. However, it happened once more after the breeze had subsided.

Keke knew that if he approached whatever was atop the stairs it would flee. He could sense the trepidation and wariness within it as though the emotions were his own. He felt another sensation within the unseen being which he somehow was certain was not human.

Wonder.

The unseen being was curious about Keke. It was astonished that Keke was aware of it. That he could perceive it in the same way it perceived him. It was certain that Keke was cognizant of its emotional state and thoughts. It was cognizant of his too. It had felt his pulse slow as he walked down the stairs opposite of where it now stood. It was aware of Keke looking for it. It knew that is what drew him here, rather than riding home for lunch.

"I know you are there. I can see you, kinda." The last word Keke spoke more to himself.

"I just want to talk. If you can talk."

Keke stood there waiting for a response. His chest heaved as the adrenaline raced freely from the chromaffin cells in his adrenal gland. Another fact which Keke could not discern how he knew.

Atop the stairs, there was another shimmer. The outline of a humanoid form flashed briefly. The creature turned and walked off to its left. Keke understood this meant for him to follow. Bud case in his left hand he jogged to the top of the stairs. Once there he scanned the area before pursuing the creature.

Keke came to a small clearing where there was a stone bench. Beside the stone bench, the creature shimmered a few times more. A tridactyl appendage waved him toward the bench. Keke cautiously approached. He stared at the creature, or at least, its shimmering outline once more. Its limb was still extended toward the stone seat. Keke saw that each digit had a long claw, the middle one was shorter and broken off on its extended arm. Keke tucked his pods in his pocket and slowly lowered himself down onto the bench.

"Hello, Ukeke."

The boy jumped to his feet. There was no sound that entered his ears, but the voice entered his head just the same.

"What the heck?!"

The creature shimmered again; its two arms extended; hands bent upward as though to assuage Keke's sudden anxiety over the being communicating with him telepathically.

"It is okay, Ukeke. I mean you no harm. I am fascinated about whether you can communicate in the way that... *my* species does."

"*Your* species?" The boy did not return to the bench, but he had stopped retreating.

"Yes. I believe your species' word for it is *telepathically*."

"You mean you are speaking to me with your mind."

"Yes, that is the way that my species communicates. We do not have a *mouth* like your species. We have no *larynx* like your kind. We do not utter *vocal* sounds as you do. We don't make any *sound* at all."

"Why do you keep saying things like that?" Keke asked.

"I am not sure what you mean?"

"The way you emphasize words like, telepathically, mouth, and vocal."

"These are not words that exist for my species or the other species that we encountered so I had to *extract* them."

"*Extract* them?"

"Yes."

"From where?"

"From you, Ukeke."

"From me? You read my mind to learn these words?"

"It is more intricate than that. But yes, my *pheromone receptors* created a *psychic connection* with yours and through them I am able to know things. Among those things are your *language* and your *emotions*."

"You mean that you created a psychic connection with me like Professor Xavier?"

"I am not this *mutant* educator from one of your *comic books,* Ukeke."

"Then what are you? And can you stop saying things like that?"

Keke huffed. Hands on his head he tried to process.

"You are invisible. You speak to me telepathically. You obviously aren't from this planet. At least, I don't think you are. Unless the military created you in a lab and you escaped. But you said, your species. Does that mean there are more of you?"

The creature took a long time to respond. Keke sensed something that wasn't quite sadness. It was worry. It was longing. It was yearning. The creature was missing someone.

"What happened to them?" Keke thought.

Night had fallen quickly that November day. The darkness of the clouds made it seem as though it were evening when it was barely after 2pm. The chill of the fall came with it. Keke felt none of the chill despite the drop in temperature. He only knew there was a chill because his breath fogged and dissipated as he exhaled.

The darkness did bring an element of security. Keke watched as the silhouette of the creature glanced around. He felt an easiness within it. It gained comfort in knowing that there was no one else traveling the woods on this cold autumn afternoon. The clouds and the tree cover created limited visibility for humans. The shimmering figure fully materialized. Keke's eyes widened with amazement. His jaw dropped, gaping at the features of the creature before him. Keke could see this alien being's frame in totality, and it was splendid.

It was a half a foot taller than the boy. Keke marveled at the smooth curvature of what would be the chin if there was a mouth as the creature glanced up at the half crescent moon. Its head was oblong. The face looked like the face shield on a motorcycle. It was a solid plate on the front of its head and completely smooth. There were three distinct muscles that bulged and throbbed on the creature's neck. A neck which was more than twice as long as Keke's and accounted for most of the difference in height. Its shoulders were roughly where Keke's sat. The thoracic portion of the creature was akin to that of an ant's thorax. It was narrower than Keke's but was quite muscular. The head and shoulder structures resembled the chitinous exoskeleton of a lobster. The thoracic area that sat atop the creature's waist was fleshy. It was like a human stomach that was ripped with a six-pack abdominal area, but the skin appeared thicker and rubbery.

The creature was bipedal. The legs were jointed halfway down like Keke's were. Only, it did not have knees.

There were two fork joints that connected the upper and lower portions, making what looked to Keke to be a muscular clevis joint, but without the pin. The lower legs were the same chitinous material as the head and shoulders. The upper legs were muscular and fleshy like the stomach. Unlike the human leg's quadricep, the creature had two large muscles on each. The feet were tridactyl like the hands. The back of the hands and tops of the feet had chitinous protective covers that guarded the small bones that were used for tactile dexterity and locomotive propulsion.

The most notable thing about the creature was the coloring. From head to toe, it was the same color. There was a sparkling cerulean, blue glow that flowed through the creature. The color hue was vivid. It reminded Keke of a cross between a Majesdanian and Isaac from the show The Orville.

"Please, sit. I will tell you *everything*."

"Can you start with why I can sense you and why I was drawn to your presence?"

"I can."

The boy sat beside the creature.

"Your ability to sense me was a *circumstance* of our previous encounter.

"Our previous encounter? We met before? I don't remember that."

"Interesting."

"Interesting, how?"

"It was a few Earth weeks ago that we encountered one another. I was walking through these woods where I have been hiding for a few days. I found it difficult to navigate your world. There are *cars, cows, deer, dogs,* other humans. When I first arrived on your planet I needed *healing.*

"You were injured. How did you get here? Do you have a ship?"

"My transport was damaged. The damage was exacerbated by entry into your planet's orbit. I had to eject from it or risk dying in the crash. It had reached what your people call *terminal velocity*. I did not understand how this happened. I ejected from the transport but did not comprehend your planet's *gravitational pull*. I fell too fast. My exoskeleton was damaged upon impact with your planet's surface."

The creature tapped at its thorax where Keke could now see that there was a blemish in the blue, chitinous cover. He looked closely and there was a slight crack.

"You jumped from your ship?"

"Yes."

"From how high?"

"I calculate that I was at the lower end of your *stratosphere*. So roughly eight and a half miles from the planet surface."

"You did an eight-mile free fall?"

"Eight and a half miles."

"And you survived?"

"That would seem obvious since I am here to explain my arrival."

"I guess so. But how? That fall should have killed you?"

"I will explain that to you, but I think it would help to start from the beginning."

Keke was having a hard time understanding how anyone or anything could fall eight and a half miles to the Earth after entering the atmosphere and only sustain minor damage and not be completely obliterated.

"Could you continue to explain how I can sense you?"

"Of course. As I stated, the fall damaged my exoskeleton. Unlike your species, humans, my kind do not have blood, a life source fluid in the same way you do. However, our life fluid does contain our genetic material, like your *DNA*. Yet, our life fluid is so much more than yours. It is a medium by which our pheromones move throughout our bodies."

The creature paused.

"What does that have to do with me?"

"You see when I landed it was a few miles from here. Your planet is much warmer than mine. The damage from the fall and the increased temperature made it difficult for me to adjust. I had to develop a new stasis in this new biome. Your days are so long, and the *radiation* hours are much greater."

"Radiation hours?"

"*Daylight* hours. The amount of time your planet receives direct *sunlight* to one area is more prolonged than my planet."

"Okay?" Keke still was not understanding but he felt it best to move along.

"My kind are different from your species. Our genetic make-up is different. We are more akin to creatures who exhibit *bioluminescent* properties."

"Like a firefly?"

"On your planet we are more akin to *sea snails*, as we use our life fluid as a means of communication. However, we are far more advanced. Our life force also carries the history of our people."

"What do you mean the history?"

"I will get to that. The day that I encountered you, I was still wounded. My body and arm were damaged. My head was damaged. My back was also damaged. I was not able to heal normally. The fall was great, and the gravity of your planet was unexpected. I was walking through this wood, and I stumbled in a stream. I landed on some stones. The algae was slippery. There were some of your kind on the trail. Humans.

I ran.

You were running further up the trail. I was retreating through the woods and crashed into you. You stumbled over the cliff into the stream. You hit your head."

"I traveled back down the trail. I checked to see if you were well. I saw that your life fluid was oozing out of your head. My *talon* had punctured your thorax. I pulled you from the stream. I pulled you back onto the trail. When I laid you down, I saw your life fluid, your blood was all over my *hands.* I had damaged them in the stream when I fell. My life fluid mixed with yours. Within a few minutes I could sense your pain. Feel your distress. Another human was on the trail approaching. I chose to leave you in the care of your own kind. They would know how to care for you. I waited for them to find you. Ensured they would care for you. I was not well and had to find a safe resting place."

"You left me?"

"Yes, as I said. One of your kind found you. This other human helped you up and delivered you to your *family*. It was the best decision for you to receive the necessary care. Your kind does not have the ability of my kind to heal. You require *medicine* and *doctors*."

"But you left me there. You hurt me and just left me?"

"We established this to be true."

The creature was not sure why Keke continued to ask the same question after being answered. He sensed pain in this but could not rationalize it.

Keke was a little annoyed that this creature hurt him and left him in the woods. He nearly killed him by knocking him off the trail into the water.

"It was that day that I began to feel you. You were distinctly different from my kind. You were of this planet. The connection was not one that should be possible. Yet, it existed."

"You can sense others of your kind?"

"Yes. I can sense all of my kind at all times."

"You can sense them now?"

"They are with me."

"They are here?"

"They are not here on your planet, but they are with me."

"I don't understand."

"My species' life fluid has multiple purposes. The first thing it does is the bioluminescent function. My world is very dark. We cannot see distant *stars* and we do not have a *moon* that is visible in our sky. Seldom can we see the *star* that holds our planet in its orbit like your Sun. Like I said, we don't have as many radiation hours.

Our life fluid also serves as a medium of *cognitive transference.* Those living members of my species are psychically connected to one another. Not only can we communicate across distances, but we have what your species calls sensory perception of what one another is experiencing. If there is a distress for one of our species, we all immediately know about it. This is how we were alert to the deception of the Wryvyn."

"The Wryvyn? Who or what is the Wryvyn?"

"The Wryvyn are a species from a planet near our *stellar system.* They arrived on our planet claiming that they sought to warn us of the impending end of our world. They said that from their world they could see our star with *devices* of *technology.* They showed them to us. They were shaped like your *binoculars* but had the capability of both your *telescopes* and *microscopes.* The Wryvyn said they saw that our star was dying. They had come to transport us to their planet as a *rescue.*"

"Their motives were not genuine. Their aim was to deceive. They had been studying our people from afar and learned of our abilities."

"Abilities?" Keke shifted his weight to one side giving relief to his right buttock that was stiff from the pressure on the stone seat.

"My kind are peaceful. Due to our connection, we had no *greed,* no *war,* no *possession.* We share a connected conscious. Our world was a place of *harmony.* We did not fight against one another. We had no reason. If one felt joy, we all felt it. If one felt pain, every member of the species felt it."

"Someone is coming!" Keke interrupted.

Immediately the creature disappeared. Keke waved at where the creature had been standing a moment ago for it to follow him up the trail in the other direction. In the waning light, Keke could barely make out where he was going. He crouched as he walked. He didn't need to look back for the creature. He could sense him mimicking his actions despite being behind him and invisible. Keke cut off the trail and found the thickest tree to hide behind, squatted and slowed his breath.

Chapter 19

The trio of teens passed by where Keke had left the trail without a glance in his direction. They were too busy discussing their preferred female fellow students and what they would do if they got the time of day. They were loud and boisterous. Their noise disturbed the quiet wood.

Once he was sure they had passed and were a good distance up the trail, Keke stood and began to walk back toward the trail. Once in the clearing, he realized his companion had not followed him.

"What's wrong?"

"I don't feel *safe.*"

"I won't let anything happen to you. If more people come, we can go."

The visitor stood his ground.

Keke nodded his understanding and walked back to the tree. He swiped at the ground litter at the base of the trunk and sat. He looked upon the wavering space that he knew was the invisible creature. Eventually, he materialized and sat beside the boy.

"How do you do that? Turn invisible."

"*Turn invisible?*"

"Yes, make it so that people can't see you."

"*Invisible.* That is a good term for it. That is a mechanism of my people's genetic makeup. Our life fluid can absorb radiation through the mechanism of our *corium's thermoreceptors*. In those rare times that our sky was clear enough to allow us to see our star, our *cells* would become *charged* with its energy. We could even pull it from the surrounding *fauna* for days after.

"So, you guys are like a cactus next to a computer?"

"I do not know what a *cactus* does in the proximity of a *computer*. When we absorb the stellar radiation, we can harness the energy for a variety of uses. Our cells are akin to that of your *Bruce Banner*. But we do not turn green. We do not grow in size from it. We turn white when we are overloaded with the energy and can move more swiftly, jump higher, have greater strength."

"In the sunlight, you get supercharged?"

"Yes, but we have the ability to store the energy that is harnessed in our cells. We do not have mitochondria *like* humans do. Our cells have *chambers* that expand as the energy passes through our...," The creature paused gathering his thoughts, or more accurately gathering thoughts from Keke's mind.

"The closest word I have for it in your language is *chitin*. Yet we are not made of polysaccharides like your crustaceans and insects. We have a nitrogen end, a potassium end, and a phosphorus end to our cells in the *shell* that covers our corium."

"Wait. You said, nitrogen, potassium, and phosphorus?"

"Yes, that is how I turn invisible. By harnessing the energy stored in my cells to manipulate my *pigmentation*."

"You absorb light energy, and that energy activates cells with nitrogen, phosphorus and potassium?"

"Yes. I was specific about these details already."

"Basically, you absorb the sunlight and become a fertilizer bomb?"

The creature pondered on the question for a minute. Keke watched as he tilted his head to the size. Keke did not know this, but he was scanning for fertilizer and bomb in the thoughts Keke had. Many of the ones for bomb were of a cartoon rabbit, or a coyote, or a video game with humans with assault rifles. Eventually he stumbled upon an episode of a television show where government agents were seeking a group of individuals called terrorists and found in a van a large device of the type that Keke had mentioned.

"No. We do not become fertilizer bombs. Our intention is not destruction or harm to others. It is just an ability that we possess and can manipulate in a variety of ways."

Keke chuckled as the creature had not identified the humor in his statement.

"You find joy in my telling of the origins of my species?"

"No. Humans sometimes laugh or smile in uncomfortable moments."

"Would you like to find an alternate sitting place. The layers of your skin are very soft, and I understand that being pressed into a hard surface for extended periods gives you discomfort."

"That's not what I, never mind."

"How is it that you have these powers, yet you didn't you use them against the Wryvyn?"

"As I said, our intentions are not meant to harm."

"But it sounds like they came to harm you. You must have understood that. You won't even harm to employ self-preservation?"

"They were *deceptive*. They came to us in a *spaceship*. They were friendly. Cordial. Their concern for our kind seemed genuine. They took a few of my kind to their world and showed them evidence that the star that our planet encircled was dying.

This evidence was manipulated. We were not in danger from our star. Our kind did not understand how their technology worked. We believe them to be superior beings with good intentions. We were *impressed* by their technology. They believed if enough of us believed them, we would go with them to their world. They were very convincing."

"Wait, if they were another species, then how did you communicate with them?" Keke screwed up his face in skepticism. "Could you communicate with them telepathically like you do with me?"

"It was not like with you. Their technology was extremely advanced. They had a device that allowed them to communicate with us. As I said. My kind were impressed."

"Oh, so why did they want you on their planet if your planet wasn't dying?"

"The Wryvyn had studied us from afar. They study many species in nearby worlds. They somehow learned how to communicate with us. The Wryvyn are a species of high intellect. They saw what our people were capable of when we absorbed the radiation. They didn't know this was the catalyst for our powers. Their *scientists* wanted to study us to see if they could harness our power through *biotechnology*. They wanted to travel to other worlds and conquer the life forms there. The scientists believed if they could harness our powers into a weapon, they would be able to create *super soldiers.*"

"So, they came to enslave you?"

"Yes, that is why they came."

Keke and the creature sat quietly for a few minutes. The gravity of his kind's ordeal weighed on them both. Keke's history was such that he understood what type of creature would do such a thing. The country's history was soiled with those types of creatures.

Scanning around Keke noted the sounds of animals, comfortable in the night. It had grown extremely dark, and he could barely see anything beyond his new acquaintance from a far-off planet.

"I should be going soon. My parents will be worried."

Keke stood wiping his hands on the back of his joggers. He wanted to hear more of his new acquaintance's story, but he didn't wish to worry his parents.

"Do you have a place to stay?"

"I do not stay anywhere too long. I will move around this wooded area until I regain my full strength."

"I mean where do you sleep? Do you sleep? Have you found shelter?"

"Your flora is not as durable as the flora on my planet. I was able to build a *hut* of sorts without tools. However, it is not truly adequate to keep out your *rain.*"

"You want to come stay with me?"

Keke waved at his acquaintance to follow. The creature stared for a moment, at least Keke took it as a stare since Keke could not see his eyes through the shield-like cover. A moment of consideration and the creature followed. It took them an hour to get back to the house. In that time Keke learned the rest of the story.

The Wryvyn had named the creatures. He had told Keke that the best translation for what the Wryvyn had named his species was Caerulusians. They called them this because the Wryvyn had referred to their planet as Caeruluziard. In Wryvyn language, this meant cold blue world. The Wryvyn were not savvy to all the abilities of the Caerulusians. Even the Caerulusians didn't know the full extent of their powers because they had never had to use them intentionally.

The Wryvyn put the first group of Caerulusians to arrive on their planet in cages. They were holding cells with magnetic fields for doors. They explained this as protocol. However, the Caerulusian prisoners discovered that they were misled when the Wryvyn began to experiment on them. The Wryvyn originally explained the cages and the experiments as testing for *pathogens* that may be harmful to their kind. After one of the original transports to the Wryvyn planet had died from being depleted of all his life fluid the ruse was over.

All the other Caerulusians were alerted to the true intentions of the Wryvyn immediately. The Wryvyn were unaware that the Caerulusians were connected psychically through their life fluid.

The Caerulusians considered escape but most of them were already on Wryvyn ships headed to their planet. Keke's blue friend explained that he was among the remaining few who had boarded the craft but not been drained. Those who had yet to board pretended to be unaware of the intentions of their would-be captors. They asked the Wryvyn how their ships operated. They pretended to be curious. They understood that the Wryvyn were *pompous* and did not expect that the Caerulusians would catch on to their deception. The Wryvyn welcomed them into the cockpit of the ship. The controls were extremely complicated. Meanwhile, others on a separate ship asked about the controls of the smaller ships. These ships were like escape pods from Earth movies. The Caerulusians decided that these would be easier to control. However, they could not all get into the pods without the Wryvyn knowing. Three of them managed to escape. They hoped to follow the Wryvyn to their planet. When the escape pods launched the main ship began to fire at them with sonic weapons. The Wryvyn knew as soon as the pods launched that their captives had figured out their deception. Their kind on board were huddled into a room with an electronic field for a door.

  The escaped Caerulusians all flew in different directions. They were not prepared and were extremely unfamiliar with the controls and flying of spaceships. They had never even left their planet before. They hadn't wanted to or considered it as a possibility. Meanwhile, Keke's companion had escaped using a larger ship. He learned enough from his people's questions to fly away.

  Eventually, the Caerulusian did something that made the ship go so fast that he could not see around him.

Once he was able to stop the Wryvyn ship and his fellow Caerulusians were nowhere to be found. He could still sense them and knew that the others in the pods had escaped.

As they turned onto Springfield Drive, Keke felt the creature stop.

"What's wrong?"

Keke noted a while back that his companion had turned invisible. It was probably for the best given the traffic on route nine as they walked along the well-lit road.

"You live in a *house*. I cannot come inside a house. I will eventually be visible while I *sleep*. Your kind will be able to see me."

Keke thought for a moment.

"We have a shed. I can get you a blanket or a sleeping bag. Nobody goes in there. You can sleep there."

The creature considered the thoughts and images he gained from his connection to Keke. Without a word, he started walking once more.

As they got closer to the house Keke saw his mother standing on the front porch. Rather than approach the house he cut through a yard that he knew had no fence. From that yard, he made his way to the back of the house. He quietly ushered his friend into the shed. There was plenty of room beside the lawn mower for him to lay down. Keke found some of their camping gear in a long black bin. He pulled out a sleeping bag and laid it along the floor. He handed his guest a small pillow. Keke turned his hands toward his head and pretended to lay on an invisible pillow. He pointed to the fluffy headrest in the creature's hand. His guest nodded his understanding. He thought to ask if the creature ate but it read Keke's mind and informed him that it did not. Keke promised the creature he would be safe and that he would check on him in the morning.

Quietly, Keke snuck into the kitchen and plated himself some dinner. The sound of the microwave beeping alerted his mother. She came in and was relieved to see him.

"Where have you been?!" She exclaimed. "I was worried sick."

Before he could answer his brother rounded the corner.

"I told you mom. He was probably out walking the trails again."

Bini stole a green bean off his brother's plate before opening the cupboards to search for a snack.

"I was. I just wanted some air. I lost track of time. I was beyond the wooden bridge before I realized it was getting dark."

"I don't care. I don't like you being out late by yourself. Next time, you had better call to check in. You just got over being sick. The doctors said there may have been a bacterial element from your fall that infected the wounds. I don't buy that and don't believe it was causing the fever. The nights are getting colder. You need to be careful in those trails after your accident."

She came over and put wrist against his forehead mimicking what Bini had done earlier that morning and found he was a normal temperature. Unsatisfied, she checked his pulse and blood pressure as he ate his pork chop and vegetables. Bini laughed in the corner as he crunched an Oreo. The crumbs fell onto his shirt as he leaned against the counter, one leg crossed over the other.

Keke just rolled his eyes at his twin brother. He was used to this type of treatment. They both were. Having a nurse for a mother came with a certain degree of coddling, poking, and prodding every now and then. Keke's mind drifted to his friend in the shed as his mother went through her routine. He felt sorry that he was so far from his people. The story of how they were tricked reminded him of how black people came to this country as slaves or how the Native Americans lost their land.

Satisfied with her check-up, Louise kissed both boys on the top of their heads and went to bed.

As their mother's footsteps faded, Keke got up from the table and went to the linen closet.

"So where were you really?"

Keke was startled by his twin's presence as he turned to shut the door. That was twice in one day.

"I was in the trails. I was just walking. Are you turning into mom?"

Bini jabbed his brother's shoulder at the insinuation that he was hovering. With a fake sigh of offense, the boy acted out donning a pretend stethoscope and pressing the pretend diaphragm to a few spots on his brother's torso. Lips pursed, he listened intently. The two boys chuckled at the performance. Still laughing, Bini marched up to the top of the stairs and went off to bed.

Keke slipped out the back door, shutting it quietly and made his way to the shed.

"You were not well?"

"I was."

"Your *mother* is a healer."

"She is. Here, take these blankets. You can use them to pad the floor so that it isn't so hard. In the morning, I can help you find a better place to sleep or maybe we can make it more comfortable in here. You can tell me more about your journey to this planet."

The Caerulusian did not take the items. Keke bent down shooing him aside. He watched as Keke laid the first blanket out in the limited shed space. He left it partially folded to increase the cushion. He did the same with the second before laying the sleeping bag over it. When he was done, he patted the blanket and gazed in the direction of his companion. When he still didn't move, Keke laid down and covered himself with the sleeping bag.

"See. You can lay down here and sleep in comfort. It isn't very warm but there won't be any wind."

"Ukeke Wallace. Is this a safe place?"

"What do you mean?"

"The last time someone tried to help me they enslaved my people."

"Oh. Yeah, this is a safe place. I won't hurt you. I won't tell anyone you are here."

"Are we *friends?*"

Keke felt a pang of sadness run through him.

"Yes, you are my friend now. Friends take care of one another. Maybe tomorrow we can come up with a plan to help you get home to save your people or something."

Keke watched as his new friend materialized before him. He mimicked Keke as he laid down, fluffed the pillow at the end of the blanket before laying his head down. He covered himself with the sleeping bag and gazed up to Keke for approval.

"Like this?"

Keke nodded and gave him a thumbs up.

He returned the nod and thumbs up which made Keke laugh.

"Thank you, Ukeke Wallace. For being my friend and not wanting to enslave me for my powers."

Keke nodded once more before turning to shut the door and heading off to bed. The creature did not tell his new friend that he was already working on a plan to return to his people.

Chapter 20

Zheng Wei set her glass of wine on the deck beside the hot tub. Her husband Henry was pulling some appetizers from the oven in the kitchen. She was thankful that he suggested returning home from their vacation on Friday evening. This gave them a time buffer when their connection flight was delayed. Arriving home late Saturday was not ideal. However, it would be much more frustrating to arrive home late Sunday and miss a day of work after having been gone for so long due to airline issues.

As the head principal, the school board looked to her to ensure that people were responsible with their usage of time. The consensus was that teachers got enough leave time with having the entire summer off and all of the school vacations. It was unspoken, but the board felt they should just have to sacrifice throughout the rest of the school year. Wei didn't consign to that ideology, and thankfully the union didn't agree. Despite having time to use, she didn't want to take any heat for missing an unplanned extra day last minute.

She wondered how well Betrand was faring during his stint as acting Head Principal covering for her. He wasn't the most diplomatic of school administrators. He didn't have the ability to garner favor with the student body the way that she did. It wasn't so much that he was incapable of caring for the students. He just didn't understand the need to develop any understanding of their personal life. He couldn't equate it to any metric of his role and performance. Therefore, he communicated with them in a cold and unfriendly manner. She sometimes felt perhaps he had chosen the wrong career field.

She and Henry were fortunate that they were laid over in the States and not in Europe. This made the extended travel a bit less stressful. Worst case scenario, they could rent a car and drive home. If their flight from Europe had been delayed, they would have been at the mercy of the airlines. She appreciated having the option to modify plans to ensure arrival on time for work. Although, that option proved to be not necessary. While their layover added an additional ten hours to their travel, they made the best of it. They were able to rest for a few hours in one of those airport pods.

She and Henry took turns sleeping to ensure that they didn't have to cram all of their belongings into the pod. When they weren't sleeping, they grabbed a few overpriced drinks in the airport bar. They even spent time looking over their vacation photos. The decision to grab a few hours of sleep in the pods meant both of them were wide awake when they arrived home. They rummaged through the kitchen to see what snacks they had on hand to prepare. They hadn't yet closed the hot tub for the winter and decided to get another night of use out of it. A romantic and relaxing night in to end their trip.

Their fifth anniversary was as magical as she expected it to be. Wei thoroughly enjoyed their tour of Italy. They even found time to sneak off to Tuscany on their schedule relaxation day. Now that they were home, she planned on having that day of relaxation tomorrow before returning to the real world of teenage angst and underpaid teachers. But first, would be a romantic evening in the hot tub with hors d'oeuvres and wine.

Wei shouted for Henry to bring the bottle of wine when he returned from the kitchen. She had already slipped off her robe and lowered into the bubbling spa.

"Sure thing, Lucy." Henry shouted back.

Lucy was her Western name. Her parent were Chinese immigrants. She kept her maiden name when she married. She used the name her parents had selected for her when she began primary school with her non-Chinese friends. It was the name that she used when she met Henry. In the time that they had been together, Henry had learned a great deal from her culture and had been around her parents often. He knew the cultural reasons she went by Lucy and not Wei. Still, he referred to her as Lucy and not Wei, and she didn't mind in the slightest.

The smell of bacon-wrapped scallops wisped past her nose. She opened her eyes and there was Henry with a small plate of treats in one hand and the bottle of wine in the other. He set them to either side of her on the deck. She smiled up at him as he crouched to kiss her gently on the forehead.

"The baked salmon bites are just about done. I will bring those out when I bring the bruschetta. Anything else before I head up to put on my suit?"

"You don't have to wear a suit?" Henry watched as his wife's eyebrows raised and a small smirk formed in the corner of her lips.

"Well, if Mr. Montenegro decides to peek out from across the yard, then he might be envious. To play it safe, I'll grab the suit."

"We really need to get a contractor over here to put up a privacy fence. It is really messing up the 'visual appeal'."

Wei smirked at her husband once more. Henry leaned his head to the side, scrunched up his mouth and glanced toward the stars. He pretended to weigh the pros and cons of wearing a suit once more. He tapped his chin with his index finger, adding to the effect. After a brief moment, Henry grinned down on his wife mischievously.

The couple chuckled playfully.

Their laughter was interrupted by the doorbell.

Neither of them had a guess of who it could be. None of their neighbors ever visited and they hadn't told their friends which night they were coming back from their trip. An unexpected drop by under those circumstances was unlikely.

Henry filled his wife's half empty glass before crossing the dining room and turning the corner to the foyer to find out who was visiting them at this late hour on a Saturday. He opened the door and there on the cement walkway stood two young men staring at him.

"Can I help you boys?"

The two boys seemed confused upon seeing Henry at the door. When they didn't respond to his initial inquiry, Henry pried further as to their presence.

"What address are you looking for?"

Again, neither boy said anything.

Henry found it to be entirely peculiar and rather concerning that neither of them were speaking, or moving, or blinking. He noted that one of them had green colored hair. He had a gas station nametag pinned to the shirt under his jacket. The other boy had blonde hair wore a white dress shirt under his jacket and wore what looked to be suit pants. The boy with the name tag looked to be of college age while the other couldn't be much older than sixteen or seventeen. They both continued to stare as though frozen in time. His patience with the two of them was wearing thin. They were keeping him from a romantic evening with his wife.

"Listen, Roger..." Henry leaned getting a partial read of the tag on the boy's shirt.

"He's not Roger." The blonde boy responded dryly. "Ok, Not Roger. You and your friend here need to work on your communication skills. I'm busy so I'm going to help you out so I can get back to my evening. You rang my doorbell. Traditionally, we humans only do that when we are visiting someone we know or perhaps soliciting some type of good or service.

"Humans, do this." Not Roger responded.

"Yes. We also communicate our purpose for ringing the doorbell upon the arrival of the occupants at the door. You obviously have the wrong address and are potentially a little bit too high to be out in civilized society tonight. I recommend you boys head on home."

The two boys looked at one another, as though processing the information that they just received.

"Well, you boys have a lovely night." Henry turned to go back inside. He stepped across the threshold, reaching for the edge of the door with his left hand.

"Wait. Are you the principal of the school?" The blonde boy asked robotically.

"I'm sorry?" Henry had not heard the question as his thoughts were on his swimsuit clad wife in the hot tub.

"The school. Are you the principal of the school?"

"No, that would be my wife, Lucy."

"Lucy." The boy echoed.

"I believe you would be calling her Ms. Zheng, young man, but yes."

The two boys stared at one another for a moment.

"Ms. Zheng. She lives here." The blonde boy confirmed.

"Yes. But I must ask that whatever business you have with her you wait until mornechkkk..."

One grey and red tentacle entered Henry's open mouth cutting off his words while another wrapped its way around his left arm. Both slender tentacles projected from Not Roger's mouth. Frantic, and on instinct, Henry whipped the door closed. Both tentacles were severed as the heavy wooden door crushed them.

Henry stumbled back smashing his back against the wall. He slid to the ground wrestling with the foreign object that had wormed its way down into his throat. It gripped tightly to his insides, a grey fluid pouring out the opposite end. He struggled to get it free but was slowly losing air. The end of the tentacle was resting right at the top of his trachea. It had expanded, blocking the passage of breath in and out of his lungs. The more he struggled, the closer he came to losing consciousness. With a last desperate effort, he wrapped the end of the tentacle around his palm, made a fist and tugged violently. The force of tug flung the tentacle out of his hands. He fell to his chest gasping for air.

In the yard, the sound of the slamming door was barely audible over the music that was playing from the deck speakers. Wei snapped her head up listening. She called out to her husband quizzically, but he didn't respond. After a moment she shrugged and assumed that he had just turned away whoever was at the door and headed up to change. She was bummed that he didn't bring the other plates of food out first. She was craving the bruschetta.

Wei took a large gulp of her wine then took a bite of her scallop. She chewed the bacon wrapped mollusk a few times before chasing it with the rest of the glass. Feeling a warm buzz in the cold night air, she slid down into the hot tub further, resting her head on the edge. She closed her eyes, just vibing to the music, hands and arms waving under the water to the Al Green tune that played. Entranced by the music and alcohol, she nearly didn't feel the footsteps on the deck when Henry returned.

She smiled as the tremors of his steps stopped close to her head.

"I hope that you elected to go without the suit."

"I have a suit, Lucy."

The strange voice snapped Wei out of her buzz. She flung herself across the tub to the other side, slipping on the bottom as she flailed in fright.

"Who the hell are you?"

She could see her husband scrambling across the floor on hands and knees inside the house. The blonde-haired boy could see it in her gaze. He turned and marched into the house toward Henry punching him in the side of the face. The force of the blow knocked Henry out cold. He turned to see Wei had exited the hot tub. She was now on the deck sliding into her robe. Wei tied the cotton belt tightly to her waist before snatching the empty wine bottle to wield as a weapon.

The boy walked toward her casually.

"Lucy, the principal, we require your assistance."

Lucy wasted no time in slinging the bottle at the boy. He didn't recognize the threat of her action. The bottle sailed directly at his head, smashed him in the face. The boy stumbled backward knocking his head hard on the tile floor just inside the doorway. The boy was still conscious as Wei ran past him to tend to her unconscious husband. She tried to wake him but found that he was unresponsive. Behind her, the boy was rousing already. She ran to the kitchen and grabbed a knife from the drawer. Wei positioned herself behind the counter waiting for the boy to attack.

Wei was incredibly surprised when he simply walked past her and out the front door, leaving it wide open. She considered running for her phone which was on the charger in the living room. However, the body of her unconscious husband drew her in. She scampered to his side across the tile floor, nearly impaling herself with the knife, slipping on one of her own wet footprints.

She propped Henry's head up onto her lap. Wei tapped him rapidly on his cheek. The action didn't garner any response. She rubbed his chest, sobbing, her robe sopping from not properly toweling off. The shock of the attack and the cold chill of the November evening had sobered her right up. Now she was shivering with chill and fear.

Wei ran to the back door and pushed it shut. She knew she needed help for her husband and to file a report. Quick as she could she then dashed into the living room and grabbed her phone. On her way back she noticed that the boy had not closed the front door. Her heart thumped in her chest at the thought of him returning. She slid the phone in her pocket and grabbed the knife from next to her unresponsive husband.

Wei crept to the foyer, listening for signs that the blonde boy was there. After a half dozen deep breaths to calm herself, she turned the corner. The screen door was shut and there was no one to be seen. She pressed herself to the cold aluminum, fumbling with the lock on the handle. She shut and latched the interior door and pulled out her phone and dialed 911. She spun quickly to run back to her husband. A wet hand grabbed her by the throat, lifting her off the ground. The boy before her had half green hair and there was a muddy substance dripping from his mouth. Wei tried to scream but the clench on her throat was fierce. The boy was incredibly strong. He had lifted her high enough to see that the blonde boy was standing over Henry, the back door which she had locked was slid open. Desperately, Wei swiped and chopped with the kitchen knife in her hand at the arm of the boy who was strangling her. She got a few good swipes in, one of which went through the fabric of his jacket. Still, the boy did not release her. He didn't even flinch as the sharp blade split the skin.

Not Roger maneuvered her in the air slamming her into the wall where the coat rack hung. She could no longer see her husband and was almost certain that they were about to die. Oxygen leaving her lungs she stared into the eyes of the boy. The fluid oozing down his chin smelled rancid. Her arm wavered at her side as she tried to fight. Just as she was about to pass out, he dropped her on the floor. Wei slumped hard onto the carpeted foyer. She writhed, back against the wall, coughing to gain her breath. Despite not being in the boy's grasp all that long, her neck throbbed from the trauma. Wei looked up to her attacker in time to see three tentacles fly at her from inside his mouth. Shocked when a pair of them flew into her own mouth. One of them was leaking that unctuous fluid. The sulfuric taste and sticky texture of the substance that oozed from the appendage made her gag. She began to retch, bile shooting up from within. A few moments later, the lights turned off for Wei Zheng.

Chapter 21

Mac woke in the morning and saw that the bedroom windows were frosting up. He thought that it would be a good time to go shopping for a snow blower. There was a full month left before the official start of winter. He knew about Upstate New York winters. It didn't have to be December twenty-first for the snow to fall. As a boy, Mac once visited his grandfather for winter recess and found himself helping to shovel away eighteen inches of cold, wet, whiteness. It was the only thing that his adolescent brain could call what had plummeted to the ground overnight. He had gone to bed on a cold clear night. He awakened to a winter wonderland. It wasn't even cloudy in the morning. The sun shone brightly overhead, yet the snow sat there heavy and wet in defiance of the celestial body. Mac recalled his fingers being pink at the end of the hour-long ordeal of clearing the sidewalk and uncovering his Grandpa W.D's Buick Skylark. That was one surprise he vowed to be ready for when the decision was made to uproot his family and move to New York.

Mac arrived downstairs to find Keke was already making breakfast.

"Your mother know that you are cooking, son?" Mac asked as he put a k-cup in the coffee maker.

It was a rule that Louise was allowed to cook for the family on the weekends when she wasn't working. She felt quite dogmatic about the tradition. Part of her language of love was feeding her family. That was her act of service. The other part was words of affirmation. A few times, the second was all that preserved the first.

Her work schedule regulated when she would have the opportunity to prepare meals for her loved ones. She made it clear a few years back that for them to disallow her endeavors was an affront on her love.

Tunes had awakened early and put a bagel in the toaster one Sunday before church. He was on a kick where he was eating cinnamon raisin bagels every day. He would pester Mac every time they went to the market to ensure that he was getting the bagels. When Louise saw him eating the bagel when she came down, the mood in the room got really somber. A nine-year-old Darius didn't understand what he had done wrong. After the service, Mac sat him and the twins down to explain some things about women. They all were mindful of the weekends that Louise was off work thereafter. Each one of them had the schedule in their phone calendar.

"Shoot! I forgot. I had to get out early this morning and wanted to eat before I go. I am starving dad!"

"Really? Where are you going?" Mac crossed the kitchen to the stove to turn off the burner. He dumped the partially scrambled eggs into a bowl and set the pan in the sink.

Keke watched as he washed the pan, dried it with a hand towel, and placed it back on the rack which hung above the island. He pulled the two slices of bread that were sitting in the toaster waiting to be toasted. He slid both slices back into the plastic bag with the rest of the loaf. He slowly twisted the tie to close the bread. As he twisted, he looked to Keke who had not responded to his question.

"Where are you off to, son?" Mac repeated.

"To the trails."

"Oh really. Been spending a lot of time there. I hope you are being careful after your accident."

"I am, dad."

Mac looked to the stove, then the countertop and then back to Keke. He took a hand and waved it in a circular motion.

Keke understood the gesture. He grabbed a washcloth from the linen closet to clean up the evidence of his near betrayal. When he returned, he saw that his father had gone out into the backyard and was heading for the shed. Keke felt incredibly famished to where he almost didn't register his father's destination.

That lasted a brief moment.

Abandoning his cleaning task, he threw the cloth on the counter and sprinted out onto the deck.

"Dad! What are you doing?" The question came out more aggressively than he planned it.

"I'm measuring the room in the shed." Mac scrupled his son, confused by the tone of his inquiry.

"Why? Right now? It's cold out here. Don't you at least want to grab a jacket?" Keke softened his tone.

"Yes, right now. I'm going to buy a snow blower today. I want to know what size will fit in there. I need to get a couple shovels and some rock salt too. No, I don't need a jacket. Any other questions, counselor?"

Keke trotted down the steps to meet his father in front of the shed.

"Let me do that dad. I will measure for you." He held out his hand for the tape measurer.

"No, I got it. It will take me as long to explain to you how to do it as it will for me to just do it."

"I can read a tape measure, dad." Keke tried to make his tone light, but his heart was racing.

"I'm already out here, son." Mack looked down at his son's feet that did not have shoes on them.

Keke tensed up as his father yanked the door of the shed open and stepped inside.

"Dad, look, I can explain." Keke stuck his head inside expecting to see a sleeping alien on the camping blankets.

"Explain what? What is the matter with you today, son. Are you feeling okay, Ukeke."

Keke was surprised to find that his alien friend was gone. He must have left early that morning. He had put his blankets away. There was no trace he had even slept, there. Keke tried to sense him like he had yesterday, and he was unable to do so.

"Uh, nothing. I had um, borrowed some of your tools. I didn't remember putting them back. But I guess I did."

Mac scratched his beard. From years of teaching and years of being a dad, he could tell that his son was not being honest with him. There was something that he expected Mac to see in the shed that he didn't want him to see. This made the father of teenaged boys curious.

Mac surveyed the room. Nothing seemed to be out of place at all. The mower, the gardening supplies, even his tools; nothing was amiss. Mac catalogued the small room. Finally, he noted the bin for the camping blankets and gear. It was not closed entirely. The face side with the writing on it was not facing out. Mac had intentionally faced the label out for ease of location. The back edge had a corner of a blanket sticking out. It was an in-the-house blanket and not a camping blanket.

He continued to look around the room pretending to not notice. When he scanned back to face Keke, the boy looked entirely uncomfortable. He could see his son staring at the bin over his shoulder. He obviously noted the blanket hanging out the corner as well.

Mac chuckled. Keke was confused by the laugh.

"Son, do we need to have 'the talk'?"

"The talk, dad?"

"You know. The one about being respectful of the house in regard to having a lady over for company."

"Dad, I'm confused."

"Well, let's pretend that somebody, has a lady friend who they are very fond of."

"You mean Tunes and Jenna?"

"No, not them. But maybe someone else. And they wanted to bring that lady friend over to the house."

"Bini had a girl over to the house?" Keke exclaimed.

Mac shook his head.

"And they maybe wanted to get comfortable with the lady friend. Now, this someone knew the rules about having a lady friend *in* the house."

"Yeah, we aren't allowed to have anyone that we are dating in our bedrooms. You told us this last year, dad. Did you forget?"

"I think someone forgot."

Keke was lost as to where the conversation was heading.

"Dad, are you okay? Why are you talking about having girls in the house? I thought you wanted to measure the space in here?"

Mac kneeled down and pulled out a tape measure. He dragged the metal tape out slowly, keeping a constant eye on Keke.

"Dad, you aren't looking at the measurement. You are talking to me about girls in the house. Where is this all coming from? Are you really measuring to buy a snowblower?"

"Nowhere, son. Just making sure you remember the rules."

"I do, dad. I don't bring girls to the house. I really don't talk to any girls anyway. Not like that."

After the odd interaction with his father, Keke went back to the kitchen. He was thankful to find his mom whipping up banana fritters, saltfish fritters, bacon, and eggs.

"Son, did your father forget that I was off today?"
"Mom?"

Louise reached to the side of the toaster and grabbed the bowl of eggs that Mac had set on the counter."

"No, it was me. I'm sorry mom."

Louise looked at him sternly. The boy hung his head. Louise crossed the room to where Keke was standing at the head of the table.

"Did you not have enough to eat last night?"

"I did, Mom. I just woke up starving. I don't know why." Keke confessed.

Louise grabbed the boy's chin, pulling his face toward her. She kissed him gently on the cheek. Keke smiled. She hugged him tenderly to her.

"She found the eggs?"

Mac didn't stop on his way to the front door. His wife and son watched as he donned his winter hat and coat and headed out to the car.

Louise looked at her son, a confused look on her face.

"He's off to buy a snowblower."

She nodded at Keke's explanation. She kissed her son on the forehead before returning to her task of preparing breakfast.

***

Keke was extremely distracted in chemistry class the next day. Emma noted that he was not taking notes and was instead looking up something on his phone. She could tell that he wasn't texting because he was scrolling up with his thumb periodically without typing. She found this to be distracting and extremely uncharacteristic of her table mate. In the past, Emma would not have noticed what the person who sat next to her was doing. It was different with Keke.

Keke had proven to be as studious as she was in class. Being his lab partner and classmate challenged her in ways that were unfamiliar to her. There had been other classmates in the past who sought to one-up her because they had animosity towards the best student in the class. She was not always the smartest. However, Emma put in maximum effort to learn every lesson and every subject and was fond of completing assignments. Her mother was a career military woman. She had reached the rank of captain before she retired the previous year. She was a decorated officer and contributed the success to the effort she put in toward completing missions and tasks with speed and efficiency. She impressed this upon her daughter.

For Emma to find another student who was her equal in intelligence and drive but provided the absence of the contempt that Emma typically found had accompanied the competitiveness was something Emma had not known she needed.

Keke also saved her from an extremely dangerous chemical burn and did not act any differently since doing so. Throughout the chaos of it all he remained calm, supportive, and endearing. He had taken the spill by covering her with his own body. For his bravery, he was gifted an interaction with the head of security and the assistant principal. This was due to the actions of a jealous classmate who saw his endearing nature as a threat to his claim on her heart. As though there were a claim to be had. Ricky Burns had tried an uncomfortable number of times to win her favor. Each time had been some uncomfortable interaction or miserable disaster of fortune for the boy.

It concerned her to see Keke distracted in a class where he typically was fully attentive. She dared consider him a friend. She was not accustomed to having friends in school. She thought about what she would like a friend to do for her if she was distracted in class. Emma made the decision to do something uncharacteristic for her.

Pry.

"Are you okay?" Emma whispered.

When Keke didn't respond, the girl looked up to the board, jotted her next note, then tapped the tabletop gently in front of him. He looked at her, concern in his eyes.

"Keke, is everything alright?"

"What do you mean?"

Emma gestured to the phone down in his lap, then to his closed notebook. She gazed up at the Ms. O'Brien who had just asked a question?

"Does anyone know what this special rate of decay that radioactive isotopes experience is called?"

The teacher noticed Emma shoot her hand up.

"Yes, Ms. Wakins."

"Half-Life."

"That is correct!"

Ms. O'Brien turned back to the smart board to continue the lesson. Keke had turned back to his phone.

"What are you Googling?" The girl craned her neck to get a glimpse at his screen.

"It's nothing."

"Keke, *nothing* would not have you ignoring the lecture. You haven't taken a single note."

"I'm listening."

Emma's face was reddening. She had done enough prying for the day and felt very much like her mother who was often overbearing and intrusive. Unable to sway her tablemate to pay attention or to confide in her she thought it better to be left alone.

When the bell rang for class Keke quickly exited and headed out into the throng of students and chaos. Emma shoved her books back into her backpack as quickly as she could and attempted to follow him.

Bini saw his brother weaving through the crowd on his way toward their lockers. He watched as his twin navigated through the other students crossing his path without ever looking up from his phone. He found it odd that he didn't bump into anyone and seemed to know just when to stop and when to speed up without looking.

Had he not been so intently watching Keke he may not have noticed the complete contrast of the girl in pursuit. Where Keke was so gracefully avoiding people, the girl was like a chip in that Plinko game on the Price is Right. His mom used to watch on her days off when he, Keke and Darius were little. Bini didn't care for the show. However, both he and Keke got a kick out of how the discs would bounce around and they would guess where it would land. Unlike Plinko, Bini knew exactly where the girl was going to end up, eventually.

Bini was busy watching the girl and allowed his brother to walk right past him and continued on his way. When the girl got to where Bini was waiting, she shot him a worried look. She craned her head towards his twin who he now had noticed had passed him by without a word.

"Hey."

"Hey. Is your brother okay?"

"You know, I am not sure of what he is lately. A lot of strange things have been happening that aren't like him."

"You mean like not paying attention and searching things on his phone the entire class."

Bini chuckled. When the girl didn't laugh with him, he realized that she was not joking.

"Wait, you're serious?"

Emma nodded.

"This is more serious than I thought."

"Look after him." The girl pleaded. "Something is not right."

"I always do."

Bini offered the girl his hand, which she grabbed gently and gave a slight shake sealing their agreement before walking off.

Bini turned to see that his brother was turning the corner at the far end of the hallway and jogged off to catch up.

Chapter 22

    Mac was pleased to see that Principal Zheng was back from her vacation. He waited until his free period to go looking for her to discuss the situation with her assistant principal Mr. Paul. He approached with a smile on his face, hoping not to be seen as a burden on her first day back. He politely inquired about her trip and asked for a moment of her time. Much to his surprise she dismissed him and continued walking as though she had not heard him. Confused, he spun around and watched her proceed toward her office. At the end of the hallway, holding the door for Ms. Zheng with a smug look on his face, was Bertrand Paul.

    Mac would not be so easily dismissed. Not when it comes to issues regarding his family. Bertrand had sent his attack dog after Mac's son. Mac had handled the situation. But he could not allow any room for a second occurrence of this nature. He had worked long and hard to raise his boys in an atmosphere that was as free of unfair treatment and racial injustice as life in Newport News would allow. Moving to Upstate New York, Mac had felt he had succeeded. The events of last week had soured that for him.

    Mac resolved himself. Arms down at his side, he marched down the hallway toward the main office. He was mindful to check his breathing and his temper. This was his place of employment. There were children about. There were other teachers moving through the hallways. Growing up in the south, Mac had learned to internalize emotions, especially his anger. Lest he be tagged an angry, black man.

From outside the office, Mac saw that Principal Zheng had been equally dismissive of Assistant Principal Paul. In an instant he sprouted a smile and passed by the office. He slowed enough for Bertrand to see his face before continuing to the teacher's lounge. Whatever the day has brought for Principal Zheng, she was in no mood to hear complaints.

Mac felt a little sorry for her. He hoped that it was not something that occurred on her vacation that had spoiled her mood. An anniversary trip should always be happy and carefree. His mother told him that before his first honeymoon. It would be the last year his mother spent on this Earth. Due to that fact, this final lesson she conveyed upon him visited him every time his family took a trip of any sort.

That Afternoon, the team had practice for the state championship that would be held that weekend at Vernon Verona High School. They would only have one more practice after tonight. The girls were all locked in. Most of the boys were locked in. A few of the boys were noticeably distracted. This was evident to their teammates. During their half mile warm up, Keke stopped halfway around the second lap. He didn't even continue walking. He cut across the field and despite Coach Halliday's adamant inquiries, he continued into the locker room.

As they rounded the turn Marshawn tapped Bini on the shoulder. He looked up to see the coach attempting and failing to communicate with his brother. The look of concern on Marshawn's face mirrored Bini's. A moment later, Taryn and Maryn jogged up alongside the two boys and gave similar inquiring looks.

Bini simply shook his head cluelessly.

"Where is Keke off to?" Anika asked.

"I have no idea."

"Has he talked to you since the other night?"

Bini did not wish to divulge anything about the fight at the pizza shop to anyone who wasn't there. Therefore, he deflected.

"I was busy the rest of the weekend. We haven't linked up yet."

"Well, you better go *link up* with him now. We need the both of you this weekend." Maryn had cut in front of Bini.

The girl stopped running. She walked backward in front of him, hands on her hips, the ghost of her breath floating above her head. Her sister spun around beside her. She too had wanted to know what was going on. It was clear that they were outsiders on an inside secret. As the seniors on the team, they felt it was their place to ensure things ran smoothly. Isabelle and Katie caught up with them and joined the pow wow. Justin, Everett, and Kenan arrived with them.

Spencer Halliday was visually irritated as his team had abandoned the warmup and had huddled up fifty meters from completing the first lap. He felt it was an inopportune time for them to lose their focus. However, Spencer had been a coach for over a decade. In that time, he had learned to watch his athletes and learn their character from their actions. Words could be deceptive. If you observe students for long enough, their tendencies will give away who they were.

What he knew about the Callow twins; they were leaders. They pushed their teammates, the girls and the boys, to be the best. This is how they captured the state championship last year. This is how they were in a position to repeat this weekend. This is how Halliday knew that whatever it was that was going on with their little huddle, those girls would ensure that it would end with the necessary resolution.

He wished they had chosen to produce their little meeting before practice. The temperature was dropping and was expected to be in the low 50s this weekend for the state championship. He wanted them to get a couple of light practices before Saturday. He was hoping today would end with a lift and then a team meeting. The team meeting was likely not needed afterward.

Halliday turned around to stare at the building, keying on the door to the gym where Keke had entered. The boy had run the best 5k that he had ever seen as a coach. Through the gossip tree, he had learned that he initially was lagging behind. This made his time that much more impressive. A few of the other coaches had contacted him with insinuations of performance enhancement. Halliday would hear none of it. Keke and his brother had run and won several meets this year. Halliday assured those coaches who contacted him that the stamina was due to all the trail running that Keke had done on his off days. Halliday expected Keke to be locked in this week. Apparently, his expectations were too lofty for his new track star. He turned to Keke's twin brother

Bini who was scowling as the other pair of twins addressed his brother's departure.

"What is up with you guys? We know something happened after the meet the other night. When we left the pizza shop you all were still there. First, Ricky goes all Obsessed over Keke's lab partner and tries to get him expelled. Now Jaali is over there running alone when he is typically chatting someone's ear off. Your brother had one of the best races ever and now he walks off five minutes into practice. Did something happen between those two?"

Before Bini could respond, Marshawn put a hand on his chest and stepped between him and the Callows.

"This one is on me."

"Explain."

"You remember how I got hit with a rock during our first meet?"

"Yeah, by that douchebag from Ballston Spa." It was clear that Isabella was familiar with Brandon and shared the sentiment the others had for the boy.

"He came into Cusato's after you all left. I followed him out. There was a fight."

"What does that have to do with Keke and Jaali?"

Marshawn looked to Bini and then to Anika. Both of them nodded.

Marshawn recounted the fight with Brandon and his companion. Early in the story, the rest of the team had joined them to see what they were talking about. He left out the part about Jenna confirming that up until that evening, Brandon had been thought to be missing. Not because he was hiding it, but because in the moment, he had not recalled it.

He explained how the boy was surprisingly strong and when Jenna had stepped in to stop the fight, the boy grabbed her by the throat and tossed her backward, sending her to the ground. All the girls gasped upon telling of the level of aggression used upon a girl trying to stop the fight.

Marshawn continued to give the play by play as best he recalled it. He detailed how Bini and Tunes immediately intervened to take the boy down.

"So where was Keke and Jaali during all of this?" Taryn asked.

"Keke was in the restroom. I was watching." Jaali's voice cracked as he spoke up from the back of the assemblage.

"You were watching him in the restroom? Keighleigh Maguire asked puzzled.

"I was watching the fight." Jaali corrected emphatically.

"Oh, that makes more sense."

"Was that the end of it."

"No." Marshawn began.

"This other dude that was with Brandon jumped in."

"You know the guy who worked the gas station that they said had a gas leak and was shut down for a few weeks?" Anika added.

"Roger Murphy?" the Callow twins asked.

"No, the other guy with the green hair."

"Eww, you mean Ethan Ramsey." Isabella added.

"He caught us by surprise. He got Bini and Tunes from behind. He was choking them. I couldn't get to them fast enough."

"Do you mean he was trying to kill them?" Maryn asked a bit too loud.

The group turned and looked toward Coach Halliday who was now sitting on the bench looking at his phone. The coach didn't look up. After verifying he had not overheard, they returned to their circle, where the telling continued.

"Yeah. He was definitely trying to choke the life out of us." Bini added.

"Ethan Ramsay?" Isabella did not buy that the guy who had played the lead in Oklahoma was suddenly some killer with unbelievable strength.

"That was until Keke came out of nowhere with a super punch!" Kenan whispered.

"Super punch?" Keighleigh screwed up her face.

"Don't you watch wrestling?" Kenan asked.

Before the girl could answer, the boy's older brother backhanded his chest.

"Keke knocked that boy out cold. He went night night."

Bini and Marshawn shook their heads in disappointment. The two boys squeezed closer together, pushing Kenan to the back.

"After that the cops came and we all dispersed." Anika ended the telling of the night's events.

"My brother isn't a fighter. Until the other night, I never saw him throw a punch in anger. This is probably what is bothering him. I will talk to him after practice. We will be ready for the next practice. I promise you."

The Callow twins considered Bini's words momentarily. Before allowing the group to disperse, they insisted that he give similar assurances to the coach. They recommended that they leave out the story of the fight. Isabella who had been watching Jaali after he said he just watched his teammates get into a fight pulled the boy to the side. She impressed upon him the need to not speak of the fight to anyone, lest Marshawn get in trouble and risk a potential scholarship being lost. Jaali nodded his understanding.

Bini was unsure as to whether they could count on Jaali to keep quiet about the fight. Even after Isabella's pep talk. The boy had not participated. He had not left with them afterward. He didn't sit with them during lunch earlier. Jaali was silent in the locker room when they got ready for practice. He was hopeful that Isabella's warning of the ramifications of speaking about it would be enough to keep the boy silent. Anything that Jaali mentioned prior to the weekend would jeopardize the chances of the team being able to compete at the state championship. Anything beyond that could impact their future.

After practice, Bini found his brother and cousin sitting outside waiting for him in front of the school. Mac was sitting in the car parked at the curb, but the boys chose to wait outside.

"We have to talk." Keke leaned in close to his brother.

"Yes, we do."

"After dinner. Basketball court. Mom and dad can't know."

Bini observed his brother, trying to read him. Tunes kept his face blank giving no indication that he knew what the conversation would be about. When they got in the car, it was Mac's turn to observe. He found it peculiar that Keke and Tunes were out front much earlier than normal. However, he didn't pry. His youngest boy had experienced a series of interesting events in the last few weeks. Mac studied the three of them. They did a wonderful job of convincing him that nothing was up. It was a little bit too much. Still, the way that the three of them were in it together, he knew that whatever it was, there was likely to be a healthy resolution. His boys always did their best when they worked together.

After dinner, the three boys cleared the table and then quickly donned their sweatshirts and marched silently down to the basketball court. The three of them, single file, hands shoved deep into their front shirt pocket. Chins tucked tight to their chest to prevent the wind from blowing at their necks. Bini was in the lead. He pulled his left hand from his pocket, turtling it up his sleeve. With a swipe he cleared the leaves and dirt from half of the bench that was alongside the fence. He sat down, waiting in silence.

On the other hand, Tune was not as patient. Keke had been standing in front of them trying to figure out how to start when he spoke up.

"Listen, cuz. You know we not gonna judge you. You were sick and probably lost some muscle mass from the illness and the injuries. I probably would have done the same thing if I were in your shoes."

Bini scrutinized the boy with a stank eye before turning back to his brother.

"Tunes, what the hell are you talking about man?" Keke asked.

Tunes looked to Bini who subtly shook his head no. Tunes didn't catch on and said what he had to say anyway.

"You see, the thing of it is, after you won that race, people started to think..."

"Think what?"

"Just shut up, Tunes. Let Keke tell us what we came out here for."

"Nah, bro. I want to hear this." Keke squatted down arms wrapped around his knees. "Continue, Cuz."

Tunes felt a bit sheepish at that moment.

"I don't want no problem, want no problems with you. But people been saying that the way you won that race you been like, 'I got problems bigger than these boys. My speed it be on steroids...'"

Keke gave Tunes the same screw-faced look that his brother did a moment ago.

"Like I said before, where the hell would I get steroids from?"

"I don't know man. You might know somebody. Maybe they thought you made it in chemistry or something."

Bini and Keke bother exploded into laughter.

"Man, forget I even said anything. I'm just trying to be supportive and here y'all go clowin' me."

"Boy, sometimes you say the stupidest stuff." Bini slapped Tunes' knee. The boy rubbed his leg as the blow stung in the cold night air.

"Okay. If you aren't doing steroids, what did you bring us out here to tell us?"

Keke was still laughing. Bini too was chuckling and shaking his head at the foolishness that his brother could've just been casually making some steroids up in chemistry lab while Ms. O'Brien was having other people do school approved experiments.

"Listen. What I am about to tell you is going to sound crazy. But I swear on the strength of great, great grandmother Ehiosu that everything I'm about to say is truth. Regardless of how crazy it is going to sound."

"You don't have to swear on Ehiosu for me to believe you, Keke. We are brothers. I got your back." Bini slapped his cousin in the chest. This time he took something off of the blow to keep it from stinging.

"We both do."

His cousin nodded his agreement.

"I'm telling you, It's crazy."

"Crazier than steroids?" Bini jested.

The twins burst out into laughter again.

"Yes, way crazier than steroids." Keke confirmed through chuckles, tears and gasps, trying to be serious.

Chapter 23

"I met an alien."

Both boys before him remained silent.

"I was in the woods. On the trail. That is who saved me that day I fell in the water."

"You mean like an illegal from Mexico, or Guatemala?" Tunes asked.

"No, I mean a creature from another planet that can walk and talk. Well not talk per se. But anyway. I met him. We talked. I let him sleep in our shed one night."

"You brought an alien home? Like a little Gizmo from the Gremlins or the Sigourney Weaver, mouth inside a mouth type?"

"Closer to the Aliens version than a Gremlin."

"And you brought it home? You might be craaazy. That makes you craazay." Tunes sang.

"I'm serious. He had this cover over his eyes. No mouth. His head was oblong. His face looked like the face shield on a motorcycle. It was a solid plate on the front of its head and completely smooth."

"Like Isaac of from The Orville?" Bini asked.

"Yes! That is exactly what I thought."

"He had big bulging neck muscles. And his neck was super long. Like that Indian dude on that old arcade fighting game.

"Street Fighter?"

"Yeah, I think so. But its body was partitioned like an ant. The thorax or whatever he calls it was fleshy like skin, but rubberier. He was skinnier than me. Not like bony. Just slim."

"Did you touch it?" Tunes asked.

"Touch it?"

"Yeah, the skin. How do you know it was rubbery?"

I don't know. It looked that way like Batman's cowl.

"Did it have like 2 legs and walk like us or did it like gallop or whatever?" Tunes questions showed that he was all in on belief.

"The creature had two legs. Only, it didn't have knees. Not really. There were these two fork joints that connected the thighs to the calves. The lower legs were hard like his head and shoulders. The upper legs were yoked like a body builder. The back of his hands and tops of the feet had this hard covering like motorcycle gloves over his fingers and toes. Oh, and there were only three on each hand with these sick claws."

Keke thought for a few minutes to see if there was anything else he had forgotten. Tune started to ask a question, but Bini stopped him.

"Oh, and his skin was blue."

"Like Avatar blue?"

"Yeah. Like that."

"Did you ask him if he was from Pandora?" Tunes was a fountain of questions.

"Stupid. It wasn't like a skin tone though. It was like a glow that changed brightness. It was crazy."

Bini sat quietly. Tunes watched for his lead because he didn't want to say another wrong thing. Keke stood up and paced around, watching his breath turn white in the night air. Occasionally, he would look back to his brother.

Bini was deep in thought. His hands were tented over his nose, thumbs pressed to his chin. The boy considered the ramifications of the truth of what his brother said. Keke was not a storyteller. He did not seek out attention with sensational information. He was quiet. He didn't want the spotlight. He was content with being ignored and left to his own thing.

Bini also knew that whatever had been going on with the race and the fight, he wasn't crazy. He didn't act out of the ordinary in any way up to this point. Bini decided in that moment that he believed his brother.

"You said this alien saved you from the water when you fell?"

"Yes. He told me that."

"Does that have anything to do with the race."

"Yes. I also think that it may also have something to do with Brandon coming back and the fight as well."

"What do you mean?"

"Boy's it is getting late." Mac announced.

"Okay Dad." Keke yelled out.

Mac stood at the end of the driveway. He had his hands on his hips. Keke could see that he was leaning forward trying to see them down on the basketball court. Keke could sense that their father was concerned. He was concerned for Keke. He had tried to hide it on the car ride, but Keke knew. Keke also knew that their father trusted them to figure it out together.

"We gotta go in before he comes down here. He's really worried."

"How can you tell that, Keke?" Tunes asked.

"That's the other thing about the alien. Somehow, I developed some of his abilities."

What do you mean abilities?" Bini stood up and dusted off the seat of his pants.

The three boys began to make their way back to the house. Keke widened his path and began to walk toward the streetlight across the road. The other two boys noticed he wasn't with them and began to divert to the light. Keke held up a hand for them to stay where they were. Both of them stopped. All three boys turned to look toward the house. Mac had gone back inside.

"I think I can do this." Keke said, mostly to himself.

"Do what?"

Tunes' question went unanswered. Keke had his left hand pressed to the cold aluminum. His eyes were closed. He shut out all sound to concentrate. The light began to dim. Bini and Tunes said nothing. Eventually there was a humming noise, like the sound of a transformer going through magnetostriction from a ferromagnetic field. Only the buzz was not coming from a transformer. It wasn't coming from the streetlight. It was coming from Keke's body. The humming continued for only a short time. When it stopped Keke opened his eyes. They were glowing a bright blue. He approached his brother and cousin at a brisk pace.

"Grab him." He gestured to Tuned to wrap his arms around Bini's shoulders.

"Grab him?"

"Yes, hurry before dad comes back out looking for us.

The boy did as instructed. Keke gestured for him to lock his hands in front and Tunes obeyed. Then, eyes still glowing, he gestured for his brother to latch on to their cousins arms in front of his chest.

Keke squatted slightly to get leverage under one of his twin's elbows. He counted to three silently to himself and then lifted both boys above his head with one hand.

Bini stared down into his brother's eyes. The blue blaze in them flickered. Bini's mouth hung open at the shock of the physical feat. Keke had just hoisted just under three hundred pounds of body weight overhead with a single arm. A moment later Bini and Tunes were back on the pavement.

"Bro, you have electro-steroids?" Tunes stumbled backward in disbelief after his feet touched down.

"I don't know what to call it. All I know is that I blew up a microwave at the gas station the other day. I can do some other things as well."

"Like what?"

"You blew up a microwave?"

"Later, here comes dad."

Tunes and Bini both looked to the door and saw nothing. As they got to the edge of their lawn, they saw that Mac was indeed standing inside the doorway watching out for them.

After Mac and Louise had gone to bed, Tunes crept into the twins' room with a pillow and blanket, like he used to when they were younger. Keke finished telling his brother and cousin all of the abilities he knew of that he acquired from his alien friend. He also told them as much of the story from his meeting with the alien that he could recall.

***

Agents Smarten and Swain spent the morning interviewing students. They weren't allowed to interrogate children and to suggest that is what they were doing was frowned upon. Agent Swain was quite familiar with these situations. Prior to joining the agency, he had several positions within municipal law enforcement. There were many occasions for him to interview children and teenagers to get witness or accomplice testimony. It was often unreliable because rumor and hearsay dominated what children or teenagers learned in a high school culture. By the time the authorities got involved, the story had already been extremely sensationalized or romanticized by other members of the student body.

Being in the know was cool. Kids would tell tales and the resulting 'knowledge' within the community was worse than that final telling in a game of telephone.

That particular morning had been no different. Early on, they interviewed siblings, cousins, and close friends of the four missing kids. Each one of them was solemn. The stories they told were pretty congruent. They hadn't seen them since the night of the blackout or the night after. None of them had any idea where the missing kids could be. They didn't have any new friends that they were aware of. No secret girlfriend or secret boyfriend that they could have run off with.

One of the students piqued both of the Agents' interests. The boy's name, Brandon Gause. His father was the local sheriff. He was a senior, star quarterback, prom king. He was not a defenseless kid. He was invested in coming to school. His absence forced an early out of the high school football playoffs for his team.

This boy's absence concerned Agent Swain. It was quite likely that they would be informing the parents that their child was not ever coming home.

The agents were joined in the principal's office by a taller boy. The file said his name was Kellan Price. He was the starting left tackle for the team. He was Brandon's best friend from the information the principal's secretary was able to provide.

"Kellan, thank you for taking the time to meet with us. I'm Agent Swain. This is my partner Agent Smarten."

Both men flashed their badges. Kellan was not looking up, so he missed the badge flash.

"We are investigating the missing people from a few weeks ago. I know you may have already spoken to the local authorities. However, there have been some other disappearances. We are trying to see if there is a link to the disappearance of your friend. Why don't you tell us about Brandon and your relationship to him."

The boy's cheeks were reddened. His eyes looked to be welling up. He swallowed the lump that was formulating in his throat and took a deep breath.

"Brandon is a cool dude. He is always making jokes. He and I started hanging out a few summers ago. We became good friends. I know something had to happen to him. He loves football. He disappeared and we needed him for the playoffs. This was our senior season. He is missing classes and that could cost him a scholarship. He wouldn't risk that. He didn't want to stay around here. He was going D1."

"You mean Division One football?"

"Yeah. He was being scouted by a couple teams. His dream was to go to Miami. We both applied. He got early acceptance. I am still waiting."

"Tell me about the last time you saw him. What was his mood like?"

"It was homecoming night. He had just won homecoming king."

"Did his girlfriend win prom queen?" Agent Smarten asked to lighten the mood.

"No, his cousin did." Kellan said blankly.

Agent Swain gave his partner an admonishing look.

"Did you guys go out and celebrate his good fortune that night? Your team just got a big win, right?" Agent Smarten made a second attempt to relate to the boy.

"Yeah, we were going to be the #1 seed. Without Brandon, we lost the last game of the season in overtime. We got bounced in the first round of the playoffs."

Agent Swain jumped right in before his partner could inflict any more wounds.

"Kellan, you were telling us about what you did the night of the prom."

"Afterward, we were all heading to one of our teammates' house. We were going to dri…"

"You were going to order pizzas?" Agent Swain prompted.

"Yeah."

Kellan explained who ended up going to the impromptu party. He told them how they never had a party and just ended up sitting around staring at their phones in the dark, waiting for Brandon. He was in charge of getting the 'pizza'. When he didn't show up, they all figured he found a girl to get lucky with and brought her back to his place. He would often skip out on plans suddenly. They would hear about a girl the next day. From what Kellan explained, Mr. Gause was prone to bragging about his conquests.

Kellan had gone by the next morning and his mother told him that she thought that he had spent the night at Kellan's because he never came home. They immediately called his father, the sheriff. Despite it not being the full twenty-four hours, a missing person report was issued. After three days, they had not found Brandon or the other three youths that had gone missing.

Ten minutes later, Kellan left the principal's office. There was a girl waiting down the hallway for him. Agent Swain asked the secretary the identity of the girl. The redhaired woman with the horn-rimmed glasses explained that Jenna was Kellan's younger sister. The agent followed up by asking if she had ever been a love interest of the missing boy. The woman scoffed.

"What did they say?" Jenna asked Kellan.

"They asked a bunch of questions about Brandon's disappearance. They wanted to know what happened the night of homecoming. Did you see him at all afterward? He was supposed to go to the party at Evan's house. He was getting the beer."

Jenna deftly slid an arm around her larger brother and started to walk him farther down the hallway. She could see the agents watching them.

"I told you already. I did not see him after he left homecoming." Jenna glanced around and lowered her tone. "But I did see him the other night."

Kellan snapped around putting his hand to her shoulder, he shoved his sister against the wall.

"Where? Why didn't you say anything? Was he okay?"

The force of the sudden shove knocked the wind from her when she hit the wall. A shockwave of pain ran through her shoulder as she was mashed between his hefty palm and the ceramic tile. The girl doubled over grabbing at her left shoulder with her right hand. Without thinking, she let the anger in.

With a jab that the boy did not anticipate, she chopped him right in his windpipe. She retracted from the blow and with the same arm punched the boy in the lower abdomen.

"You fucking asshole!" The girl growled. "You could have dislocated my shoulder.

Before the boy had a chance to recover, she reached up with her sore left arm and grabbed him by the ear. She used a slight twist to encourage him to walk. They turned the corner out of sight from the prying eyes in the principal's office.

"Listen. I saw him the other night. But he was different. He didn't even recognize me."

"Different how?" His voice was raspy.

Kellan shoved his sister away, freeing himself from the grasp on his ear. With a meaty palm, the boy rubbed at it, never moving his left hand from the spot where she had punched him.

"Are you saying he was on drugs or something?"

"If by drugs you mean super steroids, then yes. He was with some guy with green hair. They tried to fight my friends."

"Green hair? Are you sure it was Brandon. We don't have any friends with green hair."

"I know that, dipshit. Listen, don't tell his parents until I can figure out what is going on?"

"How are you going to find out what is going on? I don't even think it was him. Why would I tell his parents?"

"Good, don't. And if you see him, be careful."

"You're fricken crazy, Jenna. I'm going to tell mom that you hit me in school."

"And I'm telling Dad that you shoved me into a wall and nearly dislocated my shoulder, *in school.*"

The two siblings stepped back into the main hallway and headed in different directions.

"What do you think that was all about?" Agent Smarten asked his partner.

"I would wager that either Mr. Price knows more than he was telling us."

"Or maybe his sister knows more than he told us."

"Or both do."

Chapter 24

"Are they still behind us?"

"Yep."

"That is four stops that we made. They have been with us after leaving each stop."

"They are not great at being inconspicuous, are they? Did you notice them at the school?"

"I did not. They must have been waiting outside the school grounds. Either that or they followed us from the hotel this morning. I do have to say that a white roofing van isn't the most conspicuous vehicle for a tail."

"Who do you think it is? It wouldn't be the people who are abducting these kids, right?" Smarten posited.

"People?"

"Yeah. So many abductions happening in such a small timeframe. It would have to be more than one person."

Agent Swain grunted. He had hoped that this conversation could go unspoken.

"You saw the doppler images from lake, right? You saw the craft fall from the sky back in Hawai'i. A sonic boom was heard that caused a blackout locally on the evening that the disappearances began. I don't believe in coincidences. I think that we both know that we are going to have to concede that we are encountering an entity from outside of our atmosphere."

"You think these are alien abductions." Agent Smarten was shocked.

"You don't think that is what is happening here?"

"Well, I'm not sure. I haven't really thought about it."

"Haven't you, Brian?"

Agent Smarten looked at his partner.

"I'm serious. You were completely quiet for most of the ride here from Oswego. The evidence presented to us strongly suggests that there is life out there on another planet. Further, that life clearly has better technology than we do."

Agent Swain signaled a left turn. When he got to the corner, he circled his left hand a few times before pulling away from the wheel allowing it to correct his path. The white van made the turn as well.

"What makes ya say that?"

"Did you see the size of that ship?"

"I did. Bigger doesn't necessarily mean better."

"Okay, I'll grant you that. But tell me this partner. Have you ever heard of Proxima Centauri."

"Are those the creatures from the first Avengers movie?"

"I don't know what the creatures from the first Avengers movie are called. But, no, that is not what Proxima Centauri is. Proxima Centauri is the closest star to us other than the Sun. Proxima Centauri B is the closest exoplanet to Earth. It is about four light years away."

"Okay. Do you think that is where the ship came from?"

"That I can't say. What I can say is that it would take us a few lifetimes to travel there and back. That sweaty kid Bart sat beside me on the plane to California. He was rambling on about the potential whereabouts of the object. He mentioned that Proxima Centauri b was the closest exoplanet to Earth and that it was 4 light years away."

"Okay. So why does that mean that they have better technology than us?"

"Well, according to sweaty science boy, it would take NASA's fastest rocket close to sixty million years to get there."

"So, you are saying that their ships are faster?"

"I am saying they sent a manned vessel from wherever they came from to Earth. Whatever technology they have, it allows them to get a creature this far, without starving to death and without getting so old that they died."

"Hmm. I see your point."

"Now, I'm going to slow up at this next light and roll through it. If these fellas behind us don't blow the light I'm going to pull into the hotel parking lot and let you jump out near the bushes. I'm going to pull around back slowly. They will likely pay attention to where I park and try to casually pull in a few spots away."

"That's when I come up behind them."

"No, I want to see if they follow me into the hotel. If they follow me, then we know that they are either stupid or they are dangerous, or possibly both."

"Why do you say dangerous?"

"You tell me. You are tracking a subject. He goes inside a building that you are unfamiliar with. Do you follow inside or wait for them to come out?"

"That's not really straight forward. If I think the situation inside could be dangerous where I could be outnumbered or they could be armed, then I wait outside. If it's a public building like our hotel, I probably follow them."

"Why?"

"Because I know I'm armed, and odds are I won't be in danger. If I had backup, I would follow either way."

"Exactly. Here we go, let's see which guy this is."

Agent Swain slowed at the light and allowed it to turn red as he rolled through. The white van a few cars back was forced to stop. Agent Swain signaled his turn into the parking lot. Once he got even with the bushes, he slowed and let Agent Smarten jump out and duck behind the nearby cars.

Agent Smarten could see that there were three men in the van as it rolled by. He didn't follow them because he could see that his partner was already parking. The van came to a quick halt and pulled into the nearest spot. Agent Smarten got a little closer to being in position in case they got froggy and approached his partner. He was careful not to let them see him.

Agent Swain exited the SUV with his phone to his ear. He was talking casually, smiling. His partner could see the driver and the passenger in the front seat share confused glances. They were likely puzzled as to why there was only one person exiting the vehicle. He could see them leaning forward to look beyond the vehicles between where they parked and where Agent Swain had parked. The driver and passenger turned around and had a discussion with the person in the back of the van. There was some arm waving and other animated actions by both. When the side door slid open, a chubby man in a black sweatshirt climbed out. Agent Smarten watched as the hefty middle-aged man in black cargo pants and a tight black hoodie waddled across the parking lot toward the main entrance. He saddled up to a pillar that was just to the left of the sliding glass doors that opened to allow entry into the hotel. He glanced back toward his two accomplices in the van. Both were hanging out their respective windows. Brian Smarten had moved to the other side of the divider that split the lot. Both of the men in the van extended their forearm and flicked their fingers outward from a half-closed hand, indicating for the third to continue onward.

Clumsily, he fumbled into the front pocket of his sweatshirt and pulled out a pair of aviator glasses. He jabbed himself in the cheek trying to slide them on his face with one hand. Disguise complete, he approached the sliding doors. The sensor, alerted by his movement, parted the glass panes. The chubby man disappeared inside.

Agent Smarten turned his attention back to the van. The man in the passenger seat had exited the vehicle and stomped through the shrubbery in the divider. He was a slender guy but had the same garb as his chubby accomplice. Hands shoved in his pockets he took a conspicuous walk by the agent's SUV. He went about four cars beyond it before destroying more flora and looping back to the van. The chubby one tasked with the reconnaissance mission inside the hotel was waddling back at the same time that the slender one returned.

From where he was positioned Agent Smarten could hear their entire conversation. The chubby fella told the others that he was certain that Agent Swain had gone up to the fourth floor, but he had no idea where the other one went.

They considered the potential options. Perhaps the second agent hadn't gotten in the car at the gas station. Or perhaps he got out in front of the hotel to run inside to use the bathroom. The chubby one thought this was a great solution because he had done this sometimes when he and his ex-wife would go out for Mexican. He explained that he would pull up to the house and run in and leave her to park the car. Not difficult to see why it was his ex-wife.

After learning that they planned on waiting in the van to follow the agents if they went back out, Agent Smarten snuck around the building and used his key card to gain entrance to the building via a side door.

***

The three men watched as two young dark-skinned women left the hotel. Both of them had slender figures. The taller of the two was curvier but both were very pretty. They approached the van passing along the passenger side, climbing through the shrubbery toward a car in the next area of the lot. They presumed they were out-of-towners heading to SPAC or a night of dinner and drinks. The taller one smiled at the passenger of the van when she noticed him. He didn't smile back but his chubby friend who had craned his neck over the bucket seat was interested. As she got to the other side of the divider, she bent down to tie her shoe. Because she didn't squat, the tail of her jacket pulled up exposing her backside.

The driver was startled by a tap on the window. Standing there with a pistol pointed in his direction was Agent Swain. Agent Smarten had appeared at the passenger side door. Agent Bush stepped back in front of the van, her weapon drawn as well. The men had lost track of her while staring at Kameka.

In the conference room of the hotel the agents interrogated the three men. The first thing they did was confiscate their phones. It didn't take long for Kameka to find their discord private chat discussing the events since the blackout. They played it tough, although the chubby one was sweating profusely. They all were stunned at how quickly Kameka was able to find their conversation and provide the details.

"This one's name is Dale." Kameka pointed to the driver. "That's Tommy and my sweaty friend there is Eddie. They believe that the sonic boom was a secret Russian jet that has cloaking technology. They think the kidnappings are a setup to a Red Dawn type of scenario."

She paused, flicking her index finger against the screen of Dale's phone.

"That remake was horrible by the way."

Kameka set down Dale's phone and moved on to Tommy's. She assumed that out of the three of them, he was most likely to include someone else in what he thought. To Kameka's surprise, Tommy had no texts to anyone other than Eddie and Dale. She checked through Eddie's phone and then slid all three across the table to where Agent Bush was sitting.

"You can't go through our phones without a warrant. That is a violation of our rights."

"Oh, I'm not an officer."

"What?"

"She isn't an officer. We asked you to set your phones on the table. You complied when we asked. You guys must've left them unlocked. She didn't violate your rights because you watched her do it and said nothing."

Agent Bush smirked at the men. Dale went to stand up in protest and Agent Smarten shoved him back down in his seat. Dale knew in that moment that the dark-haired agent was stronger than he first presumed. Agent Bush stood up, looking over at Kameka to continue.

"Dale and Tommy were pretty tight lipped about everything from what I can tell. Eddie here texted his sister about his thoughts about the Russian attack and she basically told him to seek mental health assistance."

The other two men gave Eddie an accusatory stare.

"Why were you following my colleagues around town? Staking out a school is pretty cringe, boys." Agent Bush got right down to business.

"We weren't staking out the school!"

"Oh yeah, Dale. What were you doing?"

"We heard that someone was investigating the kids at the school that went missing. We were hanging around to see..."

"See what? If they would catch on that it was you? See if there were other kids you could abduct?" Agent Smarten interrupted.

"We didn't kidnap no kids! One of them was the sheriff's son. We would have to be pretty stupid to do something like that."

Agent Smarten waved his arms apart, glancing around the room as if to say look where we are.

"Ok so you just happened to be at a school, not staking it out, just sitting in a van with no reason to be there waiting for a specific someone to come along, not a kid, for you to follow them. Definitely not a stake out."

"We only followed you because you were agents. We thought that you were investigating the school for a Russian plant."

Agent Swain chuckled in the corner.

"You laugh but what else could it be?"

"It's a good theory, Dale. You are wrong. But it's a good theory. How did you know they were agents?" Agent Bush continued.

"Eddie works at the school. He called when he heard agents were coming by."

"Janitor?" Agent Bush speculated.

'Yeah. Why?"

"Lucky guess. Anyway, why would the Russians attack a New York town that has no real strategic advantage other than proximity to a great concert venue and a racetrack?"

"Well, you guys are here so we have to be right." Dale was unwilling to yield that his incredible idea was incorrect.

"Or..."

Agent Swain stepped away from the corner of the room. He dragged a chair from a nearby table over in front of Dale. He dragged it slow for dramatic effect. The legs vibrated on the carpeted floor as he pulled it along. When he got to where the men were sitting, he spun it around and sat on it backwards, forearms resting on the chair back. "Perhaps the disappearance of a number of children is something beyond the police's capability, especially since one of them is the sheriff's son. He may not be able to be unbiased in his search and needs to be with his family during this trying time."

"We didn't think of that." Eddie said rather matter of fact.

The agents continued to paint a story for the three men about the abductions being their only reason for being in town. They even provided flyers for them to take with them should they see the missing kids or hear of any leads. The flyer had a hotline number on the bottom. They added a reprimand for wasting valuable time that was supposed to be spent looking for leads. Instead, the agents were busy pulling them in for questioning. Agent Swain promised not to tell the Sheriff about their interference as long as they didn't interfere further.

Agent Bush walked the three men to their van. She reiterated that they had wasted valuable time. She also reminded them that following federal agents is not really advisable, especially when they are investigating child abduction.

"What about the attack at the gas station? The entire place was destroyed. And that worker, he was out of school. He wasn't a kid."

"What gas station?"

Eddie and Dale gave Tommy a look that he didn't catch.

"The one on route twenty-nine. A lot of high school kids go there to buy beer. The owner always employs younger kids who accept lower wages. They don't care though because they just end up giving their friends discounts and letting them slide on alcohol."

"The place looked like a bomb hit. It was the night of the sonic boom. Word is there was no remains of the clerk in the wreckage."

"We'll check into this missing store clerk. Any other places we should look into?"

Dale was shaking his head no, but Tommy was eager to provide more information to the pretty agent.

"There is also that kid."

"What kid?"

"Come on Tommy. She has real leads to chase after."

"No tell her Dale. You thought that kid was a Russian plant."

"Tell me more." Agent Bush set her hand gently on Tommy's forearm.

"Dale was the one who saw it. His niece had a cross-country event. Tell her Dale."

Reluctantly, Dale shut the van door and walked back toward the agent.

"I know what you are gonna say. It sounds crazy. But there was this boy. A black boy. He was way in the back of the race. I'm talking almost last place. Then out of nowhere he takes off running like a bat out of hell."

"Okay?"

"You know they run a couple miles in those things. This kid ran like Forrest Gump the rest of the race. Past all the other kids like it was nothing. My niece's boyfriend. He was in the race. He's going to North Carolina for track. They offered him almost a full scholarship."

"Since this boy beat him, you think he is some type of Russian plant?"

"I told you. I know it sounds crazy. But if you saw it, you would know that it was almost inhuman. He almost set a course record, they said."

"A fast kid, but not record fast. Just faster than your niece's boyfriend fast. And what school did this boy go to?"

"Saratoga Springs. Their boys finished in the top three. The girls too. Something fishy about that."

"Got it. We'll check it out. You gentlemen have a good night. Try to stay out of trouble."

"Wait." Agent Bush turned around to see Dale jogging after her.

"Listen, I know you all think we are just nuts. But you should look into the break-in at the military base. I won't give you particulars because it could compromise my source. There is something not right about what they are saying happened there over the weekend."

Agent Bush considered the man's face. He had kept eye contact with her the whole time. She got the feeling that he was trusting her with the information. Maybe he hadn't even shared that with his accomplices. The man seemed genuine, for the first time that evening.

Dawn nodded affirming that she would look into it.

**

Kellan was still fuming as he drove home from work that evening. He was pissed that Jenna had lied to him about something so serious. There is no way that Brandon would just leave his family worried like that. Jenna had to be lying. Brandon was his best friend, and he hadn't heard from him in weeks. Kellan was so preoccupied that he nearly ran a stop light. He screeched to a halt, encroaching into the crosswalk. A woman pushed a stroller in front of his truck yelling obscenities at him, waving her free arm above her head. He watched her until she got to the opposite sidewalk. When she arrived safely on the other side, she nearly crashed into a blonde boy that was walking down the street. The boy turned his body slightly to avoid the collision.

Kellan's jaw dropped.

He couldn't believe his eyes. Either Brandon being on his mind was playing tricks on him or the boy who turned down the one-way cross street was his missing best friend. He slapped his hand on the steering wheel furiously, wishing the light to turn green. He danced in his seat trying to get a better look at the boy who was disappearing into the shadows of the trees.

When the light changed, Kellan sped up the block, taking the next right and swinging around to try to catch the boy at the next corner. He whipped his truck toward the curb, parking with his tail end hanging out in the lane. Kellan slammed the shifter to park and jumped out leaving his keys in the ignition. He didn't think that Brandon could have made it to the end of the street faster than he circled the block, although when he didn't see the blonde-haired boy, he second guessed himself.

Kellan reasoned that at the walking pace Brandon would've been close to the corner. Unless the boy he saw went into one of the houses along the row, he should be coming toward Kellan. He craned his neck and jumped trying to see if maybe he had crossed over the street in the middle of the block. On the third jump he saw the top of a blonde head standing with another person halfway down the block. He sprinted, anxious, excited, confused that his friend was here in town just walking around while his family and friends were worried as to his whereabouts. He slowed to a walk and called out to Brandon when he got a few feet away.

The girl he was with side stepped to see who had approached. Kellan didn't know the girl. She had long brown hair in braids that wound about her head. She looked to be a few years older than they were. The blonde-haired boy turned, and it was indeed Brandon. Kellan was elated. He ran up to his friend and tried to hug him. Brandon stepped back, noting the aggressive approach. Confused, Kellan stopped.

"Brandon! It's me. Kellan." He began, waving his hands toward himself as he spoke. "Where have you been? Your parents are worried. I was worried. We lost the section. What happened to you?"

Brandon turned to the girl who responded on his behalf.

"Do you want us to help you find the lost section?" She asked.

"What? No, I'm not talking to you. I'm talking to my friend. Brandon. You have to come home with me now.

Everyone is looking for you. Your mother thought you were dead."

Kellan stepped closer to him and placed a hand on his friend's shoulder. Kellan had an odd feeling about the strange girl. He kept an eye on her as he moved. Distracted by the girl, he was unprepared when Brandon shoved him. Kellan exhaled hard, as the pressure of the blow sent a spiral fracture through one of his ribs on impact. Hands and feet flailing he slammed into a nearby Ford Escape. The rear passenger door panel collapsed inward with the force of the large boy's body colliding with it.

Kellan bounced off the vehicle, falling hard to the pavement. His head collided with the ground. The boy struggled to breathe, both arms crossing the midsection of his body. His ribs ached with every attempt to draw breath. Kellan writhed for several minutes, gasping, earnest to steal whatever oxygen he could from the cold night air. It seemed like an eternity before he was able to sit up. When he finally gathered a full breath, he rose to see that Brandon and his new friend were gone.

Chapter 25

The next morning Agents Swain and Smarten took a drive to the local Air Force base. Agent Swain had reported back to Washington what they had found. There would be a team arriving that afternoon with instructions from the pentagon.

There was indeed a break-in at the base. The base commander, Colonel Rodriguez, was not forthcoming with information. Agent Swain read him in on their findings when they were in Hawai'i, California, and Oswego. He laughed, thinking that Agent Swain was pulling his leg. When Agent Swain insisted that he was not, the Colonel got angry and accused them of wasting his time. He stormed off to his office leaving them with a few officers. The agents followed while the officers stared at one another confused.

Once behind closed doors, the Colonel confided that what was stolen was top secret. It was part of a project that was supposed to revolutionize aviation.

"The NGAD-2 is a seventh-generation fighter jet. It is a scientific marvel. This jet is completely undetectable by radar and sound detection systems. Imagine, a fighter jet with the noise equivalent of a Tesla that can hit supersonic speeds."

"Someone stole a fighter jet?"

"No, they stole the power core."

"What is so special about this power core that made someone risk breaking into a military facility?"

"Think Tony Stark's Arc Reactor on steroids."

"Who knew it was here?"

"Nobody. It was recently delivered. They brought it in late Thursday night. I had it delivered to an empty hanger and sealed the hanger with my personal code. Only the guard on duty at the gate and I knew we got a delivery. It was brought in under cover of darkness for a reason. It was unloaded in the hangar. There were no other personnel on duty."

"Within two days of arriving someone executed a break in and detached the power core from an experimental plane that nobody knew was on the premises? How did they go undetected?"

"We are still looking into that."

"What do you mean?"

"I mean nobody cut through a gate. Nobody drove in that wasn't identified as authorized at the gate. There was no commotion at all. They never raised any alarms."

"I presume they came at night?" Agent Swain asked.

"Yes. At night there is only the guard staff at the gates and security forces. They do periodic patrols."

"What time did you notice that it was gone."

"That's the thing. A member of security forces heard the hangar gate closing as he drove by on patrol. He couldn't get into the hangar, so he radioed the commanding officer on duty. The officer called me. I hurried right over. I got the call just after 3 am."

"How big is this thing that they escaped with?"

"Judging by the gap that it came from, I would say the size of a 5-kilowatt home generator.

"Pretend that we don't know those dimensions."

"Apologies, Agent Swain. It's a cylindrical shape, maybe three feet long, two maybe three feet in diameter."

"How many men would it take to carry it out of here?"

"Two, maybe? I can only make a rough guess as to what it weighs. Everything on that jet is next generation technology. Super lightweight but durable. But its size would require minimum two men to carry it."

"Well, we know that they didn't drive the thing out. Would it be possible for them to get to an area where they could pass the thing over a fence to others or maybe sneak through an unmanned gate."

"Not likely. The hangar is nearly dead smack in the middle of the base, and I don't see two people sneaking through the shadows with it. It would be very conspicuous."

"There goes that word again." Agent Smarten quipped.

"I beg your pardon?" The colonel retorted.

"Nothing. Other than powering the jet, what practicable application would they be able to use this for?"

"Agent Swain, this is next generation technology. There is nothing in this world that would be able to use this as a power source other than this jet."

The two agents shared a look that did not go unnoticed by the Colonel.

"What are you thinking?"

"Colonel, last night I had to inform my bosses back at Homeland and the joint chiefs that we are potentially dealing with an extraterrestrial entity. Take all the time you need to process that information. Laugh it off as a joke if you need to. Bottom line, all the things that we have uncovered lead to only one conclusion. A craft from outer space crash landed in Lake Ontario. A creature that had been aboard that craft ejected itself. We expected to have someone provide its corpse or what is left of it. There has been no mention of that thus far. We have a specialist that has the trajectory of its crash somewhere in this area. On the night it entered the atmosphere, there was a blackout locally that was preceded by a sonic boom. There have since been a number of locals that have been reported missing. They were either abducted or killed. I am not a man that believes in coincidence. I can see in your face that you aren't either. Thus, my question for you, do you think that the power source could power a spaceship that was constructed with alien technology?"

***

Kameka wandered back and forth in the main hall of the high school. The kids were all in class. There were a few security members in the hallway but not one of them was cordial at all. Those who had passed her paid her no mind, even when she greeted them. She found it weird that they were all bundled up inside the school. She had on a light jacket and was quite warm standing in the hallway. Agent Bush was in the principal's office asking about the boy that Dale told her about.

Last night, when she returned to the conference room where Kameka and the two DHS agents were discussing their three new friends, she told them about the theft at the base, the gas station, and the boy in the race. They all had a good laugh over the sleeper agent high school track star.

They agreed that it was worth investigating a theft at the base. Agent Bush told them that she and Kameka would investigate the gas station while they went to look into the military base. While Agent Bush was in the gas station speaking to the owner, Kameka decided to search for video of the boy at the race to see if there was proof or if Dale was exaggerating. She found a video of a boy sprinting up a hill in the middle of a race. There were about a half dozen boys near the top of the hill but nothing else stood out.

Agent Bush reported that the store owner claimed there was a gas line explosion that caused them to need to remodel. The clerk Roger who was supposed to be working traded with another boy named Ethan Ramsay. Ethan hadn't been seen since that night. When he didn't show up, the manager called his parents. They hadn't seen him. There was no evidence that he died in the explosion, even though the camera recordings showed they went offline during operating hours. They were hopeful that he would have turned up but as of today, no luck. The Public Service Commission hadn't yet finished their investigation, so they couldn't sell gasoline. They were opened as just a store a few days ago. Kameka showed Agent Bush the video of the boy that Dale had told her about when she passed her a coffee.

"Doesn't look Russian to me." She joked.
"No, not at all. But I was thinking..."
What were you thinking?"

"Hear me out. I don't want to sound like crazy Eddie, Tommy, and Dale. But what if he had been body snatched by an alien or something?"

"Kameka! Are you serious? You think that this boy was body snatched by an alien and the alien said you know what? I'm going to go run a hell of a time at this high school cross country meet."

"It does sound crazy when you say it like that."

"It does. Would that make you Leonard Nimoy or Jeff Goldblum?"

Kameka wore a look of surprise.

"You think because I'm an FBI agent I didn't watch old school sci-fi movies?"

Kameka shrugged.

"Listen, we don't have any other leads to look into until Swain and Smarten finish up at the base. We can head over and check out this kid if you want."

So now here she was in this nearly empty hallway with the gestapo security guards lined up all along the corridors like it was a Siberian prison camp. She had nothing to do but pretend to be interested in the trophies in the case in front of her.

Meanwhile, Agent Bush was getting a similar vibe in the office. Both the head of security and the principal were very cold toward her. It was as though they were unhappy with her presence. She understood that she had just dropped in on them unexpectedly. Still, her explanation for being there was that she was investigating missing children. Neither of them pretended to care.

Agent Bush stood before them inside the office and pulled out the video to show them. Neither looked at the screen. She paused the video.

"I'm sorry. Am I keeping you from something?"

Neither responded. Annoyed, she pressed play and shoved her phone toward them. She didn't have a chance to demand that they watch. As she hit play, the assistant principal chimed in with an announcement.

***

Bini, Tunes and Marshawn were walking down the hallway. They were chatting about the creature that Keke discovered. They didn't want to risk being too obvious, so they all agreed to refer to the alien as 'the foreigner.' The boys decided that Anika could also be involved in the secret. Of course, they told Jenna as well. The girls had been with them when Brandon and the green haired kid Ethan walked into the pizza shop. They didn't tell Jaali because they didn't trust him to keep the secret. They didn't tell Kenan because they thought he might slip up to his parents.

They were pretty sure that the alien's arrival had something to do with the disappearances. Keke assured them that the alien he met was friendly and that he must have been followed to Earth by the Wryvyn. Keke said that maybe the Wryvyn could infect people with a Slaver Virus. When they asked what that was, he explained that the X-Men fought a race of aliens called the Brood. The Brood were sent by the Shi-ar Deathbird. She used the Brood to overthrow her sister Liliana. The brood infected their hosts by implanting their embryos inside of them.

This was the only explanation they could come up with for why Brandon didn't remember any of them. They presumed that it was the reason that he and his friend were so strong. According to Keke's blue friend, the Wryvyn were scientifically gifted. They could have brain wiped people and enhanced their strength. The group had plans to get together after school to decide how they should report a possible alien invasion without sounding crazy.

The three boys stopped in front of the principal's office. In the hallway ahead of them, was a woman. She had long braids, down to the middle of her back. A shiny nose ring dangled from her septum. She wore a long coat that did little to hide her curvaceous physique. Her skin was chocolatey brown. All three of the boys were instantly enamored.

When the announcement chimed, a deep male voice called out for a student to come to his office. Kameka turned around as the announcement chimed. Through the glass window and open interior door, she could see an annoyed Agent Bush standing in front of the principal and one of the gestapo guards. She was holding up her phone, which neither was looking at. Kameka became aware that someone was staring at her. Just past the door to the main office three boys stood still in the small wave of students in the hallway. All of them had the same look in their eyes. It reminded her of Tommy from last night. She smiled at how simple high school boys could be. She appreciated them noticing her but chuckled at how out of their league they were not aware she was. Her smile faded as she noted the boy in the middle. She was certain he was the boy from the video. She quickly flipped her phone open to watch the video.

Kameka called out to Agent Bush. The FBI agent heard the yell and turned to see what the commotion was about. Principal Zheng took the opportunity to glance at the phone. She saw that the boy on the screen was a student from the school. Without warning, she grabbed Agent Bush by the left wrist and flung her across the big oak desk in the middle of the office. Agent Bush's phone drops to the ground from the intensity of Mei's grip. The startled agent watched it fall as she flipped through the air. Her back hit the top of the desk, scattering its contents. Momentum took her to the floor where she landed awkwardly on the same wrist the principal grabbed to throw her. Rolling over, she cried out as her back slammed into the radiator against the wall.

Principal Zheng grabbed the phone, shoving it into the head of security's face. He watched as the boy ran up the hill and the clip restarted. Ridgefield turned to her with a blank look, then nodded his understanding.

The noise alerted Carol out in the main office. She ran to the door to see what was going on. Marshawn and Bini pushed through the glass doors to stand beside her. Tunes stood in the doorway, eyeballing the pretty woman who had yelled.

Agent Bush got back on her feet. Her left wrist throbbed, and she was a bit wobbly. Ridgefield saw her and charged the agent who was able to sidestep his lunging attack. Ridgefield crashed into the wall face first.

Nose bloodied, he stumbled backward. Dawn kicked the chair causing it to roll behind the stumbling security guard. He fell and toppled over it, rolling to the ground before Carol's feet. The secretary had shuffled to the office entrance to see what was going on inside.

Marshawn and Bini beside her were stunned to see Principal Zheng leap up on the desk in a manner that didn't seem human. Bini noted bruises on the woman's neck. Agent Bush wasted no time. With her healthy right arm, she drew her service weapon. She backed into the corner and pointed the pistol at the principal. This did nothing to give pause to the woman hunched on the desk ready to pounce. As she leaped from the desk, Agent Bush squeezed the trigger three times. The woman's body slumped heavily to the ground, knocking Agent Bush into the desk as she moved from the corner in an attempt to avoid it. The fresh corpse nearly felled the injured agent as it toppled into her legs.

Ridgefield turned over on the ground. Looking up he saw the boy from the video. He grabbed Bini by the ankle and tried to pull him to the ground. The boy grabbed the door jamb tugging his foot free of the man's grip. Both he and Marshawn kicked the man's head while Carol stumbled backwards out of the office landing on the bench in front of her counter. Certain that the kicks would not keep Ridgefield down for too long if he was a Brood Zombie, Bini and Marshawn raced out into the hallway where Tunes was waiting with the door open.

Ridgefield was on his feet giving chase before Agent Bush could gather herself to stop him. He shoved Kameka out of the way as he exited the office. The hallway was already mobbed after the sound of gunshots. There was no way for him to know which direction the boys went. Kameka saw him running in a different direction than they had. Confident that they were out of harm's way she ran into the small office to check on Dawn.

"You okay Agent Bush."

The Agent stumbled to the doorway, her left arm hanging from where she had landed on it.

"Body snatchers." Was all that she said.

"Seriously?"

Agent Bush nodded.

***

Kenny tapped the steering wheel to the Keith Sweat tune as he turned onto the school drive. There was a couple standing around outside the school gate looking rather suspicious. They saw Kenny pulling in and both of them stared him down. After giving him a good once over, they looked at one another and shook their heads. Kenny understood the disapproving gaze as prejudice. Even in this time and place racism still had a place in the world. Kenny was used to these looks and shrugged it off. He didn't let ignorance hold any place in his mind or his heart. He parked in the faculty lot in the first available space. He grabbed his lunch bag and headed toward the entrance on the rear side of the building. He wasn't far from his car when he heard gunshots.

Instinctively, he ducked down and scooted back along the cars for cover. The shots sounded like they were coming from inside the building. Kenny scanned the area for other potential shooters. He moved out from his cover looking along the row of cars as he pulled out his phone and dialed 911. Before the operator picked up, three boys came running toward him. He recognizes them from the incident in the office last week. Immediately, his thoughts went to bad places.

"Hey fellas, what's going on?"

Kenny waved his hands in the air, wishing he had elected to keep himself hidden behind the cars. The woman on the other end of the phone had given her introduction but he forgot momentarily that he had dialed.

"Oh my god, Kenny. Are you, you?" Marshawn had a look of relief, but he took a defensive posture.

"What are you talking about, son? I heard gunshots. Was there a shooting in the school."

"Yes, there was. You have to call 911."

"I did already." Kenny held up the phone. "Hello, ma'am. Yes, there is an active shooter at Saratoga Springs High School."

"No!" All three boys screamed.

"It's not an active shooter." Tunes said.

"I think the lady was a cop. Ridgefield and Principal Zheng attacked her. She shot the principal."

"Ma'am yes. My name is Kenyon Polk. I am a security guard at the Saratoga High School. I arrived late today. I am with three students who just exited the building and informed me that an unknown woman, possibly a police officer shot the principal inside the school. I can see other students exiting the building now. Through alternate exits. Please send help." With that,

Kenny hung up the phone. In that moment, he thought of the suspicious couple at the front gate.

"Boys, tell me what happened. Why did this woman shoot the principal."

"We told you. She and Ridgefield attacked the officer. We're pretty sure she was from the FBI. The lady with her called her Agent. One minute we were listening to an announcement from Principal Paul, the next we heard a loud crash inside the office. We watched them jump on the lady. She shot the principal after warning her to stand back."

"Then she was an active shooter. An FBI agent wouldn't just shoot the principal."

"No, because after Ridgefield attacked her, he attacked us." Marshawn blurted out.

"Why would he attack you?"

"Before they could answer, the door behind them slammed open.

A bloodied Ridgefield came sprinting toward them. The boys immediately took off running in the direction of Marshawn's car.

"Hey, Martin. Calm down a minute buddy talk to me."

Ridgefield did not slow. Even when Kenny cut off his path. He knocked Kenny to the side, stumbling to the pavement as their legs got tangled. Kenny didn't hit the ground. He caught his balance by grabbing on the front of a nearby car. He wasted no time lunging onto Ridgefield's back. He quickly applied a choke hold. The taller man struggled underneath him. Kenny kept applying pressure, trying to put Ridgefield to sleep. The way he growled, he wondered whether sleep was enough. After a minute the big man stopped moving. Out of breath. Kenny got up and moved away from the body. He scanned the parking lot, but the boys were gone. He considered going into the school, but without a weapon he wasn't sure what he could accomplish.

To Kenny's relief, two more guards exited the building. It was Richie and Davis. They sometimes ate lunch with Kenny.

Kenny explained through heavy breaths what had happened. The two men walked over toward where Ridgefield's body laid. Kenny inquired about the status inside the building. Neither responded.

Without a word, they walked back over to Kenny. The two of them stood robotically in front of Kenny. The confused guard stared back at his two coworkers who had yet to speak. Uncomfortable, Kenny took a step back. Both men stepped toward him. Davis grabbed at Kenny, but he slapped the hand away. Confused, he began to back pedal, bringing his fists up in a fighting stance. Richie lunged for Kenny who sidestepped between two cars. He stole a moment to glance back at his own car. He tried to circle around but Davis moved to intercept. Kenny ran down along the back row of cars. The whole time he wondered what the hell was going on. He pleaded with them to calm down and relax but they didn't even respond.

Kenny turned his head to see that they had gained ground on him. Davis snatched a hold of his left shoulder, and this time Kenny couldn't shake free. He spun him around so that they were face to face. Kenny tried to break his coworkers' grip, but it was no use. With both hands, he grabbed Kenny by the front of his jacket and slammed him to the ground. A moment later pain shot through his back as a large boot planted hard in the middle of his spine. A second boot landed to the face, knocking Kenny out cold.

Chapter 26

Keke, Anika, and Emma were in the study hall on the second floor. They had a chemistry test in about an hour. The three of them decided to do some last-minute studying as a group. The study hall was set up just like their chemistry room. Emma sat in her normal seat, Anika sat where Keke did in class, and Keke pulled a chair to the other side of the table.

Emma noticed that there was something unspoken between Keke and Anika, but she feigned ignorance. It was as though there was something else they wanted to talk about but couldn't in mixed company. She had seen her parents act this way before the divorce. Emma thought maybe it had to do with why Keke was distracted in class. Maybe the track finals were weighing on both of them. Anika kept stealing glances at the boy across from them. In her eyes Emma noticed something peculiar. It wasn't a lustful gaze. It was closer to wonder or admiration. Keke did not look back at their tablemate the same way. The glances he stole contained what looked like concern.

There were a few other kids from their chemistry class there preparing for the afternoon exam as well. She didn't know them that well enough to join their table or else she would have given Anika and Keke seclusion to discuss this unspoken other thing. Also, she was more comfortable studying with Keke despite the tension in the air. Keke challenged her to be her best self without expressing that was what he was doing. Keke was the only person she deemed a friend in the school.

The boy was currently quizzing the two of them with flashcards. He would ask with an intent gaze as though he were willing them to be great. It was both inspiring and intimidating. He was staring deep into Emma's eyes awaiting her response to the card that he held up in front of his chest. Her freckled cheeks grew warm from the gravity of his stare. Nobody else paid attention to her in the way that Keke did. It felt good. She didn't get to give him her response as three gunshots echoed through the hallways.

There was a wave of screams outside the study hall from kids moving from lunch to their next class. Everyone inside the classroom jumped up out of their seats. Each one looked to their neighbor to their left and right verifying that they all had heard the same thing. Keke looked at Anika, the classroom door, the teacher, then back to her. Most of the kids pulled their phones from their pockets.

"I have to go help my brother. He's in trouble." The boy made a line for the door.

"Keke, wait. The active shooter drill says that we should stay put. Your brother might be safe." Emma pleaded.

"He's not. I know it." He turned to Anika with the last part. Emma didn't understand how, but whatever was going on out in the hallway that caused the gunfire had something to do with their awkwardness.

Keke arrived at the door with two girls in tow. Mr. Barnes, the teacher, saw him approaching. The man swiftly closed the gap from his desk and stepped in front of the door.

"Young man. Stop right there. Everyone, move to the back of the classroom. I am going to barricade the door."

"I have to go out there Mr. Barnes. Please step aside."

"I can't allow you to leave. I am responsible for your safety."

"Keke please!" Emma begged tugging on his shirt sleeve.

Keke reached for the doorknob, but Mr. Barnes stepped closer to the door pressing his foot to the base.

Keke looked the man in the eyes with a cold fury.

"I'm sorry for this. Barricade the door after I'm gone. Keep everyone safe."

Before the hefty man could protest further, Keke swiped him in the chest knocking the man to the ground. He pulled the door open and tried to shut it behind himself. Anika caught the door and stepped into the hallway with him.

"We're a team." Was all that she said.

Keke nodded.

The two teens began to make their way down the hallway through the mob of panicked students. Emma slipped out behind them before Mr. Barnes could shut the door. Mr. Barnes must have been slow to get up because a few other students got out and joined the crowd in the halls trying to exit the school.

The chaos was such that Anika had to hold Keke's hand to stay with him. They were salmon fighting upstream and the current was strong. She looked back and saw Emma pushing toward them. She tugged for Keke to wait. When Emma caught up, Anika took her hand as well.

"Don't let go." Anika shouted to the other girl.

Emma nodded.

She could feel her heart reverberating in her chest. It was beating so fast and the adrenaline of walking towards gunshots gave her the shakes. Emma's one hand gripped her own. Emma's other hand clung tight to Anika's hip to keep people from pushing between them.

Keke stopped suddenly causing the girls to collide into his back. Anika moved to his side and asked why he stopped. He tilted his head toward the top of the stairwell. At the end of the hallway near the stairwell was Ethan Ramsay. There was another boy with him. It wasn't Brandon. This boy was older. Dark-skinned. Chubby. Both wore heavy parkas, but Keke knew it was him. They were scanning the faces in the hallway.

Keke quickly ducked and moved tight to the wall of lockers. Anika followed suit. Unsure of what was happening, Emma crouched as well. Anika pointed across the hallway to the girls' bathroom. The three of them pushed their way across the grain and into the bathroom.

"Who are we hiding from?" Emma still didn't understand why they left the study hall. "I thought you were going to your brother."

"Foreigners." Keke said.

"That doesn't explain anything at all. We need to hide somewhere with a locked door or get out of this school. Those were gunshots."

"You're right. We just can't go the way we were planning. We need another exit."

The girl was still confused but her fear momentarily halted her questioning. Keke motioned for Anika and Emma to go inside one of the stalls. Emma didn't move so Anika gave a leading shove and did as Keke said.

Keke could hear Emma protesting as he sized up the room but there were only two options for escape. He backed up into the sunlight coming through the frosted window. Keke concentrated like he had been learning to do. He grabbed the top of the door from the first stall. With a mighty tug, he ripped the door off the hinges. Emma shuddered and stumbled back to the wall, her backside banging into the flushing mechanism on the toilet. Anika peeked out to see Keke wedging the door in front of the entranceway to prohibit anyone from coming in. He bent it as easily as the Hulk smashing a Leviathan in Avengers.

Keke shrugged at his friend as he moved back towards the corner of the room. Both girls watched as Keke leapt up on the windowsill. He grabbed the base of the lift and pulled it up as high as the window locks allowed it. He squatted, repositioned his hands at the bottom of the sash, and pulled hard.

At first, the sash wouldn't move. After about five or ten seconds the pins began to slowly move. Another few seconds and the aluminum restraints snapped off, allowing the window to open all the way to the head jamb. The noise wasn't much, but the snapping of the locks caused Emma to cry out.

Keke jumped down from the window and gazed out below. Anika leaned in beside him to see the distance.

"We are not jumping out the window." Emma protested.

"We have to Emma."

Keke held his hands low like a stirrup for Anika to step into. Using them for leverage she sprung up onto the sill. The girl crouched down on one knee, turning her body to face Keke. This time the boy hopped up on the sill, landing on his rear end. He carefully turned himself so that he could face her as well. Emma watched as they locked arms. Anika slid her legs out the window. Using Keke's grip to steady herself she pressed her body into the wall and jumped clear of the bush below her. Emma jumped up beside Keke to see how the other girl faired. She saw the top of Anika's head. Emma watched her wiped her hands free of dirt after landing in a crouch.

A loud thump echoed through the bathroom, startling Emma. Something had collided with the door with great force.

"Time to go!" Keke waved his fingers on both hands toward himself, inviting Emma to join him on the sill.

"I can't. I'm scared." The girl was trembling with fear.

"Don't be afraid. I got you." Keke assured.

"We can just stay here." She pleaded.

Another thump as someone pushed on the bathroom door trying to get through but the wedged stall door held firm.

"Listen Emma. I can't tell you how I know. What I can tell you is that my brother is in trouble. Someone is chasing him. That is why those gunshots went off."

Another thump followed by a screech as the stall door slid against the cement.

"The people on the other side of that door will kill us if we don't jump."

"I don't want to die, Keke." Tears streamed down Emma's round cheeks. Keke wiped them off with a gentle brush of his index finger. The boy dried his finger on his pants and then extended his arm for her to take so that he could pull her up onto the sill.

"But I'm not athletic like Anika. I can't do it."

Another thump and another screech told Keke that the convincing time was over. He would not leave Emma to face the two boys on the other side of the door. He couldn't. Still, he had to go find his brother.

"Fine."

Keke got down off the sill. Before Emma could protest, he grabbed her hips and lifted her high enough for her to stand on the sill. Stunned by the swift move she gasped and then froze. Once again, he hoisted himself on the sill. With a deft spin he took the girl off her feet with his legs, catching her in his arms. There was sheer terror in Emma's face. Keke weighed her fear of the moment against the fear of what would be the next. She screamed once as she fell into his arms and screamed again when he leaned forward and jumped to the ground below with her cradled tight to his chest.

Anika's eyes were wide as the two of them fell toward her. She sidestepped clumsily to get out of their way. Keke did not go to a crouch like Anika. He landed as though he had jumped down from a tall chair or stool.

Keke wasted no time. He set Emma down on her feet, took both girls by the hand and ran for the main street.

There were people running left and right. Keke had no idea who may be Wryvyn Slaver Zombies. All he could do was just keep running. Anika was able to keep pace on her own, but he did not let go of Emma's hand. The tightness of her grip told him that she didn't want him to let go. He couldn't help but think of how bad they were doing at the active shooter drill.

"Look, that's Marshawn's car." Anika pointed ahead toward the grey Kia flying out of the parking lot.

"We won't be able to catch them. We can call them when we get away from school." Keke slowed a bit feeling that Emma was dragging behind.

"Oh shit! Look out!" Anika's warning was just in time. Out of nowhere, Ridgefield came hurtling toward Keke. He released Emma's hand and leaped into the air. Keke hurdled the Head of Security, spinning in the air and landing backwards, sliding like an anime character in a fight scene. The way he changed speed and direction did not seem possible to the shocked girl whose hand he had been holding a moment ago. Ridgefield slid across the grass, missing his target. All the students around them stopped in astonishment.

"Keep going!" Keke yelled to Anika as he waved for Emma to catch up to her.

In the distance, Keke could see two more guards sprinting towards them. He turned to where Ridgefield was just getting to his knees. He channeled his energy and kicked the hunched man in the midsection. The force of the kick drove the security guard into the brick wall. He slumped to the ground with a thud. All the kids around gasped as the man was rendered unconscious.

"That is for Bini."

Keke turned and sprinted in the direction of the two girls.

"The guards are Slaver Zombies!" he called out to Anika. Emma didn't understand what he meant but she continued to run, legs burning as she tried to keep pace with the track star ahead of her.

Keke could see ahead that there was a pair of adults approaching from the entrance to the school. He presumed they heard the gunshots and were coming to provide aid.

Anika slowed to a walk as the adults got close. They were jogging over, and she began to feel safe. They wore matching windbreakers over sweatshirts. She presumed they had been out for an afternoon walk. Keke could see her pleading with the two of them to help. He started to feel relief that his friends would be safe. To his surprise, the two adults ran past Anika, Emma, and all the children running toward them. The woman nearly knocked Anika over as she reached out to her. This didn't slow the woman at all. They both ignored her and Emma's pleading and continued running toward the school.

As they got closer Keke realized that they were sprinting directly at him. He turned to see if there was another kid who could have been their child that they were so intent on getting to. What he saw was two guards running towards him. One of them, Davis, was the monitor responsible for the corridor near the gym. Like the other two adults they were sprinting toward Keke.

Anika started to retrace her steps back toward him, but Keke shook his head, holding out an arm for her to stay put. He sprinted toward her hoping to meet the two blocking his way before the two guards gained ground. Up ahead a throng of kids came running out of the door at the end of the building. They served as a wall, blocking him from maneuvering past the couple in windbreakers. Now if he got past these two, if they were indeed coming for him, he would be slowed by the kids and have to turn to deal with the guards.

As they closed in around Keke, the boy crouched into a fighting posture. At least he thought it was a fighting posture. He was relatively new to fighting. The couple moved in both lunging for him he avoided their attack but was quickly grabbed by the two guards. He used the momentum of them reaching for him to spin them off, only to have the couple in the windbreakers grab his legs. The guards were on him again quickly. They were all really strong.

Keke again harnessed the power that he had absorbed from his alien friend. The four assailants were on him, taking him down to one knee. The guards punched at his midsection while the other man tugged on his ankle. The students around watched in awe as they piled on the boy. Most presumed that he might have been the shooter and began to move away.

There was a flash of light as Keke burst free of the pile jumping back in the direction he had come.

Anika screamed for Keke to watch out behind him. He turned to see Ethan and his companion approaching. When he turned back to face her, she found that he was smiling. Anika looked at Emma. In her face was the same degree of confusion.

The two boys hit the wall with a thud. Some unseen gust of wind or force had taken them off their feet. Keke didn't have to look behind him to see the shimmering figure who moved swiftly. The alien moved like lightning as it dispatched the other two guards and the windbreaker couple. All the onlookers were incredibly confused. To them the air would shimmer around Keke's assailants and then they were felled violently. Some thought maybe Keke was magic.

"Keke Wallace, you are not safe here."

"Tell me about it. How did you know where I was?"

"I always know where you are."

"Well, how did you know that I was in trouble?"

"I discovered the Wryvyn were here. I can sense them but not like the way I can sense you. I followed two of their *zombies* here. I see that you are learning to use your powers. That is good but we must leave."

Keke noted that the alien creature had used the word zombie like the others he pulled from Keke's mind but didn't criticize.

"That way." Keke pointed, which he thought had to be odd to everyone around him.

Keke and his alien friend ran toward Anika and Emma. They didn't look back and neither noticed that Ridgefield had gotten to his feet and was giving chase. The door to the school opened once more and two women stood at the entrance.

"Freeze!!" Keke spun to see Agent Bush pointing her gun at the charging security guard. Her alert allowed

Keke to evade the attack. The off-balance guard toppled across the pavement rolling to a halt in front of Emma and Anika.

"Stay down on the ground. Nobody move!" The agent ran toward the group, Kameka following behind.

Keke had no idea who the lady with the gun was, but he assumed she was the one who fired the three earlier shots. At whom he could not say.

To Agent Bush's surprise the guard levitated in front of the two girls. An invisible entity had hoisted him and heaved him back towards her.

"Keke, what is going on?" Mac arrived, behind the Kameka."

"Dad, get to the car and get out of here."

"You have to come with me, son. I can't leave you." Mac contested.

"Trust me dad, just get home to mom. Bini already left."

Agent Bush had turned to see who the man was that called the boy by name.

Ridgefield at her feet began to stir and she pushed him to the ground with a foot to his back. Keke wasted no time waving for Anika and Emma to join him. He and his alien friend began to run toward the nearby cemetery. Keke ignored the insistence of his father to return.

"Where are they going?" Mac asked nobody in particular.

Agent Bush had trouble keeping the guard down but with Mac's assistance she was able to get his hands cuffed behind his back.

"Just shoot him already, Dawn. He's not going to stop. Do you have enough cuffs for those six as well?"

Agent Bush glowered at Kameka disapprovingly.

"I definitely do not."

Chapter 27

Keke watched as Mr. Griffin stood in front of city hall and gave a press conference about the shooting at the school. The Assemblyman did not release Keke's name but stated that there was a student who was a person of interest that the authorities were seeking. Mr. Griffin made it clear that student was not involved in the shooting and was not expected to be dangerous. He followed it up by telling the press that the FBI were handling the matter and that there is no need to be alarmed. He also made it clear that no students had discharged a firearm in the school. Keke watched him lie on television as he said that the authorities were unsure if it was indeed a firearm as none had been located.

When they got clear of the school, Keke called Bini and had him and the others meet up with them. Anika and Keke stayed with Keke's extraterrestrial friend. Emma called her father who met her and brought her home. She was still shaken by the fact that there was a shooting in the school, her lab partner had supernatural abilities, and he apparently befriended a creature from another planet.

When she saw her dad pulling up the block, she said her goodbyes to Anika and the creature. She hugged Keke tightly and told him to be safe. When she pulled away, she kissed the boy gently on the cheek then ran off to her father's car. Anika raised an eyebrows at her teammate at the parting gesture.

After Emma was gone, the three of them hung out in the woods near the back of St. Peter's cemetery. The creature had been out in the sun for a long time. Even though he had expelled some energy rescuing Keke, he still had concerns that he would involuntarily release a blast from absorbing so much radiation.

Keke explained to Anika that the way he and the Caerulusian communicated was by telepathy. Keke had gained this connection when the creature accidentally bled on Keke while saving him from drowning. Anika was in awe of how the transfer of genetic material had passed on the traits of the creature to a human. She was fascinated by the scientific aspect of it all.

She only knew that Keke had special abilities that were a new development. In the back of her mind, she had a hint that it was not the truth. Despite Tunes' animated telling of how Keke lifted him and Bini together with one hand. It wasn't until the creature arrived outside the school that she believed it was truly from an alien encounter. She was fascinated by Keke's explanation as to how the powers worked. She had seen the brightness in Keke when he had used his new abilities. She had seen a similar brilliance as the creature dispatched the people who had been taken over by the Wryvyn. Keke informed her how the creature's cells had chambers that expand as the energy passes through his *chitin*. When he told her what the cells structure consisted of, she had made the same exclamation he had.

"Wait a minute. Did you say, nitrogen, potassium, and phosphorus?"

She also had a similar conclusion about the reactive state.

"He absorbs light energy, which activates cells like a little bomb trigger and there is light emitted. It is like they are living supernovas."

He explained it all again when everyone was together at Jenna's house.

"So, what do we call him?" Tunes asked.

"I don't know actually." Keke replied.

"What's your name, alien, what's your name?"

"Tunes!" They all scolded.

Keke turned to the creature who was huddled in the corner of the basement visible to all in the room.

"I never asked what your name was. Does your species have names?" Keke asked telepathically.

"We don't. We don't have language that is spoken as we are all connected. The name the Wryvyn referred to me as roughly translates to the escaped one."

Keke relayed the information to the group.

"That's wack. You need a cool name. You don't want to take on the name given by your oppressors. You should get to choose." Everyone agreed that Marshawn had a point.

"Anika Salei said a word earlier, supernova. I like that."

Keke chuckled.

"If that is going to be your name, you need a nickname."

"What's so funny?"

Keke conveyed their new friend's choice.

"Ooh, we could call him Nova!" Tunes declared.

Jenna shook her head at the boy's excitement. Although, she had to admit that picking a nickname for an alien who had saved her friend's life was the coolest thing she had ever been part of.

Bini rolled his eyes at his cousin.

Keke relayed his cousin's suggestion, forgetting that the creature could obtain the message of others through his connection to Keke.

"Nova is a good name. I accept this as the word that you will use to reference me."

"How does it turn invisible?" Marshawn asked, staring at the cerulean entity sitting on the papasan chair in the corner of Jenna's basement.

Keke relayed the question. After a long pause he conveyed the response.

"Do you know what albedo is?" Keke began.

Marshawn shrugged.

"It's the measure of sunlight an object reflects." Keke smiled at Anika who provided the answer.

"That's right. It is measured on a scale from zero to one."

"Snow has an albedo of around point nine and charcoal around point five."

Everyone in the room looked at Anika with surprise.

"Science camp."

They nodded, accepting the brief explanation.

"Right. Spectral albedo is higher in things that are brighter in color spectrum and lower in darker looking things. Nova's species has the ability to manipulate the albedo of its external cells by controlling the radiant flux in and out of the surface."

"Radiosity versus irradiance?" Anika asked, fascinated.

"Yes."

"Cool!" Marshawn exclaimed.

"You know what these two are talking about?" Tunes asked. "Because just like a test, ju-just like a test, I cram to understand them."

"No clue. But it sounds cool."

"With that piece of business settled," Bini moved closer to his brother, "How are the Wryvyn getting people to help them."

"They are probably taking over their bodies like Invasion." Marshawn suggested.

"Nah, they probably have mind control powers." Tunes countered.

"Marshawn Fields is correct. The Wryvyn have a technology that has enabled them to perform a sort of reproduction inside of another host organism. The host organism loses much of their self in the transition. They do not transition their genetic material as was the case with you and me. They deconstruct the host organs with a secretion from their *tentacles*. This *kills* the host in a fashion. However, it is not a death the way humans see it. The mind of the host is cleared of some of the data to allow for learning of those things that the Wryvyn require to enter. The Wryvyn implant certain genetic *messages* to assist the host in adapting the Wryvyn abilities. They also remanufacture the host organ with a synthetic material. The amount of the host that remains is determined by a number of factors. However, the more hosts that are *infected,* the less of the host that is removed. It is a *learning curve.* The modified hosts can learn new information and relearn their host traits. Over time, the only difference is they have the Wryvyn strength."

"So, they are like the Slaver Virus Zombies!" Tunes was happy to understand something about this whole ordeal.

"How do you know so much about the Wryvyn and what they do to hosts?" Jenna asked staring at the blue creature in the corner. "Did they do this to your people?"

Keke didn't relay but Nova knew what she said.

"He said that they told his kind things and other things he learned on his own."

"It doesn't seem like that would be something they would tell you if they were trying to trick your kind into volunteer slavery."

There was a long uncomfortable pause. Most of the room stared at the creature. Keke and Anika stared curiously at Jenna.

"I know this thing about the Wryvyn. I cannot explain everything I know in a manner where your kind would understand. I was merely responding to the inquiry about what they had done with those humans back at the school."

Jenna was not satisfied with the answer. She found something to be off about the creature. However, she knew that it was far from its home and being hunted. Oddly, the people who were sent to hunt him he was able to dispatch with ease from Keke's telling. Perhaps they were not as strong and dangerous as the actual Wryvyn.

Still, there was no way to determine how many Wryvyn were here on Earth. She decided that she would keep an eye on Nova until she was convinced that he could be trusted.

"This is so crazy. Nova came down here like, 'Greetings, Earthlings.' And then he and Keke took out some body-snatched dudes and dipped off like two dope boys in a Cadillac. Now we're all plotting the next move, and it might just be the end of the world as we know it."

Tunes sang most of his realization. When he finished Bini put a hand on his shoulder, indicating he should calm down.

"Okay. So, what is the plan now?" Marshawn asked.

"The plan is to figure out a way to get in touch with the authorities to let them know the full scope of what they are dealing with. We have no idea how many of the Wryvyn are here or if more are on the way."

"Nova says the plan for him is to find a way to get back to his home planet and help his people."

All of them nodded their understanding.

"Looks like the government knows they are here."

Anika pointed to the television screen. The news had cut to the Stratton Base. A convoy of trucks, armored vehicles, and Humvees was driving through the gate. The news lady was interviewing a Colonel Rodriguez. Before Jenna found the remote to unmute the TV the story had changed. There was a break-in at Global Foundries, a local semiconductor manufacturer. Disinterested in the burglary, due to the current situation, Jenna turned the television off.

Everyone grew quiet, trying to think of the best way to get in touch with the military personnel without endangering Nova or Keke.

"I must go home to my kind. I need to save them, Keke Wallace."

Keke turned to his blue friend.

"But your ship. You said it crashed somewhere else. Do you think you can fix it?"

"No but the Wryvyn are here. I could use their ship to go home. I believe I can make it so that it is *modified* for me to pilot the ship. I need only to locate where they have it hidden."

"Yeah, but if you take their ship, they are stuck here. They could do to all humans what they did to the guards at the school."

"And Principal Zheng." Bini added.

"And Brandon." Jenna chimed.

"Then your *government* must kill them."

"That is a little hasty." Anika began. "How would they even be killed?"

"They have weaknesses. Extreme cold. Their exoskeletons are not as durable as mine. It can be penetrated. They are very imposing. Your kind would consider them *terrifying.* They have an armor that they wear. Still, their tentacles can be severed. That is what they use to absorb nutrients. They also use them to infest their hosts."

"Again, an encyclopedia of all things Wryvyn."

The room grew quiet after Jenna voiced her latest skepticism.

"Jenna!"

The scream came from upstairs. Jenna turned to share a look with Tunes before running up the basement stairs. Tunes scrambled off the couch where he was sitting beside Bini and followed her. Bini trailed behind him, catching the door as he pulled it shut. Bini held the door ajar allowing him to hear the conversation. This was not necessary as Kellan raised his voice when he spoke.

"Jenna! I freaking saw him! I saw him. You were right!"

"You saw who?" Tunes behind her watched as the boy panted, his chest heaving.

"Brandon! I saw him last night after work."

"Oh no! Kellan. You didn't approach him, did you?" Jenna's voice revealed that she was sincerely worried.

"Of course I approached him, Jenna. He's my god damn best friend. He has been missing. What did you expect me to do?"

Jenna stared at her brother's face. Only now did she notice the scrapes on his forehead under his coifed bangs. The boy stood oddly. Leaning just a bit as though standing upright was a challenge. Generally, Jenna held derision or hatred toward her brother when they argued. In this moment, she felt pity. While the boy paced back and forth his sister peeked at Tunes. He gave a head shake as though to say it was not their secret to share. The girl huffed but understood.

"Kellan, how bad did he hurt you?" Jenna extended her arm to rest a hand gently on her brother's shoulder.

Kellan jumped at the consoling act. This type of gesture between the siblings was unfamiliar. He winced in pain with the sudden movement.

Startled by the reaction, Jenna flinched. Tunes behind her took a step forward. The girl placed a hand to his midsection. Holding the boy back, she took a step toward her brother and placed her hand to his shoulder once more. This time, he stood still. Weary, worried eyes connected with his sister's soft brown eyes. She escorted him to the kitchen where she sat him in a chair. Jenna gathered an ice pack from the freezer and a towel that hung from the handle of the dishwasher. The girl placed the wrapped ice in a few different positions on the boy's back until he nodded. Gently, she leaned him back, allowing the back of the wooden chair to hold the ice in place.

"We have to go." Bini was there in the kitchen beside his cousin.

Jenna nodded her understanding as she pulled a chair up to sit beside her brother.

Bini tugged on Tunes' elbow, indicating that he was coming with them.

"I'll call you later."

Again, the girl nodded, adding a small smile.

Outside, the group of them surrounded Marshawn's grey Sportage.

"This is going to be a tight fit, guys."

Marshawn fiddled with his keys, clicking the unlock button a few times more than necessary. In his pocket, his phone vibrated. A series of texts from his younger brother. He had called Kenan after he and the others escaped Ridgefield. He told Kenan what happened. It was not an active shooter in the school. Zheng was dead. Avoid Ridgefield on his way out of the school. When Kenan arrived home, he told his parents what happened. Marshawn had been ignoring the calls since.

Nova stood in the shadows under the neighbor's tree uncomfortable with getting inside a vehicle again. He found the automobiles of Earth very confining. He could not stand. He had to scrunch up in the back of the SUV. While traveling to Keke's home, he would have to do so again.

Marshawn did not drop the boys off out front of their house. He pulled into the neighborhood and let them off a few streets over and let them make their way on foot. After leaving Jenna's house, they dropped Anika off at home to check in with her parents.

Mac called and told them to come home and explain what happened at the school. Carol told him that Bini was in the office when the shooting happened and that he, Tunes and Marshawn ran off. Before they dropped Anika off Mac texted to say that the police were there. He told them that he was going to the station to speak to them about the shooting at the school.

As they expected, the police left a unit outside the house. Keke and Nova waited in the woods behind the houses on Copper Ridge while Bini and Tunes made their way back to the house on foot. The two boys found it easy to creep through their neighbors' yards and enter the house through the back. They were careful not to turn on the lights. Other than Tunes smacking into a stool in the kitchen, they were rather stealthy. Once upstairs, they took turns going into the bathroom to shower and pack a bag with a change of clothes for Keke.

When Bini exited the bathroom, Tunes was gone. Bini didn't know whether to be worried or angry. Bini gathered his backpack, tossed in his brother's deodorant, grabbed them both a heavier coat and crept out into the hallway. He listened intently as he slowly made his way to the top of the stairs. He glided close to the wall but was mindful not to create any noise by allowing his jacket to brush against it. Bini got to the top of the stairs. The streetlights outside illuminated the living room enough for him to see that there was nobody there. He listened, but there was still no sound. In a raspy whisper, he called out to his cousin.

"Tunes."

There was no response. He descended two of the steps and squatted. Looking toward the kitchen he saw no movement.

"Tunes!" He pushed the air from his lungs to enhance the sound.

"Darius!"

"Yeah?" the boy whispered back.

"What are you doing?" relief washed over Bini.

"Making some sandwiches."

"You were supposed to wait for me. That was the plan. We stick together."

Before Tunes could respond the doorknob wiggled.

"Someone's here!"

Bini retreated back to the top of the steps and out of eyesight of the doorway. Tunes slid into the pantry behind him and shut the French doors. Both boys fought to slow their breath. Their heartbeats echoed in their ears.

Slowly the knob turned. The door opened. Bini heard the familiar sound of keys clanging against the wall.

There was a click from the light switch being pressed, and the living room lit up. Bini glided down the stairs to greet his mother with an embrace.

"Adesusu, are you okay?"

"Auntie Louise!" Tunes bumped the edge of the French door with the toe of his shoe as he emerged from the pantry. Bini and Louise watched as he fell face first, catching himself with his hands before he hit the floor. Despite the fall, he never took his eyes off of the mother and son.

"Darius, what are you doing?" Louise chuckled.

The woman was dressed in scrubs. Her feet ached from a long shift at the hospital. When she walked in the door, she was weary. Her husband had told her there was an incident at the school, but everyone was okay. When the other nurses and patients began to speculate about the particulars, she did not join in. She knew her family was safe and didn't need the news to tell her about it. Despite her weariness, Louise sprang into mom mode.

She pulled her son over to her nephew and with a hand, the two of them pulled the boy back to his feet.

"Are the police still parked outside?" Tunes asked.

"No, they aren't. They were driving away as I pulled up. What is going on with you two? Why are you wearing this coat in the house? Where is your brother?"

"Whoop, whoop. It's the sound of the police. Uncle Mac went to the precinct." Tunes uttered nervously.

"There was an incident at school today." Bini began.

"Your father informed me. Where is Ukeke?" She pulled her phone from her pocket and began to scroll to her son's name."

"Mom, the principal was shot. We were there."

The woman paused.

"What do you mean you were there?"

"Me, Tunes and Marshawn. We were in the office when it happened."

"Why were you in the office."

"It's a long story."

Louise glared at the boy, letting him know that the explanation given was insufficient.

"And you saw the principal get shot."

"I did, yes."

Louise hugged her son tighter wrapping a loving hand around the back of his braided head.

Bini grabbed his mother's hand and pressed send on her phone. He heard it ring a few times then he pulled it as close to his face as his mother's embrace allowed.

"Keke, it's safe. Come home."

Chapter 28

days later

Anika dove over the rail and behind the large lion out front of city hall. The teenage girl rolled, tumbling off the landing to momentary safety behind the stone staircase of the municipal building. She tucked up and covered her head with her arms. Chipped concrete whizzed past her as bullets fragmented the stone block. Anika flinched as a chunk ricocheted off her thigh. Frantically, the girl crawled back against the wall of the building. There were men in uniform leaping from jeeps and Humvees that screeched to a halt in the intersection of Broadway and Lake.

The frightened girl scanned for a path of egress. The sound of rifles and pistols firing was loud. Everything around her erupted chaotically. It all transpired so quickly and so unexpectedly. She didn't even know what was going on.

She had exited the vestibule of city hall. Climbing the steps as she passed through the doors was Assemblyman Wendell Griffin. She recognized him from his news conference. Beside him to his left was the Sheriff's son, Brandon. To his right, the green haired gas attendant, Ethan. Across the street behind them was a crowd of roughly forty townspeople in front of the post office. When she saw the Assemblyman, Anika initially thought he had called another press conference to announce that Keke had been apprehended. Then she recognized Ethan, Brandon, and the absence of press.

Jenna, Tunes, and Bini left a few minutes before her. They must've just missed the trio who had met her atop the steps. She would have too if not for the pervy clerk who held her ID on her as an excuse to chat her up. The sheriff noticed, pulled her away and followed her out. The jeeps pulled up a second later. The sheriff struck with disbelief upon seeing Brandon, shoved Anika aside as he ran to his son.

Sheriff Gause expected an embrace like Kellan had when he encountered Brandon. His missing son had marched up to the doorstep of his job. The man was elated. Instead, Brandon caught his father by the throat lifting him off his feet. With surprising strength which Anika would not have thought possible had she not known he was a Wryvyn zombie. Brandon threw his own father from the top of the steps. The man bounced on the pavement and rolled out into the middle of the road. A man with a very decorated uniform began to shout orders and within moments, mayhem.

Anika wasn't sure why, but at that moment she thought of her own parents. They had fled Belarus to find a better life for themselves and their future children. Yet here she was pinned down by military gunfire, likely about to die without ever having kissed a boy.

Through all the noise, a bastion of hope arrived as a jeep skidded to a halt about forty feet from the entrance on the Lake Avenue side. The driver leapt out. He was a private first class. The single chevron with the one arc rocker told her that much. She was too far to make out his name plate. The private slammed the door and crouched behind the tail end of the vehicle for cover. The passenger exited and took position toward the front. The driver took aim toward the men in front of the police station. He noticed the cowering girl in the corner. He alerted his partner on the other side of the jeep. The private at the front of the jeep made eye contact with Anika, then held out his hand to her, motioning for her to stay put.

He yelled something back to his partner and then opened fire on the front of the municipal building. Anika flinched as bullets clanged off the bronze lion above her. She didn't notice but the driver had made his way to the transformer at the edge of the building. The uniformed officer waved for her to come to him. Anika craned her neck towards the top of the landing, inching along the bushes, weighing the value of making the move.

The moment she reached the transformer, there was a thud behind her. Ethan and Assemblyman Griffin had leaped off the stairs. The green-haired boy had a weird-looking, black object in his hands. The thing was dark as a void. Like the boy held the darkness of space in his hand.

Anika read the private's name plate. PFC Williams turned his body so that he could grab the girl with his left hand behind his back, while keeping his pistol in his right, aiming at the approaching threats. The private tugged the girl to the opposite side of his body, positioning himself between her and their aggressors. Anika now had a clear path back to the jeep. Private Williams released Anika, bringing his hands together to grip the Sig Sauer M17, firing several rounds. The girl flinched with each round released from the chamber.

Anika sprinted to safety. She flattened her back to the large knobby wheel of the jeep. Sliding down shielding herself from any potential stray gunfire. There was an eerie sounded like a gong reverberating to her left. Anika pressed her palms to the side of her head to block the sound. The girl looked back for Private Williams. To her surprise, the private was lying in the middle of the road. His chest was partitioned up the middle like someone had sliced his torso in half lengthwise, from the inside.

Ethan continued to approach. The black object held menacingly in his right hand. The other private rounded the front of the vehicle. There was gunfire erupting behind her. Mr. Griffin was getting to his feet with blood oozing from his torso where he had been shot. Men were yelling commands. Tires screeched. Glass shattered. The echoing gong sound once more. Anika didn't know what would happen next. She only knew that she needed to move.

***

Agent Dawn Bush, Agent Brian Smarten, and Agent Rick Swain stood outside the middle cell inside the jail. Kameka Ralston sat at the foot of the stairs at the end of the hallway, out of site. The three agents sized up the boy in the cell. On the exterior, he was a normal teenaged boy. There was nothing about Keke that seemed analogous to 'the infected', as Agent Smarten had referred to them. Kameka felt he preferred infected because perhaps there was a cure. She tended to think of them more as 'snatched'. To the three Agents Keke appeared ordinary.

Kameka knew otherwise. She and Agent Bush had visited his parents' home just the previous day. His father, MacArthur Wallace and mother, Louise, were a lovely couple. Mac was a history teacher at the school. He had been there when all hell broke loose a few days ago. Louise was a nurse at a nearby hospital. They had only moved here from Newport News just before the school year began. Kameka took to them as she had been born and raised in Hampton. In the scope of the world, they were neighbors.

Agent Bush asked the Wallace's if they knew why the people who were 'infected' were after their son. Neither of them understood why. Mac averted his eyes when he spoke. Stealing a gaze at his wife while responding. Neither of them even shuddered at the idea that these individuals were after their son. Ordinary people would have asked if the 'infection' was contagious. They may even ask how the infection accounted for the feats of strength they exhibited.

When asked why he thought the guards at the school had attacked his son, Mac told a story about an incident in the principal's office that was mostly true. Both Agent Bush and Kameka could tell that he was holding back details. The part he withheld was his treatment of the guard when he arrived in the office.

Louise was a better liar.

She didn't betray their story at all. Kameka recognized the look in her eye. It was the look of someone who had to be another person while engaging certain people. Kameka's guess was that she came from a family that had a secret or perhaps a story that not too many people knew.

Kameka's dad had been an alcoholic. She had lived that lifestyle until she left for college. Her mother refused to leave him. Kameka refused to go back once she was free.

Before they left the Wallace's home, Mac gave them directions to the comic bookstore that he presumed his sons would be at. He also gave them a few ideas of locations they would go to after the store.

When they arrived, Agent Bush had Kameka go inside first. She looked around and immediately noticed the twins in the corner digging through crates. There was another boy with them. He was chatting with pretty young girl with long brown hair. The two appeared to be singing to one another, which didn't seem odd to the twins who paid them no mind.

Kameka tried to squeeze past the people standing in front of the door but none of them would budge. Eventually, she just shoved past the rude boys who ignored her pleasant requests to move aside. Kameka turned to give her ugliest glare to the group when she noticed the boy with the green hair that worked in the gas station that was 'remodeled'.

Ethan. That was his name.

Kameka last saw the boy being handcuffed while unconscious. A uniformed officer had picked him off the ground and attempted to place him in the back of a police SUV. She and Agent Bush were walking back into the school when the sound of the doors being ripped off the hinges cut through the walkie chatter that was echoing off the stone walls inside the corridor. They and the officers with them ran outside to see that the detained guards, the windbreaker couple and the boys had escaped.

Ethan didn't recognize Kameka from the school. He and his companions were staring in the direction of the twins. The other two boys with him didn't pay her any mind. She turned to see that there was a mother and daughter cashing out at the register to her right. Kameka slipped her phone out walking backwards toward the twins and their companions. She started to text Agent Bush to tell her to come inside. Before she could hit send, chaos ensued.

One of the infected boys pushed his way across the room knocking over tables of boxes that contained comic books in plastic covers. The startled store owner yelled for him to be careful. Ethan moved toward the store owner with a cold look in his eyes. Kameka stepped backward into a row to get out of his path. The mother and daughter who had just checked out weren't so lucky. Kameka looked to the door where Agent Bush hadn't entered yet then back to Ethan. The mother and daughter froze in his path. The mother could read the situation, but her daughter did not.

The cute little girl with red hair, freckles, and green overalls walked up to him. She couldn't have been any more than nine years old. The girl glanced up at Ethan smiling, holding out her Ghost-Spider issue #5 for the boy to see. The girl beamed proudly.

Both Kameka and the mother gasped as he swatted the arm holding the comic with The Jackal and Ghost-

Spider on the cover. The plastic-wrapped periodical plummeted to the carpet. The store owner marched forward in protest of Ethan's action. He was a burly, bearded man with a Mandalorian T-shirt under a blue and black flannel. His thinning coif of hair waved as he moved swiftly to the girl's aide. He was not about to tolerate unruly actions in his store. Ethan grabbed ahold of the little girl's shirt and hoisted her in the air. She protested with an angry growl. Kameka envied her courage. The girl's mother covered her face in horror.

The store owner socked Ethan strongly in the side of the face. The punch was heavy enough to concuss the average human. It stumbled Ethan a step, causing him to drop the girl to her feet. Still, he clenched her shirt in his grip as he doubled over. The burly store owner swung again. This time Ethan caught the punch with his free hand. Kameka watched as Ethan let the girl go, enabling his right hand to grab the wrist of the store owner. With unbelievable might, he performed what resembled a judo toss sending the man flying past Kameka onto a near table. While the boy was bent Kameka stole the opportunity to front kick him in his exposed midsection as hard as she could. The boy tumbled back behind the counter from whence the burly man came.

Kameka motioned for the mother and daughter to run for the door. Agent Bush had since entered and shouted for everyone to freeze. The two infected boys that were moving towards the corner and the twins turned and looked at the FBI Agent with the same cold gaze that Ethan wore.

A rumble of boxes notified Kameka that Ethan was getting back on his feet. She took a few steps backward, dukes up, ready to do her best. The store owner behind her groaned. Kameka awaited the attack, that never came.

A dark blue blur flew past her knocking Ethan to the ground. She saw that it was the boy from the video, Ukeke Wallace. The boy who they had come to find. The boy who had fought with the infected guards outside his school. Kameka watch in awe as Keke's fist lit up like the Immortal Iron Fist Orson Randall, but his qi was blue. Keke slammed the fist into the middle of Ethan's back. There was a sound of bones cracking and then the boy was still.

Keke's brother and friends followed behind him. They scrambled toward the exit. In pursuit was the boy who had started the chaos. He was tall and lean, but Kameka knew that meant nothing when it came to those infected by the aliens.

The group of them ran out the door. Dawn covered their exit, firing 4 rounds at the tall boy in pursuit of the twins. She waited for the store owner to rouse before she exited behind them. Kameka did as the teenagers did. She ran two blocks away to get distance. The group of them stopped at the corner. The girl pulled keys out double tapped the button on the fob and she and the others jumped in a truck.

Before Keke could get in, two women tackled him to the ground. They tumbled taking Kameka down in the melee. Keke landed on top of Kameka crushing her legs. The force of the fall sent her head to the pavement.

Keke recognized that she was in pain beneath him. The boy pressed his hands to the ground beside her hips, ignoring the punches from the two women on top of him. Punches so powerful that Kameka could feel the reverberation of the blow through his body.

Once again, the boy's hands lit up blue. With inhuman dexterity and force, he sprung into the air. The two women rose with him. Kameka watched as Keke pivoted in midair, defying gravity, driving the two women down into the concrete. The boy rose. Grasping each woman by an arm like a child dangles a doll, Keke applied alternating kicks, hitting them both in their torso. The kicks sent each of them into the brick wall of a flower shop. It reminded Kameka of The Hulk kicking Emil Blonksy into a tree.

Kameka could see more people were running their way. Each wore a cold stare. None of them looked to be concerned citizens. Kameka counted at least ten. The number of infected was growing.

Keke looked back at Kameka who was still on the ground. Glancing up the block to see that Agent Bush was nowhere in sight. His brother beckoned him to get in the truck. The boy leaned his head toward her, a concerned expression on his face. Bini nodded to his brother who slammed the door, telling his friend to go ahead and he would catch up with them. Without waiting for protests he returned to help Kameka to her feet.

The bruising on her thigh where he had landed with the weight of the two women on top, throbbed. It was like there was a dull blade wedged between her quadriceps. The truck squealed up the block. None of the people attempted to impede their flight. Keke considered what to do. There were too many to fight alone. Kameka knew this from the fray at the school.

Unable to fight them and protect the wounded Kameka, Keke did what Keke did best. He picked up the girl and he ran. Even with the weight of Kameka in his arms, he was able to put distance between himself and their pursuers. Kameka was stunned by the strength and swiftness. She pointed him toward Agent Bush's car. The FBI agent was turning the key to start the engine as they caught up to her. Keke tugged open the back door and tossed Kameka inside before jumping in next to her. Their sudden arrival startled Agent Bush who fumbled nervously with her keys to start the engine mere seconds ago. Agent Bush floored it up the block past the unknowing infected that hadn't noticed them get into the vehicle.

Kameka was saddened that in saving her from the infected, Keke had inadvertently landed himself here in a jail cell.

Chapter 29

"What do you want with me, Agent Swain?"

"We want to question you about the aliens." The agent said plainly.

"Aliens?" Keke's tone was intentionally skeptical.

"We aren't going to get very far Mr. Wallace if we aren't honest with one another." Agent Swain sighed.

"What does that mean?" the boy asked.

"It means that we know you are involved with these aliens!" Agent Smarten's tone was aggressive, accusatory.

"I'm not one of those crazy Slaver Virus freaks!" Keke vehemently denied the accusation.

"Slaver Virus?"

"It's used by a fictional alien race called the Brood. They escaped to the Marvel main universe from another universe. They use a virus to turn off a victim's reasoning and self-awareness. It turns them into zombies."

The three agents looked down the hall toward the casual voice that echoed off the old stone basement walls. The girl was tucked a few steps up and was out of view. After a few moments of confused silence where he didn't know whether to be perturbed at the interruption by their guest or in awe of the breadth of her nerd knowledge, Swain turned back to the boy in the cell.

"You think the aliens infected these people with a virus?"

"Do you think it is contagious? Why haven't you turned like them?" Before the boy could respond, Agent Smarten, driven by anxiety, interjected.

Keke rolled his eyes.

"Why haven't I turned like them? Really? I already told you that I'm not one of them. Why are you so sure they are aliens."

"You and Ms. Ralston both confirmed that you believe them to be aliens. So, why are you now eager to convince us otherwise."

"Typically, you government agent types aren't so inclined to believe in invaders from another planet. Extraterrestrials. Little Green Men."

"So, you're saying that they are here to invade the planet?" Agent Smarten's tone had changed an octave.

"No. I don't think they are here to invade. And it's not contagious."

"How can you be so sure?" Agent Smarten was not convinced.

"The Wryvyn have to 'infect' people to control them. Our planet's conditions are not ideal for them. I don't know if the people they infect have the ability to infect more people, but it's not an airborne thing or something you can get from coming in contact with them or anything. They have tentacles that they use to implant whatever it is that turns people into their slaves."

"That is an interesting theory Mr. Wallace. What did you call them? Ravens? If they have tentacles, why do they have a bird name?" Agent Swain wrapped his index finger around his chin, pressing his thumb firmly to his submental crease.

"Wryvyn. Not Ravens. They are called Wryvyn."

"You sound confident. How do you know what these creatures are called, Keke? Have you seen or interacted with any of them?" Agent Bush employed a softer tone. Having recently met his mother, she felt this may be a more fruitful tactic.

"I spoke with someone familiar with them."

"Familiar? Like a scientist, or one of them?" Agent Smarten reverted back to an accusatory tone, as though Keke were a suspect.

"Have you tried talking to one of those Slaver Virus freaks?" There was sarcasm in the boy's voice as he posed the question.

"No, I haven't." The Agent responded defiantly.

"Well, my friend tried, and it was like speaking to a wall. My other friend's brother tried, and he got a couple broken ribs for it. Agent Bush had a nice conversation with our school principal and the head of security. How did that go Agent Bush?"

For the first time the boy stood. He was the tallest person in the room but there was something else about him that gave the agents the sensation that he was looming over them. There was an energy within him. His body vibrated so hard it vibrated the floor of jail. Absently, Agent Smarten's hand went to rest on the Glock seventeen on his hip when the boy approached the front of the cell.

"I had to shoot the principal in the head."

There was a somber finality in Agent Bush's words. Keke could tell that it was a reluctant act.

"I bet she wasn't much for conversation prior to that, was she?"

"Not particularly."

"Let's not get off topic. Mr. Wallace, you were telling us about your theory on how the Wryvyn infect people." Swain tired of all the segues.

"I could have done this from not inside a jail cell, you know."

"It's just a precaution Mr. Wallace." Swain said plainly.

"Lock the black kid up as a precaution? There are people out there with alien-controlled brains attacking and possibly turning other people into mind-controlled zombies. There are Wryvyn, members of a dangerous alien race running around doing God knows what but I'm the one behind bars."

"Better the local jail than Guantanamo." Agent Smarten jested.

Agents Swain and Bush both glowered at the man.

"Please, Mr. Wallace. You are the only one who seems to know about these things that we've encountered. Ms. Ralston down there is an expert on astronomy."

"Astrophysics!" The voice down the hall corrected.

"Astrophysics. We don't have others here yet to provide expert analysis on what is going on. Once they arrive, we will need to get ahead of the situation. We saw their ship enter the atmosphere on Keck Observatory video. We saw where it crashed. We saw one of them falling to earth. Where did the rest come from? What do they want? Was there another ship? Are there more coming? We need to understand how the mind control or this Slaver Virus or whatever they are doing, how that works."

Keke paced back and forth as the DHS Agent rattled off questions. Keke could tell that he genuinely wanted these answers. The man seemed sincere, but his current status locked behind bars was clouding Keke's cooperativeness. He took a deep breath and the floor stopped vibrating.

"That wasn't their ship."

"I beg your pardon."

"That ship, the one that crashed. It wasn't theirs. The one with one of them falling out."

"How can you be certain? We saw the footage. It was a big black ship, and it was on fire. One of them ejected out. We presume that he died on impact."

"You presume wrong."

"Excuse me?"

"I said you presume wrong. About everything. That was technically one of their ships, but that was not the ship that the Wryvyn came on. That was a ship that was stolen from them."

"Stolen?" Agent Bush stepped forward placing a hand on Keke's fingers that were gripped tightly to the iron bars.

"Stolen by who?"

"A friend. Nova."

"Nova?" Agent Bush turned to her colleagues to see if they shared an understanding as to what it was that the boy was communicating to them.

"Who is Nova? Was he there outside the school?"

Keke, realizing he may have said too much, pulled away from the bars and returned to his bunk.

The jail was silent other than the faint sound of rapid clicking from the stairwell. The three agents came together as though in a pow wow, but no words were spoken.

"Mr. Wallace. Tell us what this, Nova, told you about these Wryvyn and how they infect folks."

"They start out very basic. The people they take over are initially like hypnotized sloths. But over time, the fluid they deposit inside learns from the host and begins to function at a higher level. The more hosts a Wryvyn infects the faster they assimilate to the brain chemistry of the new hosts. The more of a host species they infect, the less of the host they have to eradicate to convert them. It is like they learn and advance their technique. That is why I doubt it is a virus or contagion."

"This Nova tell you that part?" Swain asked.

"He did."

"And to be clear, this Nova, he's not from here?"

Keke refrained from answering.

"He's right."

Again, the agents looked down the corridor toward the seemingly disembodied voice. This time, the girl's head appears, then shoulders, then torso appeared as she leaned forward into a standing position, one hand cradling the bottom of her chromebook.

"What are you talking about Miss Ralston?" Agent Smarten asked.

"Keke's right. Another spaceship entered the atmosphere that night." The woman's braid swayed behind her as she approached.

"Are you certain, Kameka?" Agent Bush leaned over to glance at the computer screen.

"Absolutely."

"How do you know?"

Kameka paused at the sound of crunching vinyl as Keke shifted his weight on the padded bench inside the cell.

"When one of our space shuttles re-enters the atmosphere, it weighs approximately 78,000 kilograms. It re-enters the atmosphere at a speed somewhere around seven kilometers per second. The formula for kinetic energy at atmospheric entry is $K_E = 0.5mv^2$. V is the velocity and m is the mass of the object."

"This math lesson tells you that another ship entered the atmosphere how?" Agent Smarten asked, confused by the physics.

"What she is saying is that she looked at the data from when the ship that you all saw enter the atmosphere and saw that there was similar data later."

They all turned to the boy who was once again standing.

"Precisely." Kameka confirmed.

"Could it have been something else?"

"The energy released from the entry of a NASA shuttle would be around 568,000 gigajoules, if not for controlled re-entry. The alien spacecraft entry was around thirty times that."

"And there was a second of this magnitude?"

"Yes and no Agent Swain. NESDIS, the National Environmental Satellite Data Information Services, which is sort of a department within NOAA, the National Oceanic and Atmospheric Administration, tracks space junk entering our atmosphere. Approximately forty-five minutes after the spaceship we recorded entered the atmosphere, a second unexplained entry occurred at around a third of its energy release."

"So, a much smaller ship, then?" Agent Smarten asked.

"A better explanation would be the same size but just controlled rather than uncontrolled." Keke corrected.

Kameka flipped her chromebook all the way open so that the keyboard and screen were facing outward. She pointed to the screen, explaining that the trajectory of the second object was unknown as it did not fall in line with the force of gravity. Instead, it kept a steady altitude in the stratosphere before they lost it.

"Interesting."

Agent Swain again curled his index finger around his chin, this time, allowing the crook of his finger to rest upon his lower lip a bit, his thumb resting across the tip of his middle finger.

"Wouldn't we see this big flying cruise liner just floating around up there.

"Not if it landed." Kameka postulated.

"Or it could be cloaked." Keke suggested.

"What do these Wryvyn look like?" The senior agent asked.

"That I don't know." The boy said with finality.

Three government agents, a graduate student, and an imprisoned teenager considered the gravity of an alien invasion on their planet. Each of them had seen the movies. Most of the time, the good guys win. Never without innocent casualties.

In their case, the aliens were here. They were hiding. Using human host bodies to do their dirty work. None of them had any idea what would become of those hosts' bodies when the Wryvyn were finished with them. Nova told Keke that they were killed in a fashion, but he was unuse what that meant.

Would they be discarded lifeless shells? Would they be returned to their old selves? If so, might they have recollection of all the stuff they did while mind controlled? Would they be able to live with that knowledge? Or would the horror of the acts they committed drive them mad? Many of them had already attacked children and teenagers. Some likely did worse without hesitation. Ridgefield and the other Wryvyn zombie guards had killed another guard, Kenny Polk.

Agent Swain wondered how he would explain to the military leadership on their way there that it was indeed aliens. That a teenager who encountered what was probably one of the aliens had received intel on them. This teenager had provided the best lead as to how to combat these aliens and how they operate. What their potential weaknesses were. Also, this teenager exhibited strange abilities according to witness testimony but nothing out of the ordinary had been witnessed by anyone he considered credible.

The only person whom he trusted was Ms. Ralston. She had told them nothing about the encounter at the comic bookstore. She said only that Keke had kept her safe during the attack. Military men didn't like things that they couldn't explain. He knew this and worried that too much time would be spent disbelieving when problem solving was needed.

One thing for certain, those like Principal Zheng, who was shot in the head by Agent Bush would not be coming back. Neither would her husband who was found dead in their home when they had gone to report her death to him.

It was also a certainty that if the agents didn't get this under control quickly there would be more casualties. The military had begun establishing a base of operation here in Saratoga Springs. Soon the brass from Washington would arrive and take charge. They would quarantine areas where the infected had been encountered. Today they had learned a lot, but they had not gotten to the bottom of narrative of how Keke Wallace, a high school boy who had multiple encounters with the Slaver Virus zombies, managed the feats he has been witnessed accomplishing.

"What about you, Mr. Wallace?"

"What do you mean, what about me, Agent Swain?"

"I've been told you have performed some nifty tricks yourself. Mind telling us how you were able to achieve these things? Gift from your friend Nova?" Agent Swain got right to the point of the matter.

"Some folks think it's steroids."

The agent chuckled but the boy didn't even smirk.

There was a faint staccato of cracking sounds in the near distance. All three agents wheeled around to face the door, hands to their hips, pistols popping a few inches out of their holsters.

"Firecrackers?" Agent Bush asked.

The DHS agent slowly swung his head back and forth twice. He tapped his partner's arm beside him, drawing his weapon. In a single file, the three agents moved to the stairwell. A drum, drum, drum, drum, drum, of vehicle mounted artillery rattled the building.

"Stay here!" Agent Bush pointed to Kameka who had her feet glued to the cement floor since the first crack. She was no stranger to gunfire and was happy to be away from it.

"Listen! You gotta get me out of here Kameka!"

Startled by Keke's proximity, loudness and insistence, the woman jumped back flattening to the wall behind her.

"Kameka!"

"I can't let you out. I don't have the keys."

"Find someone with the keys. The Slaver zombies are here. There are a lot of them.

"How do you know?"

"I just do. Besides, who else would be getting shot at outside a police station? That was military gunfire. Unless our military has taken to firing upon civilians, the zombies are here. They are getting stronger, and their numbers are growing. They have been after me. You've seen them. They are coming down here eventually."

Kameka considered the boy's words. She didn't know what to do. The gunfire upstairs continued. She could hear voices yelling incoherent instructions.

"Kameka. If they come down here, and trust me if there are enough of them, they will. You will be standing between me and them. So, either you need to get me out of here or you need to leave."

The girl pondered her choices. Glancing around the room, there was nothing to be used as a weapon. The door at the near end of the corridor had a padlock on it. That door and the narrow windows above the cells that were barely large enough to let in sunlight were the only alternatives to venturing up the stairs.

Kameka looked Keke in the face. The anxious woman scrunched up her right eye, scrupling the boy in the cell. She realized that what he was saying was true. Back at the school, the guards went for him. The people at the comic bookstore went for him. Those people who were outside being fired upon, if they get inside, they will come for him.

"I'm sorry."

Hand over her mouth, she apologized to the boy. Kameka flipped her chromebook closed, slid it into her satchel and sprinted out of the basement.

Chapter 30

Agents Swain and Smarten exited the police station behind a cadre of officers. Each one of them sprinted up the incline of Lake Avenue towards the intersection. An army jeep was parked diagonally in the intersection. There was a private escorting a young girl to safety behind his jeep.

Agent Bush was the last one out the door. She watched as all of the men before her dropped to their knees from a noise that sounded like a large gong. She watched as the soldier at the corner fell backwards, splitting apart down the middle.

Agent Smarten eye were wide and his jaw hung slightly, the face of shock. He looked back at Agent Bush who was cowering by the entrance. The unspoken communication was an ask if she saw what he had. She nodded toward his partner. Agent Swain waved an arm in a half circle, indicating for the two of them to follow him across the street.

The three agents hurried to the other side of a GMC Terrain at the corner of the small alley just as the sound of the gong went off again. When he emerged around the backside of the SUV, Agent Swain saw four of the seven sheriff's deputies flayed on the sidewalk adjacent the police station. Their blood was splattered across the pavement. The boy at the corner held out a mysterious black object toward them. One of the deputies who had been spared the death blast took refuge in a doorway at the basement of the municipal building. The other two ducked behind the corner. There was dread in their eyes as they gazed upon the split corpses of their comrades.

Agent Bush moved to the porch of the nearby apartment building allowing her to see over the SUV to where the boy was standing. She saw that it was Ethan, the boy with the green hair that wielded the strange alien weapon. Without a second's pause, Dawn took aim and fired, putting three rounds into the boy's upper torso from about twenty yards away. The boy fell, dropping the weapon he held to the ground. She signaled to Agent Smarten who sprinted to the Tesla at the corner.

The cowering girl watched the Agent move into position. A wave of Slaver zombies overpowered the dozen or so soldiers that had taken up position to secure the intersection. They were swarming down toward the police station entrance into the gun fire of the three remaining officers. The girl ran to the awaiting agent who shielded her as they scurried back to the GMC and the awaiting agent Swain. The agent attempted to coral the girl, but she side-stepped him and sprinted down the block. Agent Bush recognized her as one of the girls who was at the school with Keke.

Agent Bush could not pursue her. The zombie mob was making its way down the sidewalk, overtaking the officers. She and the two DHS agents fired upon them, scoring a few kills. They hit many of the Slaver zombies, but some got back up after strikes to the torso. It was clear that anything less than a headshot would put them down for good. She didn't like the idea of killing innocent people that were under alien control, but she was not willing to trade her life for theirs.

Agent Smarten brazenly moved to the middle of the road to get a better aim at the mind-altered townspeople who were moving to overtake the police station. Up the road, Agent Bush saw another group approaching. Out in front of the group was a recovered Ethan. In his hand the alien weapon. The boy was pointing it toward the exposed agent in the middle of the street. She yelled his name, pointing toward the danger. Agent Smarten turned to see the boy with the curved, black object aimed directly at him.

***

Keke paced back and forth in the cell. He questioned whether his powers would allow him to break free of his cage. Kameka had run off. With her exit, so went his best chance at getting free before the police station was overrun. Now, if he was going to escape, he would need alternate assistance. With the commotion outside he doubted that any of the officers cared that he was sitting down here in a cell.

He was going to have to escape.

The wrought iron bars were solidly built into the concrete structure of the basement. He hadn't attempted to move anything of that magnitude since his encounter with Nova had inadvertently transformed him. The boy backed up to the wall, took three steps and front kicked the locked gate as hard as he could. Concrete chips fell from the ceiling where the bars connected. Other than that, his cage held firm. Not to be deterred, Keke tried three more times. Each time yielded the same result.

The futile exertion left him feeling slightly deterred.

The gunfire outside had gone quiet. That was either a good thing or an awful thing. Keke didn't spend time dwelling on it. He had to break free. If he was right, there was a mob of people outside. Each of them mind controlled by the alien Wryvyn. If the increase in numbers from his encounter at the school and then the one at the bookstore just a few days later was any indication, Keke could not fight them all. At the current moment the bars to his cell were a buffer between that inevitable encounter. However, he was not confident that they would not be able to get in given enough time. Plus, they were on the side with the keys.

Keke kicked the bars once more. The metal hummed as the vibrations chipped off more fragments of concrete. Still, it was insufficient for him to break free.

Footsteps on the stairs alerted the boy. He pressed himself flat to the wall, his breath held to prevent his chest from heaving. The person coming down the hallway did not suppress their breathing. Keke could hear the steady puffs as air exited her lungs shortly after being pulled back in.

"Keke!"

The boy was relieved to see that it was Kameka.

"I couldn't find any keys to open the cell and all the cops are dead. They ran outside and shortly after I heard screaming. I peeked out and saw Ethan with a strange device in his hand and blood everywhere."

"Ethan?"

"The boy from the gas station explosion disappearance. The one with the green hair."

Keke nodded.

"Anyway, we are stranded in here. I locked the door at the top of the stairs, but I don't think that will stop them long."

"It's okay. We are going to be fine. Come here stand close to the bars and turn your face that way." Keke pointed toward the stairs.

"Your optimistic bravado is not necessary."

Kameka did not like that the boy was so calm. It frightened her a bit that he was smiling. It wasn't a scary or sinister smile. His face was relaxed. He looked relieved. The way that he gently motioned for her to come closer was reassuring. In that moment her fight or flight receptors turned off and she engaged in an act of trust.

"What are you planning to do, Keke?" the woman asked as she slowly approached the boy.

"Me? Nothing." Keke reached through the bars. His hand rested gently against her twist of hair as he cradled her head. "Don't be afraid."

Before Kameka could ask of what, she was startled by the sound of the steel door at the end of the hallway being ripped from its hinges.

She tugged away from Keke who allowed her to go a few steps, still holding onto the inside of her right elbow with his left hand. Her right hand gripped the bars, using them as a pivot point. Before her was a boy, roughly Keke's age. He was tall with a sweet smile. He was grinning upon seeing Keke inside the cage. Beside the boy there was a shimmer of light and a creature materialized in a space where a moment before there was nothing.

Eyes wide, Kameka felt her sight betrayed her. The creature was nearly seven feet tall. There was a sparkling cerulean, blue glow that surged through the creature's skin. Kameka was taken by how vivid the pigment was. It reminded her of the neon in store signs. It seemed to ripple and be solid at the same time.

The creature had a smooth curvature to its face. There was no mouth. Its face was like a shiny riot shield on the front of its oblong head. Behind this shiny, smooth plate on the front of its head Kameka could make out a pair of sensors that she presumed functioned as its eyes. If not for the light in the hallway being directly over the creature, she might have missed this feature.

The long neck was twice as long as a human neck. Its shoulders were just higher than the boy beside it. The thorax was narrow but was quite muscular, like the neck. It was quite fleshy and resembled her own stomach that sported a six-pack. The skin looked like a superhero's costume.

The creature stood on two legs with two arms hanging from the torso. The legs had two fork joints instead of knees. The lower legs were the same chitinous material as the head and shoulders. The upper legs were muscular and fleshy like the stomach with two large muscles on each. The feet were tridactyl, as were the hands.

The creature and the boy approached them. Kameka attempted to retreat but Keke held her close.

"Kameka, this is my friend Marshawn. And this big guy, is Nova." Keke pointed to his two friends as he gave introductions.

"Stand back, Keke Wallace."

Keke heard the voice inside his head and released Kameka's arm. Once free, she retreated down the hallway. She had no desire to stand so close to a seven-foot alien.

Nova placed a hand on Marshawn's chest, ushering him back a bit. Once, everyone was clear he grabbed ahold of the cell. They all watched as the creature's skin turned from a vivid blue to a nearly blinding white. The three humans shielded their eyes as the sound of the iron lock being ripped off the door echoed through the basement of the police station.

Kameka unshielded her eyes to see Keke hugging the other boy.

"Me and Nova have a communication system now. That is how I knew to come with him to find you."

"You can hear him telepathically like I do?"

"No, we use signs. Watch."

Keke and Kameka watched Marshawn make a circle with his hand from his chest to Nova, over to Keke and back to himself, before pointing to the door. The alien responded by holding his hand aloft and swinging it past his head. He then turned and marched toward the doorway.

"Nova, wait. There is trouble outside. There was shooting."

"Some army people showed up in jeeps and JLTVs. There was a mob of the people that were taken over by the Wryvyn out there. It is pretty crazy. We gotta get out of here, Keke. They are everywhere."

Keke motioned for Kameka to come along with them. She glanced at Nova and shook her head. Keke understood that she was afraid, but he couldn't leave her behind. It was feeling a bit like déjà vu. As he approached, the woman retreated. Before he could debate with her, there was a sound of a gong like Keke had heard a few times previously.

"Keke Wallace. That sound is from a dangerous weapon. We must leave now!" Nova exclaimed.

Without a word he shimmered and disappeared. Only Keke could tell that he had exited the station. Keke could also tell that Nova was afraid. He gave Marshawn a head nod and the boy retreated toward the door.

Keke turned to Kameka. The girl stepped backward to the bottom of the stairs. The heel of her right foot had just caught the lip of the bottom step when the gong sound echoed from above her blowing the door off the hinges. She cowered as the handle and hinges ricochetted off the walls. The steel door itself got wedged between the two walls. Keke wasted no time lunging for the woman's arm, dragging her to her feet, and pulling her down the hallway in pursuit of Marshawn and Nova.

There was a screech as the door was flung from its place between the two walls and rested awkwardly at the bottom of the stairwell.

Keke looked back to see Ethan with a strange black object in his hand that looked like a small rams horn at the end of a selfie stick. The boy pointed the weapon, but Keke and Kameka rounded the corner before he had a chance to discharge. Keke did not look back as the gong echoed.

Outside it was chaos. Military vehicles flew past them on Maple Avenue. More were speeding up Lake toward Broadway. The building behind them shook from the impact of a round from what Keke presumed was a thirty-millimeter chain gun. There were pedestrians hustling to their vehicles when they saw the military vehicles and heard the gunfire. Keke was relieved to find no Wryvyn zombies in their path.

The three of them dashed through the parking lot toward the Hampton Inn and Suites. They cut diagonally through the lot and across Lake Ave. A familiar voice called out to the boys.

It was Anika.

She was sprinting ahead of Agents Swain and Agent Bush. Kameka stopped when she saw the agents. The boys jogged on through the newspaper parking lot expecting that Anika could catch up. The sound of gunfire told them that the agents had encountered the mob. The gong device sounded again, followed by crashing of glass. In that moment, Keke wondered where the other agent had gone to.

When they got to Caroline Street, Keke saw that the Agents were fleeing as the mob of zombies that exited the station in pursuit of him had been too much for them. That gong weapon must have been powerful because hearing it scared Nova off.

Keke directed his friends to head up Caroline Street toward Broadway. Marshawn thought that going that way was heading back toward the danger but said nothing in protest. The cold late-autumn air scraped their lungs as they pushed their pace up the block. When the trio got to Broadway there was a pickup truck parked sideways in the road just beyond a military barricade. Keke recognized it as Jenna's.

    Soldiers saw the three of them approaching and took a cautious stance. Keke pointed back down the streets and called out to the first sergeant that the agents behind him needed help. The sergeant called out for his men to let them through and led a squad toward the two Agents and the grad student who were struggling up the road. Behind them was a group of people. A JLTV pulled into position behind them. Keke saw that there was a mounted thirty-millimeter chain gun atop the joint light tactical vehicle similar to what he had felt rock the station.

    Bini saw his brother and ran to embrace him. He began to inquire as to how he got free. Reading his mind, Keke pointed to Marshawn. When Bini last saw their classmate, he was at home with Nova-sitting duties.

    The four of them squeezed into the backseat of the truck and Jenna sped off.

Chapter 31

Agent Swain stood beside the hospital bed in the ICU. His partner was connected to a multitude of apparatuses. The man's left arm was surgically re-attached. His left ear had been blown off. The left side of his face was bandaged. The extent to which he might recover was still unknown.

Agent Swain had done the best he could on scene, but it was not enough. When the boy Ethan aimed the alien device at Agent Smarten, Rick was able to tug his partner partially out of the way of the blast. However, it was not enough to save him. The weapon was sonic in nature. Its pulse was powerful, but it did not have a long range. That contributed to Agent Smarten not being flayed like the police officers who had been hit with a direct blast. Brian was not unscathed.

The boy Ethan appeared to be the leader of these Slaver Zombies. He was the only one of them who possessed a weapon of alien technology that they had encountered. Agent Bush did not see the weapon when she had encountered him at the school nor at the comic bookstore. This led Swain to believe that he was in recent contact with these Wryvyn. It was still possible that he had the weapon all along but didn't use it yet, but that seemed entirely unlikely.

It was alarming to Agent Swain the extent to which the numbers of infected had grown. The arrival of the aliens, both the Wryvyn and this Nova, happened weeks ago. Those who went missing went unseen for weeks. If the numbers that he saw at the station had all gone missing around that same time, then there would have been a much larger concern.

At the station, the military personnel had a tough time putting them down. If it had not been for the chain gun, he, Agent Bush, and Kameka would have been killed by the alien zombies as well.

Gently, Agent Swain patted the reattached shoulder of his partner and headed out into the hallway. He took a seat, cradled his weary head in his hands and fell asleep with his grief.

"Agent Swain."

Rick had no idea if he had been asleep for thirty seconds or thirty minutes. He gazed up into the eyes of a nurse. She was dark skinned, early forties, extremely kind eyes.

"Mrs. Wallace?"

"Where is my son, Agent Swain?"

"I am not sure, ma'am."

"You and your partner took my son into custody. You had him locked up in a cell in the station. His brother went there with his friends to try and get him out. They were told that you were holding him for questioning."

"I was, yes."

"Now, the news is reporting that a mob attacked the station, your partner is here in critical condition, the cops are dead, and the military was involved. Was my son killed."

Rick Swain appreciated the directness of the boy's mother.

"You have a special boy. He escaped. I saw him leave with my own two eyes. Both your boys. They got away."

The woman sat down next to him; her arms crossed in her lap. Relief washed over Louise to know that her boys had gotten to safety.

"Is this all really happening?" The nurse's voice was strained, her tone weary.

"Unfortunately, yes. It all is happening."

Louise nodded.

"An alien from outer space came to Earth. It wasn't some crazy alcoholic yahoo in the country who first identified them. It was an astrophysics student in Hawai'i. A second ship with different aliens chased it here. The first ship crash landed in Lake Ontario. The second one brought a species of creatures with the ability to mind control humans with some Slaver Zombie Virus. Somehow your boy is caught up in the middle and the key to all this and my partner had his arm blown off by some alien weapon. A weapon that had he been any closer would have split him down the middle like a hot dog left in the microwave too long. Every single insane moment of it. It's really happening."

Louise stared at the agent with sympathetic eyes. His face was dirty. His shirt bloodied from cradling his wounded partner before being overrun by mind-controlled civilians. He stared ahead at the blank wall, speaking with monotone sullen speech. Louise could relate to the man. Watching for her boy on the news and not knowing whether he was among the casualties was draining. It was a relief to her that her boys were together. They always did best when together. Still, they weren't quite out of the woods just yet.

***

Keke awakened outside. Lying flat on his back, gazing up at the stars, he became aware of being outside. There was a clearing in the gray cloud cover which surprised Keke because he could see the stars a moment ago. Nonetheless, the cloud break exposed two brilliant gas balls off in the distance. Unlike on Earth, the atmosphere's argon concentration made the sky a gentle violet.

The ground beneath his feet was a wavy sandstone. He could feel its grooves under the pads of his bare feet. One of the stars was a blue giant. Keke knew it was a blue giant but the ball in the sky was not blue. It was a brilliant white. The other a blue dwarf. The blue dwarf was bright blue. The dwarf star was on the verge of becoming a white dwarf, in another millennium or so. The rate at which the hydrogen was burning off generated the color. In just over a thousand years, there would be just helium left in its core.

This is the information that the Wryvyn had conveyed to the Caerulusians. Only they lied to them about how soon and which star would become a stellar remnant. Keke knew this now. All his people did.

Keke was awestruck by the brilliance of the blue in the dwarf star. He knew that a star of that type was at that moment burning warmer than it had been throughout its system's history. When it transitioned to a remnant it would be cooler.

The stellar temperature did not correlate to the air temperature of the planet. The cloud cover kept the radiation from heating the planet in a manner that would be detrimental to the Caerulusians. Without the clouds they would need shelter for most of the day or risk becoming a living bomb. The temperature was not warm, but it was not cold to his skin. To the contrary, it invigorated him. Keke stood and began to walk, tridactyl feet. There were silvery bits that periodically would glow blue. Keke surmised that there was an element akin to Actinium in the mixture. On Earth, the element is used in cancer treatment and to study the movement of fluids in the ocean. As a solid, Actinium was silvery white. However, it had luminescent properties which caused it to glow in the dark, similar to zinc oxide.

The sky above Keke looked like the Waitomo caves in New Zealand. The hydrogen in the air presented a sparkling azure glow. This is what Keke previously believed was the stars. The blue hues made a gentle two-toned rainbow across the horizon as the light from the dual stars collided with the argon molecules in the atmosphere.

Keke walked along the Caeruluziard landscape. Intrinsically, he felt his connection to the others. There were so many of them. Hundreds of thousands of them. He could feel this overwhelmingly warm sense of harmony and peace. It wasn't an emotional sensation. This was something deeper.

Each member of the species welcomed him as he passed them by. He felt them, knew their entire life in an instance. Their experiences. Their travels. Their connections. Keke had only felt anything close to this type of harmony at family reunions. However, this was less hyperbolic than aunties and uncles at the reunions. This was natural. It was normal. They cared for one another like they cared for themselves. Keke felt peace and warmth in this cold blue world. It was beautiful.

When Keke next woke, he was aboard a Wryvyn ship. There were five of them in the room with him. Their faces weren't smiling, but he could sense that they were elated. The Wryvyn each had an implant that enabled them to communicate with the Caerulusians. It was a device that their scientists developed. They had just told his people that their Blue Giant Star was dying. They told the Caerulusians that the Wryvyn scientists had discovered this, and they have come to warn them. They offered to let them come to their home planet where they can live in an area that the Wryvyn do not inhabit due to the temperature. The Wryvyn require an environment with a warmer climate. Their planet's revolution is such that one side of the planet received minimal exposure. That pole saw none at all.

They convinced some of the naïve creatures to come aboard their ship and travel back to their planet as emissaries. Keke was among them. Keke found that before they even arrived on the Wryvyn planet, he was strapped down to a table. He couldn't move anything other than his head. There was a Wryvyn in a chamber beside him. Keke was attached to a Wryvyn machine. There was a silver fluid inside the tubes that ran from a large glass canister to the device beside him. There was a similar machine in the chamber with the Wryvyn.

Keke's heart began to race. The Wryvyn scientist turned on the machine and Keke was struck with extreme pain. When Keke woke, he was drenched in sweat. Four hands pressed him to the bed as he fought to jump up. Tunes and Jenna were there trying to calm him.

"Relax yourself cuz, please settle down." Tunes' voice was less sing songy than usual. His smile was less vibrant.

"Where are we?" Keke fought against their pressure, sitting up, surveying the room.

"Home. You said you were tired. We came up to get you for dinner."

"Dad let you have a girl upstairs?" Keke asked, surprised to see the girl in his room.

"What? Oh, no. She's not a girl. I mean, she's not a girlfriend. Well, she's a friend that's a girl."

"Okay wordsmith, relax." Jenna rubbed the boy's head lovingly. "I think your dad has other things on his mind.

Keke nodded.

The girl stepped down the hallway while Keke changed into dry clothes.

"Keke, are you okay?"

Tunes lowered his voice as he leaned into the bathroom door.

"Yeah, I just had a weird dream."

But Keke knew it wasn't a dream. It was a memory from Nova. Something from his past. It gave Keke a glimpse of what his extraterrestrial friend had been through. He was sad to learn that a creature who came from a place of harmony like he had witnessed Caeruluziard to be, could be visited with such betrayal and manipulation.

Downstairs, Bini, Mac, Anika, and Marshawn had already plated slices and wings. When he saw them approach Mac waved for his son, nephew, and guest to sit as he grabbed more plates from the cupboard. Bini could sense something off about his brother. They had been through a lot in the past few days. Still, he had something weighing on his mind. Their dad had ordered a pie with Keke's favorite topping combination, sausage, peppers, and onions. Tunes reached into the box and slid out two slices to his plate. Keke hadn't touched it.

Keke sensed his brother watching him. Felt his concern. His fear that he would lose the closest person to him in his life. He smiled at Bini. Taking a slice to assuage his worry about him not touching his favorite pizza. To add to the affect, he snatched a carrot stick from Anika's plate to his right. The girl slapped his wrist, bringing a round of laughter to the stressed-out group.

Suddenly, Keke stopped laughing.

"What is it, Keke?"

"Nova."

"Nova?" Mac asked.

"The alien." Marshawn informed.

"He's outside the house." Keke informed.

"He better stay his behind out there too!" Mac exclaimed.

"Where did he go after the jailbreak?" Marshawn asked.

"I'm not sure. He says he discovered a way to get aboard the Wryvyn ship. If we can get their ship he can return to his people."

"We?" Tunes questioned.

"If their ship leaves Earth, then the other Wryvyn won't be able to track it here. He wants to strand the Wryvyn in a cold area, then they will die. They can't survive in temperatures below freezing for more than half a day. With autumn nearing its end, the Wryvyn would not be able to stay on Earth."

"He wants to strand them on Earth?" There was a hint of disgust in Jenna's voice.

"Yes, two days here in the cold and they will die." Keke responded.

"But until those two days of cold, what do we do?" Jenna charged. "Just let them keep taking over humans with their virus!"

"Whoa, whoa. It's not Keke's idea, Jenna." Anika sternly pushed back.

"it's not my plan, but he wants our help."

"Y'all are not getting more involved with this than you already have." Mac asserted. "You are children."

"Teenagers dad." The twins retorted.

"I don't care. There was a military shootout with people mind controlled by aliens and you all were the center of it."

"Well actually, Uncle Mac, only Keke, Anika, and Marshawn were in the shootout. We were safe." Tunes swung his finger around the table as he spoke.

Both twins gave him a look as if to say he should not try to help.

"I forbid you all from participating in this foolishness any further. You are putting yourselves at risk.

"But he deserves a chance to go home. To be with his family." Keke argued.

"That is true, but you kids have been involved way more than you should have been. The military is here now. They can figure out."

After a spirited debate, Keke was forced to tell Nova that he would not be able to assist with his plan.

"I understand Keke Wallace. We have helped one another as much as we can. You made sure I was safe, and I made sure you were safe. I will find the ship and do my best to get home to my people."

"Good luck, Nova."

"Good luck, Ukeke."

Tunes and Bini turned the topic and convinced Mac to let their friends spend the night. Mac argued that they should go home to their parents. Bini doubled down about keeping their friends safe after they just told one of them that they couldn't help him get home to his family.

Triumphant with their negotiation, Marshawn and Bini headed out to grab snacks for the sleep over. Mac called Louise to inform her that their boys were home and that their friends were sleeping over. He had texted her when they arrived, but she did not respond. During their call, Louise conveyed what happened to Agent Smarten and that Agent Swain was there at the hospital watching over him.

Chapter 32

While Bini and Marshawn were out on their provisions run, Agent Bush and Kameka showed up at the house. Mac was quite reluctant to let law enforcement into his home. However, he felt it pertinent to get it done before Louise got off work. She would be tired. Mac didn't wish to stress her any more than she had been today by the news stories and their son's detainment.

Agent Bush informed Mac about Agent Smarten. Mac revealed that he was aware of Agent Smarten's condition. Agent Bush assured him that the military have set up operations and are out in the streets trying to round up the people who had been infected by the alien mind control. She was hopeful that they would have everything handled soon.

Mac expressed his concern that they may have told the military about Keke. Agent Bush assured him that they had not. She and Agent Swain did not believe that Keke posed the same threat as the Wryvyn. For whatever reason, he was able to do incredible things, and this made the Wryvyn want him, but neither she nor Agent Swain saw him as a threat. Both of them actually presumed that the Wryvyn saw him as a connection to Nova and a means to get him within their grasps.

Keke thanked Agent Bush and confided that she should inform the military that the Wryvyn are not good with the cold. He hypothesizes that perhaps their infected zombies may have the same intolerances. Agent Bush stepped outside to have a call to communicate what she learned. Upon hearing this news, Kameka began a search on her chromebook, typing rapidly.

When Agent Bush returned, it was with Marshawn in tow. The boy was out of breath and flustered. Keke immediately noticed his brother's absence.

"Where's Bini?"

"Where's my son?" Mac pushed through expecting that he just couldn't see his eldest boy from where he stood.

"They took him."

"What do you mean?" Tunes chimed from behind his uncle.

Marshawn explained that they decided to run to the market. They could get a better variety of snacks. He was off getting drinks when he heard a commotion. The place was overrun by the Wryvyn zombies. Marshawn was trapped in the back. He expected they would find him back there, but they all vanished. When he went looking for Bini, he saw Brandon and a few others throwing him into a van. He tried to follow but by the time he got to the car they were gone.

"We have to find him." Keke asserted.

"I think you should leave that to us." Agent Bush pressed. "I assure you we will get him back."

"They took him because they thought he was me." Keke's voice cracked. The guilt of knowing his brother was in harm's way because of him weighed heavy on the young man.

Anika stepped forward, placing her left hand on his right shoulder and her right hand on his elbow. Tunes stepped in on the other side, placing his hand on his cousin's other shoulder.

Agent Bush immediately began to make some calls. From her position as a fly on the wall, Kameka observed the teenagers in the room. She could tell that no matter what happened, Keke Wallace planned on rescuing his brother. The boy Marshawn was willing to go along. The guilt of being present when Bini was abducted would drive him toward it. The cousin would be a willing participant. His friend, she may be the most reluctant. Still, Mr. Wallace and Agent Bush could give whatever speech they wanted. At the end of the day, these kids would be out there on the street trying to find their abducted friend. She decided in that moment that she could maybe arm them with a weapon, if she could find a local place to get the materials.

"I have bad news." Agent Bush swiped her screen ending her phone call.

"Did they find my son?" Mac closed the distance between himself and the agent.

"No. But that was the lieutenant in charge of this area. He received a report of a mob of those Wryvyn zombies approaching the neighbor. My guess is they are heading here. We need to leave now."

She turned to open the door and Keke stopped her.

"I'm not leaving." Keke held the door shut. "We need to get everyone here to safety. But I can't leave. I need to figure out what they did with my brother. My only lead is that mob of Slaver Freaks."

"Keke I am not letting you stay here and wait for them. You heard the detective. We are leaving."

"Dad, I can't. He's my brother."

"Agent Bush and the military can get your brother back. We first have to ensure the safety of all your friends. Understand me?"

"I do." Keke turned to face his friends. "You all have to leave. Go with Agent Bush. Get to safety before that mob gets here."

"We're a team, Keke." Anika and Marshawn protested.

"I'm family." Tunes added.

"You aren't staying, son." Mac repeated.

The debate ensued. In the end, Keke was able to convince his friends to leave. Agent Bush aided when she informed them that the military were on their way. Despite this, Keke refused to leave the home. There was a tense moment where he and his father had come to an impasse where neither would back down. They were running out of time. Kameka suggested that Mac and Agent Bush stay with him. Noting the attempt to resolve the situation, Agent Bush cosigned the idea. She hoped that the military arrived before the mob.

They had no such luck. Three minutes after the kids and Kameka left, more than a dozen people were standing outside the home at Eight Springfield Drive. A few minutes later, there were twice as many of them. Standing in the middle of the road, was Ethan. The boy had the Wryvyn weapon in his hands.

Mac ran upstairs to his bedroom and pulled a rifle and a box of shells out of his closet. Not one to leave her partner alone, Agent Bush followed him halfway up. She didn't take her eye off the door while instructing him to stay clear of the windows.

Keke stood in the living room; eyes closed.

Agent Bush would have taken that to mean he was afraid. However, she saw the boy in action. He had been able to take down multiple of the infected people that he called Slaver Freaks. He was brave. He wasn't arrogant. He acted with compassion despite his ability. Even when he learned his brother was taken and the mob was on their way. Keke protected everyone. She saw those characteristics in his father and her mother when she first met them.

Through the windows atop the door, Dawn saw Ethan approaching. He pointed the weapon at the house. Dawn lunged over the railing and onto the couch as the sound of a dull gong rang out. The heavy wooden door splintered. Agent Bush rolled off the couch and scrambled to the hallway for cover. Keke lunged to the hallway with her. The sound of Mac's rifle alerted them that the Wryvyn zombies had rushed in.

Keke could tell by the manner in which the bodies fell, Mac didn't need to be told to aim for the head. He dropped five of them. Keke could feel his fear as he reloaded as quickly as possible. The boy moved out into the living room to distract the zombies. He reached into his jacket pocket and pulled out an ice mold that he pulled from the freezer. He threw the mold at the next person through the door and hit the right side of the woman's face. She collapsed in front of the door. Two more fell over her. Agent Bush took out the next two who rushed through the door. Keke followed suit, with a three fast pitched hardballs. They all hit home, adding to the pile of bodies.

Once again, Keke senses Mack's fear as two of the zombies scrambled up the stairs. Mack shot the first one of them point blank sending them both stumbling back down. Mac retreated down the hallway to his bedroom. Two more stepped past the falling bodies in pursuit of the history teacher. Keke heard his father firing shots from upstairs. He charged forward charging his fists blue. Keke rained punches, but the numbers were too many to allow him to get up the stairs. The gong sounded once more. The bottom few stairs cracked as the sonic blast collided with them. The blast tore off the legs of a zombie who was trapped beneath the fallen ones. Keke lunged behind the love seat to avoid the blast.

Agent Bush aimed at the boy with the alien weapon. She squeezed the trigger twice, emptying the magazine hitting the head and shoulder of one of the mob members who ran in in front of him. Ethan raised his arm toward Agent Bush. The Wryvyn weapon would annihilate her at that distance. Keke grabbed the arm and hip of a charging zombie spinning and tossing the elderly man into Agent Bush just as the gong sounded. The force of the collision knocked her into the pantry. The blast hit the thrown man and his body split in two. The fallen agent made an 'X' with her arms to shield her face from the splattered blood and skin that plastered her overcoat. Keke charged the boy who wielded the sonic weapon and tackled him out the front door. The zombies in the house didn't notice their target was outside and continue toward Agent Bush and Mac.

Out on the lawn, Keke unleashed a flurry of blows on Ethan. The boy swung the Wryvyn weapon at Keke. The force of the blow sent Keke rolling off. The weapon had more to it than Keke expected. As he got to his feet, Keke saw that more zombies were marching up the road. He roundhouse kicked one in the midsection as it came running toward him. Ethan ran at the distracted boy, tackling him to the ground. Keke saw that the zombies had stopped running in the house and were returning toward him and Ethan. He had to get free before they overpowered him.

Keke grabbed the zombie weapon. He noted that there was a sinewy coil that wound out of the weapon that was wrapped around the boy's wrist. He grabbed the length of living material and tugged as hard as he could. The gong sounded once but it was more abrupt than before. The sonic wave hit those zombies charging in, slicing them but it did not split them. Ethan struggled to wrench the weapon from Keke's grip. Keke's free hand lit up as he arced a haymaker at the gas station attendant.

A convoy of military vehicles weaved through the quiet residential neighborhood. There were people out along Springfield Drive watching the swarm of Wryvyn Zombies attack the new family's home. The convoy rounded the bend just as a brilliant flash lit up the dark cul de sac. Blinded by the light, the driver of the first vehicle screeched to a halt. The gunman atop the light armored vehicle could only make out the silhouette of a figure sprinting between the houses. The remaining mob of people followed. Unable to open fire in the close residential confines, the leader of the convoy commanded his driver to take up position in front of the house where the commotion had occurred. He split his convoy sending the second half back out to the main road in search of the fleeing mob.

As Keke had expected, his departure led to a pursuit by Ethan and his zombie mob. This ensured that his dad would be safe. The military convoy could clean up whatever stragglers remained. The Slavers didn't tire like normal humans, so they did not give up pursuit. Keke was much faster than them before he had been bestowed with some of Nova's abilities. Now, he was able to pace himself and establish a growing lead over them. He made sure they followed him out of the neighborhood before taking off on them. Before he took off running, he charged his fist and punched Ethan in the chest. The boy tried to deflect with his arm but only served to put the alien weapon in the path of the mighty blow. The weapon shattered sending pitch black shards across the lawn.

Keke stopped running when he arrived at the wooden bridge where he first met Nova. He slowed to a walk. Unlike their first encounter, well the first that Keke recalled, the night was quiet. There were no Gnat Catchers calling. There were no field crickets chirping. However, just like that night which seemed like a lifetime ago. Keke could sense the presence of another entity. Keke walked toward the diamond-shaped center of the walk. His eyesight was now enhanced. Despite the lack of sunlight, he could see the creatures outline, vivid against the texture of the tree behind which it stood. Like before, Keke sensed wonder in the creature. However, this time, there was a hint of trepidation, a touch of caution. This sensation from the creature seemed entirely alien.

"I know you are there. I can see you."

"You are starting to read my thoughts. Soon Keke Wallace you will be able to communicate with your kind like I do with mine."

The information distracted Keke for only a moment.

"I need your help." Keke asserted.

"They have taken your brother. They believe that Ubini is you."

"Yes."

"They will bring him to the Wryvyn ship."

Keke marched up the stairs, standing face to no face with the creature.

"Nova, we have to get him back."

"If you do not, they will take him to experiment, and it will be I who is stranded here. Unless they figure out that he is not you."

"I have to get him from the Wryvyn's minions before they deliver him to the Wryvyn. Please, help me." Keke pleaded with the shimmering figure.

"I cannot while they have the weapon. It is dangerous. I am *afraid.*"

"I destroyed it."

Nova materialized before him. Keke could read his emotions. There was a degree of relief within the Caerulusian.

"They may have more."

A crack of a twig in the distance alerted both of them to a foreign presence. Keke and the alien creature listened intently for other sounds. The hoot of an owl filled the night. The waning moonlight that had done little to illuminate their meeting spot became hidden behind a cloud. Nova gazed upward toward the darkened sky. A hum as though from an electric generator resonated above them. The treetops began to rustle. The dark object above them betrayed not a glimmer or a glint as it blocked out the light from the night sky.

More twigs snapped. Branches creaked as they were broken off. The night echoed with thuds, sounding like a cattle stampede getting started.

"The Wryvyn are here."

Keke and Nova ran down the trail. The blue bodied alien didn't bother to shimmer out of sight. He just set a breakneck pace that challenged Keke's ability to keep up. Despite their speed the thudding grew louder. Keke suddenly realized that the thudding was in stereo. He nearly ran into the back of Nova sending the two of them tumbling over the edge into the falls when the Caerulusian abruptly slowed to a standstill. Ahead of him on the trail and to their right in the woods loomed three of the most incredibly hideous creatures Keke had ever seen.

Chapter 33

Keke sized up the creatures surrounding him. Each of the aliens stood eight feet tall. They made Nova look short by comparison. Their skin tone was a dull, obsidian black. If Keke's eyesight hadn't been enhanced, he would not have been able to discern them in the darkness. Unlike Nova, the creatures had round eyes with cartilaginous lids. Their mouths were the only other orifice on their face. They had no nose or ears that Keke could distinguish. The pearl white teeth inside the gaping hole that was their mouth were a contrast to the rest of the body. They were incredibly long, narrow, and pointy.

Their legs were abnormally thick. Well abnormal for what Keke would expect for a creature that size. The muscles in the lower half spiraled around the legs. There were no identifiable joints or bisections. Keke presumed they had the same flexibility and maneuverability as the tentacle arms of Doctor Otto Octavius. Unlike the legs, the arms were proportionate to what Keke would expect. Both arms and the spine had cartilaginous spikes protruding from them. The tips of the spikes were a slight contrast to the black bodied Wryvyn. They were a deep indigo. However, on the Wryvyn body it represented a vivid hue. Each one of them wore some type of protective armor that was only visible at the metallic gray seams where it wrapped under their arms and around their shoulders and waist.

Keke was busy cataloging the Wryvyn features. It was all he could do to calm his nerves. The Slaver Zombies were just people with enhanced abilities, like him, only not as strong. The Wryvyn were ferocious looking behemoths that if not for their thunderous footfalls, could sneak up on a man in the dark. They were abnormally fast. Their technology spoke to genius level intellect. Their one weakness was cold, and the temperature was dropping. That one element gave Keke hope of surviving this encounter.

One stepped forward startling Keke to the point where he took a defensive stance. The alien said no words, but Keke presumed it was using the device on its neck to communicate with Nova.

"Come back with us. Allow us to continue the research."

"You will kill me. You tried once to drain my life fluid."

"We have made advancements. We can correct the error. We know that your abilities can be transferred. That is the logical conclusion from this Earth human being able to be different from the rest."

"That is the nature of the human. Some of them are not like others."

"Do not attempt to deceive us, *Caerulusian*. We have studied the technology of this species. It is primitive. Their weapons do not even have the sophistication of those used by our younglings. Somehow, you have helped them to enhance this one of them. It is bizarre that a parasite would be the alpha species of a planet. They are incapable of this type of scientific prowess. Why would you do this for this human and not the Wryvyn?"

Keke fought his flight sensors as he stood alone in the dark woods with five extraterrestrial beings. Four of those beings were worse than any horror movie he'd seen. The only thing keeping him from running was that their zombie minions kidnapped his brother. With any luck and an incredible amount of bravery, he could follow them, and they would lead him to Bini. He just hoped he didn't get himself killed in the process.

Keke became aware of a rumbling noise behind him. The Wryvyn who had chased him and Nova through the woods was growling impatiently. One of the others fiddled with a device on his arm and began to grumble back at him. The first Wryvyn mimicked the action with the wrist device. Perhaps it was the weariness of fighting a gang of zombies twice and then being chased through the woods by goliath aliens, but Keke could have sworn that he heard them speaking Spanish. Watching the massive mandible on the obsidian behemoth bounce up and down as their vicious grunts morphed into the romance language from the Iberian Peninsula. Keke made out *hablar*, *parásito*, and *frio*.

A few more adjustments and they were speaking English.

"It is unnecessary for these parasites to use so many languages. They are one species. They have the medium to travel across their planet. They have communication technology. More than one language is unnecessary. They should focus on technology to alter their cold climate."

"We didn't have technology when our language was created. Our people were nomadic and tribal for 100,000 years."

Recognizing that they had finally selected the proper language in their module, the black beasts spoke to Keke.

"Earth Human. This *Caerulusian* is not an ally."

"Why did you say Caerulusian like that?"

The Wryvyn smirked but gave no further response.

"Nova saved my life. A few times."

"You named the Betrayer?" The Wryvyn growled.

"Betrayer? You told his people you were there to help them and then you experimented on them."

"His people?"

The two massive creatures roared heads turned upward to the sky. The dreadful noise frightened Keke. It made them look much more ferocious. It sounded like the gears in a clock tower being crushed as they spun. When they stopped the creature approached Keke. The boy took a few steps backward, but he was at the cliff face and couldn't escape further.

"We are leaving here with the *Caerulusian*, or we are leaving here with you Earth human. We understand that he helped you to develop abilities. Either of you will suffice for our needs. Which choice do you believe he is going to make when offered?"

Nova was unaware that the Wryvyn were using the device on their arm to communicate with Keke. He was busy trying to persuade his Wryvyn that he had no idea as to how Keke was able to have enhanced abilities beyond that of a normal human.

"The decision appears obvious, human. Your kind is a parasite upon this planet. In our limited observation, we have witnessed humans as they usurp your Earth's resources and dismantle the flora which are meant to support the stasis of your planet. Your species is selfish. Destructive. You want to save yourself and protect your kind. That is your species nature. Now stand aside and let us take him."

Keke was angry at the characterization of his race by these savage creatures. From what Nova told him, their species was incredibly manipulative and selfish. They had used the threat of the destruction of their world to get the Caerulusians to go along with them. Then they tied them down and experimented on them. The human race was far from perfect. However, the Wryvyn lived in a glass house and were hurling boulders.

The anger helped Keke. It quelled his fear. Gave him clarity. That clarity brought confusion. Keke found it peculiar that these monsters care about the horrors of the human race given the abominable and odious acts he had been told they've committed. But the confusing part was that they asked him to stand aside? There were four of them. They were massive. They could take Keke and Nova to their ship, and it seemed obvious that neither of them could do anything about it. Or was it? He thought perhaps the cold temperature diminished their strength. If that was the case, how much so?

The more Keke thought about it, the more enhanced his calm became. Time began to slow down. He began to understand Peter Parker's Spidey sense. For the first time he truly saw them. He originally took their positioning as tactical. They were blocking his ability to flee up the two adjoining paths. The third and fourth were in front of Nova blocking the trail where the two paths converged and ran down along the falls. Keke turned to the two blocking the trail. The one who wasn't talking, or at least not gesturing, seemed uncomfortable. Keke noted that the alien kept looking over at him. This wasn't vigilance. This was wariness. He was checking Keke's position. Ensuring he knew where he was at all times. It occurred to Keke that perhaps his arrival was not expected. Maybe they came for Nova but upon discovering Keke's presence, they took up positions to ensure their own path of egress should Nova and Keke choose to fight.

To test his theory Keke casually shuffled a few paces toward the closest of the two Wryvyn, holding out a hand before him for dramatic effect. The creature was not expecting the approach and clumsily retreated.

"What are you doing, human?" There was less gruff in the creature's voice.

Why were these behemoths afraid of him?

Keke would not get a conclusion on his hypothesis as a sudden movement caught the three of their attention.

"We must flee, Ukeke Wallace."

Keke watched as Nova sprung from the trail over the side of the cliff toward the pool at the base of the falls. His heart raced as he was now alone with four alien monsters. Knowing he needed to make a split decision Keke super-kicked the nearby Wryvyn, the entirety of his leg turned blue. The Wryvyn tumbled up the trail roaring as he flipped. Keke used the moment of the kick to follow his friend, jumping from the ledge free-falling into the icy water.

When the boy leapt from the trail he felt a slimy tentacle latch onto his arm. The grey and red appendage tugged at his forearm as it wrapped itself from his wrist to his elbow. Keke snatched at the bulbous head, wrenching it free of his forearm with a vicious tug as he spun through the night air plummeting to an uncomfortable splash. Keke swam to the side of the pool opposite of where the Wryvyn had been. He felt like he had just done a cryo freeze. His entire body temperature had dropped significantly. Across the stream, the Wryvyn ran along looking for him and Nova. He wasn't sure if it was the dark or the distance, but they didn't notice him as they surveyed the area. After a moment, they returned up the trail where there was a reverberation, followed by a swoosh. Keke watched as the massive creatures flew off on round discs.

Ignoring the cold, Keke ran home to find his block swarming with soldiers. Anika and Marshawn had been driving around looking for him in his neighborhood. They never truly left when Keke told them they should. Anika convinced Marshawn that he was going to need their help. Anika had been right. If Keke tried to get back to the house, the military would surely detain him.

Anika and Marshawn were unsure where he went after the convoy rolled in. They just knew that he had fled the scene and all the Slaver Zombies had chased him Rather than drive about aimlessly, they figured that at some point he would come back for his dad.

When they saw him jogging up the road, both of his friends sighed in relief. Anika and Marshawn were concerned seeing Keke soaked to the bone. As soon as

Keke was in the car, Marshawn cranked the heat and Keke changed into some sweats and a hoodie that were in Marshawn's gym bag. Marshawn informed Keke that his dad left with Agent Bush. Jenna and Tunes took Kameka back to her hotel.

Marshawn's phone buzzed in his pocket. The boy answered it and passed it to Keke.

"Hello?"

"Ready or not, here I come you can't hide…"

"Tunes what the hell are you talking about?" Keke was without patience for his cousin's shenanigans.

"I figured out how to find Bini. Ouch. We figured out how to find Bini. Quit it. Okay Kameka had an idea, and we know where Bini is being held."

"So do I."

"You do? Is it the steroids? Ouch. Stop hitting me, Jenna. I meant the powers. Is it the powers?"

"Yes."

"Meet us there." Keke pulled the phone away from his face.

"Wait, there's more. Kameka figured out a way to create a weapon that we can use against the aliens. We didn't have much to work with, but it will be something." Tunes couldn't help but sound excited.

"What do we need?" Keke inquired.

"We got everything. This chick is a… ouch! This lady is a genius. Like that guy on that TV show that Uncle Mac likes. The old one where he fixes things and makes tools out of everyday objects."

"MacGyver?" Keke proposed.

"Yeah. That guy. She's like MacGyver."

"You have his location now?" Keke asks.

"We do." Tunes confirmed.

"Meet us there." With that Keke hung up the phone.

On the drive over Keke relayed what happened at the house and then in the woods with Nova and the Wryvyn. Keke's description of the Wryvyn made Anika's skin crawl. She hated horror movies and now felt as though she was living in one. They were stunned to learn that the Wryvyn had developed a device that could communicate with them. When Keke conveyed that the Wryvyn referred to humans as a parasite, Marshawn sucked his teeth, but Anika nodded her understanding. When the boys cocked their heads like her pet rottweiler, she explained that technically humans were the only species that operate in a manner that harms the planet. They overuse resources and find new ways to overuse them as time goes by. The boys considered her explanation and found that it did make sense. Keke explained that the Wryvyn had stated something similar. It did not comfort the girl to be of like mind with them.

Twenty-five minutes later, the three of them found themselves impeded from making their rendezvous point by a military blockade. The soldiers forced them to turn back and gave no reason other than they had restricted the area. They were forced to turn back much to their dismay.

They decided that it would be best to make their way through the woods on foot. Keke wanted to go alone. His enhanced sight meant that he could easily navigate the woods without a flashlight, and he could move swiftly. Both Anika and Marshawn protested.

When Jenna and Tunes arrived, Kameka was with them. After hearing that the Wryvyn didn't like the cold, she had come up with an idea to rig refrigerant tanks with IBC hoses. This would allow them to spray the creatures with the tetrafluroethane inside. She fastened funnels to the end of the hose to focus the spray. On the way to meet up, she had rigged up the backpacks with the tanks inside to allow for the hose to poke out. Kameka used Velcro strips to attach the intermediate bulk container hose to the outside of a wristband. The hose was attached to the tanks at the other end. The wristband apparatus allowed them to keep the spray gun close to their hand and not have it fall to the ground if for some reason they had to turn and run. Tunes put a backpack on. He peacocked his chest a bit. He loved it because the backpack made him feel like a Ghostbuster. There were two other set ups which Marshawn and Anika shrugged on, adjusting the straps to a tight fit.

After getting the lowdown on the cold guns that Kameka had devised, Keke told the story of what happened to Tunes, Jenna, and Kameka. Like when he told the story to Marshawn and Anika, the boy left out that he thought they were afraid of him because he hadn't quite rooted out the exact reason why.

Jenna voiced her concerns over Nova disappearing. It came as little surprise to her. She reiterated her belief that they could not trust him and that he is out for himself. Tunes agrees that Nova running out when trouble comes is shady. The others nodded their agreement. Keke did not tell them that the Wryvyn referred to Nova as The Betrayer. Mostly because he didn't understand why they would call a creature they imprisoned a betrayer. He also did not tell them that they said not to trust him. However, in that moment, he was weighing their words.

Keke knew that the zombies were likely holding Bini somewhere just beyond where the roadblock was set up. There was nothing there but woods and an open corn field. They were a quarter mile away from his signal when they got turned back. Their current location where they turned off the road was about a half mile from the signal. Either the Wryvyn didn't realize that Bini's phone had tracking capabilities, or they didn't care. Otherwise, they would have confiscated it, or turned it off, or destroyed it.

Nevertheless, it wouldn't have mattered. Keke didn't need the application from Bini's phone to know where his brother was located. Keke knew that Bini was in the middle of a cornfield. He couldn't tell who else was there, but the closer he got the stronger the connection became. When they were back at the house, it was just a sensation. Now that he was less than a mile Keke could feel his brother's dread. He could smell the rotting stalks from the corn that had been harvested. He could smell the damp high grass that had grown. He could feel the vibrations of the massive spaceship.

He knew that as well as he knew his mother and father were together at a hotel. He could sense them all. The connection the Caerulusians had to one another in his dream was derived from their genetic code. Now, he was connected to his family in the same way. Nova had told him that soon he would be able to communicate with all humans in this manner.

Once they were ready, Keke, Tunes, Marshawn, and Anika headed off through the woods. Keke led the way making a speedy pace. After a few minutes, Marshawn and Anika could not see him. Tunes was twenty yards behind them. Marshawn hissed Keke's name and he slowed to let them catch up. Together the four of them jogged onward through the cold wood. They were hopeful that their rescue mission would be a success. They had no idea who they would encounter on the other end of the wooded jaunt. There was no telling how many of the mind-controlled humans were guarding Bini. As convinced as Tunes was that Kameka was a genius, there was no way to know if her cold guns would affect the zombies. There was no guarantee that they would work on the Wryvyn. With all the unknowns, Keke found it best to let his mind rest and do what he did best. Run.

Chapter 34

Agent Bush and Agent Smarten pulled in behind Marshawn's car twenty minutes after Keke and his friends went running through the woods on their rescue mission. Agent Bush tugged her zipper up a few more inches. The night air had grown frigid. Both agents expressed disappointment in Kameka for helping to develop weapons for teenagers. They both found it irresponsible to enable them in their plight to run off to fight a mob of mind-controlled, physically enhanced individuals. They had encountered them multiple times and needed the assault power of the U.S. Army to defeat them.

Kameka reminded them that Keke Wallace was not easily detained. She added that these kids were going to go after his brother regardless. At minimum, she could give them a potential weapon to protect themselves to make it less of a suicide mission.

Jenna nodded in agreement with Kameka. She had only just met the astrophysicist, but she liked this beautiful, dark-skinned scientist. She didn't stand down to the authority of these agents. Jenna shared her rebellious nature.

Kameka ended her statement of defense by informing the agents that she tried to convince them to let the military handle it. This was sufficient to acquit her of further interrogation for the acts of these other parties.

Jenna and Kameka watched as the two agents loaded up with extra ammunition for the AR-15's they strapped over their shoulders. Even in the dark Kameka could see the weariness in the senior DHS agent. She did not see the hit on Agent Smarten. She wasn't there as Agent Swain dragged him and his severed arm to safety. She didn't get to see his conflict as the zombies closed in and he had to leave his partner's immobile body behind. Once they rounded the block and the military dispersed the zombies, Agent Swain ran back to the corner where his partner's body laid with a rushed tourniquet. Luckily the hospital was less than a mile up the road and the ambulance arrived immediately. Agent Swain rode with his partner to the hospital and sat there while they re-attached his arm and saved his life. She doubted that he slept at all since they left the hotel that morning. Kameka felt exhausted from the part she endured that day. She couldn't imagine what Agent Bush and Agent Swain had endured on top of what they all had experienced together. It was hard to believe that weeks ago she was at the Keck Observatory hassling Bart Messner about being a doormat for Keilani Kim.

Oddly, had he not been doing her research, Kameka would never have noticed the Wryvyn ship speed across the screen, engulfed in flames. Then Bart wouldn't have called his friends to get confirmation. The agents wouldn't have told him to stay put and his cowardice would not have caused him to try to flee. Kameka would be back at Cal Tech sitting in classes and not knowing that an alien species had come here chasing an escaped prisoner. She would not have witnessed the behavior of human beings who were mind-controlled by implanted alien spores. Lastly, she would not have witnessed the abilities of a young boy who had an encounter with an alien from another planet. An encounter that caused him to develop superhuman abilities. Those abilities enabled him to save her life. All the loss of people did not go over her head. Still, this entire experience had been nothing short of incredible thus far.

***

Keke awoke on the Wryvyn planet. He was in a cell similar in size to the one at the police station. The door was a wall of glowing energy. As Keke got close, he could feel the static energy flowing through the electromagnetic field. He dared not touch it.

There were dull blue figures on the floor of the cells around him. Keke recognized them as the other Caerulusians captives. They didn't have their vibrant glow. Each of them was slumped over in the middle of their cells. Dead to the casual observer. However, Keke knew otherwise. The Caerulusians had quickly learned distress and distrust from the Wryvyn deception. It was a shock to their harmonious existence. The sensation the entire race felt when the first of their kind was cut into was harrowing and disorienting. Once the Wryvyn began to experiment on the Caerulusians, the entire race understood their true intentions. Those aboard the ship and those back on their planet in the region where the Wryvyn emissaries were waiting to take more of them away entered into some sort of thanatosis. Had Keke not been connected to them all genetically, he would have thought they were dead. However, he could feel each one of them. Nearly the entire species entered the state to prevent the Wryvyn from performing more experiments on them. In this state, their minds were calm. Their thoughts were of their world. The thanatosis hardened their thoracic cavity and their dermal layer. The Wryvyn found it impossible to penetrate the hardened bodies despite their sophisticated technology. Thus, their experimentation was halted. This action was akin to a turtle disappearing inside its shell. Except that shell was as hard as diamond.

Keke knew that his captors, these Wryvyn, were jealous of his kind. They believe that the Caerulusians were selfishly withholding the secrets of their abilities from the Wryvyn. Keke found it ironic because they were trying to steal the abilities of the Caerulusians under false pretense in order to use that power to conquer other worlds. The Wryvyn scientists attempted to reverse engineer the ability in the Caerulusian genetic makeup. Their hope was that this procedure would enable them to take on the power of the species they interact with. However, the Caerulusians caught on and entered their hibernation state which shuts off their abilities and access to their genetic material.

Keke noticed two Wryvyn enter the outer corridor between the cells. When they noticed Keke on his feet, they began to grin. In the light, Keke could see that the vile appearance was much more horrifying than they had been in the dark woods.

To Keke's surprise, the Wryvyn opened Keke's cell and stepped back. Confused by this but not wishing to be locked away any longer, he exited the cell standing before these two horrific giants. Keke watched as the mouths of the monsters moved about. Both of them stared at one another, adjusted a device on their neck that appeared to attach to their brainstem, if they have brainstems. Moments later he could hear their voices in his head like when he was with Nova.

"How do you feel brother." One Wryvyn on the left asks?"

Keke says nothing, but he thinks, 'what the heck are you talking about?'

"Your state of well-being. You have been asleep for many hours."

Again, Keke said nothing, but this time, he also thought nothing because he was unsure what was happening. In the back of his mind, deep in his subconscious it seemed, were a hundred voices telling him things. In the beginning, it was a buzzing, jumbled mess. After a moment he is able to sift through it all. The understanding washed over him. The two Wryvyn were surprised as he ran out of the chamber.

The voices in Keke's head were his people, telling him how to escape. Describing the layout of the ship from their experience. If they were not in stasis, Keke would already have known via his connection. Still, the Caerulusians directed him toward the smaller vessels. The Wryvyn chased him calling out for him to stop and let them help him. Keke knew they were being deceptive. However, he was impressed by how they made the concern in their thoughts seem genuine. Keke turned a corner and a bulky hand grabbed at him.

"Brother, please." The Wryvyn begged.

Keke's entire body began to glow as he pulled himself free of the grip snapping a few of the Wryvyn phalanges in the process. Around the next corridor two more beasts blocked his path. Oddly, they tossed down their weapons and tried to reason with him. They told him that it was important that they replicate the experiment. Keke was having none of that. He was through being a lab specimen for these vicious beasts.

Keke leaped over the two hulking Wryvyn landing just before the door to the terminal space dock. Keke shut the door with the panel, entered a code that he didn't understand how he knew, locking the door to the hangar. Keke turned and saw himself in the metallic surface of a crate. There he was, shining blue. He became aware of something tight around his neck. In the reflection, he could see that it was one of the devices the Wryvyn used to communicate with the Caerulusians.

Keke shuddered as he was awakened by a strike. The force of the blow tipped him. He had to fight against gravity to keep from hitting the ground. His jacket scraped against the rough bark of the tree behind him, threatening to rip the polyester exterior. Beside him, Marshawn was sitting on the ground. Both their hands were zip tied behind their backs. Keke looks around to see Brandon and five other zombies standing over them. Brandon had an odd weapon in his hand. It was not the same as the one that Ethan had used at the station and their house. This one was metallic grey. He recalled seeing them on the hips of the Wryvyn in his vision from the ship.

Upon surveying the area, he realized that Anika and Tunes were missing. Keke gazed at Marshawn with wide eyes. The boy read his concern and nodded back over his shoulder. Keke took this to mean their friends had escaped.

"We found the wrong boy. Now we have the right boy. You will come with us."

Brandon's tone was even. His face was expressionless. Keke knew that the wrist restraints could not hold him. Still, he was unsure of what the weapon Brandon wielded was capable of doing. He would take the chance had he been alone. However, Marshawn could not get loose as easily as Keke. Keke knew that it would be impossible for him to free himself, free Marshawn, wrestle the weapon away from Brandon and fend off the other four mind-controlled zombies with him. He needed to buy more time.

"You will come with us." The boy repeated.

"Give me a minute. I feel dizzy." It wasn't all lies. Keke felt a throbbing on his temple where he had fallen and hit his head. "What did you do to my head."

"We did nothing with your head." Brandon replied robotically.

Like in the vision he had, a voice from deep inside welled up. Like in the vision, it was muffled at first, unintelligible. However, since there was only one it welled up quickly to the surface like a geyser erupting.

"Brother! Where are you?"

"I'm here Bini. In the woods with Marshawn."

"Are you coming to get me?"

"Brandon has us tied up. Just for the moment."

"Can you escape? I'm scared. These monsters have me. Brandon used some sonic weapon on me, but not like the one from the jail. It was like a shockwave through the air that knocked me out. One minute I was in the grocery store and the next I was here in this field."

"I am on my way, Bini. I promise."

"Please, hurry. I don't want them to bring me on their ship. It is a black dreadnought. Blacker than these creatures. And they are really, really black."

"I know. I've seen them. Help is on the way, brother."

There was a rustle in the woods that sounded like something running across the leafy ground. Brandon gestured to two of the slaver zombies who went to investigate. A moment later there was a second rustling in the other direction. Another gesture, and a third zombie went off to investigate the second rustling noise. Next, there was motion from the first direction. The object was close enough for Keke to see that it was a human jogging crouched through the woods.

"Take us to the ship. I am ready." Keke demanded. The boy was busy scanning for whatever made the noise.

While his back was turned Keke popped off his restraints. When the boy finally turned back to his captives, he found they were no longer there. He marched forward until he was beyond the nearest tree. He glanced down at the cold forest floor expecting to see his captives cowering there. A moment later he heard a thump behind him in the small clearing where he had been holding Keke and Marshawn.

Returning, Brandon found that the Latino man that had been with him was lying unconscious on the ground. There was another rustling of leaves and a few snapping twigs. He turned to see Tunes running toward him. Before Brandon could react, he received an icy blast to the face. The boy breathed in the refrigerant as the cloud enshrouded his head. The spores inside him ejected from his body through his nose and mouth. The boy convulsed momentarily and then fell still.

Not expecting the reaction, Keke who had been crouching behind a stone turned to his cousin.

"The other one did the same thing."

"Mine did too." Anika approached from the darkness of the night.

Noticing the absence of one of their friends, Anika began to worry.

"Where…?"

Before she could get the words out, Keke pointed up towards an overhanging branch. Anika and Tunes tilted their necks back to see Marshawn clinging to the twenty-foot-high branch for dear life.

"When they see me, they be like, there he go!" Tunes chirped.

"You know Marshawn is afraid of heights, right?" Anika asked.

Keke squatted, his eyes lit up like they had when he showed Bini and Tunes his abilities. Tunes waved for Anika to step back. With impossible agility, Keke sprung up, grabbing Marshawn by the waist as he flipped over the branch. Both boys landed feet-first on the ground, Keke steadying Marshawn as he swayed. The boy covered his mouth momentarily before tugging free of Keke's grasp to lean forward spilling his dinner on the fauna.

"Do you think that they are dead?" Anika pointed the business end of her refrigerant weapon at Brandon before waving it around in a circle indicating the others that she and Tunes dispatched in the woods.

Keke knelt beside Brandon checking his pulse. The boy shook his head.

"He's alive."

"Boy, Me and Anika took them out. They didn't know what happened. You like how we were like 'drop that body to the flo'. Let me see you get low."

He ended the song by spraying the face of the Latino man that Keke had dispatched with a punch. Like Brandon, the spores crawled from the man's mouth and nostrils.

"Come on. We have to go save Bini. I should warn you all. The Wryvyn have him."

Tunes tapped the funnel end of his weapon in his palm.

"They can say hello to my little friend."

"Keep that same energy when you see these monsters. But seriously, we have to focus. If there are any more of these weapons or the one that Ethan had at the house, I won't be able to fight them all off. If it comes to it, you all need to run."

"We're a team, plus Tunes." Anika said.

The boy turned his head as though to ask why he was catching strays.

Chapter 35

When Agent Bush and Agent Swain found them, Keke and his friends were huddled behind a rolled hay bail. Approximately fifty yards away was the massive Wryvyn ship. The colossal vessel was the size of a cruise ship. It encompassed most of the clearing. Keke found that his brother was spot on when he called it a dreadnought. It did indeed resemble the Madalorian heavy class cruiser. Keke felt the design was a bit closer to the Battlestar Pegasus but on the larger scale of a dreadnought.

Two Wryvyn were standing in the clearing. In front of them was a larger version of the weapon that Ethan had wielded. Keke was certain that this massive device that looked like an anti-tank gun with a wider barrel and a pedestal would do greater damage than the smaller prototype.

In front of the weapon were two dozen Wryvyn mind control zombies. Out in front was Ethan. Beside him Ridgefield, Davis, Ritchie, and the couple from the school. Bini was tied up near the entrance to the ship. There was a light from inside illuminating the boy. From this close, Keke could see the fear in his eyes. Even if he hadn't been able to see it, he could feel it. He could read his brother's thoughts. That was how he knew that there were at least thirty military vehicles and close to seventy soldiers positioned along the roadway at the edge of the clearing awaiting their orders. z

"How is your partner, Agent Swain?" Keke asked without turning.

The other three turned to see the two agents creeping up to their position. Both had pistols in hand and rifle slung over shoulder.

"Whoop, whoop it's the sound of the police!" Tunes sang a bit too loud for his companions' liking.

Anika quickly peeked around the bail to see if the others had heard. She couldn't see but Keke saw Bini turn his head. None of the others seemed to notice or if they did, they didn't care.

"Bini said to ask you, why do you always have to be so extra, cousin?"

Agent Bush and Agent Swain shared a look but didn't ask the obvious question they both had.

Agent Swain gave Keke a report on his partner's condition and thanked him for his concern.

"Your mother is worried as well. That is why I am here. Last I spoke to her I promised her that both her boys were safe. It appears that I now have to take measures to ensure that my word stands."

"What do you mean?" Keke asked.

"I mean go home, Mr. Wallace. You and your friends. I will ensure your brother is safe."

"I..." Agent Bush began to protest but the man had already began walking toward the Wryvyn ship.

The FBI Agent began to pursue her DHS partner when Keke grabbed her arm. With a finger he pointed to the tree line where other Wryvyn zombies were marching out of the woods in the direction of the ship. It would not be long before Agent Swain was in their sights. Keke pulled her back behind the bail before running and lunging for Agent Swain. Keke covered the man's mouth as they fell in a thud into the frosty high grass.

"There are more coming." The boy whispered.

The startled agent took a few excited breaths, the boy's words taking a few additional moments to register just who had grabbed him and why he was on the ground. After a short panic, he nodded.

As they laid there waiting for the zombies to pass, Keke felt the presence of Nova on the other side of the clearing. He was making his way toward the Wryvyn ship.

"Nova, what are you doing?"

"I am going to steal the Wryvyn ship and return to my home. I stole a human device from a *base* and some *components* from a factory. These will enable me to enhance the controls of the Wryvyn vessel so that the Wryvyn won't be able to take back control. I am going to connect it to the drive reactor before I board the ship."

"You can't. Some of the Wryvyn are on board."

"I can sneak into the control hub and lock the entrance behind me. The Wryvyn will be forced to leave with me. With the device connected they won't be able to fly the ship on their own."

"But what will you do when you land? They will be waiting for you to leave the ship."

"I have not completed that part of my plan."

"They also have a weapon. It looks like an anti-tank gun."

"Stay away from that weapon. It will obliterate all organic material in its path. Its range is much greater than the one the boy at the jail was using." Nova warned, confirming Keke's fears.

"We can help one another, Nova. If I can get rid of the Wryvyn and their zombies out front, will you rescue my brother before you leave? I can try but they will see me coming. They won't see you. I will be the distraction."

"The people are not zombies, Ukeke Wallace. They are closer to mutants that are mind controlled. The spores the Wryvyn implanted into their bodies are like your parasites that take over the body to enable control and then once control is established it becomes a symbiotic relationship where parts of the host function resumes allowing them to eventually assimilate to the host society."

"We were able to get some of the spores to exit the body. They shriveled up and died. We used blasts of extremely cold gas."

"That was smart. The pheromones will still remain in the human blood stream for a while but will eventually dissipate. From what I know this has never occurred. Usually, the host bodies eventually get to a phase of *controlled parasitism* where the host body all but regains conscious function of their body."

"How do you know so much about Wryvyn?"

"I cannot say. I just know these things." Nova replied cagily.

In that moment, Keke was reminded of his vision aboard the Wryvyn ship. The way that the Wryvyn greeted him. The way that they were surprised when he fled. They had called him brother. Keke realized that these may have been memories from Nova's escape.

Still, something struck Keke as odd. When Nova originally told him about his escape, there were multiple escapees on pods from a ship. In the vision it was only Keke escaping. If the vision was of Nova's experience, then he was the only one to escape. In the vision, Keke stole a ship similar to the one in the clearing. Kameka had told them that she saw the ship enter the Earth's atmosphere. Her description of it fit the ship from the dream and the one in front of him.

Nova had lied to him. Keke just did not know why.

"Nova, will you help me if I can clear the way for you?"

A moment went by. Keke scanned the area but could not see the invisible Caerulusian.

"Nova, please."

"I will help you. I will free Ubini before I board the ship. You will need to clear a path."

Keke pulled his hand away from Agent Swain's mouth.

"Agent, if you really wish to save my brother, help me clear the people away from the ship."

"Just how am I supposed to do that?"

"I have a plan. Do you have any way to contact the military personnel over there?"

"I think I might."

***

The military moved into strategic positions in the clearing flanking the ship. A singular jeep rolled out in front. A stocky dark-skinned man with a single silver bar on the centerline of his shoulder straps, indicating that he was a lieutenant, marched out in front of the jeep confidently. From his position he could see the massive Wryvyn behind the rows of people. He had a bullhorn and began requesting to speak to whoever was in charge.

Keke watched as Ethan and the others turned toward the towering aliens behind them. The two Wryvyn guarding the ship walked forward, the swarm of humans parted allowing them to pass out front. The Wryvyn adjusted their communication modules and issued an order to the Army lieutenant. The Wryvyn demanded that they turn over the Caerulusian and they would leave.

The lieutenant did not understand but was savvy enough to know that he had to bluff a bit to get more information out of the Wryvyn. The lieutenant says that they will turn over the Caerulusian if they agree to release the people unharmed. The Wryvyn looked to one another, then to the pack of their followers behind them. A moment later, the entire group began to march toward the lieutenant. The man wore a worried look because he knew he didn't have the Caerulusian and didn't even know what the Caerulusian was.

Keke could not worry about that. They had done what he needed them to do. While the Wryvyn were distracted, he and his friends had moved in closer to the alien ship. Agent Bush and Agent Swain had posted up at the edge of the tree line, rifles drawn.

Keke, and Anika held their breath in anticipation as a shimmering figure moved from underneath the ship and began to work on the ropes securing Bini's wrists and ankles. He freed the ankles first and Bini immediately stood up.

"Behind you!"

Keke tried to warn Nova, but his warning was not in time. One of the Wryvyn had come out of the ship and snatched the shimmering figure around the neck. Had he not been working furiously to free the boy he would have been undetectable to the Wryvyn. Bini struggled to run forward but the Wryvyn snatched the rope dangling from his wrist and tugged him to the ground while pinning Nova with the other hand.

Another Wryvyn exited the ship. Before he could take note of what was going on, Tunes and Marshawn crawled from beneath the ship behind him.

"I got myself a gun!"

Tunes and Marshawn sprayed the giant with their refrigerant blasters. The beast stumbled sideways, covering his face with its muscular arm. Before he could retaliate, he was blinded by a brilliant light and a sonic boom that echoed through the night.

Keke had channeled all of his energy and rushed shoulder first into the Wryvyn who had his brother pinned down. The Wryvyn's chest cavity was crushed by the blow, the force of which sent the massive creature hurling through the night sky tumbling to the ground beyond the other two who had approached the lieutenant. A second smaller flash and the blinded Wryvyn stumbled across the grass.

Meanwhile, the Wryvyn zombies who the military allowed to walk right up to them, began to attack the soldiers. The soldiers were ready for the attack and immediately opened fire with non-lethal rounds. From the tree line, Agent Bush and Swain joined in. The Wryvyn who negotiated with the lieutenant moved in and attacked. The gunfire did nothing to slow them. A few chain guns began to open fire. The first of the two Wryvyn was knocked to the ground as a few rounds hit him in the torso. His comrade quickly dove in to cover him. A dome shaped shield engulfed the two causing the chain gun to ricochet back toward the truck that fired it. The soldier stopped firing but not before striking a few others with the ricocheted rounds decimating his comrades.

Agent Bush and Agent Swain had used the cover of the chain guns to move toward the ship to assist the teenagers who daringly insisted on freeing Bini alone. They moved tactically crouching in different positions, ready to cover the teens' escape.

Nova attempted to board the ship while the Wryvyn were down. Before he could get up the gangway two more Wryvyn exited the ship. Keke recognized that the element of surprise was now lost. The Wryvyn he had hit still had not moved, but the one that Nova had rammed was up and manning the Wryvyn sonic gun.

Keke tugged his brother to his feet, pulling the ropes free of Bini's hands allowing him to run unencumbered. He made sure that Marshawn and Tunes were clear of the ship before turning to aid Nova who was outnumbered. The Wryvyn were so focused on the their Caerulusian adversary that Keke was able charge up and kick one of them into the other. This enabled Nova a clear path to the ship entrance. Keke nodded to the blue alien before turn and running after his friends.

Agent Swain watched as the boys and Anika ran from the ship. There was a sensation of relief that welled up inside him. That was until he noticed the Wryvyn behind the weapon. The hideous black monster was turning the turret toward the fleeing teenagers. Agent Swain fired four shots in succession landing four hits on the Wryvyn's face. The Wryvyn flinched, turning the turret enough that the sonic blast missed the teenagers hitting a nearby roll of hay turning it to dust. The sound that the came from the weapon threatened to shatter every human ear drum within proximity of the ship. All but the Wryvyn found the noise excruciating. Even their mind-controlled minions doubled over at the sound emitted by the sonic cannon.

The Wryvyn turned and fired once more in the direction of Agent Swain. Despite their agony, he and Agent Bush made it to the tree line before the blast shattered the trees nearby. Both agents ducked for cover. Miraculously, neither of them was hit by the blast. The Wryvyn turned his fire in support of his kind that were on the ground, but he was out of range of doing damage to the military personnel.

"We can't hide here. We have to keep moving." Anika struggled to get the words out.

"Do you think you can make it through the woods towards where the soldiers are?" Keke asked.

"Why we wanna go and to that, that, that?" Tunes asked.

"Nova told me that if the spores leave the bodies of the human hosts, eventually they may go back to normal."

"They are attacking the soldiers. They are going to kill them."

"I know, but if they capture any or you can get there and put them down, you can save lives. They are innocent people."

"Marshawn and I will go. We're the fastest."

Keke began to protest but he read Bini's mind, and his brother told him to have faith.

"Give him your pack, Tunes." The boy started to protest but Keke cut him off. "We don't have time to argue."

"Go that way. Agent Bush and Agent Swain are hiding in the woods over there. They can cover you."

"Why do we need cover?" Keke pointed in the direction he and the others came from on their rescue mission. Brandon and the others with him were running out of the woods.

"Let's hope they think you are me and give pursuit. Nova said that the pheromones will still be in their system even though the spores left. But they should be weaker now. The cold should still work on them." The twins touched heads, then embraced. Anika and Marshawn embraced as well.

The two teens ran off with high knees through the high grass.

Chapter 36

Tunes felt exposed without the weapon Kameka had designed for him. He watched with envy as Anika's pack bounced on her back in front of him. He thought it was crazy that they were moving closer to the Wryvyn ship after they just so narrowly escaped. The boy shuddered at how nightmarish the Wryvyn truly were. Now, he didn't have a refrigerant gun. He didn't have Keke's abilities. He didn't even have a bat or a knife or anything. He was just out here running into danger with his fists and his good taste in music. The whole time he cringed every few moments as the Wryvyn fired the sonic weapon.

In front of him, Anika was also wondering why they were running toward the ship. Keke had explained that they were trying to use the ship as protection from the Wryvyn sonic cannon. Anika thought it was better to do that by running away from the ship. Still, neither issued an argument against the direction when Keke told them to follow.

What Anika and Tunes were unaware of was that Keke was going to do something incredibly stupid. He had intended to run off through the woods, then circle around to meet up with his brother. However, Nova communicated that he was cornered in the ship by the Wryvyn and needed rescue. There was something off, but Keke felt he owed Nova for keeping his word and freeing Bini.

Keke told Anika and Tunes his plan. Both were firmly against it.

"Listen, I am going to sneak aboard. I can communicate with Nova. He can tell me where to go. I will be alright." Keke assured.

"Let me come with you. You need backup." Anika pressed.

"I know. We are a team. You don't want to abandon me. This is different. You saw the Wryvyn. They are right now in a fire fight with an entire Army Unit. You saw that single Wryvyn hold Bini and Nova on the ground like they were nothing. Nova easily took out five Wryvyn zombies. These creatures are strong. They are fierce. They are smart. They won't be easy to sneak up on again. The cold outside encumbered them somehow. They may have heat on the ship which would allow them to be at full strength."

"Even more reason why you need us to come with you."

"Can we talk about 'us'? I have no weapon. I'm naked and afraid out here."

"That is why I want you to stay here. Both of you."

"Keke, you have abilities, but you are not invincible. If they hit you with that cannon, you will be dust. They may have other weapons on the ship that you don't even know about."

"They don't. The only weapons they have are the ones that Brandon used and the ones that Ethan had. They don't carry the dangerous ones onboard because they would damage the ship if discharged. I just have to be vigilant and make sure they don't see me before I see them."

"How can you be so sure?"

"I'm communicating with Nova now. He filled me in."

"You trust him?" Tunes asked.

"I don't know. But he's asking for my help. I owe him. I gave my word."

"Then let me help you!" Anika implored.

"You can help me. By staying here. If the army pushes them back and they attempt to flee before I get off the ship, I need you two to sabotage the ship."

"How the heck are we gonna do that?"

"With that sonic cannon."

Before either of them could utter another word Keke leaped onto the ship ran across the top and pulled open a hatch that Nova told him he would find.

"I'm going in." Anika stated firmly.

"I can't go for that. No can do."

Anika didn't argue with him. She crept under the ship moving toward the front. If she was being honest with herself, the danger of the situation and the fear she felt made her feel alive. She also had witnessed a selflessness in Keke and Bini and how they engage with others. As someone who was once an outsider to their group, she appreciated this and wished to emulate it. Anika knew that Keke wasn't playing the hero. He truly was trying to keep her safe. It wasn't just her. In the chemistry lab, Keke had sacrificed his body to save Emma, their classmate. He had ensured her safety once more when the Wryvyn zombies attacked the school.

The closer Anika got to the ship's gangway the more she was certain the sound of the sonic cannon would rupture her ear drums. It felt as though the noise was originating inside her head and pushing outward on her temples. She cupped her hands to the side of her head to drown it out as much as she could.

A hand reached in front of her giving her a start. Tunes held out a pair of noise cancelling ear buds. She nodded her thanks, pressing the white bulbs into her ear holes. She pointed to the Wryvyn firing the weapon. He had moved it closer to fire upon the soldiers engaging his partners. Two others had moved in to assist their fallen comrade get to safety. The soldiers had moved in on the Wryvyn. They were spread out throughout the clearing engaging from multiple directions. The four hulking figures all had shields out and were firing sonic weapons at the soldiers. The Chain guns could not penetrate the shields. The mind-controlled people were still engaging the soldiers in hand-to-hand combat as well. Their proximity made all but pistols a safe option to fire upon them. The zombies were outnumbered but they had the benefit of enhanced strength and Wryvyn biology. They also had the Wryvyn fighting alongside them. The soldiers were starting to be pushed back. It was only a matter of time.

Anika pointed in the direction of a cloud of frigid air. Another one formed close by. Bini and Marshawn had arrived and were dispatching the zombies, freeing them from the spore's control. Tunes recognized the burst from the weapon he wielded against the zombies in the woods. He smacked Anika on the arm with the back of his hand, grinning triumphantly.

Anika smiled back but her smile was brief. She knew that it was not enough to push back the Wryvyn. Unless the Wryvyn were neutralized. Anika looked over toward the gang plank. She could board the ship and go save her friend before he got himself killed or captured. In that moment, Anika made her decision. Throwing caution to the wind, she sprinted toward the Wryvyn who was firing the sonic cannon. As she closed the distance, she became aware that she was shivering. It was likely that both the night air and her adrenaline were the cause. The high grass swooshed against her pant legs as she ran.

The cloud cover had cleared, casting moonlight on the previously darkened field. She could make out the musculature of the Wryvyn's back. It reminded her of the legs of a thoroughbred. At the base of its thick neck was a device that Keke had said they used to communicate with humans and Nova. Anika pulled the conical end of her makeshift weapon up into her right hand. Using her left index and middle fingers she squeezed the trigger, blasting the device and the side of the creature's head with icy refrigerant.

The Wryvyn roared as he stumbled off of the sonic cannon pedestal. He crashed to the ground with a thud ripping at the device trying to wrench it from his neck. The cold ran through the metallic weapon into whatever cortex it was attached to. Anika wasted no time in hitting the alien with another blast of the refrigerant. This time, she stood over him shooting him in the face. A black muscular arm swiped desperately at the girl who brazenly moved in too close. The wind was knocked from her lungs as the knuckles of the creature's hand struck her in the chest. She tumbled through the night air thudding hard on the cold ground.

When the Wryvyn stood, he searched for her but struggled to see her in the high grass. The enraged alien tore at its neck once more breaking off the communication module. Anika was still struggling to catch her breath when the moonlight was once again blocked out. However, this time, it was the shadow of the angry, black giant that brought her into the darkness. She was only just able to roll out of the way as the creature slammed one of its tree trunk sized legs down where her head would have been. She rolled a few more times and with all her energy sat up, hands supporting her from behind, legs bent in the best defensive position she could muster. With a surprising quickness, the Wryvyn closed the space between them. Anika crabbed backward attempting to pull the business end of her refrigerant blaster up to fire, but it was no use. The Wryvyn was on her with surprising swiftness. It lifted its hefty leg once more. Anika closed her eyes as she knew what was coming next.

Rather than agonizing pain, there was a gentle buzzing. Anika opened her eyes to see Tunes aiming one of the sonic immobilizer weapons that Brandon had used to incapacitate Keke in the woods. The Wryvyn was on the ground, immobilized but still conscious. The boy marched over to him and fired the weapon once more and the creature fell still.

"Who shot ya? Separate the weak from the obsolete. It's hard to creep these Brooklyn streets."

"Where did you find that?" Anika's voice was still raspy from the lack of breath in her lungs.

"He dropped it over there when he fell. I scooped it up when he went for you. I was like, look at me now. Look at me now."

Tunes offered the girl a hand and tugged her to her feet.

"I was gonna use that big joint over there, but I figured I might hit you. Then I saw this on the ground, so I snatched it up. I pressed this little trigger thing here and I shut him down, shut him shut him down."

"Good Let me have that. You go get on that big gun and fire at the Wryvyn in the field. I am going to go help Keke."

The boy passed the weapon over to Anika, dapped her up before jumping up on the sonic gun to figure out how to operate it. Anika was just barely inside the ship when she heard the cannon blast ring out.

***

Keke arrived at the holding area. Two of the Wryvyn were standing over Nova. The Caerulusian was on his knees. One of the Wryvyn held a device that looked like a hand saw with a syringe plunger on the end.

Keke could not make out the communication between the two Wryvyn. However, he thought that perhaps he could tap into Nova's thoughts like he did with Bini. He closed his eyes and concentrated.

"Tell us why you betrayed us."

"I don't know what you mean."

"Don't be deceptive, brother. We need a debriefing on the experiment. We were able to transfer your genetic information and your consciousness into the Caerulusian. When you woke, you ran. Fleeing to this planet where parasites are the superior species."

"I don't know what you are talking about. You came to our planet. You warned us about the death of our star. You tricked us to steal our abilities with your science. I am not your brother."

"That is where you are mistaken. Use your Caerulusian brain. All of the other Caerulusians were diminutive compared to us. You are less so. We attempted to use their genetic material to give you the ability to be unseen like the Caerulusians. However, something went wrong. Your physical form changed to be more Caerulusian than Wryvyn. This was an unexpected adaptation."

"You lie."

"We can show you."

The Wryvyn jammed the syringe-saw into Nova's midsection. He pressed down on the plunger and the images swirled. In an instant, Nova had a recollection of everything they mentioned. The experiment on the ship. Transport to the facility on the Wryvyn world. His escape. All that these beasts said was true. Nova thought that he was a Caerulusian. He thought that he had escaped the Wryvyn and was seeking to return to save his people.

Part of that was true. A side effect of the procedure that the Wryvyn performed on him gave him the sentience and abilities of the Caerulusians. However, he also still possessed some qualities of Wryvyn. They could sense that in Nova and still counted him as one of them. Nova was not sure if this was genuine or a ploy to get him to return with them quietly. Either way, he was conflicted about how to proceed next.

Keke on the other hand, was not conflicted. He moved into the holding area.

"Let him go."

The Wryvyn turned to see the boy standing with fists balled at his sides.

"Human. Why have you come here?"

"I made someone a promise."

"Keke, you are rescuing me?"

"I made a promise." Was all that the boy said.

"You made a mistake coming here, human."

The Wryvyn pulled a sonic immobilizer from his belt clip and aimed it at Keke, the boy spun sideways ducking into one of the containment units. The hum of the weapon was followed by the clattering of items off the table in the corner.

Keke dove out of the cell, rolling to his feet. He channeled the energy he had into a punch. His glowing hand landed in the fleshy abdomen of the Wryvyn with the sonic immobilizer. The giant alien collided with the alien with the syringe device. They both fell to the ground. Keke quickly moved in and snatched the immobilizer from the Wryvyn's belt. The boy hit them both with a sonic blast for good measure. They were stunned but not unconscious.

"Ukeke Wallace. I have figured out the rest of my plan." The shiny blue alien stood and approached the boy who had just taken down his captors.

"That's good. Now let's go."

"No. You must stay." Nova shoved Keke with both hands, sending him stumbling into the next containment cell. The alien slammed his hand on the panel beside it activating the cell door.

"What are you doing!? Let me out, Nova. Why are you doing this?"

"I told you, Keke. I figured out the rest of my plan like you suggested. That plan includes you. I must take you with me."

"I can't go to your planet! I have to stay here with my family. This is crazy! Let me out." Keke fired the sonic immobilizer weapon at the door. It bounced back sending Keke into the wall.

"Save your energy Keke. I know now that I am not a real Caerulusian. There is part of me that is. You and I have that in common. Together we can free the Caerulusians that were captured by my Wryvyn brothers. You are gaining greater control over your power. Your human biology matches well with the Caerulusian pheromones I passed on to you. You will be formidable against the Wryvyn. Once we rescue the Caerulusians you can use this ship or another to return to Earth."

"Don't do this." Keke's tone was solemn.

"I am sorry, Keke. This is the only way."

Chapter 37

The ship's engines rumbled shaking the corridor where Anika crouched in hiding. The grated flooring reverberated knocking her off balance, causing her to press against the wall. She could feel the metal walls on her exposed lower back where her jacket had ridden up. Her heart thumped at the thought of rounding a corner and coming face to face with a member of the colossal Wryvyn species. Still, she was here to help her friend. A stupid friend who had gone in to save one alien from an unknown number of other aliens. But still a friend she cared for.

As though summoned, two Wryvyn came running past growling something in a language that Anika did not understand. Their footfalls reminded her of horses or cattle stampeding. Their black skin and muscular features shook the girl nearly as much as the engines rumbling. Anika trembled with fear, eyes shielded in the arm of her jacket, praying the creatures didn't take notice.

The girl waited until the sound of their footfalls quieted to check to see that they disappeared around the bend before continuing her search. She turned a few more curves in the corridor without encountering another soul. A thought crept into her mind that maybe Keke was already off the ship. The Wryvyn vessel was massive and there was no telling if she had gone the same way as he had. They hadn't entered through the same way. Her loyalty and bravery were feeling like foolishness in light of her recent consideration. Maybe she was the stupid friend in this equation.

Anika came to a section where the corridor branched off. There was a light inside the branched space that was brighter than that of the overhead lamps in the center of the corridor. Around the corner inside the room, a Wryvyn was standing before a containment cell.

"You have been fooled by the Betrayer, human. Now you will be part of our experiments to enhance the Wryvyn cause to conquer other worlds. Perhaps we will come back and rid this planet of the human parasites. Then the other species can thrive in the new utopia we will create."

Anika didn't wait to be discovered by the monstrous beast who was speaking in a gruff English. The girl raised her arm, aimed the weapon at the Wryvyn, and pressed on the firing mechanism. The weapon hummed, blasting him just like Tunes had done the one outside the ship. The creature stumbled and collapsed. His gargantuan frame crushed a nearby table as his knees buckled, dropping him on it. Anika smirked, finding the act quite gratifying.

The girl marched over to him and shot him in the face with the refrigerant gun for good measure.

"Hello, boy." Anika turned her head slowly to her left. She gazed at Keke out of the corner of her eye in an attempt to be dramatic.

"Really? I told you not to come in."
"Yet, in I came. Did you find Nova?"
"Yeah."
"And?"

"And he locked me in this cell?"

"He locked you in? Jenna was right!"

"No. Well maybe. It's complicated."

"'Splain?" The girl placed her hands on her hips, skeptical.

"He did it to force me to come to his planet to help save his people?"

"He what? That's insane!"

"Yes. There's more. But first, press your hand to that grey area on the wall right there."

Anika pressed her hand to the control panel and the shield door disappeared.

"We have to get out of here. He is preparing to take off."

"Nova is flying the ship?"

Keke nodded.

"He coupled this new military jet engine that he stole from the base to enable him to enhance the speed somehow and some components to change the controls."

The two of them ran down the corridor as the ship's engines hummed louder. They had to duck into a nook as the sound of thundering announced the approach of the other Wryvyn. The creatures were so concerned with getting to the control room of the ship that they did not notice the two humans squatting behind a half wall.

Once they were sure the coast was clear, they continued toward the exit. Anika and Keke were nearly to the entryway to the ship when they heard a loud hissing sound like steam shooting from a busted pipe. The two teens shared a worried look that was intensified when the hissing was followed by the loud clang of the gangway retracting and blocking their egress.

***

"Jenna, I'm about to lose my mind, up in here." Jenna noted that the boy on the other end of the phone was frantic.

"What's wrong? Did you rescue Bini?"

Jenna was sitting in the truck out by the road. Kameka was in the passenger seat. It had been over an hour since Jenna's friends had gone off through the woods to rescue Bini from his mind-controlled captors. The agents had shown up not long after they had gone in. Agent Swain had told them to get inside the car and lock the doors. That is what they had done. As all manners of chaos erupted in the field a quarter mile up the road, Kameka and Jenna stayed safe and warm. At times there were sounds of war that broke through the otherwise silent night. In those times the two of them shared worried looks, wondering if any of those they knew and cared for were wounded, or worse. This call from Darius was the first communication either of them received as to the status of the rescue.

"Yes, Keke had a plan. Nova rescued Bini while Keke distracted the Wryvyn."

"From the Wryvyn? They were there?"

"Yeah, there were like five of them that came out of the ship. These were scary as hell. Like imagine if Venom merged with The Hulk."

"How close to them were you?" The worry made Jenna's voice crack.

"There was a war going on outside that no man was safe from. I was up in the mix of action. I got one of their weapons and there was a cannon. I had to use it to save some no limit soldiers. (I thought I told ya)."

"So, everyone got away safe?" The girl interrupted his rant.

"Yeah, we did. But when we escaped Nova got caught. So, Keke went onto the ship to save Nova. Then Anika went in after Keke. That girl is cuckoo if you ask me. They hadn't come out yet and the door just closed. This thing is about to take off. I don't know what to do. Bini told me to shoot it with the cannon, but I can't turn it far enough. It's too big."

Jenna wasted no time. She slammed the truck into drive. The abrupt measure startled Kameka who was listening intently trying to make heads or tails of the boy's rant. She thought some of the phrases sounded familiar, but she couldn't understand why he spoke the way he did.

"We're coming."

Sixty seconds later, Jenna swerved off the road into a war zone. There were corpses and wounded soldiers everywhere. Vehicles were tipped. Other soldiers were running around restraining townspeople who had been mind-controlled. A few of the people were still running around attacking soldiers who were doing their best to subdue them with non-lethal means. In the middle of the fray were Marshawn and Bini spraying people with refrigerant.

Jenna slowed to a halt. She and Kameka scanned the field looking for Tunes. The darkness of night and the smoke and chaos of fighting alien beings made the viewing difficult.

"There!"

Kameka pointed off toward the middle of the field about halfway between them and the giant alien space vessel. The blackness of the vessel made it nearly indistinguishable in the dim lighting provided by the starless sky. One of the jeeps behind where Jenna had stopped still had its headlights on. The light emitting diode bulbs were just bright enough to highlight the silhouette of what looked like a flying cruise liner. Bouncing between the beams was a smaller silhouette. That of a boy. Where his cousins both ran with great grace and coordination, the running figure was the antithesis of grace. Knees pumping high and outward to navigate the tall grass, arms flopping about more than pumping, Darius ran to regroup with his friends.

"Didn't we tell you to stay put?"

The two young women were so busy watching Tunes' awkward running form as he approached that they were startled by Agent Bush and Agent Swain's arrival at the side door of the truck.

"We did stay put."

"Until you didn't." Agent Swain asserted.

"Well Darius called us. The ship is taking off." Jenna explained.

"Good. Let them go back to whatever part of the galaxy they came from."

"We can't. Two of the kids are on board the ship." Kameka informed them.

Tunes slammed into the other side of the truck with both palms panting for a minute as he regained his breath.

"We have to stop that ship from leaving."

"Let me guess. Mr. Wallace and the young lady with the braids are on board?"

"Yeah, how did you know?" Tunes puffed.

"Ms. Price and Ms. Ralston have brought us up to speed."

It took Jenna by surprise that the agent she had never officially met knew her last name.

Agent Swain scanned the field, but he could not make out who may be in charge of the soldiers who were scattered about detaining townspeople and tending to the wounded. His brow furrowed as he gazed upon two figures running toward a Light Utility Vehicle.

"That would be Mr. Fields stealing that military vehicle and Mr. Wallace climbing into the gunner seat." The agent pointed toward the pair as they sped off.

"There's one over here." Agent Bush was already jogging toward the other vehicle.

Agent Swain began to follow her. When he was just a few feet from Jenna's truck he heard the vehicle speed off. Annoyed that these children insisted upon throwing themselves in harm's way, he ran and jumped into the gunner seat of Agent Bush's commandeered vehicle, and they too sped off.

***

"So, Nova was a Wryvyn?" Anika asked as she and Keke ran toward the far end of the ship.

"Apparently so. The Wryvyn were talking to him about the experiment they did on him. They were trying to take the Caerulusian powers for themselves and they ended up transforming one of their own kind into a Caerulusian."

"And he had no memory of being a Wryvyn?"

"According to him he thought they were trying to trick him."

"Maybe he was lying?"

"I don't think he can lie. Plus, I was inside his mind. He was not aware and had no reason to lie."

"True, but what if he was trying to trick the Wryvyn?"

"He could have been. But he wanted to trap me to get me to help him free the Caerulusians. Even after he was convinced that he was a Wryvyn. He is connected to the Caerulusians now. I think the Wryvyn scientists just messed up their experiment. That is why they wanted to take me, and had Bini kidnapped. The zombies thought he was me."

"Crazy! Do you know where you are going?"

"Yeah, I kinda do. I have been picking through Nova's subconscious. If we can get to the middle of this ship, there are escape pods. Nova is preparing to take off any minute."

"What if we don't make it before he takes off?" There was trepidation in the girl's voice.

"Well, I also have been communicating with Bini. I told him to find a way to shoot the ship down. If that happens.

"Shoot it down! With us on board?"

"If you have another plan to save us from getting to outer space, I'm open to suggestions."

Two left turns and a right brought them to where they needed to be. However, between them and the pods was a massive black alien. It didn't seem possible, but this one was larger than the other Wryvyn. It stood closer to nine feet tall. The forearms were as thick as Keke's body. The legs were the same tree trunks that the others had. Yet, the torso was different. The abdomen was much slenderer than the rest while the chest and shoulders were massive and rounded. When it growled the guttural sound was somehow more harmonic. The Wryvyn language sounded like an array of cracking sounds and clunky clicky sounds like the tumblers on a booby trap, but hollower. This one was more like the voices of the Merpeople in the lake at Hogwarts. Less Like someone turning a big gear underwater and more like the sound of a radio underwater. Keke thought that perhaps this was a female.

The growl may have sounded more harmonic to Keke, but Anika was more terrified than ever. She hoped that the spurt of urine that escaped from inside her did not become a flow. She didn't want to die with wet pants. An involuntary whimper escaped from her. The sound caused Keke to tense up a bit. Had she not been so close to him she would not have noticed.

"Let us pass. We mean you no harm. We just wish to get back to our people."

The Wryvyn configured the mechanism on her neck to communicate with them. Keke was not afraid. Unlike Anika, the size of this new adversary was of no consequence to him. All he cared about was getting himself and Anika to safety. His focus enabled him to notice the Wryvyn's other hand reaching for the weapon that hung from its hip.

"Run, Anika." Keke instructed cooly.

When the girl stood firm, Keke reached behind him grabbing her arm and dove out of the way as a blast from the sonic immobilizer weapon hit the wall in the corridor behind them. Anika landed face down on the floor. Keke rolled to his feet, leaped upon a nearby crate and them jumped to another causing the Wryvyn to turn towards the active threat and away from the frightened girl. Anika used the distraction to scurry behind the first crate.

"We don't have to fight." Keke pleaded.

"You will die nonetheless, parasite. I do not fear your Caerulusian abilities. I do not care that our scientists wish to study you. I will dispatch you and enjoy it."

The Wryvyn aimed the weapon at Keke and fired. Keke employed a well-timed somersault to evade the blast. He rolled to a squatting position behind another crate. The boy glanced over and motioned for Anika toward the pod bays. The girl stared back at him with an incredulous look on her face. She didn't seem keen on venturing out in view of this furious monster.

Keke peeked over the top of the crate to see the Wryvyn marching toward him. There was malicious intent in her eyes. He charged his energy and thrusted the crate into the midsection of the beast. She caught the crate stumbling back under the force of the throw. Her weapon fell from her hand as she tumbled to the ground.

"Go! Now." He demanded.

Seeing the creature fall down, Anika was emboldened. She ran as fast as she could down to the far end of the large chamber. There were half a dozen pod bays but none of the doors were open. When she arrived, she frantically waved along the edge of the wall and pressed and poked hoping to find the mechanism to allow access to the escape pods.

Across the room Keke ran over to the sonic weapon. He stooped to retrieve it. Halfway down, a frustrated cry from Anika distracted him. He turned his head to see the crate flying toward him. Before he could get the weapon in his hand or dive out of the way he was struck by the crate that the Wryvyn cow had thrown back at him. The force of the blow cracked a few of Keke's ribs on impact. He rolled to the ground; his breathing hindered by the trauma. He struggled to get on his feet but did not have the strength to get up. He lurched forward but fell to the floor.

The vicious Wryvyn thundered over toward Keke ignoring the sonic weapon. With a swiftness that should not be possible for a creature so large, she closed the distance, raised a knee, and slammed it down where Keke was laying. It took all his resolve to roll the few feet that saved him from the stomp.

Keke knew he was in trouble. His breath came in painful spurts. He felt nauseated as though he may pass out or puke or both. The floor rumbled as the Wryvyn moved in for another attack. This time she reached down grabbing him by his arm. Keke struggled to get free, but it was futile. She dangled Keke aloft like a child with a ragdoll. The boy marshaled all his strength and thrust both feet into the abdomen of the Wryvyn. He kicked as hard as his condition would allow. The maneuver sent him flying through the air as he freed himself from her grip, sending her tumbling into another crate.

Keke flipped over midair, landing on his feet but stumbled, ending up on his rear end catching himself with his hands. His cheeks and palms ached with the force of the fall. Desperately, he tried to pull strength from within himself like he had so many times before. Unfortunately, he was tapped out.

The Wryvyn was back on her feet and charging with murderous intent. She closed half the distance to Keke when she fell face first, her knees buckling as though someone had turned off a switch.

Anika lowered the sonic immobilizer and switched to the refrigerant gun. Before she could spray the Wryvyn with the icy blast, she was taken down by a swift kick from the Wryvyn's heavy leg. Unlike the male Wryvyn, the blast from the immobilizer did not stun her.

Anika's knees buckled sending her crashing to the floor. The force of the blow made Anika cry out in pain. Her shin colliding with the floor brought a second yelp. The Wryvyn twisted kicking the girl once more. The kick grazed her midsection. Anika couldn't imagine what it would have been had the elephantine leg hit her square. Just the graze knocked the wind out of her and sent her sprawling. She clutched her midsection in unendurable pain.

The creature stood turning her attention to Anika. She briefly looked back at Keke grinning.

"Watch as I squash this parasite comrade of yours."

The behemoth loomed over the huddled girl. A higher pitched guttural cry escaped from its mouth. Lifting its hefty left leg, she slammed downward with all the force she could muster.

Just as she was about to crush Anika's skull beneath the immense foot, a mass thudded against her midsection. Keke tackled the Wryvyn preventing what surely would have been Anika's demise. He and the Wryvyn rolled across the ground. The weight of her body pressing into his fractured ribs stole the breath from him once more. Keke slid into the wall, adrenaline driving him to slide up into a standing position. The Wryvyn stopped short of the wall, getting to her feet as quickly as he had.

The altitude of the ship changed. The enormous vessel wobbled more than hovered. Clearly Nova was not an experienced pilot. The ship shifted like a gyroscope as the landing gear raised. The Wryvyn stumbled but didn't fall. Keke saw Anika on the ground beyond the beast before him. He knew Nova was moments away from launching them all into space. Time was running out.

He focused on his opponent, he found that she had produced some type of laser blade. It reminded Keke of a lightsaber but in dagger form. It took all of Keke's strength to remain upright. He had nothing left for self-defense. The Wryvyn charged, blade raised. Keke didn't move. He glanced toward Anika who was starting to rouse. He knew that if the beast succeeded in dispatching him, Anika would be next. He would not allow this beast to kill the girl.

Keke calmed himself and felt time stand still. He reached out to his brother, his twin. Bini was in an army vehicle on course to shoot at the ship. The chain gun pelleted the rear of the ship but did little to damage the alien vessel. Still, Bini continued to fire. If he wasn't giving up, neither could Keke. The boy reached out to Nova he could feel his angst at getting the ship to take off and save his people. Nova could feel Keke as well. He sensed his pain, his desperation. A trickle of life surged from Nova into Keke. In an instant he had his breath, and his ribs began to fuse causing the excruciating pain to dissipate.

As the Wryvyn lunged with the laser knife toward him, the boy slid his body down the wall kicking out the front foot of his attacker. The force of the kick accelerated her lunge. She slammed the blade and her face into the wall where Keke had been just seconds prior. With a second mighty kick to the midsection the hulking, black monster stumbled backward.

There was a muffled growl and a gurgling sound as she staggered. From where he sat on the floor, leg extended, Keke could see that the knife had lodged in her neck when she collided with the wall. He listened to the sound of the chain gun's staccato rhythm as the bullets collided with the hull of the ship. The enormous alien creature reeled from the unsteady vessel and the approach of death.

Slowly, Keke got to his feet. He crossed the room and leaned over Anika. The boy wasted no time on the slain alien. The girl looked up at him then gazed over at the Wryvyn corpse.

"Maybe I should have waited outside."

"We're a team." He replied.

Weary and weak, Keke was barely able to crack a smile. The girl hugged her friend as the ship began to climb.

Chapter 38

Keke helped Anika over to the wall of pods. He ran around the room looking for some mechanism to open the door to allow access into the smaller vessels. It was difficult with the ship soaring through the sky. When he finally found the panel, it took a moment to figure out how to open the pods. Eventually he did something that made the door in front of the fourth pod slide to the right. He wasn't sure how, but he said a blessing for small miracles.

"We are going to get inside this pod. I am going to figure out how to fly it. You saved me. I am going to get you home."

Keke held the girl's hands in his, looking her straight in the eyes as he made the promise. There were tears in the corners of her eyes from fear and from the pain.

The girl took a deep breath. She pulled her hands free, wiping her eyes dry with her sleeves. Keke admired her resolve.

"Ready to go?"

"Not yet."

Keke began to protest but the girl pulled him close, arms around his shoulders. She pushed up on her toes and kissed him, sweetly. At first, he was stunned but her gesture proved to be persuasive.

"What was that for?" Keke asked as the girl dropped back flat footed, arms falling from his shoulders to his lower back.

"You probably are going to kill us trying to land this thing. I don't want to die having never kissed a boy."

One eyebrow lowered and the other raised, Keke examined the girl, unsure how he felt about her trust in his ability to fly an alien spacecraft.

"What if we live through this?"

"Then I'll be able to tell everyone my first kiss was with a boy on board an alien ship in outer space."

"Thermosphere."

"What?"

"We are likely in the Thermosphere. Exosphere at most."

"Well let's get out of here before this thing breaks orbit."

As Keke discovered the controls to release the pod from the ship, he couldn't help but think about Nova. The Wryvyn turned Caerulusian had saved his life multiple times. He had helped him rescue his brother. Under other circumstances, perhaps he would have gone with him to help rescue his people. Now he would have to go alone.

"Nova, I'm sorry. I cannot come with you. I have to get Anika to safety. I hope you are able to rescue your people."

"I understand, Ukeke. I should not have forced you to come along. That was unfair of me. I brought the other Wryvyn to your home. I will take them away. I have learned many things from you Ukeke Wallace. Goodbye my friend."

"Goodbye, Nova. My friend."

Keke pulled the lever which disengaged the lock and the pod fell from the ship.

***

Marshawn, Agent Bush and a few other soldiers drove to the edge of the clearing. Bini and the others in the gunner seat fired upon the vessel until he had flown out of range.

"Nooo!" Bini screamed with great anguish in his voice.

He jumped down from the back of the truck and began to run off through the woods. Marshawn and Agent Bush gave chase.

"Bini, wait!" Marshawn called after him.

The boy was unwilling to sprint through the dark woods. He could barely see the branches that threatened to take his head off or the roots and rocks that jumped up to trip him.

"Bini, please." Agent Bush called from behind the two of them.

"I can't let them take him! He's my brother."

The boy ran on for another hundred yards before slowing. Bini scanned the sky realizing that he could no longer see the ship through the treetops. A knot thickened his throat as he swallowed hard, fighting back tears. Marshawn rested a hand on the boy's shoulder in consolation as he caught up. Bini clenched his teeth tightly, lips pressed firmly together, as his eyes began to cloud.

"What am I going to tell my mom. I told her I would protect him. He's my younger brother."

"By just a few minutes. Besides, Keke is different. None of us could have stopped him from doing what he did. Anika is with him. He is strong. She is tenacious. They will find a way to get back."

"Mr. Wallace, Bini, this is not your fault."

"It is. I got kidnapped. I wasn't paying attention. He came to save me, and I couldn't save him. He told me to shoot the ship down. I couldn't do that. My brother asked this one thing of me, and I failed."

"None of us could do that. The technology that built that alien ship is far more advanced than the cannons on those Light Utility Vehicles. You saw what their weapons were capable of. The damage that their handheld weapons alone could do was catastrophic. Their spaceship travelled light years in weeks."

The Agent crouched beside the tearful teen. She took his hands in hers.

"Bini, if there is a way to get off that ship, your brother will find it."

Through a wall of tears Bini stared into the face of the sympathetic agent and nodded.

**

"You are doing a great job of ensuring that I can't tell anyone about my first kiss." Anika screamed.

The ship spiraled as Keke tried to learn the alien control mechanism.

"You are welcome to try to fly this thing." Keke shot back.

"I don't think that is wise. But also, I think I am going to puke."

"The kiss was that bad, huh."

Head pressed against the back of her seat, she glared at the boy but said nothing.

It was difficult to tell where they were going the way the ship spun. However, Keke was certain they were losing altitude. If he didn't figure out the controls soon, he and Anika would experience eminent death. He did not have enough time to figure out how to fly the ship, not without help.

Anika watched as Keke closed his eyes. She thought he was praying so she closed her eyes to pray too. In the back of his mind, Keke was searching for the experiences that Nova had when he escaped the Wryvyn on the ship he stole. Perhaps there was a similarity between the controls that would help him evade demise.

In a moment there were a flood of memories. The memories weren't from Nova. They were of him in his childhood. His first steps. His first day at school, his first-time pitching. It was an out-of-body experience. He was watching himself do a series of acts from his childhood. He could feel the pride he felt at the successes. He could feel the sadness of failure and sometimes the pain.

Some of the experiences did not match up with Keke's memory. He saw the game where Bini had saved the day by catching a sure homerun, scoring the final out. The feeling he felt that day was regret. He felt like a failure. In the memory, the feeling was delight. He felt triumphant. He looked upon himself with admiration. Keke finally realized that these were his brother's memories he was experiencing. They weren't Keke's recollection of himself. He was literally seeing himself through his brother's eyes. That is why there was so much love and reverence.

Keke pushed deeper and found the blue aliens walking on Caeruluziard. The first encounter with the Wryvyn. The experiments. All the Caerulusians' knowledge and wisdom were in his genetic code. Genetic code that was scientifically stripped of an actual Caerulusian and mutated to be injected into a Wryvyn host. Keke finally came to the escape. He focused on how Nova manipulated the controls.

Eyes wide he realized the mistake. He was only manipulating half the controls. He lunged across Anika's body placing his hand on the panel beside her. A series of holographic levers appeared. He grabbed Anika's left hand and wrapped her fingers around the handle of a lever.

"We are going to have to do this together."

He leaned back and grabbed a hold of his own lever.

Together they maneuvered the controls to get them out of their downward spiral and into a level flight path. From the altitude they were holding it was difficult to say where they were. The aurora borealis told them they were in the Northern Hemisphere but other than that they were lost. Keke slowed their speed to something controllable and then together they manipulated the controls to lower their altitude.

"Do you want the good news or the bad news?"

"The bad news first please." Anika said dryly, still unsure whether she was about to vomit. Still in disbelief they were flying an alien spacecraft.

"I don't know if this thing has landing gear and if it does, I don't know how it works."

"What's the good news?"

"The planet's surface is seventy-one percent water so we may survive a crash."

"You can't be serious."

"Also, I think I know where we are and can get us home." Keke pointed to the clear view port as they passed the Bering Strait. "I'm pretty sure that is the Alaska Peninsula to our left. If that is true, then we can fly slightly southeast and get home."

Together, they piloted the Wryvyn craft along the Western Coastline to Vancouver Island veered over Puget sound, Lake Washington and continued eastward toward the Great Lakes.

"Any thoughts on where we are going to 'land' this thing?" Anika asked.

"Nova's ship landed in Lake Ontario." Keke proposed. "Might be fitting."

"How about someplace closer to home?

"Saratoga Lake?"

"Works for me."

An hour later they were flying over the Adirondack Park. They reduced the speed and lowered the altitude redirecting to approach Saratoga Lake from the north side. The plan was to fly low and hope that when they killed the engines they would hydroplane to a stop and float long enough to make their escape.

They lowered the craft on the descent to roughly fifty feet above the water as they traced Fish Creek down into the lake. Once they crossed the Veterans Memorial Bridge, they descended to just above the water and throttled down. The jet-black pod with the V-shaped wings bounced along the lake's surface like a skipped rock.

Their speed as they approached Brown's Beach on the other side of the lake was much faster than Keke hoped. They would not stop before they hit land.

"Can you swim?" He asked the girl.

"My ribs are sore, but I can try. Why?"

"Because either we crash, or we eject now and get wet."

"The water will be freezing." Anika protested.

"Then you want to risk the crash?"

"This thing doesn't have a reverse?"

Keke started to protest and then got an idea. He shifted his control so that the ship spun from the single thruster. The action redirected their path but did little to slow them down. Anika mimicked his action but was a bit overzealous. The thrust forced them right. The craft skidded up onto land, through the fence, it rolled as it hit the pavement. The ship tumbled loudly up the embankment to US-9P. The craft flopped in the middle of the highway and slammed to a halt.

***

The sirens blared as they made the turn off of route nine. Anika's midsection ached. Her head had a gash from slamming into the console of the pod as it flipped.

Sticky blood caked her left eyebrow. Other than that, she was unscathed.

Beside her the boy sat up holding one arm over his ribcage. With the other he caressed a knot on his forehead which he received in the crash. At first he was unsure where he was. The blow to the head had knocked him out cold. The sound of the sirens were indistinguishable from the ringing in his head and throbbing he felt where he had hit his head. He stared groggily at Anika trying to understand where they were. The girl reached out to him; a gentle hand tapped the lump. The boy winced. She pulled the hand back not intending to cause pain. He watched as her hand floated in the air before his face, her fingers trembling. The girl scooted forward cupping his cheek. She tilted his face to allow her to look at the wound. She retracted her hand, pressing it to the panel to retract the roof of the pod. The sound of the sirens were immediately intensified. The cold air brought the world back to the two teens inside the alien pod.

Anika stood looking around at the destruction the crashing pod caused. Keke stood with her. A foot apart they gazed into one another's eyes. The understanding that they had survived a fight with a ferocious alien and a spaceship crash hit them. A hint of a smile curled up in the corner of the girl's mouth. The boy reciprocated the gesture. Without warning, Anika grabbed the boy kissing him for the second time in one night.

"What was that one for?" He asked after the passionate encounter.

"I couldn't have my only kiss be a pre-death kiss in outer space." The girl smiled at him.

"Thermosphere." He corrected.

"Whatever."

Less than a minute later, Agent Bush skidded to a halt in the parking lot. Bini leaped from the back seat almost before the SUV stopped moving. The boy's eyes streamed tears as he sprinted to his twin. He snatched Keke into an embrace that shot pain through his torso. He couldn't speak the words, but their connection allowed him to convey the message. The boy pulled back arms on his brother's shoulders sizing him up.

"I thought I lost you. I thought I would never see you again."

Before Keke could respond Tunes, Jenna and Marshawn ran in to join the hugging circle. Soon the teens were surrounded by police and military officials who established a perimeter to look for whatever creature might have been inside the vessel that was the size of a pair of eighteen wheelers side by side with wings. Agent Bush and Swain ushered the kids back into their SUV and sped them off to their parents before anyone could question their presence.

s

Chapter 39

A month later, Keke, Bini, Marshawn, Tunes, and Jenna all sat in Principal Paul's office. Jenna felt out of place in the office of another school.

Agent Bush and Agent Swain were there with them along with Mac and Louise. Principal Paul was asked to leave when the Agent's showed up. They cleared the outer office and posted an agent outside to ensure nobody disturbed them or listened in.

"I hope we all can agree to keep the events of last month a secret. None of you were ever kidnapped by mind-controlled folks. None of you were involved with fighting aliens. None of y'all crashed a ship. Understood?"

All of the kids nodded.

"It is especially important that you keep your abilities under wraps Mr. Wallace. The Wryvyn corpses that the military obtained are off in some black site being examined. The weapons that they left behind went with them. If the technology can be replicated, then this would change the nature of warfare."

"Members of secret organizations or foreign governments may find you to be an asset that could level the playing field. This would put you and your family in danger. That is why Agent Bush, and I took great care to scrub you from all reports. You were never part of the investigation. You didn't have an alien encounter. The video of you at the race where you were filmed has been removed from the internet. You can go on being a regular teenager. I hope that we can trust you in this."

Keke nodded. Louise smiled at the agent.

"All of the townspeople who weren't killed in the skirmish have been treated and are back to their normal lives. Most of them have vague memories but that's about it. Those who lost their loved ones will need to find a way to carry-on as best they can."

"What about the soldiers who came to our home and were in battle with the Wryvyn? Will they remain quiet?" Mac inquired.

"They have been debriefed and informed of the chosen narrative for what transpired last month." was the only response the Agent would provide.

Louise and Jenna walked the Agents out after the discussion. None of them said a word to Principal Paul who stood at the door, brow furrowed.

Keke and Anika walked into their chemistry class and gave their apologies to Ms. O'Brien. She was teaching a new chapter so both of them grabbed their notebooks and began to copy down the example on the board.

Keke glanced over at the page of the brown-haired girl who wore her hair in a French braid. Emma smiled at her classmate sliding her notebook closer so that he could copy the previous notes. Keke smiled thinking back to his first encounter with the girl and the experiences they had together the past few months. She wasn't one of his inner circle, but Emma was indeed a friend.

The girl noticed him smiling and she smiled back. When he came out of his thought, her smile made him smile bigger. She giggled a bit to herself before tapping her pen to his notepad. This made Keke chuckle. Keke had saved her from chemical burns before he knew he had abilities. In turn, she saved him from being expelled. She had been traumatized by the events of the day the principal was killed. However, Keke had saved her and after the shock of what happened had passed she analyzed the day's events. Keke took every measure to ensure her safety. Not to be a hero like Ricky always had. He did it because it was his nature. She knew that on some level he cared for her, and she decided that was the most important thing to her.

Keke next looked over to Anika who was diligently writing notes from the board. Had it not been for her he would have been traveling off to some other planet, a prisoner on the Wryvyn ship. Together they faced an alien race, nearly died, escaped, and nearly died again. Keke was thankful for her presence in his life. He next thought of Nova and his mission to fly off to rescue his new species on their cold blue world. He was hopeful that he achieved his mission. It would be extremely difficult for him to dispatch the Wryvyn alone.

Outside the building the two agents sat in their car in silence.

"When's your flight back?" Agent Bush asked.

"This evening. How about you?" Agent Swain asked.

"I am taking some time. Going to fly home and visit family for a bit before I return to the office."

"Well, you are a top-notch agent. I am happy you were along for this ride with us."

"I am glad as well." She shook hands with Agent Swain and the two agents climbed into separate vehicles, departing for their next chapter.

Epilogue

Kameka sat in the computer lab at Cal Tech reviewing the feed from the Keck observatory. It had become a new hobby of hers. She would be graduating in two weeks. The events of last fall seemed like yesterday and a distant memory at the same time. She had grown from that experience. She could not tell anyone about the events that transpired. She had promised Agent Swain and Agent Bush that she would keep quiet.

She also promised that she would keep an eye on Bart while she was at school to ensure his lips weren't loose. Agent Swain told her that was not necessary as they would be 'monitoring' him by other means. It was a good thing because other than a passing wave from across the courtyard or a rare encounter here in the lab. She hadn't seen much of or spoken to Bart since she returned to school.

"Kameka!"

As though summoned by her thoughts, the man appeared in the doorway of the lab. He was no longer the heavy disheveled mess she knew him as when they met. Bart had started taking spin classes and lost forty pounds. He stopped wearing the Hawaiian shirts and glasses. He got contact lenses and dressed in slacks and button up shirts. He even changed his diet and started wearing medicated deodorant for the pungent sweat odor.

"Hey Bart. Just finishing up my final project. Crazy to think we are graduating next week."

"It really is. I have an interview at NOAA the Monday after graduation. If I get it, I will be moving to New Orleans."

"The Big Easy. Good Luck. I hope you get it."

"Still monitoring the feed from Keck I see." Bart pointed to the monitor in front of her."

"Sometimes I feel like the guardian of the skies. I now must be ever vigilant." She jested.

"You never told me what happened when you flew off with those agents."

"You know I can't speak about it. They made me swear."

"I understand. It was a crazy thing, and I never knew what happened to you until one day I saw you back on campus."

"Yeah, it was an experience. That is all I really can say."

"Holy shit!" Bart exclaimed.

"Yeah, I am sure you feel the same."

"No. Look!" Bart pointed at the screen.

"Ha, ha. Good one, Bart."

Bart grabbed her shoulder and turned her back so that she was facing the monitor. Two large black Wryvyn ships were hovering in place. Kameka's jaw dropped. She could not believe her eyes.

"Is that?" Bart asked.

Kameka nodded.

At that moment her phone began to buzz. She held the phone up in front of her face, unwilling to take her eyes off the screen. It was a private number. Warily, she pressed the green phone icon.

Made in the USA
Columbia, SC
28 July 2024

721b4b6d-d607-44f1-af44-adc71f50e8afR01